A Moment Like This

Anita Notaro

TRANSWORLD IRELAND

TRANSWORLD IRELAND
An imprint of The Random House Group Limited
20 Vauxhall Bridge Road, London SW1V 2SA
www.transworldbooks.co.uk

A MOMENT LIKE THIS
A TRANSWORLD IRELAND BOOK: 9781848270343

First published in Great Britain
in 2012 by Transworld Ireland,
a division of Transworld Publishers
Transworld Ireland paperback edition published 2013

Addresses for Random House Group Ltd companies outside the UK
can be found at: www.randomhouse.co.uk
The Random House Group Ltd Reg. No. 954009

The Random House Group Limited supports the Forest Stewardship Council
(FSC®), the leading international forest-certification organization. Our books
carrying the FSC label are printed on FSC®-certified paper. FSC is the only
forest-certification scheme endorsed by the leading environmental
organizations, including Greenpeace. Our paper procurement policy
can be found at www.randomhouse.co.uk/environment.

Typeset in 12/15½pt Ehrhardt by
Kestrel Data, Exeter, Devon.
Printed and bound in Great Britain by
CPI Group (UK) Ltd, Croydon, CR0 4YY.

2 4 6 8 10 9 7 5 3 1

To my readers

Prologue

Do you ever get the feeling that your life is just a series of moments, brief seconds in time when something that defines you happens, only you don't even see it? There is no big plan for life, at least I don't think so. It's really just a series of accidents, good and bad, which happen while we think we have it all under control, and before you know it – well, life has changed for ever.

That's what happened to me, Antonia Trent, or Toni, as I'm now called. I didn't plan any of this. A year ago, I was just a girl from Wicklow who sang in the church choir. And now, I'm here, backstage in The O2, waiting for an MC to call out my name. A hush falls over the huge crowd, broken by just the odd whistle, a scream. I peer around the edge of the set, and then pull back. All I can see is a sea of faces, the MC standing in a pool of light in the middle of the huge stage. My stomach flutters, the old nerves bubbling up, and I have to put a hand on my tummy to settle them. They're nothing like they used to be in the beginning, but I still get them, a churning sensation mixed with a rush of adrenaline, but now I know that it's all part of the process – that in a funny way the nerves help me to sing better. They keep me on my toes, but they don't stop me in my tracks any more, like they used to.

He's talking now, warming up the crowd, but I can barely hear him, his voice echoey and muffled. 'Get a move on,' a heckler yells, and he obliges.

'Ladies and gentlemen, this year's singing sensation, Toni Trent!' His voice is lost in the roar from the crowd.

I hesitate for a moment, then I turn around. They are all there, behind me: everyone that's meant so much to me this year. Everyone except Mum, but I know she's up there somewhere, looking down on me.

'Break a leg, Toni.' Niall squeezes my hand. I squeeze it back. And then I step forward on to the stage.

1

'BOILED EGG AND TOAST, MUM. YOUR FAVOURITE.' I PUT THE tray down on the coffee table, picking the TV remote up and turning the volume down on the television. Mum was watching *Fair City*, as she always did, but Betty next door could probably hear it, she was playing it so loudly. I had to smile.

'Here, let me move this cushion for you. Make you more comfortable.' I pushed Mum gently forward in her chair, placing a hand under her shoulder while she pulled a cushion up behind her. 'There we go. Now lean back there. Better?'

'Perfect, thanks, pet.' Mum closed her eyes for a second and relaxed back against the cushions. Then she opened her eyes again and smiled at me. 'You look nice.'

'Oh, God, Mum, I don't.' I looked at my navy trousers with the crease down the front, the white scoop-neck T-shirt that I used to wear into the office – when I had a job, that was. I used to work in an IT company before Mum's stroke, but that seems like a million years ago. I look, well, frumpy's the word that comes to mind, but then I'm going

9

to choir practice, not a nightclub. At least, that's what I tell myself. I don't exactly need to dress to impress.

But earlier, as I was getting dressed, I looked out my bedroom window to see Mary O'Donnell leaving her house in a sequinned sheath and killer heels, and I wondered what it would be like to dress like that: like a smart, confident young woman. I think I've forgotten how. Sometimes it feels as if I've never really grown up, not properly anyway. I'm twenty-five and all I've ever known is here.

'Well, you look lovely to me.' Mum smiled up at me and took my hand in hers. 'Always my lovely Antonia, with those fine curls and those big, dark eyes.' She reached up, then, and pulled at a stray lock of my golden-brown hair, which I'd tied into a ponytail. It's so long now that it hangs down below my waist. I've hardly ever had it cut, at least not in the last five years. Mum used to do it, and of course she can't now. And I'm too busy, to be honest, with the cleaning and the cooking and everything that Mum's needed since she's had her stroke. But then it's what she deserves.

I owe Mum everything, you see, and I want to look after her. Maybe I feel it all the more because I'm adopted. Until I was seven, 'home' was a grey stone convent near Bray, with girls just like me, and Sister Monica, the nun who ran it. Home meant bells ringing for homework-time, dinner-time, bedtime, and a room shared with four other girls. Not that I ever really knew I was different, until my best friend Sally told me. I can still remember: it was going-home time after school, and we were both seven. We always left the

10

yard together, saying goodbye at the school gates, when she would turn left to go to her house and I would turn right to the convent.

'My Mummy says you have no one to love you,' Sally said, and she smiled at me with her gap-toothed grin.

'Oh.' I still remember standing there with my brown schoolbag on my back, my hair in tight plaits. I didn't know what she meant, but I knew that it didn't feel right. What did she mean, no one to love me? It bothered me, all the way home and through homework and teatime. Sister Monica loved me, and Mary-Kate and Jane and the others in my room. They loved me, too. What had Sally meant? I couldn't get it out of my mind, and at story-time that night, I asked Sister Monica. 'Why don't I have a mummy, Sister Monica?'

'Well, Antonia.' She smiled. 'You live with us because your mother died when you were born.'

I knew this, of course. She'd told me many times, always with the same expression, the same calm smile. But now, I curled my fists up into tight balls. 'And what about my daddy?' I persisted. 'Where is he, and why can't I live with him?'

'I'm afraid we don't know who your father is,' she said gently. 'But you're happy here, aren't you?'

'Yes, but my friend at school has her own room, and her mummy makes her lunch and buys her nice clothes. I want that, too.'

'Well, we're your family, and I promise we will do our best

11

to look after you,' Sister Monica said, and she gave me a hug, pulling me towards her. I could smell the talcum powder she always used, and feel the scratch of her black habit against my cheeks. Sister Monica was the person I loved most in the whole world, I thought, as I returned the hug. But she wasn't my mum.

The funny thing is that when she told me that she'd found me a real mum and dad, who wanted me to go and live with them for ever, I was heartbroken. I was only seven, and it meant leaving everything and everyone I'd ever known. 'I don't want to go, Sister,' I told her, my bottom lip trembling.

'Don't you want your own family, Antonia?' Sister Monica's tone was gentle, and when I looked up at her, she was smiling at me, her brown eyes crinkling at the corners. A family of my own. I couldn't imagine what it might be like. 'I think you'll like them.' And she came around the desk and held her hand out to mine. 'Come on, let's go and meet them.'

And that's how I became Antonia Trent, and came to live here in County Wicklow, in a little country village called Glenvara, with Anna and David Trent, my mum and dad, and a room of my own painted pink, and a garden with a swing in it. It was perfect, of course, and I had everything I could ever want. But more than that, I finally understood what it was like to live in a real family. It was another one of those moments, I guess, another one of those twists of fate.

I didn't need anything else, except Mum and Dad and my room and my friends at school and, of course, my singing.

And I wasn't the kind of girl to stand out – not really. I think I was afraid that I'd be sent back if I didn't behave, but soon I just wanted to be good for the parents who'd given me everything. And I *am* kind of shy and quiet, or at least I think I am. I've been this way for so long that I can't really remember. Before Mum had her stroke, I used to go out with the other girls in the village, maybe to the cinema in Bray, or for burgers at our local café. The girls, never the boys – at the grand old age of twenty-five I'm not sure what I'd say to boys. Miss Mouse, that's me. And you know what? I'm happier this way, really.

I kissed the top of Mum's head. 'I'm off, Mum. Are you sure you'll be all right? I'll be back home in a couple of hours to take you up to bed.'

'I'll be just fine here with my television and my supper.' She smiled. 'You go on and sing your heart out, pet. That way, I'll have Sunday Mass to look forward to. Do you have a solo this week?'

I blushed a bright red. 'Well, Eithne's asked me to do "Ave Maria", but I don't know . . .'

'Of course you will. And you'll be the pride of Glenvara, pet. My little nightingale.' And with this, she patted me on the cheek. 'I'm so proud of you, Antonia. But I wish you had more of a life of your own.'

It's not the first time Mum's said that to me. Every so often, she drops hints, about whether I'd like to go out more with the girls, insisting that she could easily get

Betty next door to help out if needed, but I can't leave her. I just can't.

'I have you, don't I?' I squeezed her hand.

'Of course you have.' Mum smiled up at me and patted my cheek. 'And now, *EastEnders* calls.'

'Which means that I'm late,' I said. 'And Eithne will kill me.' I leaned over to kiss her again, and then I left her in Albert Square, a look of contentment on her face. She was happy, and I was too, and that was all that mattered.

2

I WAS LATE BY THE TIME I REACHED THE VILLAGE CHURCH, even though I'd run all the way down the main street, past the post office, the chip shop and my old primary school, brightly painted pictures hanging up in its windows. I waved at Mrs O'Brien in the sweet shop, and old Jim Dunne, who was out mowing his lawn. I know everyone here and they all know me, which is nice, I suppose, although sometimes I wonder what it would be like to spread my wings a bit more. It's a pretty place, Glenvara, but it's small. And it's funny to be a grown woman, and to have left Ireland just once, for a day-trip to Holyhead with Mum and Dad on the ferry. I've often wondered what Paris might be like, or London, and the closest I've been to New York is watching *Sex and the City,* but I try not to think about what I can't have.

I closed the church door behind me and climbed the steep steps into the choir, out of breath, huffing and puffing like an old woman. 'Sorry, Eithne,' I mouthed to the choir leader, and was rewarded with a smile and a nod as I took my place in the second row and listened to the others to find my note and then I opened my mouth to sing.

15

We were halfway through the hymn 'Hail Holy Queen', and when we reached the final note, Eithne beamed at me. 'Thank God for you, Antonia, or else we wouldn't have a note between us.' The others all laughed, and of course I turned bright red, as usual. Billy, who always stands behind me, patted me on the shoulder. I turned to catch his eye and he winked. Billy's someone I count as a friend, even though he's all of sixty and has hardly a hair left on his head – I know, it sounds a bit sad, really, but he's been so good to Mum, calling around to her almost every day, always ready for a laugh and a cup of tea. I don't know what we'd do without him. Most of my other friends are up in Dublin working or have busy lives, so without Billy and Betty, Mum's neighbour, I'd be lost.

'All right, everyone,' Eithne continued, 'let's prepare "Ave Maria" for the O'Dwyer wedding, shall we? It needs a bit of polish. Now,' and she looked at us over the top of her reading glasses, 'I need someone for a solo.' I blushed to the roots of my hair and looked down at my shoes. Please don't pick me, please don't pick me, I repeated to myself over and over again.

'Antonia. Would you like to take the first verse?'

'Well . . .' I began, desperately trying to think of an excuse, until Bridget O'Reilly piped up.

'Ah, Antonia love, would you ever not sing, just for us? When I hear your voice, sure, it's like the angels are singing . . .'

'For goodness' sake, Bridget.' I laughed. 'I'm not *that* good.'

16

'Oh, yes you are, pet. Now sing up,' she shouted, and everyone laughed. Oh, God, I thought, I've no choice now. I hate it when everyone looks at me like that. But I took a deep breath and heard the first notes in my head, and then opened my mouth as the song just came out. It's always been like that for me. I don't even have to think about it. As the notes come, I feel my heart lift – and by the time I get to the end of the first verse, I feel as if there's nothing else but the song. I forget everything. I forget about being the shy girl I am, about how I hate my hair and my clothes and the fact that I can't open my mouth in a public place without blushing to the roots of my hair and wanting to run away. I just focus on the song and the music and how it makes me feel. And, when the song is over, I feel a sense of surprise. It's as if I'm waking up from a sleep, as if the song is holding me, controlling me. I can't explain it, but it's the most special feeling in the world.

I sang the last few notes of Schubert's 'Ave Maria', and when I finished, there was complete silence. Oh, God, I've sung it all wrong, I thought. Maybe I was out of tune for the whole thing. I hardly dared look at Eithne's face. But then the choir burst into applause, and I found myself going bright red again and looking down at my feet. Bridget clutched her hands to her chest and whispered, 'I've never heard anything like it. It's like I've died and gone to heaven.'

'Beautiful, just beautiful,' Billy murmured.

Eithne smiled at me briskly and said, 'Well done, Antonia. Good work. And now everyone, let's move on to "Our

Father", will we?' And I felt a sudden burst of gratitude to her for sparing me any more of the spotlight. She knows me so well, Eithne.

'Well, that was a blast, sure, wasn't it?' Billy was smiling as he tucked his arm into mine and we walked out of the church door into the chill of the autumn evening. 'Even deaf old Mrs Ferguson managed to keep in tune for most of it.'

'Billy, you're awful.' I laughed.

'I'm not, girl, I'm just accurate. How that woman was allowed to join a choir is beyond me. Now you, on the other hand . . .' He smiled and squeezed my arm. 'Your singing just lifts my heart.'

'Thanks, Billy.' I blushed and looked down at my shoes again. But I knew he meant it. I feel comfortable with Billy, maybe because he reminds me of my dad, the first man I ever really knew. David is – was – my dad. He died when I was fifteen, and since then it's just been Mum and me.

He's solid, Billy, but fun, too, and I know that he'll always look out for me, like a big brother. And it's safer that way, I don't have to think of what to say to strangers, especially male ones. Sister Monica says it's because I never knew my real father, but all I feel is that if a man I didn't know came up and tried to speak to me, well, I'd run a mile. I know, I sound like a nun, but it's true. Sometimes I wonder how I'd manage in the real world, but I suppose I don't have to find out, not yet anyway.

'You should take it further, Antonia,' Billy was saying.

'You need to get lessons, at least. That voice of yours is just wasted on Glenvara parish choir.'

'I *like* the choir,' I protested.

He turned to look at me. The lines in his forehead were creased into a frown, and he ran a hand through his few strands of white-grey hair. 'Antonia, you deserve better. I'm sure your mammy would love to see you go out into the world and make something of yourself and that wonderful voice of yours.'

I was shocked that Billy was disappointed in me. 'I know, Billy, but I can't abandon her.' I sounded panicky, but just the thought of it made me feel a bit sick.

'Ah, Antonia, a few singing lessons wouldn't do any harm, you know that. Sure I'd keep her company while you got the bus up to Dublin or Wicklow town. You know . . .' he paused and looked at me sharply, 'If I didn't know you better, I'd think you were just scared.'

I felt my bottom lip wobble, the way it always has done when I get upset. Because he was probably right. I've been in the background so long, I probably don't know how to be any other way. I felt the tears spring to my eyes.

When Billy saw them, he put an arm around my shoulders and squeezed. 'Ah, pet, I'm sorry. I didn't mean to upset you. You've been a wonderful daughter, and you make your mammy proud every day. It's just I know she wants to see you happy, that's all.'

'I *am* happy, Billy,' I murmured, thanking God that we were at the turn to my road and that I could cut the conversation short. 'I know you want the best for me, but . . .' I didn't know how to explain to him how frightening I found the prospect of change, so instead I pretended to look at my watch. 'Oh, God, is that the time? I must run, or it'll be midnight before Mum gets to bed.' And with that, I ran as fast as I could, without even turning to wave at my front door, the way I always do. I knew that Billy would be upset, but right then, I just didn't care. I was cross with him, to be honest – probably because, deep down, I knew that he had a point.

'Mum?' the television was still blaring from the living room as I closed the front door behind me and put my house keys on the hall table. She didn't call out, as she usually did when I got back, but then she probably couldn't hear a thing over the noise of the television. She must have turned it up again, I thought, as I slipped my feet out of my navy walking shoes and into my slippers. They were huge and fluffy, with 'Antonia' embroidered on each toe. Mum had bought them for me as a joke the previous Christmas, but I loved to wear them around the house – they were a bit daft and they made me feel a bit less . . . straight-laced, I suppose.

'Mum, I'm surprised you can hear yourself think.' I laughed as I pushed the door of the living room open and walked over to her. She was slumped forward in the chair, her chin on her chest, and for a moment, I thought she was fast asleep. 'Mum?' My voice sounded odd, even with the din of the television. I put a hand on her shoulder, and it felt stiff to the touch, cold. No, please God, no. I ran out of the room, and dialled 999, trying to stop my hands from trembling as I punched in the numbers.

3

THE JOURNEY FROM HOME TO THE HOSPITAL WAS A BLUR. I wasn't even allowed to travel with Mum in the ambulance, and I had to drive behind it all the way to Dublin. I was in such a state that I couldn't find my car keys, emptying my handbag out on the hall floor and rummaging around, until I remembered that they were in my coat pocket. And now, here I was, in an alcove off the main waiting room, Mum's warm dressing gown in my hand. I was shaking violently and my teeth were chattering.

'I'll get you a cup of tea to warm you up, is that OK?' The nurse's voice was loud in my ear. I'd forgotten she was there for a moment, and then I looked down and realized she was holding my hand. I shook my head. 'I just want to know how she is.'

'Dr O'Rourke is looking after her. She's in good hands. I promise.' And she smiled and patted my knee. 'I'll bring you that tea, anyway.' And then she was gone and I was alone. I couldn't think straight. Should I call someone? Mum had a brother and sister who lived in Australia, and I found myself looking at my watch, wondering what time it would be there. But what on earth would I tell them? That Mum was unconscious? That I didn't know whether she'd live or die? I'd never felt so lonely in my life.

I realized that I must have nodded off for a while. As I listened to the beeping of the monitors I remembered I'd dreamed that I was singing 'Ave Maria' in a crowded stadium in front of a huge crowd, and they'd all been laughing, and I'd wanted the ground to open up and swallow me. And then I'd looked down to the front row and seen Mum, smiling and blowing me kisses and that had kept me going.

'Are you the next of kin?' I sat up and rubbed my eyes as the doctor sat down beside me. 'I'm sorry. You must think that I'm uncaring. It's just . . .'

'Not at all.' His manner was brisk, and when I looked up at him, I could see how distracted he was, tapping his foot, jiggling his bleeper in his hand. And then he smiled at me and his features relaxed, his eyes crinkling at the corners. He was about my age but he looked older, tired, and his fair hair was thinning on the top of his head. Probably all the late nights in this place, I thought.

'How is she?' I put a hand to my throat.

He sighed. 'She had a heart attack, but she's stable now. We'll need to monitor her carefully for signs of cardiac distress over the next few hours, and the picture should become clearer then. I'm sorry not to be able to say more now, but . . .' Abruptly, he stood up. 'Look, do you have any-one that can be with you?'

I shook my head. 'No, my dad's dead and I'm an only child.'

He nodded and looked over his shoulder as a nurse called his name. 'Friends?'

'What? Oh, well, yes, I do,' I said, thinking immediately of Sister Monica. I'd call her. She'd know what to do.

'Good.' He looked at me again, this time more kindly. 'Look, I'll check in on you again later to update you. And if you need anything . . . one of the nurses will know where to find me. OK?'

I was about to nod and say thanks, but I was interrupted by the bleeper and by the nurse again. 'Dr O'Rourke, your CT scan . . .' He looked down at the beeper and then back at me.

'Busy night.' I attempted a smile.

'You could say that.' His smile was broader this time. 'Right, must go.' And he was running up the corridor, as another nurse grabbed him by the arm and pulled him along towards one of the wards.

I wanted to cry, but the tears wouldn't come, so instead I sat with my head in my hands for a few moments, before deciding to call Sister Monica. I needed her, I thought, as I pulled my mobile phone out of my handbag. I didn't even look at the time, but when I stood outside the A & E department, mobile in my hand, the sun was just coming up, so I hoped she'd be awake.

'Sister Monica?' I was mortified to hear the wobble in my voice, like a little girl. Pull yourself together, Antonia, I thought.

24

'What is it, Antonia? What's wrong?' Her voice was strong and alert, as always, and when I heard it, I just crumbled.

'It's Mum . . .' I couldn't get the rest of the words out for the sobs.

'Is she ill? Tell me, pet. What's the matter?'

Sister Monica's voice was so gentle that I managed to blurt it out. 'She's had a heart attack.' It sounded so final that I burst into a fresh bout of sobbing, barely able to hear Sister Monica shushing me down the phone.

'Which hospital are you in? I'll be right there.'

'No. No, there's no need, Sister Monica.' At the thought of seeing my old friend again, I panicked. I couldn't get an old lady out of bed and make her come halfway across the city, I thought. But that wasn't the real reason. I knew that if she appeared, with her calm good sense, I'd just fall apart. 'Look, she's stable . . . I'll ring you if there's any change. In the meantime, will you pray for her?'

There was a pause at the end of the line, and I could tell that she was weighing up what I was saying to her. She could always read me so well, Sister Monica. 'You can't fool me,' she'd joke when I was seven and trying to get out of doing my homework. 'I can see everything with my magic eye.' And we'd laugh, and of course I'd squirm with guilt at the same time. And then she'd reach inside the pocket of her black habit, produce one of her favourite chewy Milky 'Moo' Mints, and hold it out. 'Peace offering,' she'd say and pat me on the head.

25

Now, she sighed. 'Of course I'll pray for her, and I want you to ring me the minute you have any news. Do you promise?'

I nodded. 'I promise.' And then I disconnected before I could burst into tears again. I wiped my eyes with the back of my hand. I'm alone, I thought. For the first time in my life.

By the time I got back to the waiting room, a nurse was just coming towards me. 'Antonia Trent? Dr O'Rourke has been looking for you everywhere.' She was around the same age as me, but smaller, with her hair pulled into a tight bun, and bright blue eyes above her green scrubs. She shot me a glare and I hung my head for a moment.

'I'm sorry. I was just phoning a family friend.' But her back was turned to me already, and she was marching up the corridor. I wanted to stick my tongue out at her, and then wondered what on earth was wrong with me? Miss Mouse didn't stick her tongue out at passing nurses. It had to be the stress.

I had to run to keep up with her as she walked briskly ahead of me, up a flight of stairs and in through a door marked 'Intensive-Care Unit'. My heart started thundering in my chest, and I could feel the blood rushing in my ears. I prayed that I wouldn't pass out. Think of Mum, I said to myself. Think of how much she needs you.

The nurse turned to hold the door open for me, and the expression on her face was kinder this time. 'Just hang on a second. I'll need to find Dr O'Rourke for you. He can explain everything.'

Explain what? I thought, standing beside a drugs trolley in ICU, watching the nurses rush back and forth, hearing the beep-beep of the monitors. Was Mum in one of those rooms? I couldn't bear to think of her being alone. I was about to grab one of the nurses and demand to know where Mum was, when Dr O'Rourke appeared. Even harassed and dishevelled as he was, my heart leapt when I saw him. At last, here was someone who could tell me what was going on.

As he came towards me, his lips were set in a grim line. And I knew.

'How is she?'

He shook his head and reached out to hold my arm.

'She's not—' I began.

'No,' he said gently. His fingers were warm as he steered me towards one of the rooms. 'But I have to tell you that I'm worried about her. She's very weak, and she's not responding to the heart medication.'

I put my hand to my mouth. 'Oh, God . . . she's not going to die, is she?'

I was willing him to say of course not, but I guessed the truth from the look on his face.

'It's not good, Antonia. You might have to prepare yourself.' We stood outside the door of her room, and for a second I wasn't sure about going in. I was scared, I suppose.

I nodded. 'Thank you.'

He smiled at me, and this time the smile reached his eyes. He patted me on the shoulder. 'It's difficult, I know, but we're doing everything we possibly can.'

'I know, Dr O'Rourke. Thanks,' I managed, and crossed the threshold into the room.

Mum looked so small and frail on the bed, so vulnerable. I wanted to reach out and hug her, but she had so many wires on her chest, and a tube in her mouth. 'We're monitoring her heartbeat,' the doctor said kindly.

'Mum?' I went over to the side of the bed, putting down the dressing gown I was holding, and took her hand in mine. It was warm and soft. I looked over to the doctor. 'Can she hear me?'

'Well, she's heavily sedated, but I think you should talk to her and hold her hand. She'll take comfort from it, I'm sure.'

'Thanks.' I barely heard him leave. Then the door swung closed behind him, leaving me alone with Mum. As I held her hand I remembered how she used to take mine in hers when we were crossing the road. It always made me feel so safe, my small hand in her larger one. Every time, she'd turn to me before we crossed and smile. 'Always look right, then left, then right again. Will you remember that?'

'Right, then left, then right again,' I'd repeat.

'That's it, pet.' And she'd squeeze my hand.

It was one of the first things she taught me. And then she taught me how to make scones and sew clothes for my dolls, and to remember always to say please and thank you, and how to play patience and make popcorn on the stove. And, later, how to curl my hair. She was my *mum*. I took in a deep breath and tried to push the sobs away. 'Mum? It's Antonia.' I squeezed her hand again, hoping that somehow she might squeeze back, might sit up in the bed and ask me what all the wires were for. Mum, who before her stroke had never been sick for a single day in her life.

'Mum, I just want to say . . . well, I love you.' In spite of everything, I couldn't keep the tears away. We'd never exactly been demonstrative, Mum and Dad and I. We'd never said 'I love you' to each other, but it seemed important to say it now. Funny, it was the first time I'd ever said the words out loud, to anyone. 'You're in the best of hands, Mum,' I continued. 'The doctors are doing everything they can. You don't have to worry about a thing.' Because I knew that if she could hear or see anything she'd be scared and would need reassurance. And I'd always been there to offer her that.

'I'm here, Mum,' I said to her now. 'I'm here.'

I couldn't hear anything for a moment except the steady beep–beep of her heart monitor, but then it let out a sudden long single beep, and the nurses and that harassed doctor came crashing in through the door. 'Wha—?' I opened my mouth to ask what was happening, but the nurses ignored me.

'Her blood pressure's dropping,' one murmured, examining the monitor.

'Right, we'll need CPR,' the doctor said. Then, as if he

was seeing me for the first time, he added, 'Could you wait outside, please?'

His tone was brusque, and stupidly, I felt hurt for a moment, before nodding my head. 'Of course.'

I went to the door and glanced back. They were all around Mum like a swarm of bees, pressing buttons and injecting her. I knew that it was the last time I would see her alive.

The doctor came out of her room twenty minutes later. I jumped up from where I'd been sitting, perched on a radiator outside her room, willing him not to say the words.

He shook his head. 'I'm very sorry, Antonia. We did all we could, but her heart was just too weak. We couldn't revive her.'

My knees buckled, and he had to hang on to my arm to keep me from collapsing on to the floor. 'It's OK, it's OK,' he repeated, steering me towards a row of seats at the end of the corridor. He sat down beside me and waited, while I sobbed my eyes out. 'I'm so sorry,' he said. 'If it's any consolation at all, she didn't suffer, Antonia.'

I nodded, unable to speak.

'Do you have any family or friends you'd like to call?'

I shook my head. 'Mum has a brother and sister in Australia, but I'm adopted.' I blurted the words out and then wondered what he must think of me. What had my being adopted got to do with anything? God, I sounded so stupid. But when I looked up at him his eyes were kind.

'Well, that must make you even more special then,

mustn't it?' He said. 'Your mum was very lucky to have you as a daughter.'

'Thanks,' I murmured, opening my handbag and rummaging around for a tissue. I realized then, that he was still holding my arm, and I had to extricate myself gently. I blew my nose and tried desperately to be collected. 'What happens now?' I managed.

'Well, you'll need to contact the funeral home, and they'll come and . . . take her—' he began.

'Take her where?' I panicked, and clutched my hand to my throat.

'To the funeral home,' he said gently. 'Did you do this before for your dad?'

I shook my head. 'No. Mum did it all.'

'Right . . .' he began, and then his bleeper went off. He looked at it and tutted, pressing the black button off. He was distracted again, running a hand through his hair. 'I'll bring you back to her for a moment, and then I'll have a quick look to see if there are any local funeral homes in your area. Where did you say you lived?'

'Glenvara. It's in Wicklow.'

He smiled. 'Coincidence. My brother and sister-in-law live there. Nice spot.'

I managed a smile. 'Yes, it is. I've always loved it.' But then I thought: What on earth am I doing talking to this man about the beauty of Wicklow when my mum has just died? He must think I'm out of my mind.

I stood up, more abruptly than I'd intended. 'Can I see

31

my mum now?' I tried to look as if I was in control, not a blubbering mess who didn't know what to do with herself.

'Oh.' He looked startled for a moment. 'Of course.'

'Thank you,' I said crisply, and I stood up and turned my back to him, and walked up the corridor to Mum's room. I stood at the door for a few seconds and closed my eyes, trying to pluck up the courage to go in. And then I could feel the doctor's hand on my shoulder, heavy and warm, and I've never felt so grateful to anyone in my whole life. He had to see this kind of thing day after day, and yet he still managed to be kind.

'Ready?' he said.

'Ready.' And then I walked into the room to say a last goodbye to my mother.

4

WHEN I OPENED THE FRONT DOOR TO THE HOUSE LATER THAT day, I had to stop myself calling out 'Mum', the way I always did as soon as I turned the key in the door. 'I'm home!' I'd announce as I put the shopping down. Of course, there was no one there to welcome me. The silence was oppressive, and I suddenly realized that I was entirely alone. I put my bag down on the floor, and cried until I could cry no more, wondering if Mum would mind that the tears were for me as well as her. Would she be hurt that I was thinking about myself and the life I'd have without her?

Eventually, I managed to drag myself up the stairs. I couldn't imagine that I would sleep, but it's amazing how the body has a way of telling you what it needs. I took Mum's dressing gown out of my bag and tucked it around me, huddling on her bed. The dressing gown smelled of that lavender face cream she liked, and it comforted me. In spite of everything that had happened earlier, I drifted off.

The late-afternoon sunlight streaming in through her bedroom window woke me. Groggily, I looked at my watch. It was four thirty. For a precious moment I forgot where I was, but then the memories came flooding back, and I felt the tears sting my eyes. My first day without Mum.

I managed to get out of bed and down the stairs to the kitchen to make myself a cup of tea, putting the bag in the cup and pouring boiling water over it, congratulating myself that I could do just that small thing. I *could* manage on my own. Maybe if I kept saying it to myself, it might turn out to be true. What was it Sister Monica always said? 'One foot in front of the other, Antonia.' The thought of it almost made me smile, until I remembered that I'd have to ring her, to break the news. And everyone else. I began to feel my heart flutter in my chest, that familiar feeling of panic coming over me.

The knock on the front door made me jump in fright, almost dropping my teacup, and then the letter box flapped open. 'Antonia, are you in there?'

Betty. Mum's oldest neighbour. I got up heavily out of the chair, wondering how on earth I was going to tell her what had happened. But of course, it wasn't difficult. When I opened the door to her, she took one look at me and knew that something was badly wrong.

'Oh, Betty,' I wailed. 'She's gone!'

Betty pulled me into her arms. 'Shush, shush, pet,' she soothed, as she patted me on the back.

'She had a heart attack and they had her hooked up to machines, but then she had a second one and they couldn't bring her back,' I sobbed.

'You poor child, why didn't you knock when you came

home? I'd have come in and sat with you.' She held me tight and tried to ease my pain by rubbing my back and murmuring that we would get through this. 'I'll look after you now, pet. C'mon, into the sitting room there and we'll put on a fire.'

I shook my head. 'No, Betty. I . . . can't.' I looked at the sitting-room door, now slightly ajar, and thought of Mum, in her chair, smiling as she watched the television, and of the way she'd been, the last time I'd seen her there.

Betty's soft brown eyes were kind. 'Of course you can't, pet, what was I thinking? Let's make a nice cup of tea, then.'

'Thanks, Betty,' I said, allowing her to lead me into the kitchen, feeling like a child. I didn't want to tell her I'd already had a cup. 'You must think I haven't got an ounce of sense.' I tried to smile at her.

'No, not at all, love. You're just in shock, it's perfectly normal.' She felt the kettle, nodded to herself, then refilled it, reaching up into the kitchen cupboard for Mum's favourite willow-pattern teapot. Betty knew where everything was, because she spent so much time in our house. Herself and Mum had been friends since Mum and Dad had come to live in Glenvara, and had become even closer when Dad had died. I watched her quick, economical movements, and the swish of her purple tweed skirt and tight grey curls. She was barely older than Mum, and yet so full of life and energy.

The tea made, Betty came and sat down beside me at the kitchen table. 'Antonia,' she said, taking my head in her warm, wrinkled hands and tilting it towards her. 'You have

35

been the best daughter in the world. Your mum told me that a hundred times. She said they got lucky the day you came into their lives. You just remember that.'

'Did she really say that?' I was amazed.

'She most certainly did, all the time, so you hold on to that now. And remember, I'm here for you, and so will all the neighbours be. Everyone loved your mother.'

'Thanks, Betty, I don't know what I'd do if I didn't have you here.' I smiled.

Betty paused for a second. She'd taken her hands away to lift the teapot and fill our cups. Now she put it down and looked thoughtful. 'You'd manage, my love.'

I wasn't so sure at all. But then, I wasn't sure of anything any more.

Later on, I remembered the time Mum had tried to discuss it with me. Managing without her. I'd been help-ing her out of the bath and she'd sat there on the edge, looking thoughtful, as I'd tied her bathrobe around her and combed her wet hair. 'You know, Antonia,' she'd said finally. 'Sometimes I really do wish you had more of a life of your own. And I blame myself. I should have helped you to be more independent, to go out in the world and make your own way.'

I hadn't understood her. 'What do you mean, Mum? I manage to look after us both, don't I?' I'd smiled and tucked the label of her bathrobe in underneath her collar, patting her on her thin shoulders.

'Oh, of course you do. No daughter could do more. But you know,' she'd said, as I'd put my arm around her and helped her to her feet. 'You were our little girl and, well, we only wanted the best for you.'

'I know that, Mum,' I'd replied, feeling a bit nonplussed. 'I'm happy, you know, really I am.'

She'd looked at me for a long while, and then she'd said to me, 'I know you are, love, but sometimes you have to find happiness on your own, do you know what I mean? It's not always where you think it is.'

Of course, I'd just nodded my head, hoping she'd drop the subject, but now I began to see what she'd meant. It was nobody's fault, really, but sometimes I felt that I was still the little girl who'd come to stay with Mum and Dad all those years ago.

The next two days passed in a daze, as Betty helped me to organize the funeral, phoning the undertaker and the local priest, making a list of all Mum's relatives that needed to be contacted. There was so much to do, and I felt completely at sea. 'What about food?' Betty asked me.

'Food?' I looked at her, astonished. 'What kind of food?'

'For the people who'll come back after the funeral Mass, love. There'll be a big crowd, you know.'

'Oh. I hadn't thought of that.'

Betty tried to suppress a smile, and in spite of everything, I had to smile too. 'God, Betty, you must think I'm useless.'

'No, not at all,' Betty said stoutly. 'You just don't have

37

much experience organizing funerals. Thank God,' she added as an afterthought.

'Thank God for *you*, Betty,' I said, and hugged her, pressing her tight grey curls to mine.

'Ah, will you stop? Or you'll set me off,' Betty said, turning away from me and pretending to dry the cups and saucers on the draining board. And then she said quietly, 'Will you be singing at the Mass, Antonia?'

I shook my head. 'Oh, no, Betty. I couldn't. Eithne and the choir will look after it. I just . . .' I shook my head again. At the very thought of it, my stomach churned and my mouth felt dry.

Betty turned to me, the tea towel in her hand, and the expression on her face was one of pure disappointment. I wondered what on earth it was about me – first Billy now Betty, giving me that same look. 'You know, Antonia, I can't think of anything your mum would have liked more.'

'I know, Betty, it's just . . .' I began, but then I looked at her again. 'You're right, of course. I'll sing "Ave Maria" – she always liked that.'

Betty came over to me and squeezed my arm. 'She'll be up there now, happy, pet.'

And the funny thing was, Betty was right. It's one of my big secrets, that I don't share Mum's passion for God and religion. I actually never did, even in my days in the orphanage. Perhaps it was because I couldn't believe that if God existed, he'd take away my mum and dad from me

38

and leave me alone. But of course, I knew better than to say anything, and when my new mum and dad adopted me, it seemed easier not to tell them, either. It would only have upset them, because their faith was so strong. I don't think they ever really suspected, because I sang in the choir every Sunday, sometimes at two or three Masses – but I wasn't going for the prayers, of course, but for the music and for the chance to sing, even if it was just hymns.

But in the days that followed Mum's death, I knew, somehow, that she was up there, looking down on me. I could feel her presence everywhere, buoying me up: helping me to get through every minute and hour before her funeral; to deal with the undertaker and the flowers and the constant stream of people that called to the door, wanting to remember her, to tell me just how much she had meant to them. So, even though I missed Mum more than I would have thought possible, when I walked to the altar on the day of her funeral, I didn't think about how I was standing in front of people we'd both known our whole lives, all packed into the tiny stone church in the village. Or that I was about to open my mouth in front of them and sing, something that would have made me sick with nerves just a few weeks before. I just cleared my throat and looked out at the congregation, packed into the tiny church, and knew Mum would be thrilled that so many people had come to say goodbye, and that I was among friends.

'I'd like to say a few short words about Mum. As you all know, I came into her life when I was seven, and I can truly say that no one could have had a better mum. I know that's what everyone says, but it's true.' As I said this, people smiled and chuckled gently, nodding their heads in agreement. 'Mum and Dad chose me to be their daughter, and always told me how special this made me. They didn't give me a swelled head, though,' I added, and there was another laugh. 'But they made me feel that I was truly loved, and . . .' My voice wobbled as I tried to compose myself. 'And Mum was special to me, more special than I can ever say. So, in honour of her memory, I'd like to sing her favourite song, "Ave Maria".' There was a murmur of approval and heads nodded, and Bridget, of course, gave me the thumbs up from her position in the choir.

Eithne played the opening bars to the song, and I opened my mouth and let the notes come out, soaring into the church, over the heads of the congregation. And as I sang, I found my confidence growing, my voice getting stronger and stronger, as if it was guided by someone. As usual my nervousness just disappeared. And when it was over and the last few notes on the organ had trailed away, I could see great smiles on the faces of everyone in the congregation, and knew that Mum was there, with me, and I hoped that I'd made her proud. What I didn't know then was that Mum's death, the worst thing that could ever happen to me, was a turning point. That, in the space of a few short weeks, my life would change in ways I'd never have thought possible.

5

IT DIDN'T HAPPEN IMMEDIATELY THOUGH, BUT THEN I SUP-
pose that's normal, when your whole life is about to change.
People talk about overnight success, but it isn't really like
that. There's a moment when you feel you're on the edge
of something, like you're standing on top of a high diving
board, before you decide to jump. And believe me, I spent
quite a lot of time on that diving board. But then, I hadn't
even realized what it was I wanted, until it happened.

The month after Mum's death passed in a blur, the only
comfort being that I hardly had the time to feel lonely. And
even though I knew I'd have to face it sooner or later, I was
glad not to be alone. The doorbell and phone never stopped
ringing, but I answered every time, sighing with relief at
the distraction. I opened the door to every visitor, and rang
everyone to thank them for their gifts of meals.

'You're coping very well, pet,' Betty said to me one
morning. She'd come over to help me wash and dry all of
the casserole dishes, and was carefully labelling them with
their owners' names. She looked at me steadily as she said
this, and I knew what she really meant. That I was coping

too well. That I hadn't given myself time to grieve. But the reality was, I felt numb, as if my feelings were wrapped in thick wads of cotton wool. I didn't know how to explain this to Betty, so instead I just shook my head and tried to smile at her, but my smile didn't reach my eyes.

'I have to be strong, Betty, strong for Mum.'

Betty softened. 'No, pet, you don't. Nobody would blame you if you cried a bit. You've just lost your mother, after all. You know, you need to grieve, it's normal. What do they call it? "Acting out".'

I laughed, and Betty had the grace to look sheepish.

'You've been watching too many American self-help shows on TV, Betty.'

'Ah, sure, I know. They cheer me up, knowing that everyone else is a worse basket case than myself. But,' she continued, giving me that look again, 'they're right. You can't bottle it up, love, it'll only do you harm in the long run.'

'But I'm so . . . useless at life,' I said, 'that I feel it's the least I can do: have a bit of dignity about it, for Mum's sake.' And then I took her hands in mine. 'Thanks, Betty, I know that you're trying to help. And I appreciate it, I really do.'

She tsked and shook her head before replying. 'It's all right, I suppose.' And then her shoulders dropped and she put the tea towel down on the counter with a flick. 'C'mon, we've a pile of letters to answer.'

We spent the rest of the afternoon sifting through the huge pile of letters and cards of sympathy from friends and family. Mum's brother and sister from Australia had been at the funeral, but I hadn't realized she had so many distant cousins and friends. There were cards from America, where she'd worked when she was young, as well as a hand-stitched card from her sewing group in Glenvara. It was good to know she had so many friends. As I turned the cards over in my hands, I couldn't help wondering who would be there for me when I died – silly, I know, but I felt so alone right then. I wondered if anyone would really notice if I just wasn't there any more.

And then I shook my head. What on earth was I thinking? That I wanted to die? No, it wasn't that, it was just that I didn't feel I had a life that mattered. I sighed. And whose fault is that, Antonia? I said to myself. You've been living like a nun in an enclosed order for the last few years. Is it any wonder you're alone now, and you don't feel you have a life? Get a grip, for God's sake.

'Everything all right, Antonia?' Betty was giving me that look again. The one that said she was worried about me.

'God, yes, I'm fine, Betty. It's just . . .' I said, waving a white letter in my hand. Unlike many of the others, it was addressed to Ms Antonia Trent, typewritten, with the logo of Celtic TV on it. Who did Mum know there? I wondered, slicing the envelope open with her silver letter opener. She loved things like that, Mum – letter openers and tea cosies. She was always ordering them from catalogues or buying them from a local country shop she loved, and it made me laugh. 'Don't you have about a dozen of them already?' I'd tease her, as she filled in the order coupons for yet another knick-knack.

'You can never have too many tea cosies,' she'd smile back, signing the form with a flourish.

I turned my attention back to the letter, pulling the crisp white paper from the envelope and unfolding it.

The logo on the top of the letter was Celtic TV's, and I scanned the lines rapidly, then re-read them, unable to believe the words.

Dear Ms Trent,
Thank you for applying for Celtic TV's newest show, *That's Talent!* We really value the fact that you took the time to contact us . . .

But I didn't, I thought to myself, as I read on.

Even better, we've listened to your audition CD and we just love it! And we'd like to see more of you, Antonia. We'd like to invite you to the auditions for the show, taking place in Dublin on Friday 7 October at 9 a.m. Come early, as there's bound to be a crowd!

I put the letter down on my knee, open-mouthed. The fact that it was seriously cheesy didn't even register, because I was so . . . gobsmacked is the only word.

'What is it, pet?' Betty stood up and came over to me, pulling the letter gently out of my hand. She scanned the lines for a moment, her face gradually breaking into a smile. 'But that's fantastic, Antonia! I love that show. I didn't know you'd applied!' She shot me an admiring glance.

'I didn't,' was all I could say.

'You've probably forgotten, love, with everything else that's been going on.'

I shook my head, adamant. 'I didn't apply, Betty, honest. You know me, it's the last thing I'd do, sing on television. Do you seriously think I'd apply for something like *That's Talent!*?'

'Well, no . . .' Betty looked thoughtful. 'But someone did. I wonder who?'

I shook my head. 'Doesn't matter. I'm not doing it.'

Betty put both her hands on my shoulders and turned me around to face her. 'Now you listen to me, young lady. You have a gift, and your mammy would want to see you make the most of it, do you hear me? You're right. It doesn't matter a damn who sent the CD in, what matters is this is a chance, can you not see that? A chance to change your life, pet. Don't you think? Wouldn't your mammy want that for you, after everything you've done for her?'

I nodded, not daring to say anything else. I'd never seen Betty so . . . vehement.

'That's more like it,' she said, interpreting my silence as evidence that I was actually agreeing with her. Well, let her think that, I thought, taking the letter from her and putting it carefully in the envelope. She doesn't need to know, does she? I made a mental note to put the letter on the fire later.

*

I'd just got to the bottom of the pile of letters, having ushered Betty out the door a couple of hours earlier. I hadn't even stopped to make dinner, throwing a frozen pizza in the oven instead, and eating a couple of slices as I thanked another person who'd been kind enough to remember Mum. Frozen pizza. Mum would have had a fit. She'd always insisted on home-cooked food, made with fresh ingredients. She'd haunted the farmers' market in Ashford every Sunday, picking up fruit and veg and quizzing the stallholders about farming methods. She'd taught me to cook, and I wasn't bad, actually. I could make the kind of wholesome food that we'd both liked. But I hadn't got the heart for it now.

I was about to go into the kitchen with my plate when the phone rang. I debated for a bit whether to answer it – it was probably another of Mum's friends wanting a chat – but I sighed and lifted the receiver. 'Hello?'

'Antonia Trent?' It was a woman, about my age, by the sound of it, crisply efficient and remote.

'Yes,' I said cautiously.

'It's Dublin University Hospital here.'

At the sound of the name, my heart started beating faster and I felt my chest tighten. 'Yes?' I managed.

'Please don't worry, there's nothing . . . amiss,' the woman said. 'It's just that we've been, erm, finalizing your mother's file, and we notice that we still have one of her personal effects.'

Finalizing. That was one way of putting it, I thought, as

46

my grip tightened on the phone. 'What is it?' I knew that I sounded sharper than I should, but did she have to be so . . . impersonal, I wondered?

'It looks like her wedding ring.' The voice was softer now, apologetic. 'We're very sorry not to have returned it to you . . .'

How on earth hadn't I noticed that it was missing? Her wedding ring, of all things. 'No, that's not a problem. It's just, you see, I had no idea—'

'I understand.' The woman was almost warm now, her voice kinder as she realized how upset I was.

'Can I come in and collect it?'

'Well, we can send it to you by registered post if you like.'

'No, no,' I said. 'It's just, I wouldn't like it to get lost.'

'I understand. Well, the office is open Monday to Friday, nine to five. I'll put it in an envelope and mark it for collection. Is that OK?'

Suddenly, I found myself unable to talk, and so I just nodded, thinking all the time that of course, the woman wouldn't be able to see me. Speak, Antonia, for God's sake, I told myself.

'Are you still there?'

'Yes,' I managed. 'Yes, that's fine. I'll come in. Thanks.' And I slammed the phone down and sat down on the floor and cried so hard I thought I'd die. I'll never see Mum again, I kept saying to myself, over and over again. I'll never see her again.

6

I TRIED TO EMPTY MY MIND ON MY WAY UP TO DUBLIN, AND just drive on the motorway, past the Sugar Loaf Mountain in its coat of autumn purples and browns, and past the country shop which Mum used to love to visit. 'Just for a treat,' she'd say, and I'd roll my eyes to heaven, thinking of where we'd fit another tea cosy or trinket. Don't think of anything, just drive, I told myself, as I reached the edge of the city. And then the logo of Celtic TV caught my eye as I drove through the suburbs. The office was on the main road into the city, a row of low-level grey buildings, the bright yellow logo splashed on the wall above the main entrance. Funny, I hadn't thought about the letter. Not once. I hadn't even wondered who'd entered me. Not that I had any intention of going, it was just . . . who on earth could it have been? 'Oh well,' I said to myself out loud in the car. 'It doesn't matter anyway.'

I managed to keep my focus all the way to the hospital, pulling up in the car park and forcing myself through the entrance before I had the chance to change my mind. I went straight to admin, to be told that her 'effects' were still at the

48

nurses' station in the ICU. I debated for a moment whether to leave, just run back to the car, and to ring later and ask them to post the ring to me, but then I changed my mind. Just for once, Antonia, be brave, I told myself, as I walked up the corridor to the ICU, my feet feeling heavier with every step. I could feel the panic rising, and I had to fight hard to push it down, opening the door to the busy department and walking over to the nurses' station.

The nurse in there didn't see me at first. She was on the phone, wearing a brightly coloured set of scrubs. When I caught her eye, she raised a hand to me. 'Just a minute,' she mouthed, before continuing, 'But I'll need that bed sooner rather than later, Sister. Right . . . thanks.' Replacing the phone in the cradle, she looked up at me brightly. 'What can I do for you?'

'I've come to collect my mother's—' I began, before realizing that I couldn't get the rest of the words out.

The nurse looked at me expectantly. 'Your mother's . . . ?'

I shook my head, fighting the tears, clutching my throat and feeling faint. And then I felt a hand at my elbow. 'Come on, sit down.' I allowed myself to be led to the row of seats near the room where Mum had died. I sat down on one, rubbing my forehead and trying to catch my breath.

'Just breathe deeply.' The voice was gentle and vaguely familiar, and I looked up. That wisp of blond hair, the tired eyes. I couldn't remember his name, until I looked at his name tag. 'Niall O'Rourke, SHO.'

'Thanks,' I managed. 'It was just such a shock, coming back.'

'I'm sure it was – most of us don't have to, so you must be here for a reason.' I looked at him now and noticed the tired eyes were kind.

This time I could say it. 'My mother's ring. It was left behind.'

'Oh. For goodness' sake! They should have sent it out to you! What were they thinking, making you come back here for it?'

'I don't know,' I whispered, willing myself not to cry.

'Well, let's get you out of here quickly, shall we? Do you have the ring?'

I shook my head.

'I'll get it,' he said. 'Just wait a second here. OK?' and he patted me on the arm. Damn it, I thought, he's so *kind* . . . and I'm so pathetic.

I suddenly realized that my chair was the very same one I'd sat on just a few weeks before, waiting for Mum, hoping for a miracle.

The doctor was holding something in his hand when he came back to me, an apologetic look on his face. 'Here you go.'

'Thanks.' I didn't say another word, just looked at the small clear plastic envelope with her wedding ring in it, a slim gold band. She'd never had an engagement ring. She'd joked that Dad was too cheap to buy her one, but it was really that she liked things simple. She hated making a fuss about anything.

I took the ring out of the bag and turned it over before slipping it on to the third finger on my right hand. It fitted perfectly, which was funny, because I didn't have my mother's long, slender hands. Mine were small, my fingers short. When I was young, I'd wondered who I took after – my birth mother or father – but as soon as I put my real mother's ring on, I knew. I belonged to Mum and Dad. Here was living proof of what Mum meant to me.

The doctor's voice broke into my thoughts. 'I've a break coming up just now. Let me buy you a coffee.'

I looked up from examining the ring. 'Sorry?'

He looked sheepish. 'I just thought, well, that you might like a chat.' He nodded towards the ring.

He's feeling sorry for me, I thought, unable to suppress a flicker of annoyance. Everyone was feeling sorry for me. 'Look, I'm fine—' I began, but his hand on my arm was firm.

'I know you're fine, but I need coffee. Urgently.' And he smiled.

I had to laugh. 'OK. As long as you let me buy.'

'Deal. Now, let's get out of here, shall we?' And before I could argue, he took me by the elbow and steered me out of the ICU, keeping up a constant stream of pleasant chatter about the weather. Only when the doors had closed behind us did he go silent for a bit, merely pointing to the sign for the hospital café.

'You didn't have to do that, you know,' I said. 'But thanks.'

He stopped for a second and looked at me sharply. 'Look, it's poor hospital policy to make relatives come back for effects. Causes unnecessary distress.' And then, as if realizing that he sounded almost angry, he cleared his throat and smiled at me. 'And you look as if you could do with a cup of coffee.'

I managed to smile back. 'You're right. I could.'

I was grateful to Dr O'Rourke for not asking me anything, just sitting beside me at a table in the huge hospital café, with its view of the grey sea and the brown strip of sand which seemed to stretch all the way to Howth. He'd placed two cappuccinos and my change in front of us, having wound his way back to our table, saying hello to several of his colleagues on the way. He didn't ask me how I was feeling, or how the funeral had gone, and I was so relieved. I'd refused the doughnut which he'd offered to buy me, and which he was now tucking into, a shower of sugary crumbs falling on to his scrubs.

'Excuse my table manners,' he mumbled through a mouthful of crumbs. 'We don't get to eat much, and I've developed terrible habits.' He grinned and his eyes crinkled at the corners, making him look less tired. His face came alive when he smiled, I noticed.

'It is kind of disgusting,' I joked.

He shrugged and took another huge bite. 'Sorry.'

I shook my head. 'So, how long have you worked here?'

'Three years, in answer to your question. Three years

without food or sleep.' He grinned again, wiping the crumbs off his mouth with a paper napkin.

At least he had *some* manners, I thought, unable to suppress a smile. 'Sounds tough.'

'It is, I suppose. Sometimes we do five nights on the trot before we get a day off, and all I have the energy to do is veg out in front of the TV. It takes a day or two to get back into a normal routine. Then just when you do, it all starts again. And there's no social life, which is why everyone hates night duty.'

'It sounds a bit lonely,' I said, suddenly wondering if he had a girlfriend and, if he did, how on earth she put up with it.

He shook his head. 'Not lonely – far from it. You can't get away from people in here – it's like a family. I suppose it makes up for the lack of any kind of outside life. And I like it, believe it or not. And if you like something, it's easy, isn't it?' He looked at me expectantly.

I said nothing, just nodded my head and wondered what it would be like to enjoy a job that much. I'd never really liked the IT firm – the work was dull and monotonous, and it was the only job I'd ever really done, so I was hardly qualified to judge. But then, I supposed singing was my passion, now that I came to think of it. Not that I'd ever go further than the church choir. There was just no way, I thought, an image of the cheery letter from Celtic flashing into my mind.

'Does it run in the family?' I asked, trying to change the subject.

As soon as I asked the question, I regretted it, because

Dr O'Rourke shifted in his seat uncomfortably and stared into his coffee.

'Have I said something wrong?'

He looked up at me, as if seeing me for the first time. 'What? No, not at all.' And he leaned back in his seat again, arms crossed behind his head. 'In fact, Dad was a surgeon and Mum a nurse, so I suppose you could say that it runs in the family . . . yes.'

I couldn't for the life of me work out what it was I'd said, and yet I'd clearly put my foot in it in some way. I wanted to ask him, but of course, I couldn't. I didn't know him well enough to probe further.

'What about you?' he asked suddenly.

'What do you mean?' I replied, leaning back instinctively in my chair, away from him.

'What's your thing . . . you know, your passion in life?' He was gazing at me expectantly, as if I'd say skiing or basketball. I shrugged and blushed again. I said nothing for a while, hoping he'd change the subject, but when I looked back at him, he was still waiting for an answer.

'Well, singing, I suppose.'

'Really, oh, wow.' He leaned so far back in the seat that it tilted, the front legs off the ground, his hands crossed behind his head so that his elbows pointed upwards. He looked interested, surprised.

'You'll fall over if you do that.'

'You're right.' He grinned and leaned forward in the chair again. 'So tell me about it.'

'The singing? Well, I only sing in the church choir, it's not much . . .' I began.

'But you love it.' He looked at me intently.

'Well . . . yes, I do. How do you know?'

'Because at the very mention of it, your eyes light up.' He took a sip of his coffee, then placed the mug carefully back on the table. I noticed his hands for the first time – strong and tanned with long, tapering fingers.

I blushed and stared into my coffee cup. 'Do they?' I pulled at a lock of my hair and twisted it round and round, the way I always did when I was thinking about something. 'It's just, it makes me feel so . . . peaceful.' And then I examined my coffee, blushing to the roots of my hair again. Why was I telling this complete stranger my innermost thoughts? And then I blurted, 'Actually, I've got into a talent competition.'

'Well, that's exciting. Congratulations!' I thought for a moment that he was being sarcastic, but then I looked up at him and he was smiling broadly. 'It takes guts to enter something like that.'

I shrugged. 'Actually, I didn't. I mean, I didn't know about it.'

'Oh?'

'Somebody entered me. I've no idea who.'

'Well, they must think you're pretty good,' he said, as if it were the most natural thing in the world. That I'd be talented and someone else would recognize it.

'Oh, no, it's not that,' I said. 'I'm sure they mean well, whoever it is . . . it's just, well, I won't be doing it.'

'Oh. Why not?' He took another slurp of his coffee. He drank like he ate: messily. It should have been revolting, but it wasn't, strangely enough.

'Oh, God, I don't know. Mum made me join the choir, and I like that because I can hide up on the balcony and sing without anyone seeing me. It's a bit pathetic, but—'

'It's not. Shyness isn't an illness, you know.' He picked up a sugar packet and began to twist it around in his fingers. 'I used to be shy, believe it or not.'

'You? I find that hard to believe.' I laughed. Then, when I saw the expression on his face, I added hastily, 'I mean, having to talk to complete strangers all day and deal with their worries. How did you become less shy?'

'Practice,' he said. 'That, and working here. You're right – you can't be shy if you're meeting people every day of the week. And generally they're in distress, you know. So you have to overcome it to be the best doctor you can be.'

'You're right. And you're very good at it.'

Now it was his turn to be embarrassed. 'Thanks. I've had to work at my bedside manner, to be honest.' He smiled ruefully, twisting the coffee cup in his hand. 'Now what's this competition?'

I cleared my throat and said, *'That's Talent!'*

'Wow. That's big. All the nurses watch it in here. You must be pretty good. When are the auditions?'

'Well . . .' I began.

'Well, what?'

I shook my head. 'As I said, there's no way I can do it. Absolutely not.'

'Oh?' He looked at me as if I was talking Greek. 'Why not?'

Oh, God, how could I tell him that if I had to stand up on my own in front of an audience of people I didn't know, well, I'd just . . . dry up? Mum's funeral had been a fluke, I knew that. I'd sung there because it was the very least she deserved. But I knew that if I went anywhere near a talent show or an audition, I'd open my mouth and nothing would come out. I knew it. I loved singing, but only if I thought no one was actually watching me, or at least not a bunch of complete strangers.

'I'm a bit of a bedroom singer,' I eventually admitted. It was half the truth, I suppose. I'd never sung in the orphanage – there were too many others around for that, and I'd been afraid they'd laugh at me, but when I came home to Glenvara, it had just started. One day I'd been standing in front of my bedroom mirror and a song had just come out of my mouth. I can't even remember what it was, just the feeling.

I'd been so surprised that I hadn't even noticed Mum standing behind me at the bedroom door until she'd come up, wrapped her arms around me, and hugged me tight. 'My little nightingale,' she'd said. And the name had stuck.

'Bedroom singers hardly get on talent shows, do they? Don't they spend all their time singing into their hairbrushes?' Niall's voice interrupted my thoughts. He was smiling.

'I suppose they do, but it's just that . . . well, I do get very nervous if I sing in public.'

He leaned towards me so suddenly that I jumped back in fright. When he spoke, his voice was steady, but intense. 'We all get nervous, Antonia, but if we don't face the nerves, we don't get anywhere in life. We just . . . stand still.' He accompanied this last statement with a gesture, hands up-raised as if to say 'stop'.

There was something about the way he said it that unsettled me, that made me feel as if the ground was suddenly shifting beneath my feet. I found myself standing up out of my seat, hands shaking as I pulled my handbag up on my shoulder. 'I think I need to go now. Thanks for the chat.' And I turned on my heel, cheeks burning.

'I'm sorry, I didn't mean to cause offence.' He was up and beside me before I had the chance to make my exit. He touched my arm and I pulled it away. 'Antonia, I'm really very sorry. I don't know you, and I didn't mean to presume . . .'

'It was nothing, really,' I blurted, before running out the door as fast as I could.

'How dare he?' I ranted as I sped along the motorway back home, overtaking all around me in an effort to get home as quickly as possible. Home, where I was safe, where no one could bother me. I pulled up to the house, parked the car, let myself in, made dinner, put on a wash, all the time trying not to think of anything at all. If I don't think about it, it'll go away, I kept telling myself. It was only when I sat down in Mum's chair to watch television that I couldn't avoid it any longer. The truth. That doctor had been right, even though he didn't know me from Adam. I *was* standing still. Here I was, twenty-five years old, sitting alone in front of the television, with no job, no boyfriend, no close friends of my own age. Oh, I had my friends in the choir, of course, and the girls in the village who I hardly ever saw, but was this the life I really wanted, that Mum would have wanted for me? Of course it wasn't. And I had no one to blame but myself.

The tears came, of course, but I wiped them away. I wasn't going to wallow. Not this time. I stood up abruptly and walked into the kitchen. I hadn't burnt the letter from Celtic TV. Something had stopped me. It was on top of the fridge, under a pile of leaflets for takeaways and free patio installation. I pulled it out and looked at it, at the cheerful invitation to audition to sing in front of three million people every Saturday night. Could that be *me*, Miss Mouse? Antonia Trent? At the very thought of it, my stomach started doing somersaults. Oh, God, I thought. I can't. But I didn't put the invitation back on top of the fridge. Instead, I left it on the kitchen table, where I couldn't forget about it, and went to bed.

*

59

Later that night, I had the weird dream again. The one where I was standing in front of an audience in a huge stadium, the lights hot on my face. My armpits were clammy and my stomach had tightened into a knot. This time I opened my mouth and nothing came out, not one single note. Booing began, and a slow handclap, and I wanted to turn and run. But I didn't. Instead I looked out at the front row, to see my mother there, a huge smile on her face. She waved at me and blew a kiss, and her lips formed the words, 'My little nightingale.' And then I opened my mouth and sang, and as I did, I had the strangest feeling, a tingling sensation from my head to my toes. I can sing, I thought, as the notes poured out. I can really sing.

7

THE INVITATION WAS STILL THERE THE NEXT MORNING. RIGHT where I'd left it. I tried not to look at it as I ate my morning porridge and listened to the news. I glanced at the clock above the cooker. Only 7 a.m. I could hardly ring them now, could I? So I decided to put it off for a bit. I'll go for a walk, I thought. I used to love walking. It was something Dad and I had done every Sunday after Mass, while Mum had cooked a huge roast: long walks over the Wicklow hills, stopping in the Hilltop Inn for what Dad would call 'a medicinal beverage', winking at me as he ordered a hot whiskey for himself and a Coke for me. The thought of it now made me smile.

I hadn't really walked much at all since Mum's stroke, I thought, as I went to the cupboard under the stairs in the hall and poked about until I found what I was looking for: a pair of battered brown walking shoes. They were Dad's, but they fitted me perfectly – I remember he'd often used to tease me about my big feet. I laced them up carefully underneath my old tracksuit bottoms, and pulled on an ancient green windcheater – also Dad's. I look a fright, I decided, catching a glimpse of myself in the hall mirror, my hair sticking up at the back of my head and my face still blotchy from all the crying I'd done the night before. Oh, well, no one will see me at this hour anyway, I thought, letting myself out of the front door on to the street, which was eerily quiet.

I wasn't sure where to go for a moment, but then I remembered that Dad and I used to love the walk along the river, the one which ended near the valley. That's what I'd do, I thought, striding purposefully down the road until I reached the bridge, where I turned left and took the path along the river. It wasn't a long walk, just a couple of miles – ideal for a rusty walker, like me, who hadn't pulled on a pair of hiking boots in five years. The path was thick with damp, rust-coloured leaves and there was a smell of autumn damp, and as I walked I began to feel myself relax a bit, the tension leaving my shoulders as I inhaled the soft air. I didn't think about anything for a bit, just allowed my mind to empty as I walked steadily along the bank, humming to myself. After about half an hour, I came to a small waterfall and sat down to watch the brown river rush over the stones. Dad and I used to love standing on these stones, I thought, keeping a careful eye for the flash of a passing brown trout. I waited there on one of the rocks, still singing under my breath. And then the sun broke through the clouds and I tilted my face up to feel its warmth, the notes coming louder now, until I realized I was singing out loud, alone in the middle of the woods. I must be completely mad, I told myself, resisting the sudden urge to giggle.

'You're in fine voice, Antonia!' The voice was so sudden behind me that I jumped and let out a little scream, putting my hand to my throat in fright.

'Oh, I'm sorry . . .' the speaker began, and I turned around to see Sally O'Rourke standing behind me, her large lab, Lola, sitting obediently beside her. Sally was the wife of Gerry O'Rourke, the local garda, and a lovely woman not much older than me. She was in the choir, too, and had a sweet voice.

'God, Sally, you gave me such a fright,' I gasped. 'I'm sorry, here I was, just warbling away to myself—'

'It sounded beautiful, of course.' She grinned, then her face became more solemn, assuming that look of concern that everyone had around me these days. 'How are things?' I knew that she meant well, but I wasn't sure how much longer I could stand it: the sympathetic looks, everybody's kindness. I felt I just didn't deserve it.

'I'm fine, Sally. You look great.' I nodded at her jeans, her silky jersey top and sheepskin gilet. Even the wellies she was wearing were stylish – bottle green with tiny yellow flowers on them. Her hair was long and golden and beautifully highlighted. I thought of my horrible tracksuit bottoms and blushed to the roots of my hair.

'Ah, sure.' She shrugged her shoulders as if it were the most natural thing in the world, to go around the place looking a million dollars.

'How are the kids?' I asked politely, rubbing Lola's head as she came close to me, nuzzling my hand and licking it

63

gently. Gerry and Sally had two young boys, bundles of energy who fidgeted and giggled throughout Sunday Mass.

'Oh, they have my heart broken, but they're just wonderful, of course.' Her eyes lit up at the mention of them, and I wondered what it would be like to be a mother. It seemed such a ridiculous thought, somehow, as I'd barely kissed a man, not to mind doing anything else. What kind of mother would I be? Like Mum or like the woman who'd given birth to me?

We were silent for a few moments, small talk exhausted, until Sally said, 'Well, I'll leave you to your practice.'

'Thanks.' I smiled. 'It was good to see you.'

'Good to see you, too,' she said politely. 'Come on, Lola. The boys will be driving Dad mad and I still have to buy the papers.' She turned to go back up the path towards the village, but then turned and said, 'I just remembered, my brother-in-law's been trying to contact you. You know, Niall?'

I shook my head, puzzled. I didn't know any Niall.

'Niall, Gerry's brother?' she said hopefully, as if this would jog my memory.

'Sorry, Sally, I don't know any Niall. I can't remember ever meeting anyone of that name.'

'He's a doctor at University Hospital,' she said to me gently. 'I believe he treated your mum before . . . well . . .' her voice trailed off.

Of course. Dr O'Rourke. How had I not guessed? Why on earth was everyone in this place related to everyone else?

And of course, his full name had been on his tag. 'Niall . . . I didn't . . . I forgot that was his first name.' I stiffened as she continued to look at me earnestly.

'Antonia . . . he wanted me to give you a message. Something about your mother's wedding ring?'

I thought of the ring, at home in my jewellery box. 'I don't understand. I have it at home . . .'

'He said that you should ring him. He said you'd understand.'

'Oh, well, sure, Sally. I'll do that, thanks,' I said. 'And now, breakfast calls.'

I pulled myself up from my perch on the large rock on the edge of the river, brushing my horrible tracksuit bottoms down and wishing, for the millionth time, that I'd thought to get dressed properly that morning, but Sally interrupted me. 'He told me to give you his mobile . . . hang on . . .' she said as she rummaged in her gilet for her phone. Here it is . . . O'Rourke, Niall – in case I forget which one I'm married to.' She smiled, and I smiled back in spite of myself. '087 . . . do you want to write it down or something?'

'I don't have a pen . . .' was my lame excuse.

'Hang on.' She rummaged further in her gilet, pulling out a pile of receipts, a bit of Lego and a small pencil. 'The boys are always dumping their stuff on me.' She grinned. 'Now, all I need is a clean bit of paper . . .' she muttered to herself.

I stood there on the path, my thick hair greasy around my shoulders, my eyes caked with sleep. I could hardly run off now, could I? She'd think that was just too weird for words. So instead I just waited, feeling foolish, while she tore off the remains of a Lotto ticket. 'Hope these aren't my winning numbers,' she joked, as she consulted her phone, then carefully wrote down the number. 'Here you are.'

'Thanks, Sally. I'll give him a call,' I lied. 'It was great to see you.'

'Will you be back at choir practice next Friday night? Everyone really misses you, Antonia. And no one can sing in tune without you.' She laughed.

'Sure. Of course I will, Sally. Wouldn't miss it.'

Of course I didn't ring Niall. Because I suppose I was too angry with him for pointing out my shortcomings, and because I knew that he was right. But I did do one thing. I picked up the phone and dialled the number in the Celtic TV letter. I don't know what came over me. Maybe it was that dream, or even meeting Sally, but somehow I knew that Mum was up there, looking out for me. And that this was something she'd want. If I couldn't do it for myself, I'd do it for her.

'We loved your demo, Toni, so I'm really looking forward to meeting you,' the girl at the other end, who'd introduced herself as 'Karen, the PA', gushed.

'You did? That's great. I'm really pleased.' And then I couldn't think of another thing to say. 'Thank you for inviting me to the audition,' I burst out. 'My Mum died and . . . well, this could be just what I need right now.'

'Oh,' Karen sounded immediately sympathetic. 'I am so sorry. Are you OK? It's not too soon?' she wanted to know.

What on earth did I say that for? I thought, as I added, 'No, no it's fine. In fact, it helps, if that doesn't sound too odd. It just . . . well, it helps me, to focus on something else,' I told her.

'Of course, I understand.'

'Ehrm, do you mind if I ask about what to sing at the audition? I have some ideas, but I'd really like to know what it is you're looking for . . .'

'Well, your demo was a classic, and it sounded just beautiful, so you could try something like that again – you'd stand out because we have a lot of pop chart stuff. I'm trying to showcase other types of music, as our audience will be very broad.'

'Well, my favourite song is "Bridge Over Troubled Water". Is that too old-fashioned?' I'd no idea where that had come from, it just seemed to pop into my head. I hadn't heard it for years. It was one of Dad's favourites – that and 'The Boxer'. I remember that it was his party piece.

'Actually, that sounds perfect, Toni. Shall we pencil that in for you? And if you change your mind you can call me any time.' Karen sounded so enthusiastic that I resisted the urge to tell her that my name was Antonia. Nobody called me Toni.

'OK. But I haven't sung it in ages, so I'll need to practise . . .'

'Oh, of course,' Karen said warmly. 'Don't worry, the

auditions are very . . . informal, just the production team, really. We pre-select for the judges, and you'll only meet them if you get to the heats. And then, we start rehearsing with the band, et cetera, and you meet the musical director and so on.'

I swallowed. 'Rehearsing?' 'Band?' What on earth had I let myself in for? 'Perfect, thanks.' I managed to sound breezy, confident.

'Well, brilliant, then, fabulous,' Karen gushed. 'Can't wait to meet you, Toni!'

When I got off the phone, I was drenched in sweat, and my heart felt as if it was beating at a mile a minute. I had to close my eyes and count from a hundred backwards, the way Mum had always told me to do when I got into a flap, until I could feel my breathing settle and my heartbeat slow. If I was in this state after just one phone call, I'd be lucky if I managed to get to the auditions at all.

The papers lay, unread, on the kitchen table, and I picked one up and then put it down again. I didn't feel like reading.

And then I had it. I'd ring Sister Monica. She'd know what to do. She always had done, ever since I was a little girl.

The phone rang for a while, and I could just imagine her rustling up the convent stairs in her long, old-fashioned habit. She'd never changed into the light grey dresses all the other nuns wore. 'I'm far too set in my ways,' she'd said. And yet she was the most modern woman I knew.

'Antonia!' Her voice sounded surprised, and I felt guilty for a minute. I hadn't spoken to her since the funeral over a month ago, and I hadn't realized just how much I missed her. Even though it was a full eighteen years since she'd waved me goodbye, standing at the front door of the convent, as I drove away with my new parents, up until recently we'd still spoken every single week.

Of course, she didn't give out to me, not a single, 'Where have you been?' or 'Why didn't you ring me?' Just, 'It's so good to hear your voice.'

'Hi, Sister.' I'd been hoping to sound different, normal, but instead my voice came out in a croak. Oh, no, I don't want to sound like this, I thought. I want to sound as if I'm coping, managing just fine.

'Oh, Antonia, what's the matter?' Her voice was calm and even, just as it had been when I was seven and I'd sat on her knee, telling her about my day at school. I'd always been able to tell her everything.

'Nothing.' I snuffled.

'You can tell me, you know that. You can always tell Sister Monica,' she coaxed.

'Well . . . I've entered a talent show. At least, someone else entered me, I don't know who. And so I rang, and the auditions are on Friday week, and I'm scared out of my mind . . .' The words came out in a rush, and I felt foolish all of a sudden. 'Sorry, I'm gabbling, it's just . . .'

But Sister Monica laughed. 'Well, isn't that great, Antonia? Fancy having the courage to do that. Your mum would be just thrilled, I know she would. She was always saying what a wonderful singer you are. Good for you.'

'Yes, but it wasn't me, Sister. I didn't do it.' I knew I sounded pathetic, but I didn't care right now. I was just too scared.

'Sure, what does it matter who did it? Someone obviously thought you were good enough. And you are,' she added firmly.

'But I'm terrified, Sister.' There. I'd said it out loud.

'Of course you are, Antonia. It's normal, but who is it that said, "Feel the fear and do it anyway?" I can't remember. Now, let me think – was it Betty Ford? No, don't think so. It might have been Mrs Nixon – no, she had no personality . . .' As she went on, I smiled. I'd done the right thing, ringing Sister Monica. It wasn't that she knew everything, even though she nearly did. It was just . . . she had this knack of always saying the right thing, somehow. The one thing that would make you feel better, or stop and think, or learn something.

Feel the fear and do it anyway. It was Susan Jeffers. I knew because after I put the phone down to Sister Monica, I googled it. And ordered the book. It looked like I might be needing it.

8

'ANTONIA. WELCOME BACK!' AT THE CHURCH DOOR, BILLY
pulled me to him and gave me a big hug, patting me on
the back and murmuring, 'There, there,' until I had to
disentangle myself.

'I'm fine, Billy, thanks.' I had to smile. 'Really.'

'Ah, sure, how could you be? But boy, are we glad to see
you. Mrs Ferguson has my ears scalded with her warbling.'
And he grinned, squeezing my hand.

'Thanks, Billy, I really appreciate the welcome,' I said.
'The last few weeks, well—' I began, before he interrupted
me.

'They've been horrible, and you have no idea when the
pain will end, but it will, believe me. It'll fade, and you'll
still have the memories.' His hands were warm around
mine, and I looked up into his watery blue eyes. Of course,
his wife Celia had died four years ago, and he'd told me once
that he'd thought he'd die too. 'But then I realized that I
just had to keep on living.' He smiled. 'Because Celia would
have wanted me to. And because I have such a lot to live for.'

'Thanks, Billy. I'll try to remember that.'

'Good for you. Now, I need you to keep Bridget away from me. She has me driven mad altogether.' He rolled his eyes to heaven.

'Trying to chat you up again, is she?' I said.

'God Almighty, she is. She's a nice enough woman, I suppose. Bossy, of course, but then so was Celia in her way. It's not that, it's just the idea of the whole thing, at my age.' He grimaced, as if the very idea of Bridget liking him was too painful to contemplate.

'It's never too late, Billy. And, sure, you're only a young man,' I joked.

'A mere sixty-one.' He puffed out his chest in pride. 'But enough of this nonsense. Eithne will kill us if we're late.' He looked up the stairs to the choir loft. 'After you.'

'Thanks, Billy. You're a gentleman,' I said. 'I can see why Bridget likes you.'

'Very funny, Antonia.' He smiled, patting my shoulder. 'Very funny indeed.'

'Hi, everyone.' I was shy for a moment, when I got to the top of the stairs, and just stood there, before Billy, bless him, saved the day.

'Now, everyone, a warm welcome for Antonia. We'll be singing in tune again before you know it.' The laughter broke the ice, and the others came up to me and shook my hand or hugged me.

Bridget gave me an extra squeeze and whispered, 'Save me from Mrs Ferguson, for God's sake, Antonia.' At which we both giggled like schoolgirls. Fortunately Mrs Ferguson was deaf, and too busy ferreting in her handbag for her reading glasses to see us. Only Eithne, the choir leader, seemed a bit, well, cool is the only word for it, merely nodding at me, 'Antonia,' before flicking through the pages of music on her lectern. She said briskly, 'Right, everyone, "God is Our Saviour". From the top.'

I was a bit hurt, to be honest, and couldn't think for the life of me what I'd done. I made a mental note to ask her as I sung my way through Sunday's hymns, racking my brains to work out how I could have caused her offence. She'd been training me as a singer since I'd started secondary school, giving me extra lessons on Wednesday evenings, which I hadn't been able to make recently. Maybe that was it? I'd made sure to involve her in Mum's funeral, as I knew it would mean a lot to her to do the hymns, and she'd been delighted, so supportive. It was funny, really, to see Eithne so frosty, because she was normally so sensible and reserved. She wasn't given to big displays of emotion. And she'd never given me the cold shoulder before. I'll have to ask her, I thought, in the middle of 'The Lord is My Shepherd', feeling my stomach tighten at the very idea. I've never exactly been good at that kind of thing. I've never really had to. God, I thought, not for the first time, I wish I wasn't like this. I really do.

But in the end, Eithne got there first.

'OK, everyone, let's have a break, shall we? Rest our vocal chords a bit.' She removed her glasses and put them in their case, closing it with a snap, tidying up the sheets of music. Then she looked at me and nodded briefly. 'Antonia – got a minute?'

Oh, God, she's going to kick me out of the choir, I thought, as I nodded, and followed her into the dusty office behind the gallery. That must be it. Perhaps I've just missed too many rehearsals.

She closed the door behind us and went to the tea and coffee area, flicking the switch on the kettle. She said nothing for so long that, in the end, I opened my mouth to speak, 'Eithne, I know I haven't been around much recently, but it's just—'

Eithne turned around to me and shook her head impatiently. 'For goodness' sake, Antonia, I don't care about that. You're always welcome here, no matter when you come.'

'I am? Well, thanks for saying that, Eithne. I'll be here every Friday from now on.'

'Well, I'm not so sure about that, Antonia.'

I looked at her, mystified.

'I have a confession to make, and I hope you'll forgive me.'

'What?' I managed. What on earth could Eithne of all people have done to upset me? She'd only ever been encouraging and supportive, giving me extra lessons after practice, and pressing me to listen to all the great singers, from Maria Callas to Ella Fitzgerald. It was thanks to Eithne that I'd broadened my musical horizons and worked on my voice. She knew that I wouldn't have the time or inclination to go to Dublin to get lessons, so she'd made it easy for me.

'It was me, Antonia.'

'You what?' I looked at her blankly.

'I sent the letter.'

'What letter, Eithne? You'll have to explain . . . Oh,' I said, as the realization dawned. 'To Celtic TV?'

She nodded. 'I'm sorry, Antonia, but I knew that if I didn't do *something*, you'd just waste that remarkable voice of yours, and then where would you be? You've got such a talent, my dear. Far more than is needed for Glenvara parish choir. You must know that.' She smiled at me and I noticed that her eyes were watering. 'Of course, I had no idea your mother would pass away—'

'Oh, Eithne, it's all right, really it is,' I moved towards her and gave her a big hug. She felt tiny in my arms, like a little bird, and I realized how old she was, how fragile. 'I can't believe you'd do that for me.'

'You're not angry?' she looked at me eagerly.

I had to shake my head. 'Of course not. Terrified, maybe, but not angry.' Because I *was* terrified. Every time I thought of it my insides turned to jelly. But Eithne didn't need to know that after everything she'd done for me. 'I needed something, Eithne, to get me out of this awful rut I've been in for, well, for ever, and you've given me that chance.' I didn't want to tell her that I still wasn't sure that I'd have the nerve actually to go along to the auditions. That was another day's work.

'Well . . .' She blinked. 'If you're sure—'

'Of course I'm sure,' I said, giving her another quick

squeeze. 'It's an opportunity that I can't afford to miss. Mum was a great believer in signs, and this is a sign. She must be up there, looking down on me.' I attempted a smile. Feel the fear, Antonia, I said to myself. Feel the fear and do it anyway.

'I'm so glad, Antonia.' For the first time, I saw that Eithne looked truly happy. I'd never seen her so animated, clasping her hands to her chest, a big grin spreading across her dainty features. 'Would it be all right if I told everyone?'

'Oh God, Eithne, I'd be mortified,' I said, but then I saw the disappointment on her face. 'Look, there's nothing I'd like to do more, but let's see if I get through the auditions first, and then we'll go from there. I'd hate them to get all excited and then be disappointed.'

'Well, if you insist.' Eithne nodded solemnly. 'Although I have no doubt whatsoever that you'll breeze the auditions. Oh, they'll all be thrilled when they hear. One of their own, on their way to *That's Talent!*'

'What's that about *That's Talent!*?' a voice interrupted us, as Billy stuck his head around the door.

Eithne jumped and looked guilty. 'Well, we were just saying what a great show it was and . . .' She turned and looked at me pleadingly.

You are a hopeless liar, Eithne, I thought, nodding at her silently, whereupon she clapped her hands together and said, 'Antonia's got into *That's Talent!* Can you imagine!'

Billy whooped so loudly, my ears rang, and he promptly turned on his heel, yanking open the door and yelling, 'You'll never guess, Antonia's in *That's Talent!*, everyone.'

Oh, Lord, I thought, that's torn it, as they all poured through the door, squeezing into the tiny meeting room, hugging and congratulating me.

'Tell you what, let's go to O'Brien's for a pint to celebrate,' Billy said. 'Drinks are on me.'

'Oh, well, if you're offering, Billy, mine's a treble brandy,' Bridget said, and they all roared with laughter.

I found myself blushing again, a bright, livid scarlet as the tears pricked my eyes. How could I ever have imagined that I was alone? The thought that Eithne would do something like this for me, that they would all support me in this way. I was astonished, well and truly. 'I don't know what to say . . .' I began, as they all gathered around me. 'I really hope I won't let you all down.'

'Ah sure, he'll only use it as an excuse to make you buy the drinks, win or lose,' Bridget joked, nodding at Billy, and they all laughed again.

But then Eithne interrupted, the expression on her face serious. 'This is an opportunity for Antonia to show the world what we know – just what a lovely voice she has. It isn't, however, a test, so relax, Antonia, we're all behind you.' And she squeezed my arm.

'Hear, hear,' said Billy. 'And now, to the pub!'

I hated to spoil things for them, but I just couldn't face the pub, walking in there and everyone clapping and cheering and knowing that I – Miss Mouse – was going to audition for *That's Talent!* Word travelled fast in this village, and I knew that Bridget would probably ring the *Wicklow People*, even though I was only going to an open audition, and . . . no, I couldn't. Not yet.

'I'd love to, everyone, but I haven't even got to the heats yet. Can we just wait until we really have something to celebrate?'

It was Bridget who understood first. 'Of course, pet, you're right. But we will be celebrating, you mark my words. Now, who's going to be styling you?'

'Bridget O'Reilly.' Billy snorted. 'Where are you going with your "styling"? You've been reading far too many of those glossy magazines.'

Bridget shot him a look. 'Well, isn't that what they call it? Won't Antonia be needing someone to tog her out for the thing and, you know, give her a makeover?' She nodded, and her bright red hair caught the lights, and I thought that Bridget was actually rather pretty.

They all looked at me and I realized that the only respectable thing I had was a navy work suit. Hardly talent-show material. And my hair was now an unruly mass of curls, hanging down my back, which had barely seen a hairbrush in the past few weeks, not to mention a salon. I shrugged my shoulders.

'She's a natural beauty. Aren't you, Antonia?' said Betty.

The others murmured in agreement, and I blushed a bright crimson. God, I really am that bad, I thought, that people feel they have to say nice things to me, to bolster my confidence. I really need some help here. And I didn't even know where to start.

9

AFTER CHOIR PRACTICE, I WAS SO SHATTERED BY THE EXCITEment that all I wanted to do was drag myself home and make a cup of tea. But as I put on the kettle, I realized that something had slowly unclicked inside me. I knew that, because I could feel it. I couldn't put my finger on it and yet I felt a little lighter, somehow, a little brighter.

That evening, I decided to sleep in my own bed for the first time in six weeks. Every single night up until then, I'd switched off the TV at 11 o'clock and gone to Mum's room, curling up under her eiderdown, in her dressing gown, and crying myself to sleep. Tonight, though, I passed her door, closing it firmly as I did so, and went into my own room, with a hot-water bottle and the three glossy magazines which I'd bought in O'Dwyer's on my way home. I pored over pictures of colour-blocking and 'on-trend' peep-toe shoe-boots, and wondered how on earth I could ever get myself to look like some of the women on the red carpet. How am I going to be able to strap myself into something like that? I thought, as I looked at a photo of Cheryl Cole at Cannes, wearing a white trouser suit, slit to the stomach.

How had she held herself in in that? I wondered. And then I found myself doubled over with laughter at the very thought of it, at the thought of *me*, Antonia Trent, strapped into a tiny white trouser suit. And I hunched over the magazine, laughing until the tears rolled down my cheeks.

It was as I was nodding off that I thought of my old friend Mary O'Donnell, in her sequinned sheath and her latest nude shoes. Surely she'd know what I should wear? She always looked fabulous. I made a mental note to call over to her and ask.

For the first time in six weeks, I slept the whole night through. I was used to witnessing the dawn chorus, but when I woke up the next morning, all that greeted me was silence. I looked at my watch. Ten fifteen. Oh my God. I couldn't believe I'd slept that late. I jumped out of bed, my head feeling clearer than it had been for some time.

And for some reason, the first person I thought of was Niall O'Rourke. He'd been so kind. Kinder than he'd needed to be to a complete stranger. And surely he met people like me every day of the week, grieving relatives? I'd been silly, I knew. Silly and oversensitive. But I couldn't ring him now – after all, I hardly knew the man. Best just to let things lie.

The second person I thought of was Mary O'Donnell, but of course she was an estate agent and worked Saturday mornings. That's what normal people did: they worked and then they came home and made dinner and watched TV. Maybe that's what I needed to do – get a job. I didn't even know where to start. What qualifications did *I* have that would be of any use to anyone?

'Don't think like that, Antonia,' I said out loud to myself. 'You have lots to offer. And before you go entirely mad and start talking to yourself, it's time to get out and about and *do* something, for goodness' sake.' I knew that I didn't need to, financially. Mr O'Doherty, Mum's solicitor, had told me that – but I needed to prove that I could stand on my own two feet. And auditioning for talent shows didn't count.

I started with the shop window in O'Dwyer's newsagents, scanning it for anything that might look promising. There were lots of ads for dog-walking, and there was a vacancy for a gardener in Glenvara nursery, but as I didn't know anything about either dogs or plants, those would hardly be any good. I sighed. Surely I could think of something? Maybe if I went home and made a list of all the things I could do, that might help. It'd be a very short list, but still . . .

My thoughts were interrupted by the humming of my mobile phone. I didn't recognize the number but pressed 'accept' anyway, realizing as I did so that it might be someone from Celtic TV – and that, in spite of myself, I was quite excited about the prospect.

'Hello?'

'Antonia?'

I didn't recognize the voice. 'Yes?'

The person at the other end of the line cleared his throat loudly. 'Hi. Ehrm, it's Niall O'Rourke.'

Oh, God no. I wasn't prepared for this at all. What on earth would I say to him?

'I'm ringing to apologize—' he began, but I interrupted him.

'No, it's me. I should say sorry. It's just, well, I was being a bit oversensitive.'

'And I was being the opposite,' he said, and I could tell that he was genuine. He cleared his throat again. 'Well, that's all I wanted to say, really. And I hope that you are well and everything . . .'

'Would you like to go out?' The words were out of my mouth before I could stop them, and I covered my mouth. Oh no. What on earth had I said? 'I'm sorry,' I blurted.

'No, that's all right.' He sounded amused. 'As it happens, I was about to ask you the same thing.'

'You were? I mean, good. That's great,' I mumbled, wishing that the ground would just open up and swallow me up. I had absolutely no practice at dating. When I should have been getting practice, I'd been looking after Mum, and I didn't have a clue. And boy, did it show.

'As it happens, I'm coming down to Glenvara the Sunday after next to see Gerry and Sally for lunch. Maybe we could go somewhere afterwards?'

'Great,' I managed. 'That's great. I'll see you then.'

'Right.'

'Great, well, see you then.' Oh, God, I'd said that already. He'd think I was a complete fool.

His response was interrupted by the loud beeping of his

bleeper. 'Better go.' He was businesslike all of a sudden. 'See you Sunday.' And he clicked off.

I was left looking at my mobile and thinking that I'd really have to go and see Mary now. I couldn't wear a blue business suit on a date, now, could I?

I'm embarrassed to say that I lay in wait for poor Mary, pretending to make a list of my skills and qualifications on an A4 pad. It was a short list, as I'd predicted, and I was beginning to feel a bit depressed about it when I saw her little silver Polo pull up. I waited a polite twenty minutes or so before I called over.

'Antonia!' Mary was wearing a pink velour tracksuit and even I could tell that it was Juicy Couture. I'd heard of it, even in my cave. Her face was radiant and her long blonde hair cascaded around her face. She looked perfect, even in her after-work clothes: sleek and groomed and polished. I looked at my old grey sweatshirt and couldn't suppress my mortification.

'How are things?' Mary was polite, but I could tell she was waiting for me to get to the point. And I felt sad, all of a sudden. Mary and I had been great friends when we were children. We'd loved to play dolls in her bedroom and, later, I'd been her willing model while she tried out new hairstyles and make-up. But then, Mary had grown up, I suppose. She'd started going to discos at the youth club and then into nightclubs in Wicklow town, and I'd got left behind. Well, there was no point feeling sorry for myself now, I thought. Not when I needed Mary's help.

'It's . . . you see, I've been selected to go on *That's Talent!*—' I began, and was interrupted by her screech as she threw her arms around me.

'Antonia, that's fantastic.' She hugged me tightly and then released me, holding me at arm's length and examining me. 'You are such a dark horse, do you know that?'

'My ears are ringing, Mary, but thanks.' I smiled. 'Look, I need help. I look like . . . well . . .' I looked down at my tracksuit and indicated my hair.

'Raw beauty, I call it.' Mary snorted with laughter.

'Funny, you're not the first person to say that.' I laughed, thinking of Betty.

'C'mon in, and I'll see what I can do,' Mary said, holding the door open and leading me into her immaculate living room, filled with pretty things. On the wooden mantelpiece was a large framed photo of a handsome young man on a motorbike, giving the thumbs up.

'That's Dave, my boyfriend,' Mary said. 'I hate that motorbike, but it's his baby, and I know better than to compete with it . . . or rather her. He calls her Mary-Ellen, can you imagine?' She rolled her eyes to heaven, but I could see how in love she was – her face lit up at the mention of his name. Not for the first time, I wondered what it would feel like to be in love. And then, for some strange reason, I thought of Niall O'Rourke. I blushed to the roots of my hair and had to look down at my shoes for a full five minutes, hoping that Mary wouldn't notice.

We spent the rest of the afternoon gossiping and leafing through women's magazines for inspiration. 'See this?' Mary would say, pointing out a picture of someone I'd never seen before in my life. 'That girl's really working the feathers trend. She's not overdoing it – just a few touches on the sleeves of her jacket, but it works.'

I nodded, confused. The woman looked like a miniature peacock to me. 'Oh, yeah.'

'You haven't a clue, Antonia, have you?' Mary laughed.

'Well, no. I have one suit to my name, and I haven't worn a pair of trendy jeans in my life,' I admitted. 'I'm a fashion disaster, Mary. How on earth am I going to be able to go on a talent show looking like this?'

'Well, you won't be going on in your trakkie bottoms, will you?' Mary giggled. 'Now, I can make you look OK, but I have this friend Colette, who's a buyer for one of the big stores in town. She does some styling on the side. Why don't we start with her?'

I had a vision of myself decked out in something completely unsuitable, my hair in an awful asymmetric shape, and muttered, 'Mary, I'm not sure. It's only the auditions, and what happens if I end up looking like her?' I pointed to a girl who was wearing a hideous floor-length maxi with a pineapple design on it, and a pair of huge brown clumpy heels.

'Show me? Oh, that's . . .' Mary mentioned another name I'd never heard of. 'She's a real trendsetter, but she takes too many risks in my view. Colette will only help you to find

85

something that suits *you*, Antonia. And you are gorgeous, you know, underneath that nunlike exterior.'

I punched her arm. 'Get lost.'

Mary grinned. 'You'll thank me when you're looking a million dollars.'

I nodded. 'It's been great, Mary, doing all this,' I indicated the magazines and the empty coffee cups strewn on the living-room floor. I realized then how much I missed having a real proper girlfriend.

Mary leaned over and hugged me. 'I missed you, Antonia. I know that it's been hard for you the last few years, with your mum and everything.'

I nodded, feeling the tears come to my eyes. 'I only realize now that I had no life, Mary. But then I feel guilty because it's disloyal to Mum.'

Mary squeezed my arm. 'Don't feel guilty, Antonia. You gave everything to your mum. But now . . . well, now you have to have your own life. You deserve it. And look, you've already taken the first step, haven't you? And a pretty big one at that. You should be patting yourself on the back, do you know that? Not giving yourself a hard time.'

'I suppose you're right, Mary,' I managed. 'I don't feel very brave at the moment,' I said. I opened my mouth to tell her about my date with Niall, but stopped. I wanted to hug it to myself for a bit, to get used to the idea. And I couldn't imagine saying the words: 'I have a date . . .' No. Not Miss Mouse.

'But you are, Antonia. You are brave, and gorgeous and

talented and I want to kill you,' Mary joked, and we both exploded into giggles again.

In the end, I promised Mary that if I got through the auditions, the first thing we'd do was go and see Colette, because for the next week, I didn't want a single distraction. I wanted to focus on getting the song just right, so that I wouldn't let anybody down. I kept hoping that time might slow down, somehow, might magically stop before the auditions, but it didn't, of course. That's not the way life works. It just keeps racing past, and you can't hold it back.

I'd dug out as many versions of 'Bridge Over Troubled Water', as I could, including one by Elvis. Mum used to love Elvis, I thought, as I watched him on YouTube. I'd never been a fan, but I had to admit that his version was amazing, so rich and vibrant. That's it, I thought, as the song came to an end, that's the sound I want – something big and dramatic, that really grabs you by the heart. Must have been Mum, up there looking down on me. Mum – and Eithne, who made me come to her house every day to practise, going over and over key phrases until I had them pitch-perfect. 'Fail to prepare, prepare to fail,' she said darkly.

I spent the rest of the week listening and practising every morning, and job-hunting in the afternoons. I'd been applying for every job I could think of, but kept being told the same thing. 'You don't have the right kind of experience, sorry.' Even the dog-walking service turned me down. How hard could dog-walking be? I'd thought bitterly as I put the phone down. All of a sudden, I felt useless, as if I were chasing some silly dream, thinking that I could emulate Elvis, of all people. Get real, Antonia, I told myself. I even debated not turning up for the auditions, telling myself that I needed to do something sensible instead, something real.

10

BUT THAT FRIDAY MORNING, I CRAWLED OUT OF BED AT 6 a.m., made tea and toast, which I had to force myself to eat, and climbed into my car to drive to the auditions, on an industrial estate to the west of Dublin. I don't know why I didn't talk myself out of it – it was like something was driving me on, even though I wasn't even sure where I was going, and needed to stop several times to consult the map in the glove compartment of the car. It was an ancient AA map of Dad's, which he always kept in exactly the same place. Dad liked things to be orderly. 'A place for everything, Antonia, and everything in its place,' he'd often say to me. If only he could see me now, I thought, as I turned the map the wrong way around, trying to find the estate's location, searching frantically in my handbag for the address Karen had given me. I'm going to be late to my first ever audition, I thought. Maybe it's a sign. But then I shook my head. 'C'mon, Antonia. You've got this far, just take it one step at a time,' I said out loud to myself.

When I found the place at last, it looked completely

deserted. 'It can't be here,' I muttered to myself as I drove into the empty car park, but then I noticed a small, printed sign on a traffic cone at the side of the building. *'THAT'S TALENT!* AUDITIONS THIS WAY'*, and an arrow that pointed to the rear of the huge warehouse. Maybe nobody's turned up, I thought, parking the car and following the sign around the side of the building. I was practising my scales, la-la-ing up and down, and then trying out a few bars of the song to relax myself, when I walked around the corner, stopped dead and did a double take.

'Oh my God,' I said out loud. The queue snaked ahead of me for at least half a mile, up one side of the building and down another. I gulped and blinked in sheer panic, fighting the urge to run.

'I know, crazy isn't it?' The voice beside me made me jump, and I turned to see a girl of around my own age standing beside me. She was an absolute knockout in skinny black jeans and a faded grey T-shirt, tossing her flame-red hair over her shoulders. She extended her hand to me. 'Amanda, from County Meath. Thought she had a chance until she heard you. Not a bit bitter about it.'

I laughed and shook her hand. 'Antonia from County Wicklow. Feel as if I'm about to die of panic.'

Amanda laughed, revealing perfect white teeth. 'It's the biggest talent show in the country, baby. Everyone, but everyone, wants to get on *That's Talent!*'

'Oh,' I managed, my confidence plummeting to my boots. How on earth had I ever thought that I even stood the slightest chance? There was nothing for it, I decided. I'd just have to turn around and go home.

'I know. It's tough, isn't it?' Amanda said, having seen the expression on my face. 'I'm going to slink off now, my tail between my legs.' She grinned.

'That's just what I was thinking,' I said.

'Well, from what I just heard, I think you should hang in there a bit. Even your scales sound good.' She laughed. 'I'm not sure I'll even get past the door.'

'What is it that you do?' I asked shyly. Normally, I wouldn't chat to a complete stranger like that, but there was something about Amanda that put me at ease, something about her self-confidence, her poise.

She shrugged and flashed that grin again. 'I'm a singer too, rock numbers mainly. I'm a big Metallica fan.' She smiled. 'Not that I'll be trying them out for this audience, mind you. "Total Eclipse of the Heart" is more the style here. You know, some big ballad that gets the mobile phones waving.'

'Oh,' I said, feeling like a complete fool. 'All I'm doing is a cover of "Bridge Over Troubled Water".'

'That's a great song,' Amanda said enthusiastically. 'That Elvis version really rocks.'

'You've heard it? Isn't it just fantastic?' I said.

'It sure is,' she said. 'And if you sing it anything like you sing your scales, you'll breeze through the auditions, believe me.'

I shook my head. 'No, I don't think so.'

'Well, I do. Believe me, I've been to enough of these things to know.' And then she paused, as the queue inched forward. 'So what's the big plan?' she asked, pulling her hair into a ponytail and then letting it fall loose again over her shoulders, so that it spread out like a curtain of red over her tiny leather jacket.

I smiled, 'Ehm, well . . . I don't really have one. I thought I'd try the auditions and then see what happened.'

Amanda looked at me quizzically. 'Oh, so you're one of those, then.'

'One of those what?' I shook my head, puzzled.

'One of those dark horses, who says she can't sing a note and doesn't want to get anywhere in the competition, and then ends up winning the thing.' She was smiling, but there was something about her tone that unsettled me. Was she joking, I wondered?

But then she flashed that grin again. 'I'm joking, you know.'

'Oh. Right. Well, I really am just taking it one step at a time. Honest. My mum died recently and . . .'

Immediately, Amanda's expression softened and she reached out and patted me on the shoulder. 'Hey, I'm really sorry to hear that. I didn't mean to be catty, I apologize.'

'Don't worry. It's just, well, she always wanted me to do something with my voice, and I thought I'd do it for her.'

'That's sweet,' Amanda said softly. 'I really hope you do well, then.'

'Thanks.' I nodded as we inched forward again another few feet.

'Tell you what, why don't I help you out with your make-up while we're waiting? It'll pass a half an hour or so. And everyone else is doing it.' She pointed to a gaggle of teenage girls in the queue ahead of us, who all had their mirrors out and were applying thick slicks of foundation and dark eyeliner, giggling all the while. It looked fun, and they were clearly enjoying themselves, as if they were at a party, not an audition. Maybe I *could* relax a bit, I realized.

I shot back, 'A half an hour – am I that bad?'

'Well, you're lovely, of course, but . . . unfinished. You have a raw natural beauty,' she added tactfully.

I burst out laughing, and she looked at me, surprised. 'You're not the first person to say that,' I explained. 'Perhaps you could work some of your magic on me.'

'Sure thing,' she agreed, opening up the large, expensive leather satchel she'd brought with her, and bringing out a very impressive-looking selection of bottles and jars.

'Wow,' was all I could manage. 'All I have in my make-up bag is five-year-old mascara and an ancient jar of moisturizer.'

'Well, look and learn, baby.' Amanda grinned, un-screwing the lid on a tube of foundation. For the next fifteen minutes she rubbed and patted make-up on to my skin, until at last she declared herself satisfied. 'There. All done. Want to look?'

I nodded. 'I'm nervous.'

'Don't be. I've just enhanced your natural assets.' She

smiled, handing me a small jewelled compact with 'Chanel' written on it in discreet diamonds.

I snapped it open and gasped at my reflection. I still looked like me, only better – my eyes looked bigger, my lips fuller, and my face had a golden glow to it. 'I look . . .'

'Amazing?' she added.

'Well . . . yes,' I said, staring at myself for another bit. 'Wow, thanks, Amanda. If I get through this audition, it'll be down to you.'

'Nonsense,' she said crisply. 'If you get through, it'll be thanks to your own talent. Not that it'll do any harm if you look good, mind you.' She glanced at me appraisingly. 'Fake it till you make it, that's what I say.'

I looked down at the pair of navy-blue jeans and plain scoop-necked navy T-shirt Mary had lent me – 'so you don't appear too middle-aged' – and wondered why I couldn't be trendy, like Amanda, why I couldn't wear skinny jeans and leather jackets. 'Well, thanks anyway, Amanda. I really owe you one.'

She shrugged her shoulders and gave a toss of that beautiful red hair of hers. 'You can repay me some time when I really need it, OK?'

'Sure thing,' I said. 'I won't forget.'

We stood there for another hour in the chilly autumn wind, chatting like we'd known each other for ever. By the time a young woman with a huge set of earphones on her head and a clipboard in her hand finally approached, I felt that I'd made a real friend. And it was great to know that I could go out into the world and talk to someone my own age – that I wasn't a completely lost cause. The young woman lifted a megaphone to her lips and yelled, 'Right, this section of the crowd, we'll take you in groups of five at the back entrance there.' She indicated a red door with a handwritten sign taped to it, reading, 'Group P'. So just line up and we'll call you then, OK?' She smiled briskly, before disappearing again.

And then we all shuffled through the door, and turned left on to a long corridor, which was thankfully warmer than outside. 'Here we go,' Amanda said, bending down to touch her toes, then stretching her arms as high as they would go. 'The moment of truth. Break a leg, Antonia.'

'You too, Amanda,' I said, trying to focus on my breathing, to keep it steady and even so they wouldn't hear the tremor in my voice.

The girl with the earphones appeared again and introduced herself as 'Karen, the production assistant.' So this was Karen, I thought, recognizing her cheerful tone, and that was what 'PA' meant. She was tiny, with bright blue eyes, a mop of blonde curls and a preoccupied expression on her face. No wonder, I thought, looking down along the line at the various contestants fidgeting and jigging around, practising dance moves, or humming under their breath. How on earth did she manage this lot? There was absolutely no way I could have.

'OK guys, I'll take you in fives into the audition suites, and then we'll call you in one by one to listen to your pieces, and we'll be letting you know straight away if you've got through. If you haven't, we'd ask you to leave promptly to avoid a squeeze, all right?' There was much nodding from the contestants, all of whom seemed to have done this before, but I had to resist the urge to scream. Keep calm, keep calm, I kept telling myself, but my palms were sweaty, and my heart was pounding.

When she called us into the 'suites' as she'd called them, we sat on orange plastic chairs outside a green-painted door and waited for our turn. Amanda went in before me, and just five minutes later she breezed out, a broad grin on her face. She gave me the thumbs up. 'I've made it to the next call-up, can you believe it?'

'The next call-up,' I squeaked. 'You mean, we have to go through this *again*?' But then Karen was calling my name and Amanda grabbed my arm and squeezed it tight.

'You'll ace it – I'll wait here for you, OK?'

I nodded silently, and walked in through the door, into the tiniest room I'd ever seen. It was more like a broom cupboard, with nothing in it but a health and safety leaflet on the wall and a Formica-topped table, behind which sat Karen and a man of about my age, dressed entirely in black, a pair of huge black glasses perched on his nose.

'Hi there!' Karen said brightly, then looked down at her list. 'Toni! Good to see you.' She stood up enough to lean over the table and shake my hand. 'Right, you're going to sing for us, aren't you?'

I willed myself to open my mouth, to speak. '"Bridge

Over Troubled Water"', I managed finally, a hoarse rasp. I cleared my throat nervously, hardly daring to catch her eye.

'Well, that's great!' she said enthusiastically, shooting the man beside her a glance.

He nodded. 'Yeah, great.'

Oh, God, I thought. I can't do this. I felt the panic mount, and I had to fight the impulse to make a run for it. And then Karen said, 'Off you go, Toni.'

I opened my mouth, which was as dry as sandpaper, and croaked the first notes, before stopping dead. 'Sorry,' I muttered. 'I'll just try again.'

Karen nodded, her expression less enthusiastic now. She was probably well used to people drying on her, I thought. And then a voice in my head said, 'Well, not me.' I didn't know where the voice had come from, but this time, when I opened my mouth, the first few bars came out true and strong, and then, just like every time I sang, the song just took over. As I got into my stride, I could see Karen's expression change.

She began to relax, leaning back in her chair and grinning, and when I got to the end, she jumped up and said, 'Bravo!'

Even black-glasses man looked enthusiastic, mustering a 'Yeah, great.'

'Toni, that was just wonderful,' Karen enthused. 'You have a lovely quality to your voice. Well done – you're through to the next call-up.' She beamed.

'Well, that's great,' I said, feeling my breathing slow. 'Ehm, what's the next call-up?'

Karen smiled at me, and I felt about five years old. 'We have so many contestants that we have to whittle them down over the day by having more than one audition. So, you've got through here, and then you'll see Sandy, the producer, and she'll make a decision, and then the executive producer will take a look. And then we're all done!' she said brightly.

I could have cried with distress at the very thought of going through this one more time, let alone twice, but I gritted my teeth and nodded and smiled. 'Thanks a million, Karen. I look forward to it.' Even though it feels like a long visit to the dentist, I told myself.

Amanda screamed so loudly when I told her I'd got through, I thought my eardrums would burst, grabbing me in a bear hug and twirling me round and round in the corridor. 'We're through, we're through,' she kept yelling. I was mortified.

I wasn't used to this kind of thing, so I just shushed her gently and said, 'It's fantastic, I know, but we've got to do it again . . . twice.'

'Twice, schmice.' She yelled again. 'We are going all the way, baby!'

'That's great, Amanda, but can we take it a bit easier, please?'

She looked at me as if I was a complete spoilsport, then shrugged her shoulders. 'Cool. We'll wait and see, then.' Something in the tone of her voice told me that I was being just too uptight, but I decided to ignore that for a bit, and focus on the next call-up, singing and warbling the notes as loudly as I dared in the crowded corridor. Amanda jogged up and down on the spot beside me, occasionally blasting out a few bars of 'Total Eclipse of the Heart'. She had a real rock chick's voice, loud and raw.

'Wow, you sound amazing,' I said.

I was surprised at the look of sheer pleasure on her face at the compliment. 'Thanks, Antonia. I've really busted my balls on this one, to get the sound just right. I think it's OK, but . . .' She chewed her lip and I thought, my God, she's nervous. There was I thinking she was totally cool, and inside she feels just like me.

I reached out and squeezed her arm. 'It's more than OK, Amanda. It's great, believe me.'

'Thanks, baby.' She grinned. 'Here goes.' She nodded as another production assistant came towards us, clipboard in hand.

The next call-up went just fine, as Sandy was a lovely woman, who told me that I was 'amazing', but the third one was the one I knew really mattered. As I waited outside the tiny meeting room once more, this time for the executive producer, my teeth were chattering with nerves. I can't do it. I can't do it, I kept telling myself. Then, I can do it, I can, over and over again, until eventually, the door opened and Karen stuck her head out. I jumped with fright when she called my name.

'Toni – all set?'

I nodded, unable to open my mouth, and then in I went again, and stood in front of the same Formica table and looked at the same health and safety advert. The executive producer was a small, chubby man who extended a warm, sweaty hand to me and introduced himself as Martin.

'Now, Antonia, I've been hearing great things about you from Karen and Sandy. Shall we see what you can do?' And he smiled at me in a way which made me nervous. I shifted uncomfortably from foot to foot.

He looked at me expectantly. 'In your own time, Antonia.'

'Sure,' I said, clearing my throat noisily, then murmuring the opening bars of the song, controlling the sound tightly, just as Eithne had taught me to do, then letting the notes swell as the song took flight.

I was just getting into my stride, when Martin put both hands up. 'Thanks, Antonia, thanks. I've heard enough.'

'Oh.' I felt like bursting into tears. He hadn't even listened to the whole song, and already he was dismissing me. 'I can sing better,' I began. 'It's just nerves . . .'

He leaned back in his chair and laughed out loud. 'I'm saying I've heard enough because you're through, Antonia.' And he stood and offered his hand, a broad grin on his face.

For a moment, I didn't react, just stood there, until I remembered my manners, extending my hand and gripping his as firmly as I could. 'I can't believe it,' I whispered. 'Thanks, Martin . . . that's all I can say.'

He smiled and scratched his head. 'You don't need to say

anything else, just repeat that performance at the heats – OK?'

'OK,' I said and, before he could change his mind, I bolted through the door, closing it firmly behind me and standing there for a moment, trying to quieten my breathing, hearing my heart thumping in my chest. I'm through. I'm through, I kept saying to myself. I couldn't wait to tell Amanda. I opened my eyes, blinking, and looked around for any sign of her, but she was nowhere to be seen. My heart sank a little – I really hope she gets through, I thought. Then, in a daze, I walked slowly along the corridor, under the watchful gaze of all the performers sitting waiting to be called, and out the door into the car park. I climbed into my car, turned the key in the ignition, pulled out of the car park, and headed towards home, and all I could think was, I'm through to the heats of *That's Talent! Me*. Miss Mouse.

11

'COLETTE SAYS THAT STYLING SOMEONE FOR *THAT'S TALENT!*
is an opportunity she can't afford to miss,' Mary said,
chattering away as I looked out the car window. 'It'll get her
name around as well, so it's good for everyone. And she says
she has some really cool things to show you.'

'That's good,' I said, noncommittally, watching the
mountains flash past as we dashed along the motorway
into Dublin. Mary was relishing styling me for the heats of
That's Talent! I didn't like to argue with her because she was
so enthusiastic, but sometimes it was a bit overwhelming.
Sometimes, I felt I just wanted to get back into my comfy
tracksuit bottoms and sit in front of the TV, but that would
be going backwards, I knew, and anyway, the cat was
well and truly out of the bag now, just two days after the
auditions. I'd told Mary first, who'd nearly hugged me to
death, and then she'd rung her mother, who was head of
Glenvara County Guild, who'd rung Bridget, who was also
in the Guild, who'd rung everyone in the choir, and before I
could take a breath, all of Glenvara was queuing at my door,
or ringing my phone to congratulate me. I'd been mortified

and chuffed at the same time. I hadn't even managed to call Eithne first to tell her that all her hard work had paid off, but I needn't have worried – she was as pleased as punch and not a bit put out.

'All that matters is that my star pupil has triumphed,' she'd said to me, when I'd called around to her. 'I'll be able to put it on all my business cards now – "Eithne Fitzsimons, singing teacher to the stars".' She'd smiled. I felt that I had a kind of family around me, all supporting me – maybe it was Mum, I thought, looking down on me, making sure that I was OK. Either way, I felt somehow more confident, walking taller to O'Dwyer's to fetch my morning paper, smiling and waving as another person yelled, 'Can't wait for Saturday night, Antonia!', when once I would have cringed and run away.

But being styled professionally was another matter. I dressed boringly, I knew, but I felt safe that way. I knew that I needed to change, but the prospect seemed daunting, somehow.

'She won't make you look a fool, Antonia, if that's what you're worried about,' Mary was saying kindly as we drove along.

'I know,' I said. Not that I *did* know. I could end up looking a complete fright. But I supposed I just had to trust in Mary and Colette.

'Listen, what song are you singing on the show?'

'Well, I did "Bridge Over Troubled Water" for the auditions, but maybe that's too old-fashioned for the heats,'

I mused. 'Eithne and I have to sit down and have a think about it.'

'Isn't that by those two old guys, Garfield or something?' Mary asked.

I laughed. 'Simon and Garfunkel. It's a classic, Mary.'

'You could sing anything, Antonia, and make it sound good. What do the TV company make of it?'

'Oh, they really like it,' I said, thinking of Karen, the lovely production assistant at Celtic, and Martin, who'd been so enthusiastic. It felt right, somehow, to sing the song again – it suited me.

'Colette has a few hair and make-up ideas for you as well,' Mary's voice interrupted my thoughts. 'She's got a friend at the store who does it for fashion shows.'

'Great!' I tried to sound enthusiastic and to focus on Sister Monica's advice: 'One foot in front of the other, Antonia.' Because if I thought about everything, it was just too overwhelming for words . . . the competition, the clothes . . . my date with Niall. No. That was something I definitely couldn't deal with right now.

'Thanks for seeing me, Colette. I'm not very good at shopping,' I said apologetically to her, when she greeted me with a warm smile and a firm handshake. I'd been afraid that she'd be intimidating, too fashionable, but she wasn't, she was just . . . cool, with a quirky edge, a cap of black hair cropped tightly around her pixie face, her dark eyes sparkling with mischief – she looked fun, Colette.

'I like your shoes,' I said, nodding at her suede mules. They were a rich burgundy with a platform and an outsize gold buckle on them. They should have looked like something out of a Shakespeare play, but instead they were modern and totally fresh. I looked at my own sensible ballet flats and skinny blue jeans – the product of a quick shopping trip to Arklow with Mary, so that I wouldn't look like a nun when I met Colette.

'Thanks. And don't worry – I should be thanking you for giving me the chance to style you for *That's Talent!* – you've no idea what it'll do for my profile!' Colette laughed. 'Now, let's have a little wander around – no pressure. We'll just pick a few things that you think look nice, and take it from there, shall we?'

An hour later, I was sitting in a large dressing room, on a comfy velvet sofa, surrounded by expensive outfits – mortifyingly expensive. I'd tried to explain this to Colette. 'Eight hundred euro,' I'd said, examining the label on one of them. 'Colette, this is out of my price range . . .'

'Don't worry. If you see something you like, I can just contact the designer and let them know that you'll be wearing their creation on the country's biggest talent show, and, sure, they'll be only delighted to let you "borrow" it.' She grinned. She had a broad country accent and such a down-to-earth manner that I felt immediately at ease. 'And anyway,' she added, 'you have a fabulous figure – any designer would be delighted to see you wear their stuff. Now, this one, I think, don't you, girls?' She picked up a short silver-grey dress. 'The body is silk, but the sleeves are soft leather . . . perfect . . . or the silver silk-chiffon? Both would look perfect for auditions. And as you have such great legs, Antonia, you can really get away with showing a fair bit of them. What do you think, Mary?'

Mary nodded her head knowledgeably. 'Got to be the silk-chiffon. Those metallic sequins are just fab. And Colette's right, Antonia, you should be showing those legs off!'

'Not now, I won't.' I laughed, thinking of my milk-bottle legs, so white they were almost blue.

'Nothing a bit of fake tan won't sort out,' said Colette, guessing my thoughts. 'Now, try it on,' she held out the exquisite silver dress. The sequins weren't shiny, but a dull metallic silver which rustled and shone when it moved. I was terrified to put it on, afraid I'd put a big rip in it with an elbow.

'It looks very short,' I said doubtfully.

Colette just nodded her head, and insisted, 'Go on, put it on.' And she helped me pull it over my head, tugging it gently over my hips. Then she stood back, a look of concentration on her face. 'Good . . . good . . . just hang on a sec,' and she bolted out of the dressing-room door.

'Surely I don't look that bad,' I joked.

Mary shook her head. 'You look a million dollars, Antonia. Honestly, I wouldn't have thought it – sorry, that sounded so rude.'

I leaned over to her and squeezed her arm. 'It doesn't,

Mary. I haven't worn anything even remotely fashionable for so long that I honestly don't know how. I've you to thank for this,' I indicated the silver dress, and the chunky sequins which swished as I moved. 'And now, I'd better stand up straight or I'll rip this dress.'

There was a swish of the dressing-room curtain, and Colette reappeared, this time with a pair of shoes in her hand. 'Nude Loubs should do the trick.'

'Nude who?'

'Never mind, just try them on. I guessed you were a size six,' Colette said, kneeling down to help me slide my foot into the shoe. It was a gorgeous pale pinky beige with just the faintest sheen to it.

'Oh! Louboutins! I've read about them! I'll never be able to stand in them, though,' I protested.

'Oh, yes you will.' Colette looked up at me and grinned. 'They've this great platform which makes them so much more comfortable, believe me. Now, try walking in them.'

I shuffled forward hesitantly at first, then more confidently. 'You're right, I feel just fantastic in these.'

'And you look it,' Mary said admiringly.

Colette nodded, ever the professional. 'That's it, Antonia. That's the look. Now, what about your hair? Any ideas who'll be styling it?'

'Ehm, me?' I said.

Mary and Colette both burst out laughing, before Mary patted me on the shoulder. 'I don't think so, Antonia, do you? Any ideas, Colette?'

Colette nodded her head eagerly. 'Oh, yes. And he's quite cute, by the way.'

I shook my head. 'I'm not sure, girls, really. I've always done it myself . . .'

'Which is why you look like an American pageant queen – all tumbling locks and big teeth. I think we need something sharper, lighter. That doesn't make you look as if you should be wearing knee socks,' said Colette. Mary nodded eagerly, and I found myself agreeing. What did she mean, 'pageant queen'? I wasn't sure whether to be offended or not.

'I'll book Richard for next Friday morning. I assume the heats are on Saturday?'

'Ehm, yes, next Saturday are the rehearsals, and then the Saturday after, the real thing. It's always recorded on Saturday morning for transmission that night.'

'Right. Well as long as you don't move your head for the rest of the week, you'll be fine,' Mary said.

I punched her on the arm. 'Very funny. But thanks, Mary, and Colette, I can't believe that I look so . . . grown-up.' I examined myself in the mirror again, unable to believe that this tall, slender woman was actually me. That I had legs and hips and looked actually OK. Miss Mouse. I could hardly believe it. I swallowed and tried to fight back the tears.

'Sexy, Antonia. You look sexy. Ditch the big hair and you'll knock them out. Now, group hug,' Mary ordered, pulling me towards her in a cloud of perfume and hair, and Colette, too. 'Better?'

I nodded, afraid to say anything in case I burst into tears. 'Thanks so much, girls. I don't know what to say.'

'You can thank us when you win *That's Talent!*, OK?' Colette said.

'Deal,' I said, and the girls hugged me again. It felt so good, I realized, to have women friends my own age. I couldn't believe I'd been missing out on this for all these years. On simple friendship and shopping and . . . fun. And then, of course, I felt a sharp jab of guilt. I knew I shouldn't be feeling like this, not now. It was too soon. I'm sorry, Mum, I said to myself. I haven't forgotten you, you know.

I was more or less silent on the way back in the car, answering Mary's excited chatter with the odd 'Yes' or 'No' until eventually she said, 'You must be exhausted, Antonia.'

I pretended that was the reason. 'It's all the excitement, Mary. Honestly, I feel like a small child that's been to Disneyland.'

Mary laughed. 'Well, enjoy it, Antonia, you deserve it. And you looked fabulous, you really did.'

'Thanks,' I said, for what felt like the hundredth time. Because I didn't want to tell Mary how I really felt. Confused. It seemed wrong, somehow, to be going out and enjoying myself so soon after Mum . . . it was as if I was neglecting her somehow. Oh, I know I wasn't needed any more. That she was no longer there for me to care for, but still, it felt wrong, to be trying on expensive outfits. But of course I couldn't tell Mary that. It would be so ungrateful after everything she'd done for me. I turned to her and put on my biggest, brightest smile. 'Tell you what? Why don't I order us a takeaway? I don't feel like cooking after all this.'

Mary smiled politely. 'Thanks, Antonia, but I'll have to pass. Dave's taking me up to Dublin to see *Grease* at the Grand Canal Theatre. He booked the tickets ages ago.'

'Oh, sure, that's great. You lucky thing.' I tried to sound enthusiastic, but I couldn't help it. Just for a moment, I felt jealous. That Mary had this normal life, with a boyfriend whom she'd known for ever. Apart from a couple of boys in school, I'd never really had a proper boyfriend – I'd hardly been kissed. Oh, God, every time I thought I was coming out of my shell a bit, I was reminded of how useless I was at all this. At life.

'We'll do it another time,' Mary said kindly.

'Oh, sure,' I said, and gave her my brightest smile. 'As you know, I'm a bit tired after all the shopping, anyway. And I need to listen to the song and practise a bit.' And when she pulled up outside the house, I managed to thank her and hug her again, and then I walked in the door of my house and clicked on the light. I was alone again.

12

OF COURSE, THE GANG IN CHOIR PRACTICE WERE DYING TO know every detail of the auditions, gathering around me at break-time during rehearsals and firing questions at me.

'Did you see anyone famous?' Bridget wanted to know. 'I always liked that Aaron fellow that presents it.' Her eyes lit up with a mischievous grin. 'He's hot.'

'He's too young for you,' Betty blurted, her arms folded across her chest, her mouth set in a tight line. Betty disapproved of Bridget, but she never really explained why. 'She's a flibbertigibbet,' was all she would say on the subject. Bridget, on the other hand, thought that Betty was frosty, uptight, didn't know how to let her hair down. They were always finding some excuse to bicker, and I often had to keep the peace between the two of them.

'I just wanted to know . . .' Bridget murmured now, looking like a sulky child.

'No, Aaron wasn't there. It was just a huge queue of people and a day-long wait for the auditions.' I smiled. 'I thought I'd die of boredom. It really wasn't that glamorous, believe me.'

'But imagine just being there, singing your heart out and hearing that magic yes. It must have been amazing.' Bridget was getting carried away now, and Betty tutted and rolled her eyes to heaven.

Billy interjected, 'I'm sure Antonia did us proud. I'd have loved to be a fly on the wall there.' He grinned. He was trying to soothe Bridget's ruffled feathers, I knew, and I tried to smile back, but I wished the ground would open up and swallow me. I know that they meant well, that they just wanted the best for me, but the attention was overwhelming, and I hadn't even got to the heats yet. God knows what they'd be like then.

Thankfully, Eithne came to my rescue. 'For goodness' sake, everyone, give Antonia some room. She can hardly breathe with the way you're all pressing in on her.' She flapped her arms in the air in a shooing motion. 'Now, no offence intended, but this is choir practice, not *That's Talent!*, and we have a job to do. Back to the practice room, everyone, please,' she said, briskly clapping her hands and winking at me as she did so, to soften her words. But I didn't mind. I could have cried with relief.

The rest of the practice was spent going over a tricky new hymn for the Holy Communion Mass. The harmonies were so complicated that it took all of our concentration to master them. Never had I been so glad of the distraction, I thought, trying to drown out Mrs Ferguson, who was singing completely out of tune beside me. Now, hopefully everything can get back to normal, I thought. And then I remembered my date with Niall, and my heart started to flutter all over again.

'Wow, you look—' Niall did a double take on the doorstep in front of me. He stood there for a moment, in hiking boots, thick socks and a woollen fleece, as if he were ready for a hike up Mount Everest.

'I know. I just had it cut yesterday. For the show.' I felt self-conscious all of a sudden. My hair was about six inches shorter and had been styled into soft layers, the golden colour now with warm honey tones through it. It wasn't that radical a change and yet I felt completely different. More grown-up, somehow. Less girlish.

Niall looked puzzled for a while, before the penny dropped. *'That's Talent!*? You're doing it? Well done, Antonia.' He sounded so genuinely delighted for me that I felt a surge of warmth towards him. 'That takes guts,' he added.

'Thanks.' I blushed, thinking of the rehearsals earlier that morning at Celtic TV. The lights in the rehearsal studio had been pretty hot, but somehow I'd managed to keep the nerves under control and just pretend that I was in command of things. 'Fake it till you make it,' as Amanda had said the previous week. And it had worked, helped by the band, who were amazingly friendly.

'All set, Antonia?' Bill, the band leader had said, before the pianist played the opening chords to the song and I took a deep breath. And then I was away, the words of 'Bridge

Over Troubled Water' coming out of my mouth, flowing out as the sound of the orchestra built up behind me. And that was it, then. The song ended and there was a silence, before the violinists began tapping their strings. They're warming up for the next act, I'd told myself, replacing the microphone in the stand and muttering, 'Thanks.'

'They're applauding you, Toni,' Karen had come over to me, a set of earphones on her head, a clipboard in her hand. Bill had nodded his head in approval and given me the thumbs up, and I'd blushed. 'That will simply blow the judges away on Saturday. I can't wait.' Karen had clasped her hands together like a girl.

I'd blushed again, wishing for the hundredth time that I didn't keep going red every time someone spoke to me. 'Thanks.' And even though I knew that Karen probably said this to all the contestants, it sure felt good to hear it. It's funny how some small remark can change your day. Karen's praise had me floating on a cloud, unable to believe how much I'd enjoyed myself. And the nerves had just faded away. For a short while I forgot everything, including my date with Niall, until there he was, standing in front of me. It was probably just as well – I'd have worked myself up into a complete state about it otherwise.

'You look as if you're ready for anything,' I joked, nodding at Niall's walking gear.

He smiled and looked down at his boots, and I noticed again the way his hair was thinning just a bit at the top of his head. Maybe he was older than I'd thought. 'Well, I like to go walking whenever I get the chance. I thought we might go to Powerscourt and look at the waterfall,' he said.

'Sure, that sounds great. I'll just dig out my own boots, and we'll be all set.' I turned to go into the hall, 'C'mon in,' I added.

'Thanks.' He looked embarrassed for a moment, before stepping over the threshold, bending slightly as he walked through the front door, which made me realize just how tall he was. 'You have a pair of boots, then?'

'You sound surprised.' I laughed.

'Well, I don't know you that well . . .'

'But you wouldn't put me down as an outdoor girl?' As I spoke, I thought how funny it was that I could talk to Niall like this. Like I was confident. Maybe it was the new hair-cut, I thought. That and the shopping trip, and the talent show. It seemed as if, after all this time, I was changing, and the feeling was . . . strange, somehow, unfamiliar, and yet not unpleasant.

'Well . . .' He looked sheepish.

'My dad loved hiking. I used to go for walks with him on a Sunday morning after Mass. I only gave up when Mum got ill, really.' I had turned my back to him and was rummaging around in the cupboard under the stairs.

'How long ago did your dad die?' I couldn't see him, but his voice was soft.

I turned to face him, standing up, a pair of hiking boots

in my hand. 'Ten years ago,' I said. 'I can hardly believe it, really, that both of them are gone.'

'That's tough, Antonia. I'm sorry.' He put his hands in his pockets and hunched his shoulders in his fleece, but the expression on his face was one of concern, of sympathy.

Don't, I thought. Don't feel sorry for me. 'Niall, that's life. I was lucky to have them for eighteen years. I have to look at it that way.' Or else I'd dissolve in a mess of self-pity, I silently added. 'OK, all set?' I tried to sound cheery as I tied the laces on my boots.

'Sure,' he looked at me steadily, before smiling at me, that smile that changed his tired face entirely. 'After you.' He made a motion to usher me through the front door.

'No, I have to lock up.' I laughed.

'Oh, of course,' he said. Then he walked ahead of me, bowing his head again as he stepped through the doorway. 'Your car or mine?'

'Oh, wow,' I said, when I caught sight of the car. 'Definitely yours.' A navy-blue vintage Mercedes, it had soft leather seats and a shiny dashboard made out of walnut. It looked gorgeous.

'Thanks.' He laughed. 'It was a gift from my parents when I graduated from medical school.'

Some gift, I thought, running a hand over the shiny paintwork, thinking of the set of CDs Mum and Dad had bought me when I got my school-leaving exams.

'I know what you're thinking, but my uncle owns a garage, and he always has a couple of vintage cars knocking

116

about. We did this up together. Took us the best part of a year.'

'It's beautiful.'

'Hop in.' He opened the passenger door, then ran around to the driver's side and jumped in. Even in a car as big as this, his head nearly touched the roof. I had to stifle a smile.

'What?' He glanced at me as we pulled out into the road.

'Nothing. It's just . . . you're very tall.' As I said it, I blushed and felt a complete fool. God, what was I thinking? I sounded like a five-year-old.

He didn't seem to mind, just nodding and saying, 'Yep. It makes reaching the top shelves in supermarkets a cinch. And nobody ever had to pass me the butter at home.'

At home. I realized that I'd never asked him about his family. 'Do you have many brothers and sisters?'

He paused for a bit, but then he said, 'Three of each. Big family. I'm the youngest. Dinner times were interesting in our household.'

'I can't imagine what it must be like to have a big family.' I sighed.

'Noisy.' Niall laughed. 'And you have no privacy and nothing belongs to you, but other than that, it's just fine.'

I smiled. 'I know what you mean. Even though I'm an only child, when I was in the orphanage, I shared a room with four other girls. We weren't too strong on privacy,' I said.

'That must have been difficult.' He was trying to be diplomatic.

117

'Well, I didn't know any better, to be honest. And I was never alone.'

'You don't like being alone, then?'

I shook my head. 'No, not really. And yet, it's funny that I've ended up that way. I think maybe when you're an orphan, you always feel it: the sense that you're basically alone, do you know what I mean?' I turned to him, wanting him to understand, unable to believe that I even thought like that, and didn't mind saying it out loud. 'No, of course you don't,' I added hastily. And then I shrugged and changed the subject. 'The countryside is so beautiful at this time of year, isn't it?'

'Sure is.' He sounded too enthusiastic, as if he were relieved at the change of topic. But then he added, almost under his breath, 'But I do know what you mean.'

There was something about the way he said it. I just didn't want to push, and so I said nothing. The rest of the journey was spent discussing the beauties of Wicklow, the ring of mountains that circled the bay, the soft reds and yellows of the autumn leaves. 'Not that I get to see much of it,' Niall said, as we drove through the gates of Powerscourt demesne. 'I work such long hours. But whenever I get the chance, I visit Gerry and Sally and the kids and go for a good long walk. Lola is a very energetic dog who sometimes drags me up to the top.' He laughed, pulling into a parking space beneath the sheer green cliffs of the waterfall.

'Sounds blissful,' I said, looking up at the cliffs above me and the long stream of water gushing from the top, a torrent of grey-white crashing against the rocks at the bottom.

'It is, and the kids are great fun. They love racing up to the top, and trying to pull each other back if one of them gets too far ahead. It's hilarious.' He laughed.

'I know, they're great kids, aren't they?' I said.

'They are,' he agreed.

There was a silence again, before I said, 'I used to mind the babies in the orphanage.' Why on earth did I say that? I thought, the minute I'd opened my mouth. It was hardly first-date material.

'Oh?' I saw a flicker of distress cross his face.

Oh, God, I'm boring him to death, I thought, and I had hastily to add, 'Oh, no, I loved it, it was my favourite chore. All the other kids hated it because sometimes you had to change nappies and mop up sick. But for me it was heaven, because they always smiled the minute they saw you. I think they were alone for so much of the time,' I told him.

He nodded silently.

'It wasn't neglect, the nuns were great to all of us, it was just that there were so many children. The nuns never stopped working, and they were very kind. They get such bad press, so I always feel I have to tell people that.' Shut up, Antonia, shut up, I kept telling myself. He doesn't want to hear this.

Niall was silent for a long time. 'Was it tough?' he finally asked.

'I didn't know it was tough, and Sister Monica took me

under her wing, so I was fine. I suppose what was missing really was one-to-one attention, so that's where I learned that if you're quiet and say nothing, you get by far easier. It was only when I came to live with Mum and Dad that I realized that life wasn't all about a strict regime, rules and bells. Does that make any sense?'

'Perfect sense.' The way he said it made me look at him, but he was staring straight ahead, the expression on his face unreadable. Then, suddenly, he reached over and squeezed my hand. And then the moment was broken, as we reached the bottom of the waterfall.

'Wow, I'd forgotten how spectacular it is.' I had to raise my voice above the din of the water.

'It is, isn't it?' Niall roared back, and we both laughed. 'C'mon, there's a nice path around here.'

We spent the next hour walking along the edge of the waterfall, scrambling around on the rocks with all of the children out for walks with their families, listening to them scream and shout as they tried to avoid being splashed by the water. We didn't say much, just clambered over the mossy rocks, Niall occasionally extending a hand to help me, before we took a steep path which led up the side. I could feel my lungs burning with the effort of the climb as I scrambled along after Niall, who kept up a steady pace, but I wasn't about to tell him that I hadn't had this much exercise in a long time. Finally, we reached the top and I leaned over, my hands on my knees, trying to catch my breath.

'Sorry, was I going too fast?'

I shook my head, unable to speak, before standing upright to take in the view, which was spectacular, from the Sugar Loaf right out to the sea. 'It's beautiful.'

'It is, isn't it? I often pop up here to take it all in. It's so peaceful.'

I couldn't resist a smile. 'Pop up? The climb nearly killed me,' I joked. And when he looked at me apologetically, I said, 'It was worth it, though, for this,' indicating the view. 'And I'd forgotten how much I liked walking. It's so relaxing.' And I sound like a woman making polite conversation, I thought. I sighed. Why couldn't I think of something decent to say, something that might show Niall that I might be in the slightest bit interesting? That I was a woman with opinions. Except of course, I wasn't. Why on earth would he find me interesting, when I had done so little with my life?

'Penny for them.' When I looked around, he was watching me, amused.

'Oh, I was just thinking that I'm probably not the most exciting date you've ever had,' I said.

'I'll be the judge of that,' he said dryly. 'Now, why don't you tell me all about *That's Talent!*? What made you decide to enter after all?'

'Well, I thought I had nothing to lose. And I suppose I wanted to prove something to myself: that I could do something that really mattered, you know? Mum was always telling me to use my talent, but I never really did. I told myself that it was because I was too busy looking after her, but it wasn't really. I was scared, that was the real reason. And I'm still scared, but I have to do it.'

'Feel the fear and do it anyway,' Niall said.

I smiled. 'You've read the book, too.'

'Hah, yeah. You could say that.' His expression darkened, and I wondered why he'd have needed to read a book like that. But it didn't seem like the moment to ask. And then he was looking at his watch. 'I'd better head back down. I'm on at ten tonight, I'm afraid to say. And it's a Saturday night, so all hell will break loose.'

'But you love every minute of it,' I said, and was rewarded with that smile.

'I do, actually.'

'What do you do when you're not working?' I asked him on the way down.

'Well, pretty boring stuff. We get so little time off as SHOs that I end up doing a pile of washing or paying bills. But every so often, I get the chance to come up here. And I play the guitar, very badly,' he said.

'Oh, really? Maybe you could accompany me on the show.' I laughed.

'If you are planning on getting no further than the heats, sure. I do a mean "Hound Dog".'

'I don't think that's quite what the producers have in mind, but thanks anyway.'

He laughed, and then looked serious for a moment. 'I really enjoyed this, Antonia,' he said. 'Let's do it again.'

'Sure,' I agreed. 'I'll be focused on the heats for the next few days, but after that would be great.'

'The heats, of course,' he said. 'Will you have anyone there?'

I couldn't tell if he was dropping a hint that he wanted to come or not, but I decided to bite the bullet. 'Apart from the entire village of Glenvara, hardly a soul. Why, would you like to come along?' Oh, God, here I go again, I thought, sticking my neck out. But he seemed genuinely pleased to be invited.

'Thanks, Antonia, I'd love to. Won't wear my scrubs,' he joked. 'Or this,' he nodded, indicating his fleece and walking boots.

'I'd appreciate that.' I laughed. 'Not that I'll notice, I'll be so nervous,' I added, feeling the butterflies in my tummy at the thought of it. 'I've been thinking about it for so long, but now that it's real, well . . .'

'You'll get through it, Antonia. More than that, you'll triumph, I know you will. It's your time to shine. And you'll feel great that you did it, no matter what the judges say.'

'I'll try to bear that in mind,' I said dryly. Because it was only when Niall said it that I realized how much I wanted to succeed. I didn't want just to try my best, I wanted to get through to the next round, and my feelings surprised me. 'I really want this, Niall,' I blurted.

He put his hand on my arm, and gave it a brief squeeze, and for a moment, all thoughts of the show left my mind. 'I can see that. I can see how much it matters to you, and

123

that focus will really keep you going. That and knowing that we're all rooting for you. So next Sunday morning, when we come out here for a walk again, you'll be well on your way to being a singing star.'

'A *walk*?' I joked. 'Do you think I'm going to put myself through this again?' But we both knew that I'd say yes. That I wouldn't miss it for the world.

13

AND THEN, SUDDENLY, HERE IT WAS, THE DAY OF THE FIRST heats of *That's Talent!* It had come at last, in spite of my best efforts to slow time down. I was sitting in Mum's armchair, Colette and Mary fussing around me. 'We'll wait until we get to the studio, and talk to the make-up girls then,' Colette was saying. 'We don't want you plastered in slap, even with the studio lighting. They always overdo it on Celtic, and they all look like Kabuki dolls, honestly.' She was standing, hands on hips, in a pair of the skinniest skinny jeans I'd ever seen, a torn T-shirt and a pair of grey suede shoe-boots, looking every inch the rock chick.

'You should be doing the competition, not me.' I tried to joke with her, nodding at her clothes. It was hard to talk, though, because of the lump in my throat, which wouldn't go away.

'No, I shouldn't, because I sound like a bag of cats,' she said crisply. 'And you sound like an angel. Which is why you are going on *That's Talent!* and I'm not. Now, all set?' she looked at me sharply, and I nodded, unable to speak. Colette had a habit of saying it as she saw it, and I'd had to get used to that, working with her, but I was grateful, because she was the only one who told me the truth, and I knew that I could rely on her.

I let her lead me in my heated rollers to the car, the precious chiffon sequinned dress over her arm, and then we were driving to the studio, a huge cavern of a place. Mary had insisted on taking the morning off work and driving me up, 'as your personal consultant', and kept up a stream of chatter in the car, which saved me having to reply, I suppose.

'Will the others all be there?' she asked me, and I nodded, thinking of my motley bunch of supporters. Eithne and Billy from the choir, of course, and Betty, because she'd been like a mother to me for the last six weeks.

Sister Monica said she wouldn't miss it for the world. 'I love *That's Talent!*,' she'd said when I'd called to invite her. 'Although you'd want to watch out for that Maurice Prendergast, he's very tough on the contestants.'

I hadn't a clue who Maurice Prendergast was. One of the judges, I supposed. 'Well, you know more about it than I do,' I had to admit.

'Maybe. I watch it every Saturday night along with the rest of the country. But the thing is, we're only the viewers, not performers,' she insisted. 'What matters is that you show them just how talented you are. And you'll melt their hearts, Antonia, I know you will.'

I tried to remember this as we neared Dublin, tried to remember that Sister Monica had always been there for me, and she was here for me now. She and all those who really mattered in my life. It was funny how this group had gathered around me, to help me. Maybe Bridget was right when she'd said, 'There's something about you, Antonia. Something that makes everyone want to look after you.' I wasn't so sure that I liked the sound of that – it made me sound like a bit of a victim, when I really wanted to learn to stand on my own two feet – but right now, I needed all the help I could get.

I had never seen so many people in one place, from the crowds thronging the pavements, hoping to catch a glimpse of their favourite star, to those self-conscious girls and boys, just like me, hanging around the corridors backstage. 'Who *are* these people?' Colette said, as Mary nudged the car gently into the studio car park.

'You sound like the Queen,' Mary joked. 'I assume they're all the contestants and . . . other people,' she said doubtfully, trying to take in the crowds. 'Now, where are we supposed to go?'

'Backstage Area 3,' Colette said. Then, looking at me, 'OK, Antonia?'

I couldn't speak. I'd literally lost my voice for a moment, rooted to the spot.

'Antonia?' Mary said, taking me gently by the arm. 'C'mon, we'll find it together, nice and easy now, OK?' she was talking to me as if I was an old woman, guiding me gently along the corridors to a pair of double doors, above which was written 'Backstage Area 3', with a handwritten sign below it. 'Performers R-Z.'

'This must be us.'

I stopped in front of the doors. 'I can't go through,' I said.

'Yes, you can, Antonia, one step at a time, OK?' Mary said gently.

I nodded dumbly and was about to open the stage door when I felt a presence beside me. I turned to see a man in a leather jacket standing beside me, a broad smile on his face. He seemed to have appeared out of nowhere. 'You must be Toni,' he said, extending a hand. 'Dave Byrne.'

I didn't know what to do for a moment, and then remembered my manners, offering him my hand in return.

'Dave Byrne from where, exactly?' Colette interrupted, her tone sharp. She had that fierce look on her face, the one she reserved for people she didn't like.

He grinned and gave me a 'who's-your-friend' look. 'Dave Byrne from the *Sunday Star* newspaper. Just trying to get some background on the contestants. You're the girl from Wicklow, aren't you?' he asked me.

'Ehm, yes, how did you know that?' I said.

He winked at me, and of course I blushed bright red. 'Oh, we have our ways,' he said mysteriously.

'I'm sure you do, but we're in a hurry,' Colette said and tried to brush past him, but he stuck a hand out to stop her.

'Just one quote, Toni?' That grin again.

Karen had told me to be friendly to the media, so I plastered a smile on my face. 'Sure. What do you want to know?'

'How does it feel to come from nowhere to the biggest talent competition in the country?' He was businesslike now, pulling a battered notebook out of his pocket and flipping it open, pen at the ready.

'Well, I wouldn't call Glenvara "nowhere",' I ventured, thinking of what Bridget would say if she read *that* in the newspaper. 'But it's amazing, Dave. I think I'm dreaming, to be honest.'

He nodded, scribbling. 'And how far do you hope to go?'

'Ehm . . .' I was startled by the question. 'Well, I don't know, I'm just taking it week by week,' I began, wondering if this was the answer he was looking for.

'She's going all the way,' Mary said proudly. 'And you can quote me on that. Mary, from Glenvara,' she said help-fully.

'Well, Mary from Glenvara, she's lucky to have you as a friend, that's all I can say.' Dave looked up from his note-book and smiled. 'Thanks, Toni. Good luck!' And then he was gone, in search of another contestant, weaving through the crowds in the car park.

'God, what an asshole,' Colette said loud enough for him to hear.

'Colette, he can hear you,' Mary said. 'And anyway, he was harmless enough.'

'Oh, yeah, "Mary from Glenvara".' Colette guffawed, so that Mary blushed bright red.

'Well . . . I just wanted to show my support for Antonia,' she muttered, looking embarrassed.

I could see that she was hurt, and so I hastily said, 'Girls, there was no way I could have faced him without both of you there beside me, so thanks.' I put an arm around them both and squeezed.

'You are entirely welcome.' Colette smiled. 'And now, deep breath everyone. Here we go.' She pushed the door open, to reveal a huge space, lit brightly from above, around which bustled TV staff with earphones and clipboards.

We all stood there for a moment, and I swallowed. 'Oh my God.'

'It's not Glenvara parish choir, that's for sure,' Colette said, and then Mary shot her a look.

'C'mon, Antonia, let's go and find Karen,' she suggested.

I allowed myself to be led across the studio, trying not to trip over wires, to keep focusing on breathing in and out, steadily, to calm my nerves, and to put 'one foot in front of the other', as Sister Monica would say. Oh, Lord, Sister Monica. She'd be in the audience with Billy and Bridget and Betty and all of the others. And then I thought of Niall, and my stomach flipped. I had absolutely no idea how I was going to do this.

'Toni!' Karen was in front of me, her ever-present earphones around her neck, a welcoming smile on her face. 'How are you feeling?'

I opened my mouth to speak, but no words would come out.

'She's a bit nervous,' Colette offered.

'That's natural.' Karen beamed. 'We'll look after you,

Toni, don't worry. We'll make sure you're well prepared and nice and relaxed.'

I couldn't imagine how, so I just nodded as Karen walked in front of us. 'I'll show you to the contestants' dressing room. It's a bit crowded in there, but I'm sure you'll squeeze in.' She was talking as she raced across the studio floor, a walkie-talkie attached to her belt crackling away as she did so. 'Now, here we are,' she said brightly as we arrived at a tiny, scuffed grey door. She knocked briskly and then opened it. 'Hi – everyone decent, I hope?'

There was a chorus of yeses and noes, and then we were ushered in, and before I had the chance to ask any questions, the door was firmly shut behind us. I took in the scene: the room was tiny and crammed with people, all pulling on dresses and applying make-up, even though Celtic had a huge make-up department. Maybe Colette was right, I thought, and they'd end up plastered in the stuff if they didn't do it themselves. There was a roar of chatter, but I could barely hear it above the din of the hairdryers. Nobody looked at me or said hello: they were all too absorbed in their work. Some girls were practising their scales, snatches of songs I half-recognized wafting towards me. One of them sounded really good – she had a strong, distinctive voice – and my heart sank. What was I thinking of, that I'd be the only one with a good voice here?

As if in a trance, I sat in the only available chair, a battered red vinyl one, and stared at myself in the mirror. The girl who gazed back at me was deathly pale, her eyes two dark circles in her face. I swallowed down the nerves again, wondering if I should have brought something to help me stay calm. Mum had always liked brandy, but I didn't drink, so that would hardly help.

'Here,' Mary was waving a small yellow bottle under my nose. 'Rescue Remedy' was written on a small yellow label on it.

'What's that?'

'It'll help you stay calm,' she soothed. 'Just a couple of drops on the tongue.'

I looked at her doubtfully. 'Will it send me to sleep?'

She guffawed. 'For God's sake, I'm not giving you drugs. Now take the stuff. You look as if you need it.'

I did as she told me and then stood up, like a robot, to let Colette pull the dress over my head.

'Wow,' she said, standing back to admire me. 'Some slap and you'll be sorted. Now, I'm not prepared to leave you to the tender mercies of Celtic's make-up department, so lie back, please.'

I sat gingerly on the chair, feeling the sequins scratching the back of my legs. I tilted my head back and let Colette smooth foundation over my face, feeling myself relax a little and my shoulders drop. 'That stuff seems to be working,' I joked.

'Good,' Mary said. 'Now, just remember: regular deep breaths from the diaphragm, to loosen your throat muscles.'

In spite of my nerves, I tried not to laugh at this advice from a girl who cheerfully admitted that she hadn't got a note in her head. All the time, I was practising silently, the words of the song playing over and over, on a loop. I longed to open my mouth and let the notes fly out, but felt suddenly shy in front of all these people. But once Colette had finished tugging at the hem of my dress and pushing my feet into the nude Louboutins, I jumped up out of my seat. 'I need the loo.'

'Are you going to be sick?' Colette asked.

I shook my head. 'Don't worry, I'm fine.' I gave her a wobbly smile. In truth, I did feel queasy, a tight knot in my stomach, but I just wanted some peace and quiet for a few moments.

Once in the corridor, I took a gulp of the slightly cooler air and wandered along until I found the bathroom. Inside the cubicle, I gratefully sat down on the closed lid of the toilet and took a deep breath. Silence at last. What on earth had I let myself in for? I closed my eyes and let the words of the song come into my mind, and then I opened my mouth and sang. Even in the cubicle, it didn't sound that bad. If I could manage to sing even vaguely in tune, I wouldn't embarrass myself that much, I thought.

After I'd practised a couple of times, I got up and went out into the bathroom. I longed to splash cold water over my face, but of course, I'd ruin my make-up. I looked at myself in the mirror: the pale face was now warmer-looking, a slick of rosy blush on my cheeks. My eyes looked smoky and dramatic and my dress glittered in the lights.

'That was some singing you were doing in there.' The

voice beside me sounded amused, admiring even, and I turned to see Amanda. She looked amazing. Her hair had been combed into a huge, wild mass of red, and her eyes outlined in smoky grey. She was wearing jeans so tight they looked as if they'd been sprayed on, and a fringed suede jacket.

'Amanda!' I was so thrilled to see her that I pulled her into a hug. 'I tried to find you that day, but you'd disappeared, and then I wasn't sure . . .' my voice trailed off.

'Well, I got through, and here I am.' She did a little twirl, her green eyes flashing. 'What do you think?'

'I think you look just the part,' I said. 'Bonnie Tyler isn't a patch on you.'

'And so do you.' She stood back to admire me, and as usual, I blushed bright red. 'I can see you've had professional styling.' There was that edge to her voice again, that tone that I couldn't quite make sense of. You're being paranoid, Antonia, I told myself firmly. Amanda's beautiful, and clearly talented, and a friend. And after all, it wasn't as if I'd had much practice in judging other people's characters, was it?

I looked down at my dress. 'A couple of friends helped me out,' I said quietly.

'Well, they've done a brilliant job.' She was smiling at me now, and that tone was gone. 'You know, your singing is utterly sublime, and you've instantly made me jealous, because you will blow us all out of the water.' She was her old, warm, laughing self again.

I smiled back, relieved at the change of atmosphere. 'Oh, don't be silly, Amanda. I'm a bag of nerves.'

She extended a hand and placed it on my shoulder, her green eyes gazing into mine intently. 'May the best woman win, Antonia.'

'Sure.' I fidgeted nervously, unnerved by her gaze. 'Good luck, Amanda.'

'You too, baby,' she said, turning from me to examine her face in the mirror. 'You, too.'

And then there was no turning back. Karen reappeared and ushered us to the back of the stage, like a crowd of schoolchildren on a tour. She put her finger to her lips, then whispered. 'Quiet, please, while the acts are on.' Then she read out the order in which we'd appear. 'Toni, you're last.' She nodded at me. 'We'll all go back to the hospitality room, where you can watch the show on the TV there, and we'll call you in order. When it's your turn, David will come and mike you up and bring you here, and then you'll wait for your name to be called. Don't annoy the judges with too much chat. Just answer their questions briefly and then Bill, the band leader, will play you in, if needed. OK?' She was all business, but then I supposed she had to be, with all of these contestants to whip into shape.

We allowed ourselves to be led back to the hospitality room, which was thankfully a bit larger, with a water cooler and a tray of unappetizing-looking pastries. The others spread themselves around, but I was too nervous to sit. I could see the show on the monitor, the audience screaming and cheering, but it seemed to be happening elsewhere. There was no sign of Amanda, and I realized that I felt a bit disappointed. I could do with a friend to distract me. Then I remembered what Niall had said to me, that it was my time to shine, just like in the song. I sat down and sighed, wondering if I could hold on to that thought until the show was over. I looked at my watch and couldn't believe my eyes. I'd been here for five hours already. Suddenly, a wave of tiredness swept over me, as if all the adrenaline that had been pumping around my body for the last few hours had suddenly ebbed away. I had the strangest sensation of not being able to keep my eyes open, and I felt myself begin to drift off.

Suddenly, there was a voice in my ear, 'Toni?' And a tap on my shoulder. I jolted awake.

It was Karen, and she was smiling at me. 'You must have nodded off. You're up in about fifteen minutes, and I'm going to take you to the backstage area now, OK?'

I nodded my head, unable to say anything. My stomach was churning and my palms were sweaty. I didn't know what my make-up looked like: hopefully my mascara hadn't run and I wouldn't appear on national television looking like a clown.

I followed Karen down an endless corridor and through a set of heavy double doors, hardly listening to her chat. 'Have you been to a TV recording before? It's not as bad as it seems, really. The lighting is bright, but I'll show you where your spot is, and all you have to do when your name is called is walk to the spot and smile and introduce yourself. Easy-peasy.' She grinned.

'When you put it like that it sounds simple,' I said, 'but my nerves are killing me. I'm not sure I'll be able to stand up.'

'Just focus on the song and you'll be brilliant. I've heard you, Toni, and you'll just blow them away tonight, OK?'

'OK.' I nodded. 'Thanks for everything, Karen.'

'All part of the job,' she said, leading me to a quiet area just behind the stage. I could hear cheering and clapping, but the sounds were muffled behind the thick drapes at the sides. 'Right, after the judges have given their verdict on this act, I'll come and get you to bring you on. Would you like anything while you're waiting?'

'Water,' I croaked.

'Sure, back in a tick,' she threw the words over her shoulder as she jogged towards the double doors again. And then she was gone and I was alone for the first time that night. And I found myself thinking of Mum. Of how much she'd have loved this – the 'greasepaint' as she always called it, all the lights and the drama. She'd loved variety shows when I was younger, making me sit through the Royal Variety Show and commenting on every performer. But when I stood out on that stage – the first time I'd ever been on a stage in my life – she wouldn't be there, cheering me on. I could feel the tears welling in my eyes. Mum, if you're up there, I said to myself, please help me to get through this.

I don't know how I'm going to get on the stage, but if I do, I'll know it was thanks to you.

And then I suddenly felt a little bit calmer. It was a strange calm, like the calm before a storm, a sudden complete silence. I've never been a believer in any kind of paranormal stuff, but right then, I knew I wasn't alone any more. I looked up at the dark ceiling above the stage lights. 'Thanks, Mum,' I murmured.

And then Karen was beside me, a plastic cup of water in her hand. 'OK, Toni, have a little drink, and then I'll take you to the waiting area to be miked up by David, and then we'll wait a few minutes for your call.' And with that, she led me gently on.

The next five minutes passed in a blur. I was led to my spot and then back to wait for my name to be called. I stood at the side of the stage, a roaring in my ears as the audience whooped and cheered. 'And now, our next contestant from the Garden County of Wicklow, Antonia Trent!' I stopped dead for a second until I felt a gentle nudge in the small of my back. And then I was walking across the stage, the lights blinding my eyes. Somehow I found my spot and stood there, feeling my stomach flutter, my knees wobble. I could hardly make out the audience beyond the edge of the stage, but out there among them were Sister Monica and Billy and Betty and Colette and Mary and Niall, and all my friends. Funny, I'd made more close friends in the last six weeks than I had in my whole life. And they were out there somewhere, beyond the bright stage lights.

You could hear a pin drop as I stood there, until I heard a tiny voice cry out, 'Way to go Antonia,' followed by a loud whoop. Bridget. It had to be. I felt myself begin to smile, in spite of myself.

'Hi, Antonia, where in County Wicklow are you from?' The voice made me jump, and I realized that I was facing the three judges. The first one, a slim, glamorous blonde, smiled at me, obviously trying to put me at my ease.

I opened my mouth to say 'Glenvara', but for a moment, no sound came out. I stuttered and there was a deafening silence. 'A-a-a village called Glenvara,' I eventually managed, and was rewarded with a beam.

'And what are you going to sing for us?' The third judge, a man in his late fifties in an oddly battered-looking dark-blue suit, had a forbidding expression on his face and I was reminded of Simon Cowell for a moment.

'"Bridge Over Troubled Water".' Now the words came out in a rat-tat-tat rush, and I felt myself blush, and the colour filled my cheeks. Oh no, they'd think I was a complete fool.

'A classic, eh?' he said, raising his eyebrows. 'And what do you hope to achieve tonight?'

Achieve? My mind was suddenly a complete blank. I blinked and swallowed and tried frantically to gather my thoughts. Eventually, I blurted, 'Just being here is an achievement for me. I haven't thought any further than tonight.' Which was the truth, I realized, as I said it.

The man said nothing, tapping his pen against his pad. Finally, he said, 'Right, Antonia. In your own time.'

I managed to nod my head at Gavin, the pianist, who played the opening bars. I listened closely for my cue, praying that I wouldn't come in too early. I tried to remember how Elvis had done it in that recording on YouTube. Twice, Gavin played the opening riff, and then I opened my mouth. '"When you're weary . . ."' Oh, God, I thought, as I sang the opening few bars, I'm out of tune. I could hear my voice wobble and tears welled in my eyes. My big moment, and I was about to blow it.

And then it happened, as it always did. The song just took over. All I had to do was trust the music and let my voice do the rest. I sang the first verse and then the band picked up the tempo, and the backing singers began to come in, echoing my words, and I was sailing along, letting the song carry me. And then it was all over. I couldn't believe it. I just wanted it to go on and on.

When I finished, I held on to the microphone for dear life, and the audience burst into loud whooping and cheering. My ears ringing, I managed a smile. It's over, I thought. I've done it. Feel the fear and do it anyway. I felt like shouting and cheering myself.

Eventually, when the applause died down, it was time for the judges to give their votes. My heart started thumping in my chest so hard I thought it would burst.

The nice blonde lady spoke first. Clasping her hands, she gushed, 'Wow. Well, what can I say?'

I wasn't sure how to react. Surely it hadn't been *that* bad, I thought to myself.

'That was absolutely superb. You really blew me away with the power and the sheer emotion of it. A definite yes from me.'

I nodded and smiled, feeling foolish, as she gave me the thumbs up, as did the other judge, a young music producer. Two out of three, I could hardly believe it. But the toughest judge was to come. I couldn't meet the eyes of the Simon-Cowell-alike, as he cleared his throat and looked disapproving. Oh no, I thought, he's going to send me home. I stared at my feet, in their Louboutins, and suddenly felt a fraud.

'Antonia, you were nervous when you started, but once you got into your stride, you sang beautifully. I can honestly say that that was the best interpretation of that song I've heard in a very long time. A yes.' And with that, the audience erupted. And I stood there, rooted to the spot, realizing that it was another one of those moments in life when everything changes in an instant. And I looked up to heaven and mouthed, 'Thank you.'

14

'TOLD YOU ELVIS'S VERSION WAS THE BEST,' NIALL WAS IN A corner of Fitzsimons Bar in Glenvara, waving a pint of what looked like lemonade, deep in argument with Bridget.

'Not at all. Whitney Houston, the only woman who could really give it some welly. Apart from Antonia, that is,' and Bridget leaned over and hugged me. 'Antonia Trent, heat winner, absolutely ran away with it, you did, pet.' And then, for the hundredth time that night, she shrieked with excitement.

Good old Bridget. Never one to hold back, I thought, as I returned her hug. The truth was, I was still in shock, sipping from my glass of champagne and nodding as everyone crowded around me, congratulating me. Sister Monica was so delighted that she had a glass too. 'For the first time in my life.' She laughed. 'But there's always a first time for everything, isn't there, Antonia?' And she winked at me. I didn't like to tell her it was my first alcoholic drink, as well.

A first time for everything. Sister Monica was right, as usual. I tried to cast my mind back over the evening, but I couldn't remember much. It was all a bit of haze, really, a blur of hot lights, sweaty dressing rooms and an awful lot of sitting around. And yet, somehow, I'd won. I'd come ahead of the talented boy band, even of Amanda, who had really impressed me with her raunchy rendition of Pat Benatar's 'Love is a Battlefield'. I'd thought she was amazing, and looked totally the part, and couldn't believe I'd come in ahead of her. I was relieved when she came up to me afterwards to congratulate me, pulling me towards her in a hug.

'I didn't know you were that good, or I'd have had you killed,' she joked in that way she had, never entirely serious, but never entirely joking either.

I managed a laugh. 'Too late. I'm on to the regionals now, and so are you, so you're stuck with me.' As runner-up, Amanda was going forward to the regional heats with me. The winner and runner-up of those would go to the national competition just before Christmas.

'Oh, I can have one of my agents take you out before then, don't you worry. Seriously, though,' and she held me at arm's length, 'you've a fabulous talent. You're going to go all the way, do you hear me?'

I shook my head. 'The competition will get tougher, and I'll reach my limit sooner or later, but thanks for the thought, Amanda.' I didn't even want to think about the next step. This one had taken every ounce of my strength. I'd told the Simon-Cowell-alike judge that I hadn't thought beyond the night of the heats, and I really hadn't, because I hadn't imagined I'd get any further than that. I sighed, thinking about

143

the mountain I had to climb, and then I remembered what Mum always used to say. 'Live for the moment, Antonia. That way, you won't have any regrets about life, because you'll know you lived it to the full.'

Perhaps that's what I was doing now: living life to the full, or beginning to, anyway. Doing things I'd never have thought of in a million years.

'Penny for them.' Niall was beside me, a glass in his hand. He looked entirely different, in a floral print shirt that would have looked ridiculous on another man but on him kind of worked, and a pair of dark denim jeans.

'Oh, I was just thinking about how Mum always said to seize the day. To live for the moment.'

'Well, you've certainly done that tonight.' He smiled gently. 'How does it feel to be a heat winner on *That's Talent!*?'

'Oh God, I don't know. Good, I guess, although I have no idea how I did it. I don't even remember singing now – it's all a bit hazy.' How could I tell him that, in fact, I was in shock, and feeling guilty that here I was, on top of the world, while the one person who would have loved this more than anything wasn't here to see it?

As if he'd read my mind, he said, 'Don't feel guilty, Antonia. Your mum would be so proud of you, no matter what.'

I nodded. 'Thanks, Niall. I know that. It's just . . . sometimes I'm not sure if I should even be here, enjoying myself, when she's not there to share it with me, you know?'

He nodded. 'But I'm sure she'd want you to have your own life, Antonia. Didn't you tell me that she was always encouraging you to go out and use your talent?'

I couldn't believe he'd remembered that, but he was right. 'And,' he added, trying to lighten the mood, 'your singing was unbelievable tonight. Better than the King himself.'

'Now, that's a lie, I know that for sure.' I laughed.

He clinked his glass against mine. 'Here's to you and the regionals.'

'Cheers,' I said and then I nodded at his drink. 'That looks like lemonade. Are you on duty later?'

He shook his head, and looked sheepish for a few moments. 'Actually no. I promised Betty I'd drive you home after the competition and, well . . .' he took a sip out of his glass. 'Lemonade is quite nice, actually.'

I burst out laughing. 'Well, that's very chivalrous of you. It'll make me enjoy my champagne all the more.'

And I did enjoy it. A little too much. Every time I put my glass out, someone refilled it, and by the end of the night I was feeling quite tipsy. I surprised myself by being able to let my hair down, for a change. Maybe it was because of what Niall had said, but I let myself relax a little bit. I laughed with Colette and Mary about the judges. Of course, I hadn't recognized any of them, but apparently they were really well-known. The blonde lady was Mary Devine, a presenter on a national news channel, the music producer was Michael Smyth, and the Simon-Cowell-alike was Maurice Prendergast, a well-known record producer. 'Fancies himself as a cut-price Simon Cowell,' Colette said sarcastically.

'Oh, I thought he was quite good,' I argued. 'He seemed to know his stuff, musically speaking, and he was tough but fair.'

'Did you see Mary Devine's face? What's she had done?' Mary shrieked. 'Botox at least.'

'Oh, I'd say she's had a bit of work,' Colette said, pulling the skin at her eyes really tight. 'What d'you think – makes me look ten years younger?' And herself and Mary burst into giggles.

I didn't have the nerve to laugh at the judges who had voted me into the next round, so I just looked at my glass of champagne, until Mary noticed and put her arm around me. 'Those judges clearly recognize talent when they see it, anyway,' she said, giving my shoulder a squeeze. And then she nodded over at Niall. 'As does he, I might add.' And then she grinned at me slyly.

'What do you mean?' I looked at her, open-mouthed.

'Oh, c'mon, Antonia, it's as plain as the nose on your face. He really likes you.' And she giggled like a schoolgirl.

'He's just a friend.'

'Oh, sure,' said Colette and then they both exploded into giggles, until Mary saw that I looked hurt, and pulled me into a hug.

'C'mon, Antonia, we're only teasing you.'

I blushed to the roots of my hair. I didn't mind that they

were teasing me, but I simply hadn't dared think of Niall like that. 'I know, but it's just . . . I've got enough on my plate now, to be honest.'

'Of course you do, love,' Colette said, shooting Mary a glance above my head.

'I saw that,' I said, and then we all burst out laughing again, and there was another toast, and another glass of champagne and more cheering and shouting. I began to feel dizzy and light-headed and realized that I hadn't eaten since the morning. As if on cue, my stomach started rumbling and I felt a wave of exhaustion come over me. Time to go home, Antonia, before you turn into a pumpkin, I said to myself.

I wobbled across the bar to where Niall was still chatting to Sister Monica, nodding his head as she talked, for all the world as if she was the most fascinating woman in the world. Of course, to me, she was, but I felt a surge of affection for Niall, that he would be so nice to an elderly nun, would understand what she meant to me. And then I thought of what Colette and Mary had said and I didn't know what to think. How would I know if a man liked me, anyway? Were there any tell-tale signs? Why on earth wasn't there a manual for women like me, who hadn't a clue?

As I walked towards him, I tripped over one of my huge shoes and tilted forward, my champagne glass in my hand. Instinctively, Niall reached out to support me under the arm. 'Whoops.' He smiled, taking the champagne glass out of my hand and putting it gently down on the bar. 'All set?'

he said, as if he hadn't had a tipsy woman practically fall into him. I felt like crying with gratitude, and managed to remember my manners and hug Sister Monica and wave and smile goodbye to everyone. It had been the night of my life.

15

THE LAST THING I CAN REMEMBER IS THE CHILL OF THE night air as Niall opened the car door to let me in. I don't recall sitting in the passenger seat or strapping myself in, or one single bit of the car journey. I must have fallen asleep, because the next thing I knew the car had stopped. I opened my eyes and blinked. 'Are we home?'

'You nodded off.' Niall sounded amused. 'Must have been my scintillating conversation.'

'Sorry,' I muttered. 'It's just . . . after everything that happened today . . .'

He shifted in the seat, rubbing his eyes, and I felt suddenly guilty. He was clearly tired, and probably didn't need to be driving me about Wicklow before going all the way back to Dublin.

'Of course. It's a once-in-a-lifetime thing, isn't it?' he said agreeably.

I nodded. 'I suppose it is. I just can't take it in, to be honest. One minute I was singing in the choir at Mass, the next I was on stage in front of thousands of people.' I shook my head. 'I can't think how that happened, somehow.'

'It happened because you made it happen, Antonia.' And then, before I had time to react, he leaned across and planted a kiss on my cheek. At least, I think he meant to kiss my cheek, because at the last minute, I turned my head and he kissed me half on the lips.

My face was burning with embarrassment and I looked down at my knees, wishing that I knew whether I was supposed to kiss him back. Would that be too forward at this stage? Did he just want to be a friend, or something more? He'd been so . . . brotherly, I suppose, that until now, I hadn't been sure.

'Sorry.'

I looked up at him, expecting him to look sheepish. But instead, he was grinning broadly.

'No you're not.' I laughed.

He shrugged and gave me that smile again, the one that transformed his serious expression, and made him look like a naughty nine-year-old boy. 'Well, no. But I didn't mean to embarrass you,' he added hastily.

'It's fine, really.' I said, hating myself for sounding so prissy. 'You didn't. Embarrass me, that is.'

'Well, good, then.'

'Right.' I couldn't honestly think what else to say, so I reached my hand out to open the door and then I turned to him. 'Thanks for everything, Niall. It meant a lot to me.'

This time, he wasn't grinning. His eyes searched mine. 'You're welcome, Antonia,' he said, and there was something about the way he said it that made me stop in my tracks. It was a tone he'd never used before. I opened my mouth to say that I felt it too, but then the spell was broken, and he was back to brotherly mode again. 'Now get some sleep. I'll be around nice and early tomorrow morning.' He smiled.

'Tomorrow? Oh, God, Powerscourt, I forgot.'

'Sure you don't want to have a lie-in?'

'No,' I said. 'The fresh air will do me good.' Not to mention the vertical climb, I thought to myself. To be honest, I didn't feel particularly enthusiastic, but Niall had been just fantastic, so I could hardly say no, could I? And it would do me good, after all the stress of the day.

'You don't sound too convinced.'

I turned to him. 'I'd love it, honestly. And you can buy me a coffee in the café afterwards. Deal?'

'Deal.' He thumped the steering wheel.

I wasn't sure I liked the brotherly thing any more, but I nodded and got out, running up the front path to the house, which was in darkness, fumbling for my keys in my hand-bag. Niall waited until I'd opened the door and switched the hall light on, waving me goodbye as I closed the door behind me. And then I was alone.

I leaned against the wall in my after-show jeans and T-shirt and replayed every moment of the day in my head, ending with Niall's kiss. I wasn't sure what to make of it: was it more than just a friendly kiss? Was I reading too much into it? But then, what did I know? And anyway, it just seemed overwhelming, on top of everything else. It just goes to show that once you start to change, well, everything changes, doesn't it? It's like a runaway train, and you've no idea where you're headed. It was exhilarating, scary and unfamiliar, all at once. I sat there, chewing over everything, until hunger drove me into the kitchen.

Of course, I hardly slept a wink. I spent the whole night tossing and turning, snatches of the day on a loop in my head, until eventually I fell into a fitful sleep, from which I awoke with a jolt, unsure of where I was for a second. Had I been dreaming? I wondered, as I rubbed my eyes and looked at the thin early-morning light streaming in through my bedroom window. I looked at the bright red numbers on my digital alarm clock. It was only 6.30 a.m. I swallowed, feeling that I'd die of thirst, sensing a headache behind my eyes. Must have been all that champagne, I thought. I wasn't used to it. I usually didn't drink at all, even at the choir Christmas party, when all I'd have was a Coke, for goodness' sake. 'I'm pathetic,' I said out loud, then giggled.

Because, for once, I didn't feel pathetic. I felt . . . well . . . different somehow.

Not that this realization had helped me to sleep. After what must have been three or four hours' sleep, my eyes felt scratchy and my legs like lead, but I knew I wouldn't doze off again, and so I gave up and went down to the kitchen. I looked out the window, at the familiar front garden, at my little car parked at the end of the path, at the small crescent of quaint semis that I'd known ever since I was seven, and thought that they looked new, all of a sudden. It was as if I was seeing them for the first time. I boiled the kettle, humming away to myself, already beginning to wonder what song I'd do for the next round, when my mobile rang. I debated not answering for a second, after all, who on earth could it be at this hour? But as the ringtone shrilled out into the empty kitchen, I picked it up and said a cautious, 'Hello?'

'Toni!' the voice at the other end said. 'You're up early!'

I might say the same about you, I thought, before asking, 'Who is this?' I knew that I sounded rude, but I wasn't used to people ringing me at six thirty in the morning.

'Oh, God, sorry, it's Karen, the PA at Celtic. Look, sorry to ring you so early, but I forgot to mention it last night. There's a photocall today for the contestants in St Stephen's Green, you know, the lucky Dubliners going through to the next round etc. Can you make it there for eight thirty?'

I swallowed. 'Ehm, sure . . . how long will it take?' I was thinking of Niall and our date, if that's what you could call it, in Powerscourt. 'Ten o'clock, sharp,' he'd said. If it didn't take more than half an hour, I could leave Dublin at nine thirty and make it back to Wicklow in half an hour, if I really put the boot down.

'Well, an hour, give or take? We'd love it if you could be there, Toni. It's really important for the production company, and it'll get your name out there in the media. Nice piece in the *Sunday Star* by the way,' she added. 'Dave Byrne's a bit cheeky – he should really have come to see me first – but you handled it well, clearly. A real Cinderella story, he called it.'

I had no idea what she was talking about, and then I remembered. The man in the leather jacket outside the studios. 'Oh, great,' I said, hoping that he'd quoted Mary from Glenvara, or else she'd kill me.

'So, we'll see you there?' Karen said.

I could tell by her tone that this wasn't a request, and besides, what normal person would say they couldn't do a photocall, whatever that was, because they were too busy hill-walking? 'I'll be there at eight thirty, Karen,' I said, hoping I sounded businesslike enough for her.

'Great! Well, see you there. Oh, yes, and don't forget to wear something eye-catching for the camera!' And she was gone before I could ask exactly what she meant by 'eye-catching'.

I checked my phone. I could hardly ring Mary at seven in the morning, surely? But I had no clue what to wear for a photocall, so I'd just have to bite the bullet.

Mary's voice sounded sleepy, and I felt a start of guilt. 'Sorry to call you so early.'

'S'all right,' she murmured sleepily. 'I need to get up early today anyway, because it's Sunday.'

I could tell that she was joking – just. 'Look, I wouldn't call, Mary, except it's an emergency,' and I explained about the photocall.

'I'll be right over.' She disconnected so abruptly, I was left holding the phone in my hand. I was still holding it when I heard the knock on my door. When I opened, she was standing there, a huge make-up bag in her hand, in what looked

154

like her pyjamas, albeit clearly designer ones. Oh, God, I thought, she'll kill me.

I reached out to hug her. 'Mary, you're a lifesaver.'

'I know,' she muttered into my shoulder. 'Now get off me and I'll see what I can do.'

Half an hour and two cups of coffee later, I was transformed. 'An ugly duckling into a swan,' I said, admiring myself in the mirror.

'Less of the ugly duckling, if you don't mind,' said Mary, pulling a few strands of hair around my face. 'You look drop-dead gorgeous, Antonia.'

'Thanks, Mary, I don't know what to say . . .' I began.

'You can thank me when you win this thing.' She smiled, and then she looked serious for a moment. 'You know, Antonia, you've really surprised me.'

I turned from the mirror to look up at her. 'What do you mean?'

'A year ago, you would no more have rung me at seven in the morning because you had a photocall than flown to the moon. Oh, don't get me wrong,' she continued when I tried to interrupt. 'I'm thrilled to see how much more confident you are. And I'm sure your mum would be thrilled, too.'

I nodded, feeling the tears behind my eyelids. Every time I thought of Mum, I wondered if I really deserved my success. If she were still alive, well, what would I be doing now? Bringing her up a tray with a boiled egg on it and two slices of toast? Was it wrong to miss her and yet not to miss the life I'd had?

Mary's voice interrupted my thoughts. 'Now, don't cry, or your mascara will run. Do you want me to drive up with you?'

I shook my head. 'You've done enough, Mary. I'm a big girl.' I smiled.

'You certainly are, Antonia,' she said approvingly, and then she grinned at me slyly. 'You even have a boyfriend.'

'Don't start.' I blushed. 'Anyway, he's not my boyfriend.'

'No?'

'No,' I said firmly as I thought of Niall's lips brushing against mine, and realized that I'd liked it. That I liked him. Oh, God, life was so complicated sometimes.

I knew that I was going to be late for Niall when I looked at my mobile for the hundredth time and saw that it was already nine thirty, and nothing had happened. Not one single thing. We'd been standing in St Stephen's Green for a full hour now, shivering in the chilly autumn wind. I hadn't thought to bring a cardigan to throw over the designer sleeveless red dress Mary had lent me, and my arms were a riot of blue goose pimples. I couldn't understand why it was taking so long. The photographers were there – a middle-aged man from one of the big Sunday newspapers, with a shock of white hair and a silver earring in one ear – and a few younger photographers, as were 4Guys, who'd come third, and Amanda of course. I was thrilled to see her: she was funny and bright and talented, and I felt she was a real ally. And the boys were really sweet, only seventeen and a real laugh. We spent the first half an hour larking around in front of the fountains in the Green, the boys pretending to splash each other with water, much to Karen's horror.

'Boys, please, no messing. I can't have a photocall with you all soaking wet,' she begged.

But after an hour, we all began to get a bit miserable, the cold sinking into our bones. I could feel my make-up clogging my skin, and I badly needed a drink of water. I nudged Amanda. 'What's the problem?'

'They're waiting for the National TV crew. They were supposed to be here ages ago, but obviously there's no sign.'

'Can't we just make do with what we've got and then all go home?' I said, anxiously checking my watch.

Amanda snorted with laughter. 'God no, if the great god television calls, well, who are we to argue?' Amanda had been through it all before, of course. She'd been dancing since she was five, and had just graduated from the Gate Dance School. I hadn't a clue, but just wished it could all be over before I got hypothermia. I glanced at my phone again. Oh, God, almost ten. I'd have to call Niall.

'Got a date?' Amanda looked at me and then at my phone.

I blushed. 'As a matter of fact, I have,' I said. 'I'm supposed to be in Powerscourt now, climbing the waterfall.'

She laughed. 'He must really be special, if you're planning to throw your first shot at fame to climb a waterfall.'

I didn't say anything, just scrolled down through the list

of numbers until I found his and dialled. Just tell the truth, Antonia, I told myself. Don't make some silly excuse.

Of course, the way he was so understanding only made it worse. That and the fact that, of course, he'd already driven the twenty miles down to Wicklow and I hadn't thought to tell him earlier. 'Look, you just finish up there. It sounds as if it's really important.'

'Thanks, Niall. I'll buy you lunch and then we can tackle the walk after, how does that sound?'

'Ordinarily, it would sound just great, but I'm on shift later, so we'll have to do it another time.'

'Oh. OK.'

'Look, you have to snatch the opportunities when they're offered to you,' he said. 'You can't afford to let them pass you by.'

'I know, it's just . . .'

'Just nothing. Now, relax and enjoy the shoot if you can, and we'll do it again next week.' Why did he have to be so nice about it? I thought, clutching the phone to my ear. I didn't deserve it.

'Niall, I promise, I won't let you down the next time.'

'I know . . .' And then there was a pause before he said, 'Bye, Antonia.'

'Bye.' As I put the phone down I thought, I've hurt his feelings.

'The price of fame,' Amanda said dryly, nodding at my phone.

'Is it always like this?' I said.

158

'No. It's worse.' She laughed. 'Sometimes you wait around for a whole day because somebody famous is supposed to be turning up, and of course they never do. But you wouldn't dream of walking away, because that could be the one person who could make a difference to your career. And so you wait and wait, and in the end none of it makes a blind bit of difference.'

'You sound bitter,' I said, unable to keep the tone of surprise out of my voice. I couldn't understand it, really. If she was that fed up with it, why bother? Why not get a nice job instead?

'I'm not bitter, not really. I'm just . . . resigned.' She grinned. 'I keep entering these shows, and I do well, but I know I'm not good enough, not really.'

'That's not true,' I protested. 'You're an amazing singer . . .'

'And the world is full of them. I'm not exceptional, Antonia. Not like you. And I know it, but still, there's nothing I want more.'

I shook my head. 'I'm not exceptional . . .'

'Oh, come on, Antonia, you know you are. You've got a voice like no other, and star quality. I know it when I see it, believe me. You'll go all the way, if you really want it badly enough.'

I didn't know how to answer, because I wasn't sure if I *did* want it badly enough, or even what that meant. I know that I wanted something more than the church choir, but what, exactly? But then I supposed I'd got a glimpse of it, hadn't I? The disappointment in Niall's voice, the hurt. After everything he'd done for me. Was it worth it, I wondered?

'OK, everyone, we're on,' Karen's voice interrupted my thoughts. 'Toni, can you stand in front of the fountain with the boys behind? Great, just great.'

I smiled and waved at the cameras and pretended to lark around with the boys, to hug Amanda, and then afterwards I stood in the chill, my skin goose pimpling, to talk to the reporters who'd been hanging around for the last couple of hours, just like us. I couldn't believe that they found us that interesting, but Karen had warned me that we'd be 'tabloid fodder', whatever that was, for the next few weeks, so I supposed I'd have to get used to it.

'Hi there, Toni, congratulations on getting through,' it was Dave Byrne, in the same leather jacket, a thick stubble on his cheeks, and that same broad grin, the one that made me feel that he was a friend.

'Hi, Dave.' I greeted him warmly, looking around for Karen, so that she could tell me what to say. 'You look as if you haven't gone home since last night.'

'No rest for the wicked.' He laughed. 'What did you think of the piece?' He smiled and looked at me expectantly.

'Oh, ehm, I haven't seen it yet,' I replied, assuming he meant the Cinderella story Karen had mentioned.

I was about to ask him exactly what he meant, when he said, 'Ignoring the press already?'

'Oh, I didn't mean it like that,' I said hastily.

I didn't want him to think I was a complete princess, but

he smiled then and said, 'Well, relax, it's a nice one. And we're friends, honest.'

'Great,' I smiled. 'Well, thanks for the publicity—'

I went to turn away, but he put a hand on my arm. 'Just a few more questions for your fans in the paper?'

I hesitated for a second, but then smiled. 'Sure.'

'I think you had a fairly rough start in life . . .' the note-book was out again, and he was looking at me, expecting me to answer.

I shifted nervously from foot to foot. Where *was* Karen? I had no idea what to say to him. 'Ehm, do you mean my being adopted?'

He nodded. 'Yeah, and the children's home and all. Must have been fairly Dickensian, don't you think? All that slaving for the nuns, and they must have treated you pretty badly. After all, it was the bad old days. Didn't they make you wash tons of laundry and polish floors and all that?' And he grinned that grin again.

'No, it wasn't like that at all,' I began. 'The nuns were really great and—'

I was trying to compose my reply when I heard Karen beside me, her voice loud. 'Now, Dave, you know you're not supposed to speak to the performers without going through me, you cheeky bugger.' But she was smiling, and I wondered if they all spoke to each other like this in this business. 'If you want an interview with Toni, queue up, like the others.'

Dave put his hands up in a gesture of surrender. 'Fine, fine, love. I've got what I wanted anyway.' And he was gone again, disappearing into the crowds now filling the park. I couldn't suppress the feeling of dread at the pit of my stomach, and tried desperately to remember what I'd said.

'Be careful of him, Toni,' Karen said. 'He's friendly enough, but they're all complete rats in the tabloids. Check any media requests in with me, will you?' And Karen gave me a friendly pat. I felt like a naughty schoolgirl all of a sudden.

Later I waved everyone goodbye and belted down the motorway. If I couldn't make my date with Niall, I reasoned, at least I could turn up to sing at twelve o'clock Mass. It'd make me feel grounded, I thought. I didn't even have time to change, tottering up to the choir in my high heels and my silly hair, accepting everyone's admiring looks, the round of applause that greeted me.

'You look a million dollars, Antonia,' Billy said as I shuffled into place beside him and picked up my music sheets, scanning the hymns to see if there was anything particularly challenging.

'Thanks, Billy. I feel completely ridiculous,' I said. 'I'm just not used to all of this. It doesn't feel like me, do you know what I mean?'

He nodded, his blue eyes twinkling. 'It'll take time to get used to it all, pet, but remember, it *is* you. That talent is really yours. And you're still our Antonia!'

'Thanks, Billy.' I smiled. 'That means a lot to me.' And it did. The whole media circus was just so unreal, and it seemed that everyone was pretending to be a friend, even if they weren't, but here, in the tiny church, I knew that I was among real friends, the kind who would stick with me. And after the first couple of hymns, I managed to relax. The singing always helped me to do that, to feel at ease for a change, to feel like myself.

I was sitting quietly, saying a prayer after communion, when Father O'Hanlon stood up and said, 'And now, everyone, I just want to talk about someone very special in our congregation this morning . . .'

My heart sank. Oh, no. I prayed that it would be someone else. Betty, Bridget. Anyone but me, but no: Father O'Hanlon turned in my direction, looking at me with a broad beam on his ruddy face.

'Antonia Trent has been a member of this choir for ten years and she has graced every single Mass, wedding and Holy Communion with the gift of her beautiful singing.' He paused. 'God doesn't bestow on everyone a gift like that, only on his chosen ones. Sometimes, it is those who have faced special challenges in their lives . . .' As he droned on, I felt the colour rise to my cheeks and it was all I could do not to make a run for it. I knew that he meant well, but I just couldn't take any more of the attention.

'And of course, everyone remembers Antonia's mother, who was the heart and soul of the village . . .'

There was a murmur of agreement in the congregation, and several people muttered, 'May she rest in peace.'

I felt the tears spring to my eyes, and all I could think was that I really wanted Mum beside me. And then Father

O'Hanlon continued, 'And we just want to wish our special girl all the luck in the world as she takes on this new challenge. I'm more of a football man myself, but do you know, I think I'll be tuning into *That's Talent!* every Saturday night, Antonia!' And there was a huge cheer in the church, as everyone rose to their feet, clapping. Every single head in the church was turned towards me, and I had to smile and wave, and all the time I was thinking how much I'd prefer to be climbing Powerscourt with Niall. Be careful what you wish for, I thought. Because it might just come true.

16

OF COURSE, ONCE I'D CLIMBED ON THE ROLLER COASTER, I decided the only thing I could do would be to hang on for dear life. And so I did. For the next six weeks, I sang in heat after heat, from the regionals through to the nationals, and every time, I seemed to glide on through. I wasn't sure how I was doing it. Call it beginner's luck, or something else, but all I know is that after that first time, it seemed almost easy. Every Monday morning, I'd meet Eithne and we'd discuss what I was going to sing in the heat. Then we'd spend the next few days rehearsing the song, before practising with the TV orchestra on Friday night. And then on Saturday, I'd drive to the venue with Colette and Mary – if she'd managed to get the morning off – and sit and wait for my turn. And I'd come out on stage and walk to my spot and talk to the judges, who knew me by now, and who smiled at me as if I were an old friend. And every Saturday night, I'd tell them the same thing: that I hadn't planned any of this, that it had come as a surprise to me, and that every week on the show was a bonus. And it was.

It was almost as if I was someone else. Not Antonia Trent,

Miss Mouse, but Toni Trent, professional singer. It was as if I was playing a role. And I let myself be swept up in it, carried along, because I was enjoying myself. I discovered that I liked applause and praise and attention. That it made me feel good. The more people applauded, the happier I became, and the more I could lose myself in it, in the song and the moment. It was intoxicating.

And, if I kept on winning, I could forget about other things, like Niall. He'd come along to all the heats, sitting in the audience and clapping like everyone else. He'd even come to the pub celebrations afterwards, but he hadn't said much to me, not really. I kept telling myself that I'd make it up to him, that sooner or later, my luck would run out and then we'd have all the time in the world to climb Powerscourt waterfall. I hardly knew Niall. I'd only met him a few times and yet, I knew there was something there. Something I chose to ignore. Amanda had been right all along. I suppose that deep down, I knew I was making a choice.

Amanda and I became close. Every time I won my heat, she was runner-up – and if she wasn't pleased about coming second to me, she never said. She just hugged me tight and told me how thrilled she was that we'd be going on together to the next round. Once, she had to go head-to-head with a young singer-songwriter called Sean, and just about scraped through, and my heart was in my mouth. I didn't know what I'd do without Amanda, to laugh with and to share gossip about the other contestants. She'd seen it all before, Amanda, and she was so reassuring. We'd sit in the dressing room and share make-up and swap stories, and she'd see another contestant out of the corner of her eye and nudge me. 'See him? He's entered every competition there is. Thinks he has the ability to "go all the way", but frankly, I've got more talent in my little finger.'

And she was always right, even if privately I thought she could be a bit cruel sometimes. I knew that some of the other contestants didn't like her – they were afraid of her sharp tongue – but to me, she was my ally, the only one who knew exactly what I was going through.

Colette had even said it to me once. 'Watch out for Amanda, Antonia, will you? You don't know her that well.'

'What do you mean?' I'd protested, and I'd looked so shocked that Colette immediately backtracked.

'Nothing, nothing, pet, it's just . . . well, she's been around the block, and she's a bit cynical maybe, do you know what I mean?'

'No.' I shook my head, bewildered, and she'd let it drop, but not before she'd tugged my hair as if I was a child and smiled. 'You're a true innocent, Antonia, do you know that?'

I knew, of course. Because I had practically zero experience of other people, I had to take them all on trust. And so far, that trust had been repaid. I had Colette and Mary and Sister Monica, even Niall, all of whom had surrounded me with love and support. The press had been lovely too, even the tabloids, and I'd had to laugh at the portrait they painted of a country girl who'd hit the big time, although I suppose

167

it was fairly accurate. The shy young girl who'd found her voice in the local choir, who hadn't left Wicklow, not to mind Ireland, in all her life, except to go to Holyhead, who preferred jeans and a T-shirt to a designer dress. It seemed to touch a nerve with everyone, and it was true. I was that girl, even though I didn't see much of her these days.

But the press attention was overwhelming, even with Karen's support, and I took her advice to pull back on it as much as I could. 'Look,' she'd said to me after the regionals, 'it helps if one contestant doesn't appear to be getting all the publicity, I've seen it backfire on people.'

God, 'backfire'? What did she mean by that? It sounded terrifying. I thought of Dave Byrne and his questions, the regular profiles he'd been running in the paper. It was all fairly innocuous, but I had an uneasy feeling about it all the same. I managed, 'Well, I'll be guided by you, but just know I'll do anything you ask. I realize how lucky I am to be here,' I told her.

'I think we should keep your first big interview until later in the competition, and so do Sandy and Martin. Your life story is quite unique, and there will be a lot of interest in it, so we're happy to hold back for now. There will be a bit of a question-and-answer session with the judges in the semis, but we'll be writing the questions so there won't be any surprises, OK?'

'OK,' I said doubtfully. I must have looked like a rabbit in the headlights, because Karen unexpectedly reached over and squeezed my hand. 'We'll take care of everything, Toni.

You are a very precious commodity to us, and it's our job to look after you.'

'Commodity', sounded a bit clinical, but I nodded and smiled, because even after the last six weeks, I felt I knew what she meant. I was filler for newspapers, big glossy photos of me in my sequinned dress with the caption 'The Nation's Sweetheart' underneath. It was as if it was happening to someone else.

And then came the night of the semi-finals. It was another one of those moments, I suppose, those twists of fate that seem to shape life, whether we like it or not. It seems that no matter how much we think we're in control, well, we're only 'blowing in the wind', aren't we?

It was a wet Saturday in December, just three weeks before Christmas. My first Christmas without Mum, and I'd never been so glad of the distraction of the competition. I'd have to buy presents for Colette and Mary, of course, and Sister Monica, but putting up a tree just seemed like too much trouble, really. Mum always loved Christmas, inviting half of Glenvara around for Christmas drinks and making sure that we had turkey and ham and all the trimmings, even if it was only the two of us for dinner. Not that it ever was, really, because Mum would invite Sister Monica and Betty and anyone else at a loose end. Without Mum, I just didn't have the heart – and anyway, the competition absorbed every waking moment of my life.

And now, it was reaching the semi-final stage, and I

wasn't sure how I felt about it, or what on earth I'd do afterwards. It had kept me going for weeks, and the future looked uncertain. Of course, I didn't dare think about winning it. There were so many talented artists at this stage from all over the country. A singer-songwriter called Damien was so talented, and gorgeous, too, and if I were to be honest, I thought he was in with a better shot than me – I could see that the girls in the audience just loved his cheeky grin and his quiff. And there was a fantastic street-dance troupe from Cork, too. All I could really do was my best, as Dad always said.

I woke up that Saturday morning with a feeling of dread in the pit of my stomach. My head felt as if it was full of cotton wool and my throat felt as raw as sandpaper. We'd all had to hang around the studio till midnight the night before because of a technical glitch, and by the time it came for me to rehearse, I'd been alternately shivering and sweating. I'd chosen my favourite song of all time, 'Yesterday', and yet when I sang it, it didn't work, at least not as well as I'd wanted it to. My voice kept cracking on the top notes, and by the end of the run-through I was frustrated and embarrassed. Paul McCartney would have been horrified if he could have heard me murdering his song. And what's more, the semi-final would be live, so there would be no second chances if I messed up.

Karen had tried to be reassuring. 'Not to worry, Toni. It's been a long day. It'll be all right on the night, promise.' I'd been mortified, slinking off from the studio without a word, trying to ignore the sympathetic looks from the others, and Amanda's gentle hand on my arm.

'C'mon, love, we all have bad days.'

'I know, and all I want to do is go home and curl up under the duvet,' I'd said.

'Well, you do that. Tomorrow is another day, eh, Antonia?'

'You're right. What would I do without you, Amanda?'

'Oh, I don't know, be slightly less brilliant than you are?' She'd smiled, and for a moment, I'd hesitated. I hadn't been quite sure what she meant, but then she'd hugged me tightly and I'd felt reassured.

I'd gone home, buoyed up by Amanda's words, climbing into bed with my hot-water bottle and curling up tightly to keep warm. I was just dozing off, when I heard my mobile bleep. I'll ignore it, I thought, because it was always going off nowadays. It seemed that every person in Glenvara had got my number and texted me five times a day to wish me luck.

I sighed. Suddenly I was wide awake. I shifted in the bed and reached out to my mobile, blinking in the dim light. I didn't recognize the number, but pressed the message button, sure that it was another local well-wisher. Who on earth had handed my number out to half the town? I thought as I scanned the message.

I had to read it a couple of times before I could make sense of it. 'YESTERDAY ISN'T THE RIGHT SONG FOR YOU. KISS GOODBYE TO THE SEMIS.' I felt cold all of a sudden, and pulled the duvet more tightly around me. 'What on earth . . . ?' I said out loud in the darkness. Only a handful of people knew my song choice for the semis, so who would have sent a text like this? Hardly Eithne, or Karen. Maybe the media had got hold of it? That had to be it. I thought of Dave Byrne and his cheeky grin. Maybe I should ring Mary, I thought, or Colette, but then I looked at the clock and saw that it was 2 a.m. I could hardly ring them now. I'd have to manage this one alone.

C'mon, Antonia, you're a big girl, I told myself, pressing delete. There, all gone. I lay back down in the bed and tried to sleep, the words 'kiss goodbye to the semis' going round and round in my head.

And now, I'd woken up with the mother of all colds. I opened my mouth and tried a 'C', to see if I could sing, but all that came out was a hoarse rasp.

'Shit!' I croaked, and then chastised myself. Mum would kill me for swearing, but what on earth was I going to do? I could hardly go on national television to do my impression of a bullfrog, could I? And then I thought, maybe my texter knew something I didn't. I'd have to go to see Dr Murphy and see what he could give me.

I dragged myself out of bed, feeling my head swim, and shuffled downstairs to the phone and dialled his number, which I knew by heart. And of course, it being a Saturday, the surgery was closed. I listened to the answerphone message about his emergency contact number, before putting the phone down again. A cold was hardly an emergency, was it? And Dr Murphy was in his seventies – I couldn't drag him out on a Saturday morning.

A thought began to form in my head, which I dismissed at first, but then, I thought, I have to. I have nobody else. Niall. Maybe he has a miracle cure, I thought, dialling his number.

'Niall?' I croaked.

At first, he didn't recognize that it was me. 'God, Antonia is that you? You sound awful.'

'Is that your professional medical opinion?' I tried to joke, but was cut off by a loud sneeze.

'It's not exactly a difficult diagnosis, is it?' He sounded friendlier than he had in a while, less reserved. I don't think he'd entirely forgiven me for cancelling, but I'd never had the chance to talk to him really, because the competition had been so all-consuming. I'm using him, I thought now, but I have no choice in the matter.

'I'm ringing . . . look, I need some help, Niall. I can't speak, let alone sing. Do you think you might be able to prescribe something?' I ventured. I wasn't sure if Niall could prescribe: he wasn't a GP.

Niall immediately went into doctor mode. 'Look, take a glass of hot water and dunk a couple of teaspoons of honey and a squeeze of lemon in it, and drink that. I'll drop around later with something a bit stronger to get you through to-night.'

Don't, I thought, as he spoke. Don't be brotherly. I don't

173

want it. And yet, part of me was grateful. I had a feeling that no amount of medication would get me right, but still, I had to try. I couldn't go on stage in front of thousands like this, could I?

I wasn't sure when Niall would appear, so I thought I'd sit on the sofa and rest for a few minutes, closing my eyes and feeling them red and swollen behind my eyelids. I must have fallen asleep, because the next thing I knew, there was a loud knocking. 'Coming,' I tried to shout, but nothing came out of my mouth. Not one sound. I dragged myself to the front door, and caught a glimpse of myself in the mirror. God, you look awful, I told myself. All the strain of the last few weeks was etched on my face, my eyes were red and itchy, my nose swollen. How on earth could I let Niall see me like this? And then I remembered that night in the hospital. He'd seen me in those daft fluffy slippers, for goodness' sake, with 'Antonia' on the toes. I'd just have to swallow my pride.

'You look terrible,' were his first words when I opened the door. He was in his blue hospital scrubs, a black bag slung over his shoulder. He looked dishevelled, and I realized with a start of guilt that he must have been up all night already.

'Thanks,' I whispered ruefully. 'I *feel* terrible.'

'Are you going to let me in?' He smiled, and my stomach flipped.

'Oh, sure,' I said, moving back to let him in and ushering him into the living room. 'I'm really sorry about the mess. I've been too tired to tidy up.'

'That's OK,' he said doubtfully, looking around at the untidy living room, strewn with half-drunk cups of tea and used tissues, the remnants of late-night dinners on the coffee table. I thought with a sudden jolt of mortification that Mum would have been horrified at me receiving visitors in this state. She always insisted that the living room be spick and span before anyone was allowed in the door. 'Treat your guests the way you'd like to be treated yourself, Antonia.' What on earth would she think now?

I perched on the edge of the sofa, unable to think what to say. 'Look, Niall, I really appreciate you coming . . .'

'It's fine,' he said, the smile not quite reaching his eyes, opening the black bag he'd been carrying and extracting a few packets and boxes out of it. 'Right, let's treat the patient, shall we?'

'So how have you been?' I tried, as he shook the thermometer in his hand.

He didn't reply, simply ordering me to, 'Open, please.'

I did as I was told and held the thermometer in my mouth for a minute.

He extracted it and looked at it. 'Hmm, you've a temperature all right. The Neurofen will see to that. Now, let's have a look at your throat. Say aah.'

Obediently, I did as I was told, nodding as he told me I probably had a throat infection. 'Hmm, it's very red, and you've got some yellow spots on your tonsils. A sure sign. I'm not certain you'll be able to sing in this condition—' he began.

'Kiss goodbye to the semis.' The words of the text flashed into my mind. I jumped up on the sofa and grabbed his arm. 'I have to be able to sing!' I croaked. I was aware that I sounded like a complete madwoman, but there was no way that I wasn't going to perform.

He looked at me and then nodded. 'Well, it's your choice, but you could do more damage to your voice if you sing in this condition, you know.'

How could I explain to him that if I didn't, that was it? I was out of the competition. *That's Talent!* didn't take sick notes. 'It matters a lot to me, Niall . . .' I began. 'I feel that I have to see it through, do you know what I mean?' And as I painfully whispered the words, I realized that they were true. Funny how something that had scared me so much had now become the centre of my life. I could truly say that I wanted nothing more than to win *That's Talent!*

'I know,' he said, looking me directly in the eye.

I knew what he was implying. I took a deep breath. 'Look, I'm sorry about our date, but I couldn't help it, really . . .'

He shook his head. 'It doesn't matter. We'll do it another time, when you're less . . . busy.'

'You think I'm selfish, don't you?' I blurted.

'No, no . . .'

'You do. You think I'm selfish and self-absorbed and I don't have my priorities right.'

'Antonia, that's not true. Look, you have talent, real talent, and of course you want to see how far you can go

176

with it. It's just . . . I can't pretend to understand what this life is like, but it seems to be all-consuming.'

'Well, so is yours,' I retorted. 'How many hours a week do you work?'

He looked sheepish for a moment, before muttering, 'Ehm, eighty, a hundred?'

I thumped the sofa. 'See? What did you say to me that time in the hospital about passion, and facing my nerves if I wanted to get anywhere in life?'

'You're right.' He nodded bleakly. 'It's just . . . if you come from, well, a background like yours, ehrm, it can leave you unprepared for disappointment.' He fiddled with the strap on his bag and looked at his feet.

'What do you mean, a "background" like mine?'

'Well, you spent the first seven years of your life in an orphanage, Antonia. You don't have that core of self-confidence that others have, that have been brought up with families.'

I felt a sudden wave of anger. How dare he be so patron-izing? What on earth did he know about being brought up in an orphanage? 'Excuse me, that's not true. I may not have had the best start in life, but Mum and Dad gave me every-thing. They more than made up for it.'

'I wasn't implying that they didn't . . .'

'Oh, no,' I said indignantly. I could feel the colour in my cheeks now, and my voice, such as it was, was shaking. 'You weren't implying anything other than the fact that I'm somehow deficient as a person and that I only have myself to blame for it. Well, you know what, Niall, I don't need your help, thank you very much,' I said, jumping up from the sofa. 'Please go.'

He looked genuinely shocked. 'Antonia, I'm sorry if I offended you. It's just—'

But I put up my hand. 'You are judging me, Niall. And finding me wanting. I don't need it. Thanks for the medicine,' I said, summoning all my strength to usher him to the door, which I shut behind him as firmly as I possibly could. And then I collapsed on the floor and sobbed my heart out. Why did it always have to be like this with Niall – what was it about me, or him? I knew that he really cared about me, but why was that tension always in the air? Except for that one time in Powerscourt, when he'd seemed to relax a little – until I'd asked him a question about his family, and he'd frozen again. And then I thought about him kissing me . . . 'Oh, for God's sake,' I said out loud in the living room. 'I can't think about this *now*.' I supposed at least I'd put an end to it, throwing him out of the house like that. I knew we wouldn't be talking any time soon.

And then I thought of the text. Surely Niall wouldn't have sent it? But that was just plain silly. Unless he wanted to protect me in some way, save me from disappointment. He'd seemed so adamant about my 'background' and everything. 'For goodness' sake, Antonia, that's ridiculous,' I said out loud to myself. And it was ridiculous. If I was to survive tonight, I'd have to put that text right out of my mind.

I spent the rest of the day fielding phone calls from well-wishers and trying to gather myself, gargling with salt water and, every so often, croaking out a note or two. All that came out of my throat was a kind of a whistle. I tried not to panic. I had until eight o'clock to sort it out, or later, depending on what time I went on. Mary arrived and stuffed me full of throat lozenges and painkillers, so by the time Colette dropped by, I had fooled myself into thinking that I was feeling marginally better.

Then Colette put me straight. 'Oh. My. God.' She looked at me sternly. 'You look like nothing on earth.'

'Thanks for the compliment,' I said shakily, feeling the tears spring to my eyes.

Seeing that I was about to cry, she pulled me to her in a hug. 'There, there, c'mon, you'll be fine,' she soothed as I blubbed into her shoulder.

'But I feel terrible,' I wailed.

'I know you do, but after tonight, you can lie in bed for the rest of your life, can't you? You can just take to your bed and drink champagne and eat foie gras and celebrate being the rightful winner of *That's Talent!* Because that's what you're going to do, Antonia. You're going to win it. Because you deserve to, OK? All you have to do is concentrate on the song, and it'll be OK.' She sounded more convinced than she felt, clearly, because I saw her shoot Mary a look. One that said, 'I'm not sure about this.' But I knew that I had to go ahead. Ducking out now was not an option.

'Yesterday' *is* the right song for me, I thought. And I'll prove it.

17

AND THEN WE WERE PULLING UP TO THE O2 FOR THE LIVE semi-final. It was a huge venue, and I should have been quaking with nerves, and yet this time, I didn't feel that tightness in my stomach, the tingle of anticipation as we pulled up to the performers' entrance. Instead, I felt hollow and tired, my mind spinning with thoughts of the row I'd had with Niall, of the anonymous text. It had cast a shadow over my day and I just couldn't shake it off. That and the feeling that he was the last person in the world I wanted to upset. Oh, God, I'd made such a mess out of everything, hadn't I?

The dressing rooms were even more crowded than usual, with make-up people, stylists and lots of other hangers-on. There are always so many people at these things who just seem to be hanging around. You have no clue what they're doing, but you're afraid to ask, in case they turn out to be someone really important. I could see Amanda in one corner of the room, practising her scales whilst Jenny on make-up brushed out that gorgeous red hair of hers. When she caught sight of me, she waved and gave me the thumbs up and I had to force a smile, even though it was so hot in there, I thought I'd pass out.

'Cow,' Colette muttered under her breath. 'She'd sell her granny to be famous,' she muttered to Mary.

'I'm not deaf, you know,' I said. 'Amanda's a friend. You've misjudged her, Colette.' I knew how sharp Colette could be. It was something I really liked about her, but sometimes it was just too much.

'Sure,' Colette said dryly, but when she saw the stricken look on my face, she backtracked. 'Let's just concentrate on you for the moment, sweetie. By the time we've finished with you, you'll look and feel a million dollars.'

I doubted it, but let her lead me to a cramped corner of the dressing room, and allowed myself to be pulled into shape by both her and Mary – and by Valerie in make-up, because as the heats had progressed Celtic had insisted on their make-up artists having a say in how I looked. Colette hadn't been impressed. 'They think we're amateurs,' she'd murmured, although she'd eventually had to admit that Valerie did a good job.

Fifteen minutes later, I was told to stand up. 'Wow,' Mary said. 'You sure do scrub up well, pet.'

I looked at myself in the mirror. The ugly duckling had turned into a swan. Valerie had managed to camouflage the worst of my red nose, and with careful applications of Optrex and plenty of mascara my eyes looked almost normal. And the dress – well, it was a show-stopper. Colette had urged me to risk it and bring a leather dress with silk sleeves, which she'd matched with a pair of black suede ankle-boots. I didn't recognize myself, but unlike before, I didn't enjoy the feeling as much. It didn't seem to be me, to be who I really was. I felt like an alien in the dress – it was just too sexy. Maybe if I told Colette that I felt uncomfortable in it . . .

My thoughts were interrupted by a loud knocking at the door. Karen opened it and bellowed, 'Right, all artists to the backstage area for the run-through!' and the door slammed behind her. It wasn't too late to back out now, I thought. I could still withdraw.

'Break a leg, Antonia,' Mary said, pulling me towards her in a hug. Feeling like death, I followed the others out to the huge backstage area. The audience had yet to be admitted, so it felt eerily quiet.

'Right, everyone, you know that the judges won't be in position just yet, only the crew, so you know what to do. Walk forward to the spot, pretend to answer the judges' questions, and then off you go.' Karen beamed.

'She makes it sound so easy,' a voice beside me said. I turned and smiled at Amanda. We'd been through the drill a million times by now, but still, it always felt like the first time.

'You look a bit peaky,' she said, her voice full of concern.

'I've just got a cold, that's all,' I said, attempting a watery smile. Because how could I really tell her how I felt? How could I explain this ominous feeling inside, the sense that my world was collapsing around me? I shook my head. This was just silly. Whatever happened to feel the fear and do it anyway? Colette was right. I just needed to concentrate on the song and it would all fall into place. I tried to look at Amanda and pin a smile to my face. 'I'll be just fine. I'm looking forward to it, in fact.'

She gave me a long look. 'Good for you,' she said eventually, squeezing my hand. I squeezed back.

After the run-through, we were herded back to the hospitality room, to huddle around the television set, whilst the audience filled The O2 and the technical crew did their final checks. The room was hot and crowded and I thought I'd faint. I closed my eyes and tried to hum a few notes, but all that filled my head was a wheezy squeak. My heart sank. Because it was the semis, most people were doing a big stage number, pulling out all the stops to make the final. I know that Amanda had done a whole new routine, getting a professional choreographer to help her. 'I want to blow the judges away,' she'd said to me earlier. I'd nodded and wished that I hadn't opted to keep it simple now, of all times. I didn't need any dancers or backing singers for 'Yesterday'. It was the perfect song for a voice like mine, strong and rich, Eithne had told me. But I didn't *have* a voice, not now anyway.

I should have been panicking, I suppose, but with all the cold treatments inside me, I was just too woozy, my head feeling as if it were filled with cotton wool. I sat on the fake leather sofa in my sexy dress and ankle-boots, my head swimming. I tried to keep positive and focus on what it would feel like to give absolutely my best performance, running through the song in my head, feeling the notes soar in my mind. C'mon, Antonia, you can do it, I said to myself. I knew that everyone believed in me, and all I had to do was believe in myself, too. Believe in myself and open my mouth and sing, just as I had every Saturday night for the last two months. It was simple, really.

And before I had time to change my mind, Karen was beside me, her hand on my elbow. 'All set, Toni?'

I nodded. 'This cold is really getting me down,' I said, 'but I'll do my best.'

Karen gently squeezed my arm. 'You'll be terrific, Toni, I know you will.'

I nodded and followed her to my spot backstage, unable to hear myself think above the din of the act currently onstage, a guitar band, who were brilliant, snappy and fun, but tonight, they made my eardrums bleed. And the audience were in a frenzy, cheering and whooping louder than ever for their favourite act. I peered around the side of the stage and the lights were blinding, the audience a loud blur behind them. I swallowed hard and waited for the band to finish, accepting their handshakes as they came off stage. 'Good luck, Antonia,' Mark, the lead singer, said.

I nodded, and, feeling Karen's hand on the small of my back, waited for my cue. It was so hot and loud, I thought, and I felt so woozy. I just wanted to lie down for a bit. I tried to shake myself out of it by thinking: C'mon Antonia, this is your moment, your night, not time for a little nap.

I tried to buoy myself up, like a boxer before he goes in the ring, listening to the applause as Aaron, the presenter, worked up to introducing me. 'Ladies and gentlemen, from church choir to singing superstar, the girl from nowhere, Antonia Trent!'

I walked unsteadily on to the stage, trying to smile and wave as the applause grew deafening. I scanned the audience, as usual, for my gang. Bridget said she'd be waving a poster with 'Go Glenvara' on it, so I'd know, but it was all a blur. I walked to the spot and stood there, trying to smile so hard my teeth hurt, my ears ringing with the screaming from the audience.

'Wow, Antonia,' said Maurice Prendergast, trying to shout over the din. 'You've certainly won the hearts of this audience.'

'Thanks,' I managed, praying that my voice didn't sound too squeaky.

He smiled at me warmly, clearly unaware of what he was about to hear. 'So, Antonia, what's the dream?'

I looked at him blankly for a moment, before remembering where I was. 'Just being here is a dream come true,' I told him. 'If anyone had told me that a month after I buried my mother a letter would arrive telling me I had been chosen to audition for a TV show, I would have had them committed.' I smiled. 'So it's gotten me through a very difficult period in my life, and no matter what happens I know I will give it my best shot tonight.' I smiled as the audience burst into applause, even though my insides had turned to jelly.

'Well, I don't think anyone can ask for more than that, so good luck.' All of the judges seemed to be smiling. They like me, I thought, and they're rooting for me. 'Now, what are you going to sing for us tonight?' Maurice said.

I cleared my throat and prayed that something would come out. '"Yesterday",' I managed, relieved that my voice was working for the moment.

Maurice raised his eyebrows. 'A brave choice, because the voice really has to carry it. What made you choose it?'

I thought for a moment, before saying, 'Because I like its simplicity. It's just the perfect song. It only takes two minutes and yet it says everything.'

'I agree.' He smiled. 'Right, Antonia, in your own time.'

I nodded and turned to where Declan, the guitarist, was sitting. We'd agreed that he'd sit about ten feet to my left so that I'd be able to hear the intro, but with the applause and my cold, it seemed muffled, and as soon as I began, I knew that there was something wrong. I'd fluffed my entry, I thought, as I sang the opening words. Oh, God, Declan was about two bars ahead of me, I panicked as, gamely, Declan tried to adjust, playing the same bar three times, until we were in sync again. I felt the colour drain from my face. My voice didn't sound like mine at all: it was nasal, with a rasp to it on the top notes. Concentrate, Antonia, I kept telling myself, concentrate and let the song do the rest. I hit the second verse, feeling the orchestra swelling behind me, and my voice gaining in power and control, but still rasping on the higher notes. I had to keep going to the end, I just had to. I knew that my voice wasn't right, but maybe, just maybe, I could pull it off. Mum, if you're up there, please give me a hand, I thought, as I felt the song carry me along, and when I got to the end, I bowed my head and didn't even dare look at the judges. Out of the corner of my eye, I could see my gang on their feet waving and generally going mad, a huge banner above their heads, just as Bridget had promised.

Aaron came over, a sympathetic look on his face, and gave me a hug, whispering, 'Well done,' into my ear, before turning to the audience. 'Now, ladies and gentlemen, you may not know that Antonia sang tonight with a very heavy cold, and I think she deserves a special round of applause,' he urged, at which the audience whooped and cheered louder than ever.

I was mortified. Don't feel sorry for me, I thought, waving weakly and trying to smile, as the judges conferred and the applause reached a crescendo. It was as if the audience was willing them to get me through, even though I hadn't sung my best. I felt a surge of gratitude to them, and I suddenly realized that that was what I really loved about performing. The support of the audience, feeling them going with me, buoying me up as I sang. But would it be enough tonight? My knees were knocking as I waited for the judges to speak.

I knew it was all over when Maurice Prendergast just looked at me and said kindly, 'I don't think you gave the performance you were capable of tonight, Antonia, but then I'm sure you know that.'

I nodded, trying not to cry.

'You've wowed us here, week after week, and I think I can say you've given some of the strongest performances we've seen in this competition,' he added, as a chorus of boos rose in the background. I wasn't sure who they were booing: him or me.

'There's nothing I'd like to see more than you going through to the final, but I have to judge you on your performance tonight. It's only fair on the other contestants . . .'

As he went on, I knew. That even though I'd managed to hold it all together, it probably wasn't enough. The dream was over.

I was ready to march off the stage, never to come back, and hardly heard his next words, 'But even a less-than-perfect performance from you is worth somebody else's absolute best, and I know the best is yet to come, Antonia, so it's a yes from me.'

I nodded my thanks to Maurice and waited for the other judges. It was a yes from Michael Smyth, if not an enthusiastic one, and then there was only Mary Devine left. She was just gorgeous, with her long blonde hair and Grecian gown, and she'd always been so enthusiastic about me, such a supporter, that I knew I'd probably just scrape through.

She sighed and looked at me apologetically. 'Antonia, what can I say? You chose a really difficult song and . . .

well, your voice let you down on the night. Now, I know that you weren't well,' she added hastily as the chorus of boos gathered pace again, 'but as Maurice said, we can only judge your performance on the night. And, well, it just wasn't right. I'm sorry, Antonia.' She smiled at me, her hands clasped, ignoring the chorus of booing. 'I just can't say yes, so you'll have to take your chances with the audience vote.'

I nodded and practically ran off the stage. I didn't realize that my knees were knocking until I got backstage, where I almost collapsed into Karen's arms.

'I blew it,' I blurted, the tears springing to my eyes. 'It was live and I blew it.'

'No, you didn't. You gave a terrific performance, believe it or not, and I'm amazed how well you did, even with the flu. You are a real trouper, Toni. Don't mind that cow,' she nodded in the direction of Mary Devine, before covering her mouth. 'Forget I said that.'

I managed a grin.

'Now, look, we'll have an hour break while another programme goes out before the results, so I'll get your gang to come backstage – I know they'll give you the support you need.'

'Thanks, Karen, for everything,' I said, and she smiled, before ushering me towards the supporters' area backstage.

On the screen, Aaron was saying, 'Join us in an hour to see who will make it to the final,' as, one by one, our faces flashed up. When it came to me, I could see how stressed I'd looked, how tense. God, it really did show, I thought. I needed to see the gang, but I wasn't sure I had the nerve. After all their support, I'd let them down. Because of course I knew that I was out of the competition. Nobody would vote for me after that, and if they did, well, I didn't want people voting because they felt sorry for me.

'Antonia—' I was aware of Amanda tugging at my arm, but I shook her off.

'I just need a few moments,' I breathed, brushing past her and praying I wouldn't trip and fall as I made for the audience area. I didn't want to talk to Amanda. I just wanted to see my friends, my family.

Bridget was first, bless her, to hug me tight and say, 'You were brilliant, Antonia, just brilliant.'

Of course, surrounded by all the love and support, I broke down. 'But I've let you all down,' I wailed. 'I'm so sorry. My voice . . .' I croaked.

'It's fine, and you haven't let us down.' Sister Monica shushed me, stroking my hair and dabbing at my tears with her hankie. 'You gave your very best, in very difficult circumstances, and that's all anyone can ask. I know plenty of people who wouldn't have had the guts to go on at all, not to mind singing that song, and singing it well. You did us proud, Antonia.'

'Hear, hear,' Billy said. 'We are so proud of you, pet, and so is everyone in Glenvara.'

'Thanks, Billy,' I said. 'I really don't know what I'd do without you all.'

'Oh, you'd be fine, but us? Don't know about you lot,

but this is the most excitement I've had in years!' Bridget trilled, and everyone laughed. I even managed a smile, even though my heart felt like lead. I longed just to go home, climb into bed and pull the covers over my head, but of course, I couldn't. I had to sit in the green room, or in the audience area, for the next, nerve-racking hour, waiting for the votes to come in.

And I found my thoughts going to Niall, even though I'd told myself I wouldn't do that. Although I willed myself not to, I just couldn't help looking, craning my neck to see if there was any sign of him.

Betty seemed to read my mind. 'He was here, pet, but he got called away. He said he'd call as soon as he could.'

'Oh.' I blinked back the tears. 'OK.' All I could do now was wait.

18

THE HOUR SEEMED TO CRAWL BY. I TRIED NOT TO LOOK AT the clock in the backstage area, as Bridget held my hand and offered me sips of tea from the flask she'd brought with her. In spite of everything, I had to laugh when she pulled it out of her shopper. 'Bridget, how did you get that through security?'

'I have my ways,' she said darkly. 'I told that nice young man that I was with you, and that they were trying to poison me with the coffee in this place, and he just waved me through. Quite a handsome young man he was, too.' She grinned. 'If I was twenty years younger, I'd have a go, that's for sure.'

'For goodness' sake, Bridget,' Betty chided. 'This is hardly the place for that kind of behaviour.'

'Oh, I'd say it's exactly the place, wouldn't you, Antonia, my love? Lots of attractive young men about . . .' And she winked at me. I winked back. I knew that she was trying to distract me, and I was glad of it, to be honest. My stomach felt as if it was one huge knot, and my forehead was clammy, my ears ringing in pain from my cold.

'I need to sit down,' I managed, and Betty took me by the arm and led me to a sofa, pushing aside a pile of coats and bags to make room for me.

I sat there while she held my hand and soothed me. 'Your mammy would be so proud, love, no matter what happens.'

No matter what happens. I knew what I wanted to happen, of course. I wanted to win. Especially now that I'd made such a mess of things. Until yesterday, all I'd wanted to do was my best, to sing as well as I could and see how far it took me. Miss Mouse hadn't wanted to *win* anything. That was for ambitious people, people like Amanda. But maybe, I wondered now, I was more ambitious than I'd thought. Maybe Niall was right. I was getting sucked into this whole thing. But then it was hard not to. He didn't understand how all-consuming the round of rehearsals, run-throughs, photocalls and performances actually was. You didn't have a moment to breathe. It seemed funny that I'd been looking for a job just a few weeks ago – now, I couldn't even imagine how I'd find the time.

The clock had ground forward to the hour, and the audience votes were in. Karen came to the backstage area, a loud-hailer in her hand, and bellowed, 'Acts to backstage, acts to backstage!' at the top of her voice.

'Oh, God, that's me,' I said, getting shakily to my feet. 'Wish me luck, everyone.'

Sister Monica squeezed me hard. 'You don't need luck, Antonia. You have a God-given talent and everyone will see

194

that. Besides, I believe in the power of prayer, and I've never prayed so much in my entire life.' She smiled.

'Well, say another few Hail Marys, everyone,' I managed.

'Good luck, Antonia!' I was smothered in hugs and kisses before Karen tracked me down, chiding me gently for being late. I allowed her to lead me to the backstage area where the acts had gathered, all of us jittery with nerves.

I found Amanda and hugged her tightly. 'Here goes,' I said.

'Oooh, the nerves are killing me,' she said tightly, clutching her stomach. 'There's no way I'll be able to stand up on stage for the results.'

'You won't need to. We'll do it together,' I said. 'OK?'

She nodded. 'OK. You and me. Like sisters.' She grinned.

'That's it.' I nodded. 'Like sisters.'

We held hands and walked out on to the stage together, waving and smiling enthusiastically as the audience's cheering grew to a roar. It was deafening, only subsiding after several attempts by Aaron to get them to be quiet.

'And now,' he said. 'The moment you've all been waiting for. The votes are in, and the phone lines are now closed. The results will be announced in reverse order with only the last three contestants going through to the live final, here, next week. Ladies and gentlemen, let's see which of these brilliant acts you've voted into the final of *That's Talent!*'

The audience roared again, as one by one, photos of the acts flashed on to a big screen above our heads, along with our numbers. By this stage, Amanda was squeezing my hand so tight, I thought she'd cut my circulation off, and I leaned over to her and whispered, 'It'll be OK.'

She gave me a watery smile and looked dead ahead, for the cameras, as one by one, the acts' names were called out and the unlucky ones left the stage. And then there were only four of us: Damien, the talented singer-songwriter, 4Guys, Amanda and myself. One of us had to go, and I knew, just knew it would be me. I hadn't done enough tonight, surely?

It seemed that Aaron deliberately slowed everything down then, leaving a huge pause after he said, 'And the final act to be leaving us tonight is . . .' It seemed that the world stood still. I could see that the audience was screaming with excitement, but I couldn't hear them for the roaring in my ears. I thought I'd faint, and found myself leaning on Amanda for support. I didn't hear the name being called, except suddenly she was pulling her hand out of mine, and walking away from me across the stage. She didn't even look back, just kept on walking as I stood there, my mouth open in surprise, nearly falling over as Damien threw himself on me.

'We're through, we're through,' he kept yelling, but it still didn't sink in, until I was pulled into the centre of the stage and Aaron announced our names one by one.

'And, going through to the grand final, in this same spot next week, in third place . . .' and he called out the name of 4Guys, who whooped and cheered, and one of them, Karl, did a cartwheel on the stage.

'And in second place . . . the nightingale herself, Antonia

196

Trent!' As he called my name, I closed my eyes for a second, and when I opened them, I was still there, on the stage, the lights hot and bright on my face, and Damien was hugging me and the tears were pouring down my cheeks. I'd made it. In spite of everything, I'd made it. Whoever had sent that text had been wrong. I'd proved them wrong. Mum would have been proud of me. I knew that.

Backstage it was complete mayhem, with crowds milling about, all wanting to get near to us, it seemed, as if some of the magic would wear off if they did. Maybe everyone wants to be famous these days, I thought. Somehow, Karen managed to find me in the chaos, taking me by the arm and steering me firmly down a narrow corridor to the press room. 'The Sundays want a photo, so we'll get that done now,' she said briskly, opening the door so suddenly I was blinded, flashbulbs going off all around me. I could hardly believe it, and just stood there, blinking and trying to smile.

'Toni, how does it feel, having got through after the night you had tonight?' one of the journalists asked, before Karen interrupted.

'Not now, guys, Toni is exhausted. But talk to Jean and she'll arrange interviews, OK?'

'Just one quick question. Toni. What would your mum say if she was here to see you?' a cute guy with a kind face asked me.

I swallowed, thinking that she was the only reason I'd got through tonight, and took a deep breath. 'Well, I think

197

she'd be proud and delighted for me, but I am just still in shock that I've gotten this far,' I said. And I was in shock. After that performance, I couldn't see how I'd made it, and yet the audience had been kind to me, had seen something that maybe I hadn't. Either way, I'd made it. I felt a pang for a moment, for Amanda, and I wondered if I should go after her, see if she was in the dressing room still. I felt I needed to say something to her. She'd given the performance of her life and, well, I hadn't. I knew that. Somehow, it didn't feel fair, and yet I didn't really know what I could do about it.

I was distracted by Karen. 'OK, guys, that's it, this is just a photo op,' she said, and led me out of the room.

'You OK?' she asked as soon as we were outside.

'Yeah, but wow, that was wild.'

'Well, you're the star of the show tonight, that's for sure.' She grinned.

'But Damien won,' I protested. 'And he deserved to – he should be the one getting all the attention.'

'He'll get his share, don't you worry, but you've really hit a nerve, Toni, do you know that?' Karen said. 'Everyone loves your story, the way you came from nowhere and made it to the finals, because it could be theirs, except they don't have the talent, of course.' She laughed. 'You're living their dream, Antonia. That's why they love you.'

'Oh,' I said, unable to think of anything sensible to say, except, 'I'm not sure I'm ready for all of this. All this attention . . .'

'Oh, you are, Toni. You're stronger than you think,' she

said. 'And don't worry, we'll mind you, that's part of the job,' she continued as we headed for the backstage green room and once again my gang went wild.

Even Sister Monica was grinning from ear to ear as they all hugged me. 'Antonia, my prayers were answered,' she said as everyone gathered around me, congratulating me and opening bottles of champagne.

'Didn't I tell you you'd do it?' Bridget said triumphantly.

I nodded, feeling a sudden wave of dizziness wash over me. 'I'm wrecked,' I had to admit. 'All the adrenaline kept me going, but now I just want to lie down and never get up again.'

'Of course you do,' Billy said reassuringly.

'And you should have seen the amount of photographers we had to meet,' I said to them. 'I'm really not sure I'm up to all this.'

'Yes, you are,' he hugged me again and I thought of Karen's words, 'You're stronger than you think.' I wasn't so sure that she was right.

'Oh, don't get me wrong, I want it all, but I just can't take the attention,' I told Billy. 'It terrifies me.'

'Well, just take it one step at a time, OK, pet? And we'll mind you, won't we, gang?'

There was a chorus of yeses and I had to smile. 'Thanks. Just knowing you lot were here is what got me through.'

'My God the tension waiting for the result! They sure know how to milk it. Sister Monica nearly broke my arm she had me in such a grip.' Billy laughed. 'Then when your name wasn't called out she started praying out loud.' We all laughed, including Sister Monica, who was sipping from a glass of champagne.

She nodded and said, 'I could get used to this. I'll tell you, it's going to be hard getting back to prayers on a Saturday night when all this is over.'

'I think I owe God a major thank you,' I said. 'God and you lot,' and everyone whooped and cheered again. 'But now, I have to go home, everyone. I'm just beat. I hope you all understand.'

There was a chorus of agreement. 'I'll go and get your things,' Colette volunteered, clattering off to the green room in her platform heels, as everyone finished up their champagne. It was funny, the whole thing felt a bit anticlimactic. I had spent the day feeling worse than I had ever done in my entire life, and it had taken everything for me to perform. It had been such a grind that now, I simply felt drained.

Later on, in the car, I remembered to switch on my phone. My in-box was crammed with good wishes from everyone, from the florist in Glenvara to the girls in Mary's office. It seemed as if the whole country was rooting for me. But there was only one message I really wanted to see.

I kept Niall's for last. I could see the envelope and his name beside it, but I waited before opening it. 'So sorry I can't be there for you tonight, but I'll be watching every step of the way. Promise. Love, Niall xx.'

I put the phone down on my lap and wondered for a

moment, then I looked at the message again. He'd had an emergency at the hospital, so he'd had to leave. That was fine. I understood, and I was relieved that he was still talking to me after the row we'd had. But 'Love, Niall'? What did it mean? I was probably just reading too much into it, I thought. Everyone said 'love' nowadays. Still, I dithered, wondering how to reply. If I said 'love' would that mean what I thought it meant? Oh, God, I was tying myself up in knots. Eventually, I took a deep breath and composed a reply. 'Thanks – really appreciated the support, and hope to see you soon.' Does that sound a bit businesslike? I wondered, my finger hovering over the 'send' button. I added, 'Antonia xxx' and pressed 'send'.

And then, when the car pulled up outside the house, I waved goodbye to Colette and Mary, opened my front door, went straight up the stairs and threw myself on the bed, still in my leather dress. I felt my bedspread under my cheek as I tried to keep my eyes open for a second, just long enough to try to persuade myself to remove my eye make-up and brush my teeth. But it was no good. I just didn't have an ounce more energy. I was beat.

19

WHEN I WOKE UP IT WAS STILL DARK. I SAT UP IN BED, GROPING
around for my mobile phone. I blinked at its harsh light and
looked at the time. Six o'clock. I couldn't believe I'd only
slept for four hours – must be all the excitement, I thought.
Perhaps I just couldn't wind down, not yet. Still, at least
I could take off my make-up now. I felt a lot better – my
temperature seemed to have gone down.

I put on a dressing gown and shuffled to the bathroom,
brushing my teeth and attempting to remove some of the
make-up from my face. It was a hard job, because they really
trowel it on thick for these shows, but ten minutes and two
applications of face scrub later, I was just about presentable.
It was funny. My face looked so different without a thick
layer of foundation and the smoky eyeliner Colette liked
applying to my upper eyelids. I looked younger, somehow,
fresher, I thought. Odd, people kept telling me how much
better I looked with an inch of foundation applied to my
face. I hardly recognized myself with it on, but still, the
natural look would probably not work well on television. I
giggled to myself.

I had just finished when I heard a loud noise downstairs. My heart stopped. A burglar. It had to be at this hour. I crept to the bathroom door, and stuck my head around it. There was a rustling at the letterbox and then it flapped open and a voice shouted, 'Antonia? Are you in there?'

Niall. I ran down the stairs thanking God that I'd brushed my teeth, which was an odd thought, I supposed, but still. It was only when I opened the door that I realized I still had my pink fluffy dressing gown on over my leather dress. Too late, I thought.

He was obscured by a huge bouquet of flowers, so big he had to crane his neck around them to say hello. 'Hi. These are for you,' he said shyly.

'Well, I should hope so.' I grinned. 'Otherwise, you are breaking into my house with a large bunch of flowers.' And then I thought, was that the right thing to say – something cheeky, jokey – after what had happened yesterday morning?

I knew I was OK when he laughed out loud. 'Very droll,' he said, handing me the flowers. 'Congratulations.'

'Thanks,' I replied, taking the huge bouquet into my arms. I could barely hold them, and the heavy scent of lilies filled the air. I love lilies. 'They're beautiful. Are you just off shift?'

'No,' he looked surprised, and I thought, of course, he couldn't be. He was dressed in jeans and a skating hoodie that I'd never seen him in before – it was olive green and it suited him. Made him look less . . . uptight, I thought,

203

although perhaps it was better not to mention that.

'It's just . . . it's quite early . . .' I began.

He shook his head. 'It's dinner time, Antonia. Six thirty. On Sunday.'

I put a hand to my mouth. 'Oh my goodness. I must have slept for the whole day!'

'Are you just *awake*?' He looked at me as if I'd lost my marbles.

'Well, I must be, I suppose.' I burst out laughing, and so did he.

'You're worse than me,' he joked.

'Sorry, it's just I was so exhausted, with the cold and the semis and everything . . .' And then I remembered my manners. 'Come on in.'

He shifted from foot to foot. 'Ah, no, I'll leave you to it—'

'To what?' I interrupted him. 'To my exciting evening washing my hair and ordering a takeaway?'

He shrugged and grinned. 'Oh, well, maybe we can do it together. My hair needs a wash. Not that it'll take long,' he said ruefully, patting his thinning blond hair.

'Very funny,' I said, ushering him in the door, wondering why it was we got on so well sometimes and others, well . . .

He stood in the living-room doorway for a bit, looking uncertain. Searching for something to do, I said, 'I'll just put some tea on.' Before he had the time to reply, I scuttled off to the kitchen and busied myself filling the kettle.

'So, how does it feel to be in the finals?' he shouted from the living room.

'Strange,' I replied. 'The whole thing was a bit of a blur, to be honest.' I took my time putting the tea bags into the cups, pouring over the boiling water, sniffing the milk for signs that it was still fresh. The truth was, I didn't know what to say to Niall about the row, and yet I knew that I should say *something*. We couldn't just pretend it hadn't happened, could we?

But I didn't have to, because he came straight into the kitchen and took the mugs of tea away from me, putting them down on the counter. 'There, we'll leave them to brew for a few minutes,' he said, and then he took my hands in his much larger ones. 'I'm sorry about yesterday, Antonia, I was way out of line—'

'Oh, so was I,' I interrupted. 'You see, I was feeling just so bad and so guilty that I'd dragged you out—'

He silenced me by putting a finger to my lips. I felt my stomach flip. 'It's not you, Antonia, it's me.'

'*You?*' I looked at him incredulously. I didn't understand. I was the selfish one, surely, with my all-consuming, well, 'career' was probably not the right word for it, I thought – my life. Because it *was* my life right now.

'Yes, me. I haven't been entirely honest with you, and I've blamed you for it. And I'm sorry.' He looked so upset that I wanted to hug him, but didn't dare, in case he got the wrong message.

Instead, I shook my head. 'I don't understand . . .' I said.

'C'mon, let's go and sit down,' he said, taking me by the hand and leading me into the sitting room, where he pulled me down beside him on the sofa.

I waited for him to talk, looking at him as he ran a hand through his hair, the way he always did when he was harassed, his forehead creasing in concentration. Eventually, he took a deep breath. 'You remember when I talked about your background, and how it didn't give you the confidence that everyone else has?'

'Yes.' I looked at him suspiciously, hoping that he wasn't going to rake all that up again. Because I'd made my peace with that when I was seven, and didn't see the need to go over and over it.

'Well, it's just, I know exactly how it feels to lack that confidence, to feel that instead of what everyone else has. It's just a void—' he began.

'But I don't feel that way, Niall,' I interrupted him. 'I was lucky in that my mum and dad gave me everything, all the love and attention I could possibly want.'

'I know,' he said seriously. 'It's not you, Antonia, it's me. You see, my family are just great, couldn't be better, but they're not really mine, you understand?'

He was talking in riddles, and I had to shake my head. 'Niall, I don't understand. And I don't know what's bothering you, but it's not a problem, honest. I know that you just want the best for me—' I began.

He interrupted me. 'I'm a foster child too.' He blurted it out, and then put a hand over his mouth, as if it were too late. As if the words had just escaped.

'Oh.' I was at a loss to know what to say for a moment. So *that* was why he got so uptight whenever we strayed on to touchy subjects like his family. And that would explain why he'd been so pushy about me doing *That's Talent!* Because he understood about not being like everyone else – not having the same foundation of security that they had. Because he was right. Being an orphan – or a foster child – did mean that there was something missing: that 'confidence' chip in the brain that others had naturally.

'Oh, Niall, why didn't you tell me?' I tried to reach out to him, but he flinched, and so I sat still beside him on the sofa, waiting for him to relax a bit.

'God, I don't know,' he said, putting his head in his hands. 'I'm not ashamed of it or anything, it's just, well, the timing never seemed right, and I thought if I said anything, you'd think I was . . .'

'What? Not the kind of guy I'd go for?'

'Well . . .' he looked sheepish.

'But that's just nonsense, Niall,' I said, feeling hurt that he could think otherwise. If he was inferior because he hadn't grown up with his own family, well then, so was I. And one thing I knew, I mightn't be the most outgoing person in the world, but I'd never felt inferior. Mum and Dad had made sure of that.

Niall's voice interrupted my thoughts. 'Look, I know that, but as far as I know, you had a wonderful mum and dad.'

'And so did you,' I retorted.

'You're right,' he said. 'My foster family . . . well, I couldn't wish for a better one. They were just fantastic, and I love my brothers and sisters as if they're my own flesh and blood.'

'Well, you're lucky then, aren't you?' I said.

He nodded. 'I'm very lucky . . . But you never knew your family, Antonia. You could begin a whole new life. I knew exactly who my family were,' he said bitterly.

I said nothing, willing him to go on. I knew that if I opened my mouth, the spell would be broken and he'd tell me that it didn't matter, that he didn't want to talk about it, and so I remained silent.

'I don't remember much about my childhood, because I was fostered at an early age, but apparently I was taken into care because I was found alone one day, wandering the streets in just my nappy. The social worker told me that I had a teddy in my arms, a blue one, and that I was freezing cold and dirty.'

'Did you know where you'd come from?'

He nodded grimly. 'I was the youngest of six, and I re-member a lot of shouting when I was a kid. That and the cold and feeling hungry all the time,' he said. 'I must have blocked some of it out, because apparently, the flat where we lived was an absolute dump – there was rubbish all over the floor, and my parents were either drunk or stoned all day. We were just left to fend for ourselves.'

'Did you have brothers or sisters?'

'Two older sisters and a brother. He was just a baby at the time.'

'That must have been hard . . . in a way, I was lucky to end up where I did, because the nuns were so kind and always did their best.'

He continued, as if I hadn't spoken. 'I went back one day a few years ago, to the flat, to see if I could remember anything, and my old neighbour came out. She told me that one day she'd called around and we were all in the place by ourselves, including the baby, and my *mother*,' he said the word bitterly, 'had just gone out to the pub the night before and left us. My sister had spilt a tin of powdered milk all over the floor because she'd been trying to make the baby a bottle. I mean, how on earth did these people get to be parents?' He sounded so bitter, so hostile, that I felt a jolt of sympathy for him. I reached out and squeezed his hand.

'And yet, you found good parents and overcame it.'

He nodded. 'I did. It was thanks to Jim and Eileen. They fostered me when I was three, and, really, my life began from the day I moved in there with my brother.'

'What about your sisters?'

'Jim and Eileen already had four foster children and they couldn't take any more, so my sisters went to another family down the country.'

'Did you see them again?'

He shook his head. 'Once or twice. We didn't really get on. It was as if we'd never been related. Odd, really.'

I nodded, knowing that it wasn't really odd. They'd never been brought up to live as a family, more like a pack of wild animals. No wonder they didn't see each other that way: they just didn't have that bond. But then I supposed, neither did I. I had no 'family' of my own, not like Niall, anyway.

I realized that Niall was talking again, but I hadn't been

listening. I'd just been too wrapped up in my own thoughts. 'My foster family,' he was saying, 'they're my only family now. And I've done everything I can to make them proud.' He was rubbing the knee of his jeans, over and over, in a nervous reaction, and I had to put my hand on his to get him to stop.

'And you have made them proud. You can't get better than being a doctor,' I said. At the same time, I was thinking that it must be an awful responsibility. He must never be able to relax, thinking that he had to make his parents proud of him, and never give them a moment's cause for concern. 'You must have been a real swot,' I tried to joke.

He laughed. 'God, I was. I spent every moment studying. Didn't misbehave, unlike my baby brother.' He grinned. 'He really made up for me: out all night, girls, fun . . .'

'You sound envious.'

'I was, a bit. Sometimes I feel as if I've spent my whole life doing the right thing, you know?' he said.

I know, I thought to myself, and then said, 'I know exactly what you mean, because so have I. I was the perfect daughter for my parents because I was afraid that, if I wasn't, they'd send me back.'

He looked at me and I looked at him, and in that moment we realized that we were alike. That we'd both been through the same thing, and it gave us a bond. Niall said, 'I thought if I misbehaved even once, I'd end up back there, with those people,' he said, a look of distaste on his face.

'But instead, you decided to make something of your

life, Niall,' I said. 'And that takes guts. Your parents must be so delighted.'

'They are,' he grinned. 'But they're happy with all of us, even my ne'er-do-well brother.' He smiled. 'Matt got away with murder, and yet they loved him just as much. I only realized lately that I don't have to please them all the time to make them love me. Do you know what I mean?'

I nodded. 'Yep, only in my case, now it's too late.'

He put his arm around me and drew me towards him, and I allowed myself to rest my head on his shoulder. It felt good: as if I could finally truly relax with someone, put my trust in them. Of course I trusted Mary and Colette and Sister Monica, but I felt that I was always a tiny bit on edge with them, never sure exactly how just to let go. But Niall and I, well, we were alike.

'You know, it's not too late, Antonia,' his breath was warm on my ear. 'Because you're doing it for yourself and not for anyone else. And that,' he said emphatically, 'takes real guts.' And then he enveloped me in a tight hug and I thought again of how good it felt to be held like that, tightly; to feel safe and protected. We held on for just a bit too long, and then pulled away, unsure of what to do next. We both looked at each other for a long time, his eyes taking in mine, his hands smoothing over my face.

'You've got a red nose,' he said eventually.

'And you've got no hair on the top of your head,' I responded smartly.

'Touché,' he said, and then he kissed me, a long slow

kiss which seemed to go on for ever. Everything seemed to stop and yet I could still hear the ticking of the clock on the living-room wall. His lips were warm and tender, and I found myself returning the kiss, running my hands through his hair, feeling the curls at the base of his neck. I'd never felt anything like it: a tingling sensation that went right through me.

Eventually, he pulled away. 'Wow, that was a first.'

'What do you mean?'

'Kissing a girl has never felt like that, I can tell you.' He smiled.

'Oh, how many have you kissed?' I tried to make it sound light, but really, I was covering up for the fact that at the grand old age of twenty-five, I hadn't kissed anyone – not really. Not a proper, grown-up kiss like this.

'A few. Not many. And nobody famous,' he said, his face straight.

I punched him playfully on the arm. 'Chancer.'

'What about you?' he said, and he looked friendly, curious.

Oh no. I looked down at my knees. 'Well . . .' I began.

'So many you've difficulty remembering?' he joked, but when he saw my face, he changed his expression. 'Antonia, I'm sorry . . .'

'Don't be.' I attempted a smile. 'The truth is, Niall, that I haven't ever kissed anyone, not really. Not to mind . . . anything else.'

There was a long silence and I thought: Oh, no, what on

earth must he think? I hardly dared look at him. Finally, I blurted, 'You must think I'm from the Victorian era.'

I'd expected him to laugh, but instead, he pulled me to him again, and this time his kiss was gentler, softer, as he held his face in mine. 'I think you're wonderful,' he finally said. 'And I don't care if you've never kissed another man in your life, or if you've kissed a hundred. It doesn't matter, because when I kiss you, it feels as if I'm kissing a woman for the very first time.'

'Bet you say that to all the girls,' I joked.

He held me at arm's length and looked at me seriously. 'I don't, because I don't fall in love with other girls every day of the week.'

I swallowed, wondering what on earth I was supposed to say to this. Because I didn't really know what love meant. Was I in love with Niall? How on earth would I know? But if it meant feeling like this . . . well, I supposed it must be love, then. Because I'd never felt like this in my whole life.

'What have I been missing?' I said, only realizing as I did so that I'd spoken out loud. And we both burst out laughing, before collapsing into each other's arms.

Later, much later, we were lying on the sofa, wrapped up in each other. My head was against his chest, and I could hear his heart beating, a steady thump-thump. We were silent and sleepy, the remains of a Chinese takeaway on the table in front of us. 'You know, this is the best date I've had in ages,' Niall said.

I turned my head to look at him. 'Me, too. And we didn't even set foot outside the door.'

'Well, it'd be difficult, what with the dressing gown and all,' Niall teased, nodding at my pink fluffy number.

I shrugged. 'Oh, I don't know. Now that I'm famous, I'm sure I could get a table at Chez Maurice, even in my dressing gown.' Chez Maurice was a tiny, exclusive French restaurant just outside Wicklow town, which was famous for being booked at least a year in advance.

He wrapped his arms around me and pulled me close, planting a kiss on top of my head. 'Well, when you win *That's Talent!* I'll take you there, OK?'

'It'll be booked up,' I retorted smartly.

'Well, they'll open it specially for Toni Trent, pop star.'

'Oh, God, don't say that. I managed to forget about the show for one whole night.' I groaned.

'Sorry.'

'No, it's OK, it's just the semis were so hard, I'm not sure I have the stomach for the finals. It feels as if I had to drag the performance out of myself, and I'm not sure I can build myself back up again for the finals. It's such a big mountain to climb,' I said, the very thought of it making me begin to panic. I put a hand to my throat and sat upright, so Niall shifted uneasily behind me.

'Just take it easy, OK?' he said, stroking my hair and kissing me gently on the forehead. 'Start with the song, and then the practice and the run-through, and just think about each stage as it comes. Simply focus on the moment, and the future will take care of itself. And I'll be there, remember, every step of the way.'

I nodded. 'Thanks, Niall. But you've got your own life and—'

'Not for a few days, I haven't.' He smiled. 'My girlfriend's in a talent show this week. Now, what song are you thinking about?'

Had he just said 'girlfriend'? For a moment, I was stunned. I'd never been anyone's girlfriend. 'Ehm. Well, I was thinking of Whitney Houston, some big showstopper like, "I Will Always Love You". It seems to fit the occasion, somehow.'

He proceeded to warble the opening lines of the song, clutching his chest and throwing his arms into the air until I had to punch him playfully. 'Shut up. It sounds better when *I* sing it.'

'I should hope so.' He laughed. 'Seriously, I think it's a great choice, because you have the voice to carry it.'

'Thanks. If the cold goes, I should be OK. I'm not sure I can take a repeat of last night.' I shook my head, willing myself not to remember.

'It won't be,' he soothed. 'You've been through the worst, and the rest will be plain sailing.' And then he asked the question that I hadn't dared ask myself: 'What about after?'

I pretended not to understand. 'After what?'

He looked at me sharply, as if to say, 'You know what I mean.'

'Oh, God, I don't know. Is there life after *That's Talent!*?'

215

'Well, that depends,' he said. 'What do you want?'

'Honestly? I never thought I'd get this far, not to mind to the finals. I've just been concentrating on the competition. I haven't a clue what'll happen after. I'll probably go back to my old life and the choir and all that. Oh, and I need a job,' I added.

I was surprised and a little hurt when he guffawed. 'I can't see you working in the supermarket in Glenvara, somehow.'

'How do you know? I'll need something to do.' I was a bit dismayed that he thought me incapable of doing any kind of real work.

'You won't be going back to the way things were, Antonia. No matter what happens. You do realize that, don't you?'

I shook my head. 'Next Saturday night, it'll all be over, Niall. And we can get on with normal life.'

He laughed again and tousled my hair. 'Life will never be the same again.' And then he kissed me and I managed to forget everything for a while.

20

'LIFE WILL NEVER BE THE SAME AGAIN.' HOW OFTEN DID I think of that phrase the following week, and in the months that followed? Because Niall was right, of course. I'd been kidding myself. I'd imagined that, win or lose, *That's Talent!* would be a fantastic experience, after which I'd go back to being Miss Mouse again, and not Toni Trent, pop star. Well, how wrong I was.

It started with the media. Niall had bought all the papers that Sunday, when he'd gone out to get the takeaway. 'I'll pretend to read them while you pretend to make me dinner,' he'd joked, as I took the Chinese cartons into the kitchen to serve up on plates. He then proceeded to read me out the headlines, until I had to beg him to stop. 'Brave Toni Sings on in the Face of Illness' 'The Girl from Nowhere Who Captured Our Hearts', 'The Nightingale', 'Our Pop Princess'. It just went on and on. The *Sunday Star* had even commissioned its own poll, inviting people to ring in and say who they wanted to win. 'Toni Trent by a Mile', the paper announced in block capitals.

I was speechless. It seemed as if they were writing

about someone else, not *me*. I had spent my whole life out of the spotlight, and now here I was, in every newspaper in the country. I had only gone on the show to sing, and the thought of what that might bring me hadn't even entered my head. But now it was becoming more and more real. Part of me wanted to spend the next week in hiding, until the show was over, to slide in under the duvet and not see anyone until the whole thing was finished, but the other part was so grateful for all the support. I'd slept through Mass on Sunday, but Betty called around specially to tell me that the parish priest had said a special prayer for me and that the whole village had planned a *That's Talent!* finals party in the parish hall, where they'd screen the final live. I was mortified and chuffed at the same time. Maybe being the girl from Glenvara wasn't so bad after all.

The curious thing was that as the night of the finals drew near, just two weeks before Christmas, I found myself strangely relaxed. My choice of song had worked really well, in spite of Niall's teasing. With my cold on the wane, I was able to stretch my voice a bit more, and hit the top notes in the song. It sounded great with the orchestra, and we had a ball practising. In fact, the whole thing was fun. It was odd, with so much at stake, but Damien and the boys from 4Guys and I just larked around, joking with each other and generally enjoying ourselves, probably because after all the grind of the last few weeks, there really was nothing we could do except go out there and do our best. We'd proven that we were good enough to get this far, and the rest wasn't up to us. Not any more.

Of course, I missed Amanda. She'd been like a sister to me, and it wasn't the same without her to giggle about the boys' haircuts or Damien's attempts to chat up the production assistants. I'd met up with her once since the semis, but it hadn't been a success. We'd had coffee together in town, and for a while it had seemed like nothing had changed. We'd chatted about music, and she'd teased me about the 'new man' in my life. I'd found myself opening up to her, the way I always had done, even telling her about Niall's past. 'It means we really share something,' I'd said, blushing.

'Peas in a pod,' she'd joked.

But then I'd opened my big mouth. Later, I could have kicked myself, but all I'd wanted to do was to clear the air, so we could be friends again. 'So, how've you been since the semis?'

She'd put down her coffee cup on the table, so that it clattered against the saucer, and then she'd looked at me steadily, her expression unreadable. 'I've been great.' Her voice had been flat.

'Look, Amanda, I know it wasn't fair—' I'd begun.

She'd put up a hand to stop me. 'Please. Don't.' And then she'd shrugged. 'Look, I'm a big girl and this is a tough business. I know the score.' She'd fixed a smile on to her face, a smile which I knew wasn't genuine. She'd shrugged then. 'I'll get over it.' And then she'd leaned over and picked her bag up off the floor. 'Gotta go.'

'I'm sorry, Amanda. I just want to be friends.' It sounded so pathetic, but it was true. 'I couldn't have got through it all without you.'

She'd sat there for a second, her bag on her shoulder, and her smile had been sad, and I'd felt a rush of sympathy for her. She'd wanted this so much.

'I know, kiddo. Good luck.' And then she was gone. Since then I'd tried calling her, but her phone had always gone to voicemail. Eventually I'd had to make do with a text: 'Really missing you. Hope you're OK. Catch up soon? Toni xx.' Hopefully, she'd text me back in a few days.

Part of the reason I was so laid back, I suppose, had to do with Niall. We were both busy, but we still found time to text each other regularly throughout the day. There were silly jokes, of course, but every couple of hours, he'd text to ask how I was getting on, and whether the rehearsal had gone well. And every night after I got home, I'd curl up on the sofa and call him, and we'd spend the next hour just chatting. It was odd that we'd ever been awkward with each other, and I couldn't imagine why now. Perhaps him being there on my mother's final night had given us a special bond. Or maybe that had come about because he'd finally told me the truth about himself – whichever it was, deep down, we now both knew that we were the same. And that we were lucky to have found each other.

I was dying to tell Mary and Colette about him, but at the same time, I felt shy, because what exactly was I supposed to say? 'I've got a boyfriend, girls.' It made me sound about

220

seven, and it couldn't go anywhere near the way I felt about him. And yet, I wanted to tell everyone, because he meant so much to me.

Eventually, Colette let me off the hook. She'd called around to run a new outfit by me for the finals. Karen thought it should be something showstopping, to go with the song, something with lots of sequins and feathers, but Colette thought it should be edgier, because the song spoke for itself. I hadn't liked the leather dress at all, and was praying she'd go for something more conventional, sighing with relief when she pulled a bright fuchsia chiffon shift out of the bag. 'It's simple, but that colour really pops,' she said, 'and it'll suit that lovely olive complexion of yours down to the ground.'

'I like it.' I looked at it, thinking that it was just perfect. Soft and girly, and yet the strong colour made it more grown-up, somehow. And when I tried it on, it was gorgeous. It was a bit short, but I was getting used to that. 'I suppose I can't wear leggings with it?' I joked.

'Ha. Ha. If you want to look like an eleven-year-old, maybe. But you're a grown woman now, Antonia. And you have great legs, you cow.'

'Thanks. Lots of fake tan covers up a multitude.' I smiled as I stood in front of the mirror.

'Still have to sort out the shoes . . .' She was talking to herself. 'Maybe the nude Louboutins again, or I've a nice pair from Jimmy Choo.' And then she looked at me appraisingly. 'There's something different about you.'

It was a statement, rather than a question, but still, I feigned surprise.

'There is?'

'There is. You look like the cat that got the cream.'

'Oh.'

She smiled at me. 'Do you remember what you were like last Saturday?'

'God, I was a wreck, I know. It was the cold and everything. I have never felt worse in my whole life.'

'I know, but you got through. That took guts, pet.' And then she looked thoughtful. 'But it's more than that. It's that guy, isn't it?'

'What guy?'

'Oh, for God's sake, "what guy"? The hospital doctor. Wouldn't mind seeing him in his scrubs, I can tell you.' She chortled.

'Colette!'

'Oh, c'mon, don't tell me you've never thought about him like that. And don't give me the "just good friends" spiel.'

I blushed and looked down at my feet, the way I always did when I was embarrassed.

Colette guffawed. 'Told you so. And you know what? I'm thrilled for you. You deserve it, Antonia.'

'Thanks.' I blushed again, but realized that I was grinning from ear to ear.

'And he's a great guy.'

I nodded. 'I know.' And I realized that I did know – Niall *was* a great guy, and I was lucky to have him in my life. I continued, 'But it's funny the way everything happens at once, isn't it? For years, my life was the same, just Mum and me, and I honestly thought it would go on like that for ever. And now . . .'

'And now, you feel as if life will never be the same again, eh?' Colette said gently.

'Well, yes, but then I think of how grateful I am for the opportunity—' I began.

'Hang on a minute, Missy,' Colette interrupted. 'This so-called "opportunity" is one you created yourself, because you have real talent, remember that.'

'I'll try,' I said.

'Good.' Colette patted me on the shoulder. 'Never forget that you made it happen, Antonia, nobody else.'

I didn't like to tell Colette that if Eithne hadn't entered me in the competition, I'd still be filling out job application forms and singing at Mass on Sunday. Colette had made me sound like a single-minded and ambitious girl, who'd simply gone for what she'd wanted and got it. But it wasn't like that. I was Miss Mouse, after all. A lucky Miss Mouse, but Miss Mouse all the same.

I remembered what Niall had said to me when he'd left me that Sunday night. He'd stood on the doorstep and wrapped his arms around me. 'No matter what happens, we won't change,' he'd said. 'Even if you win and become famous, you'll still be Antonia to me, the girl from Glenvara.'

'And you'll still be Niall, dedicated doctor and moun-taineer,' I'd joked.

He'd laughed. 'You're right. But I mean it, we won't change. Whatever happens,' he'd repeated. 'Promise?'

'Promise.'

Over the next few weeks and months, I'd replay our promise to each other many times in my head as my world became more and more of a roller coaster, and my old life came to seem like something of a dream. It was odd that I saw less and less of my friends and family in Glenvara, all the people who'd loved and supported me for the previous months. It seemed so unfair, somehow. 'That's fame for you, pet,' Colette said to me once. 'And if you dare complain about it, I'll strangle you with my bare hands.'

I didn't complain, not about any of it, even when I got another taste of what fame was really like, the day of the finals. Colette and Mary were sitting beside me when it happened, trying to make me drink wine at eleven o'clock in the morning. We'd been laughing about how like a wedding the whole thing seemed. 'All this fuss,' I'd said, taking a large sip from my wine glass, and accepting Colette's proffered bag of crisps. 'The clothes, the make-up, I feel like I'm getting married.' Just as I spoke, Betty dashed past with a huge tray of sausage rolls, a pot of hot tea in her hand for all the well-wishers who were turning up in their droves to wish me the best.

Betty was terribly excited about finals day, as she kept calling it, and was relishing her role as chief caterer, rushing around with sausage rolls and offering visitors cups of tea, whether they wanted one or not. 'They've hired a tour bus to take the gang from Glenvara,' she told me proudly. 'Imagine! That many people want to see you.'

I should have been daunted, I suppose, surrounded by all the fuss and noise, but instead I felt curiously relaxed, sipping on my wine and allowing Colette and Mary to style my hair and try out some make-up ideas for the girls in the Celtic TV studio. I suppose I was in the eye of the storm, and it was strangely quiet there, still, even.

'I think that gold shadow with the dark-brown mascara, don't you?' Mary was saying to Colette, who was nodding her head. 'I'll tell Valerie in make-up.'

I tried to stifle a smile. Valerie in make-up didn't like taking instructions from Colette, who, after all, wasn't a make-up artist, but Colette made sure she listened – and did what she was told. Nobody argued with Colette if they had any sense. But she'd transformed me from a dowdy young woman to a real pop star. Because of Colette, I looked like a grown-up – confident, assured and trendy – and I was grateful to her. It's much easier to play the part of a pop star if you look like one, after all.

And that's what I was doing, I realized. Playing a part. Of course, I didn't *feel* like a pop star. I was still Antonia from Glenvara, but once I realized that all I had to do was to act like one and nobody would be any the wiser, I found that I could relax a little. It was just acting after all.

'You know, this is probably the most exciting thing that

has ever happened in Glenvara,' Colette joked. 'And the most exciting thing that will ever happen again in this one-horse town, I would have thought. This place makes my home town look like New York.' Colette was from Youghal, a pretty fishing village in Cork, that she jokingly called the 'end of the world'. It was hardly a city, but I supposed it must have been a bit livelier than Glenvara.

I bristled a bit. 'Hang on, Colette! Glenvara may be quiet, but everyone's been so brilliant . . .' thinking of Betty and Bridget, Eithne and Billy, and how they'd been there for me every single step of the way. As I spoke, I could just see Bridget standing at the front door, intercepting callers, deciding who she did and didn't like the look of, and either inviting them in or sending them packing.

'Now, Ellen, I'm sure you'll understand that Antonia is indisposed at present . . .' we could hear her say to a local, and we all burst out laughing.

'"Indisposed." She makes you sound like something out of a Jane Austen novel.' Mary giggled. 'But seriously,' she continued, shooting Colette a look. 'It's at times like these, you realize how fantastic it is to live here – even if Colette thinks it's a one-horse town. Everyone rallies around and wants to be part of the whole thing. Although, it's true, we haven't had this much excitement since Barney O'Brien won the National Ploughing Championships a couple of years back.'

'The National Ploughing Championships?' Colette burst out laughing. 'Crikey, I rest my case, I really do.'

'You're just a snob,' Mary said tartly. 'Anyway, Antonia, it's your big day, well, almost. How are you feeling?'

I shifted in my chair and took another sip of wine, before putting my glass down on a table out of reach. I wasn't used to drinking, and I didn't want to end up singing in the finals half-drunk. 'I actually feel OK,' I admitted. 'I thought I'd be quaking, but instead it all just feels surreal. It's all too strange, really, for me to feel worried about it. Does that sound odd?'

Mary shook her head. 'Not at all. I suppose you've been through the worst of it, anyway, with last week and everything . . .' Her voice trailed off, and she looked at me nervously.

I reached out and touched her arm. 'It's OK, Mary. You're right. Last week was an absolute disaster, but I'm still standing, so from now on, everything is a bonus. At least, that's the way I look at it.'

'Good for you,' Mary said, reaching out to squeeze my hand. 'You'll blow them away, Antonia. I know you will.'

'Thanks, Mary—' I began, and then my phone bleeped. It was the hundredth time that morning, message after message, wishing me good luck, and I'd stopped answering them, just glancing at them occasionally to see who they were from. I picked up the phone now and took a quick look, seeing a bit of the message flash up on my screen. 'BITCH . . .' It seemed to begin. My heart stopped. I knew that I should delete it. That reading it would only make me feel bad, just like the previous one, but something made me press the 'open' button to reveal the whole text. And then I gasped so loudly, Colette looked up from her work, combing out my hair after the heated rollers.

'What is it?'

I didn't say anything in reply, just held out my phone so that she could read it. Her mouth moved as she said the words to herself under her breath: 'BITCH. HOPE YOU BREAK YOUR NECK IN YOUR SILLY SHOES TO-NIGHT. YOU HAVEN'T A PRAYER.'

She didn't say anything for a moment, her lips set in a thin line.

'What, what does it say?' Mary pulled herself up off the sofa, from where she'd been sitting, and came around to stand beside Colette to read the text. Her hand flew to her mouth. 'Oh my God, who would send something like that?'

'I don't know,' Colette said grimly. 'Somebody deranged and nasty, by the looks of it. Antonia . . .' she said warningly, looking at my chalk-white face. 'You are to delete this text and forget all about it. That's the problem with success – it makes people very jealous, and they hide behind anonymity to say all kinds of nasty things. You mustn't let it affect you.'

I nodded silently. I didn't have the heart to tell her that it wasn't the first text I'd gotten like that. 'I just can't believe somebody would write something like that . . .' I said.

'Oh, Antonia, pet, you are one of the nicest people I know,' Mary said gently. 'But there are some not very nice people in the world as well, you know, and it can be hard to accept that, but you have to try to ignore this. It's just some-

228

body sad ranting on. Try to hang on to the fact that you are in the finals of *That's Talent!*, and you've got there because you are good and you've worked hard, and whoever it is can go to hell.' There were two bright spots of colour on Mary's cheeks now, and she was fighting to keep her voice under control – Mary, who was always so sweet and patient.

'I know,' I murmured. 'It's just . . . after all the support, I suppose, I didn't expect something so . . .'

'Vitriolic, deranged, sad?' Colette said. 'It's just some nutter, Antonia.'

'That's fame for you, Antonia,' Mary said gently. 'Colette's right. It brings out the worst in some people, I'm afraid.'

I nodded. 'I know.' Of course, I didn't know. Until the night of the semi-finals, I'd thought that everyone was happy for me. It had honestly never occurred to me that people might be envious of my success. It seemed I still had a lot to learn about life.

I looked up to see two pairs of eyes looking anxiously back at me. I knew that Colette and Mary were waiting for me to say something, to show them that this text hadn't got me too rattled. They were relying on me to stay calm, not to be affected by it. Imagine if they knew about the other text! I thought. I couldn't tell them about it, I just couldn't. Instead, I put a big smile on my face. 'You know what, I'm going to delete this message and forget all about it. It's clearly from some crackpot and I'm not going to let it get the better of me,' I said firmly.

'That's the spirit, Antonia,' Colette said warmly. 'Now,

why don't you let me have your mobile for the rest of the day so I can screen out any crap?'

I shook my head. 'Thanks, Colette. I appreciate it, but I'm a big girl, honest. I can take it, and if I don't like something, well, I can just delete it.' And anyway, I thought, I don't want to miss any messages from Niall.

She looked at me doubtfully. 'Sure?'

'Absolutely,' I said, more firmly than I felt, pressing the 'delete' button and tossing the phone on to the table. 'There, all done. Now, let's get on with the day, shall we?' I beamed.

'Sure thing,' Mary said, picking up on my tone. 'Let's forget all about it and concentrate on what really matters. Now, group hug,' she ordered, and we all huddled together in a warm embrace.

'What would I do without the two of you?' I said, pulling away to look at them.

'You'd be fine, I suspect,' Colette said dryly. And I knew that she was right, I probably would, but my life wouldn't be nearly as much fun. Because even though I tried to forget it, the text had rattled me. It hung around the edge of my thoughts for the rest of the day, even with all the fuss and distraction, even when I'd set off for The O2 in Billy's large comfortable car – which, he proudly pointed out, he'd had valeted specially – even when we pulled up to the backstage entrance. I'm not a bitch, I know that, I kept telling myself, I've worked hard for this. But I wasn't sure I believed it, not deep down, where it really mattered.

It was only when I got out of the car at the studio that the thought occurred to me that it had to be someone I knew. Who else would have known the song I'd chosen for the semis? But then I shook my head. What did it matter who'd sent them? My response had to be the same: not to let this person win, to show them that I wasn't Miss Mouse any more.

'Nervous?' Valerie in make-up was standing over me, brushing powder over my face as I lay back in the chair in my dressing room in the vast backstage area of The O2. With a capacity for twenty thousand people, The O2 was a cavernous place, a warren of tiny dressing rooms and corridors backstage. The show wouldn't start for another four hours, but Karen liked to have us ready early. I was still amazed by how much sitting around was involved in this so-called glamorous world.

'I don't know,' I answered truthfully. 'It's like I'm in a dream. Sometimes I feel the nerves and then . . . well, they just go again. It's as if it's too late to be nervous, do you know what I mean?'

She nodded. 'I know. Now, close your eyes . . . great. I'll just apply some of this lovely gold that Colette gave me,' she said dryly.

'Oh, she got to you,' I joked.

'Ha. You could say that. You know, it's funny you should say that about the nerves; I had that lovely singer here the other week . . . what was her name, Judy?' she yelled over to the other make-up girl.

231

'Leona Lewis.'

'Oh, yeah, Leona Lewis. Lovely girl.'

'Leona Lewis?' I nearly jumped out of my chair. 'She's a huge star!'

'Yes, but you wouldn't know it. She's really unaffected and natural. And anyway, she wasn't always a star,' Valerie said calmly. 'She was just like you once, you know. A real girl next door until she won *Britain's Got Talent*.'

'I think it was *The X Factor*,' I said.

'Yeah, whatever, but fame hadn't changed her one bit, sure, it hadn't, Judy?'

I found it amusing that she couldn't even remember what show Leona Lewis had won. Mum and I had watched every single episode of that season's *The X Factor*. I'd had to make dinner early so we could sit down and watch the whole thing from start to finish. Now I wondered if it was because, secretly, we'd both thought that one day that could be me. It is, Mum, I said silently. It is me.

Judy was shaking her head. 'Nope, she was really down to earth. Like you, Antonia.'

'That's right. You're so fresh and natural. That's what people like about you. They look at you and think it could be them. And that you can be famous and still be yourself,' Valerie said.

'Hmm,' I said, non-committally. Because the truth was, I wasn't myself, not really. And if I wasn't myself now, what chance might I have if I won the thing? 'BITCH . . .' the words of the text flashed into my mind, before I shook my head. 'I can't even think about winning, Valerie.'

'Oh, you'd better think about it. You're the hot favourite, do you know that? Sure, I had Maurice Prendergast here only half an hour ago, and I asked him who he thought would win, and do you know what he said?' Valerie was standing, her hands on her hips, a make-up brush clamped between her teeth.

I shook my head.

'He said if he were a gambling man, he'd put all his money on you. So there,' Valerie said. 'And now, you look gorgeous.'

She turned me round to look in the mirror and I gasped. Colette had been right, the gold was perfect: dramatic and rich. I looked like an Egyptian princess. 'And you think I'm just being myself,' I joked to Valerie, 'looking like this.'

'It's what's inside that's real,' she said. 'People see that, Antonia, and they like it.'

'Quite the philosopher, aren't you?' Judy said from across the room, ducking as Valerie threw the brush at her.

'My work here is done,' Valerie said, helping me out of the gown which covered my dress. 'Now break a leg, Antonia,' she said. 'Make me proud.'

'I'll try,' I said. And I would, I thought. I'd make them all proud of me.

Even though I was in the final, it was still an amazing experience. Celtic TV had pulled out all the stops, and every Irish star was on the show. Sitting in the green room, watching on the monitor, I felt for a few moments that I was at home in front of the TV, enjoying the spectacle, instead of here, at The O2, about to sing in front of twenty thousand people. A fabulous dance troupe from Cork, who'd got to the semis, had been called back to do a number and, not for the first time, I wished that I could dance. I might be able to sing, but I knew that I had two left feet and felt faintly envious as I watched them strut their stuff on the stage. They were all so talented, I thought – who on earth was I to have got through to the finals? Sometimes I felt like an impostor. And then, for some reason, I thought of Amanda. What would it be like for her, sitting at home watching dancers like this, when it could so easily have been her? How I missed having her here with me, cracking jokes.

I was relieved that Damien was on first, because I loved listening to him. He wrote all his own songs and I was dying to do more of my own songwriting. I could play the piano and had begun to pick out a few tunes, because I knew that it was really important to write my own material. Lots of people had good voices, but original songs – that was another matter. Damien was really charismatic, too, and a funny, cheeky guy, and I had to admire the way he was able to stand out there on stage with nothing but a guitar and entertain thousands of people. I needed the orchestra around me: it made me feel much more secure.

Of course, this time, I found it hard to concentrate. I swallowed the lump in my throat which seemed to have got bigger and bigger, and shook my hands out to calm my nerves. Tentatively, I tried a few scales while I was waiting for Karen to bring me backstage, and was relieved to find that I could still sing. Ever since I'd had that cold, I'd been paranoid about losing it on stage in front of everyone, friends and fans. I thought of the Glenvara gang, sitting there in the audience, waving and cheering, and then I thought of Mum. They were all rooting for me, and all I had to do was what I always did: let the song carry me with it.

'Mum, if you're up there, wish me luck,' I murmured.

And then, the next thing I knew, Karen was touching me on the arm. 'Ready?'

I nodded but couldn't speak, and just let her lead me to the backstage area, where I watched as Aaron took the stage. It was my turn next, and I waited for him to do his piece, to cue me in, but Karen shook her head. 'Not yet. Another ten, OK?'

I nodded, surprised, and turned my attention to Aaron, who bounced on stage with his usual enthusiasm. 'And now, everyone, I know you're all waiting for the lovely Toni Trent to make her appearance and blow us all away with *that* voice, but before we do, we have an extra special surprise. Will you please welcome on to the stage . . . Jude!'

My heart was in my mouth. Jude were Ireland's biggest boy band, winners of the last *That's Talent!*, who'd gone on to have a massive career with three number ones in a row in Ireland *and* had just broken into the UK top ten. The audience roar was deafening as they swept past me on to the stage, all boyish energy and slick charm. Follow that,

Antonia, I thought to myself, as they bounded into their latest hit, a bouncy, upbeat number that had the audience on its feet. They were fantastic, I had to admit it, and I was absolutely dreading going on after them. I'd have to put on one hell of a performance, I reckoned. Feel the fear, Antonia, I said to myself as the number drew to a close.

The boys bounced back off the stage, throwing kisses to the screaming girl fans. I clutched my chest, feeling the nerves circling, ears ringing with the roar from the audience. The lead singer, Graham, bounded towards me like an eager puppy, his hair slick with sweat. I edged back to let him past, but instead he leaned over and planted a kiss on my cheek. 'Good luck, Toni, we think you're deadly.' He grinned.

'Thanks,' I managed, feeling the laughter bubble up inside me. What would Niall make of it, me being kissed by a seventeen-year-old? I stifled a giggle, in case Karen thought I was entirely mad, *laughing* before the biggest performance of my life. I tried to compose myself, shaking the tension out of my hands and feet, shuffling from foot to foot, feeling the sweat breaking out on my forehead. It was nearly my time. My time to shine.

Aaron was warming the audience up again, but I could barely hear him for the roaring in my ears. 'If you think that was spectacular, here's the nation's sweetheart, the girl we've all taken to our hearts over these past few weeks, with her version of Whitney Houston's "I Will Always Love You". It's Toni Trent!'

I stopped for a second, hovering, taking in, dazedly, that Aaron had called me 'Toni Trent' for the first time. Then I felt Karen's hand in the small of my back. 'Off you go, Toni, hurry!' I'd long since learned that the timing on the show was split-second, and if I missed my cue, chaos would result, so I practically ran on to the stage, praying I wouldn't fall over in my high heels. I trotted over to the spot in the centre of the stage, and felt the lights hot on my face. The audience was a blur beyond the footlights, the orchestra just to my right. I stood there, waiting for the applause to die down, feeling like a small child in the middle of the vast stage.

Maurice Prendergast was in good humour. He smiled at me and said, 'Well, well, Toni. Here we are. On the brink of fame. How does it feel?'

I blinked for a few seconds, before collecting myself. Even Maurice was calling me 'Toni' now. 'Well, Maurice, it's nerve-racking, but I can only do my best.'

He nodded. 'But you're still prepared to take on Whitney Houston. That takes guts. Some would say it's foolish, even.' He was being mischievous, I knew that, and I had to hold my nerve. Some people thought all of this was scripted, but he always caught me on the hop. He liked to keep contestants on their toes. We all hated it, but we respected him because he knew what he was doing.

'Maybe,' I said, more confidently than I felt, 'but I've been working hard on it all week, and I'll give it my best shot.'

He smiled at me thinly. 'Well, you've been under a lot of pressure. People have been expecting great things from you. How have you been coping?'

I looked at him blankly. Why didn't he just let me get on and sing the song? I took a deep breath. 'You know, I'm nervous, really nervous, but I can feel a lot of support in the room tonight.'

And I nodded towards the audience as they screamed back at me. Some of them were standing in their seats, waving madly and shouting, 'Come on, Toni!'

'And really,' I continued, 'the only thing I can do is sing the song and hope that you like it.' I thought of the gang from Glenvara, somewhere out there, but most of all, I thought about Niall, how he'd come to every single show, organizing changes in his roster to sit and support me, even though I knew he thought the whole thing was madness. I'd do it for him, I thought now, him and Mum.

Maurice nodded at me, and I opened my mouth on the low notes, feeling my voice gathering strength as the song took off, the orchestra swelling behind me. I could feel the audience responding slowly but surely. Of course, I couldn't see anyone, but I could feel it, a wave of support which buoyed me up, carried me along to the final chorus. The song was a huge number with a swooping chorus, and we'd discussed ending on a top note, but in the end had opted for a hushed, muted conclusion, and as it drew near, I realized that it had been the right choice. I'd brought the audience with me as I whispered the closing notes.

I stood there, head bowed, microphone in my hand, down by my side, and I thought, That's it. It's all over. I took a huge breath and exhaled, and all the stress and tension of the past few weeks seemed to leave me. There was a second's eerie silence in the hall, during which you could have heard a pin drop, and then the place erupted. The audience was standing on its feet, a roar of applause rippling up to the back of the stadium, and then the judges were standing, too, and Mary Devine had tears pouring down her cheeks.

I had no idea what to do. I just stood there, and said, 'Thank you, thank you,' over and over again. I wasn't sure who I was thanking: the judges, the audience, my friends, or Mum. Maybe all of them. Because it was truly the greatest moment of my life. It didn't matter now whether I won or not, because I'd had this experience. I'd understood what a true performance could mean, and how it could make people feel. There was absolutely nothing better than that. I looked up and mouthed, 'Thanks, Mum,' and bowed quietly and waited for the thunderous applause to die down. And then Aaron was walking across the stage, enveloping me in a huge hug.

'Well, Toni, that was the performance of a lifetime, and with all the pressure you've been under this week, it took real guts. Well done,' he said, trying to shout above the din of the audience.

The verdict of the judges only surprised me. Maurice Prendergast said to me, as I stood there in the centre of the stage, 'Do you know what, Toni? You look and feel like the real deal. A star is born.'

Michael Smyth nodded. 'I couldn't agree more,' he said.

And Mary Devine clutched her hands to her chest and said, 'After last week, Toni, I had to admit I doubted you. I thought that you hadn't got the feeling for the big moment. But now I see how wrong I was. You've got it in spades. You are going to be a huge, huge star . . . well done.'

The applause was deafening, and my ears rang as I walked off the stage, remembering my manners, to wave and smile, my knees like jelly. I wanted to see my gang, to get a hug from Sister Monica, to have Bridget say something outrageous. And most of all, I wanted Niall: to feel his arms around me. To feel safe again.

Karen was the first to greet me backstage, hugging me as I stumbled off. 'That was just amazing, Toni. Well done.'

I nodded, unable to speak.

'C'mon, let's find the gang for you.' Clipboard in hand, she led me down the corridor to the green room, steering me through the banks of photographers. 'Later, guys. There'll be a press conference and you can take all the photos you want then, OK?'

'Toni, is there any truth to the rumour about you and Damien?' one journalist shouted, pushing a microphone in my face.

I stopped for a second, baffled. 'Ehm—' I began, before Karen interrupted.

'No questions, understand? You'll get your chance later.'

I looked at her, bewildered, as she led me into the green room. 'What's this about me and Damien?'

She looked doubtful, shaking her head. 'God, I don't know. Don't worry about it now, for goodness' sake – you have the rest of the show to do, and two more costume changes, so forget about it.'

She sounded really hassled, and I blushed in shame. 'Sorry, I know you have other things to be thinking about right now . . .'

Karen's look softened. 'No, it's fine, but you're going to have to get used to this, Toni,' she said to me gently.

'Get used to what?'

'The gossip and rumour. Most of it won't be true, but you won't have any easy way to prove that, so you'll have to develop a thick skin, I'm afraid. But don't think about that now. It's not the time, OK? And I'll take care of you, don't worry.'

I shrugged my shoulders and smiled. 'Sure, I know how it works, Karen. And it's fine, really.' I thought of the text again, 'BITCH . . .' But I hadn't tripped over my silly shoes, had I? I'd given the performance of my life instead.

'That's the spirit.' Karen grinned. 'Now, let's get you to the gang, so you can relax for a bit.'

The door of the green room opened, and I saw a blur of excited faces. And then I was enveloped in a sort of group hug, as Betty, Bridget, Sister Monica and Billy all congratulated me.

'That was amazing, Antonia, just out of this world,' Bridget said, and there were tears pouring down her face.

'Oh, Bridget, don't cry,' I said. 'You'll set me off.' And before long I was crying, too, all the tension of the past few weeks pouring out of me.

'There, there, pet, let it all out,' Bridget was saying, rubbing my back. 'You've done us proud, do you know that?'

I sniffled into her shoulder and sobbed. 'I can't believe it . . . it's all done. Finished . . .' and then I cried again.

I could hear Betty beside Bridget now, patting and stroking my hair. 'You're right, pet. All done now, and it's in the lap of the gods.'

At which Bridget snapped back, 'Do you have to be so fatalistic? Antonia's given the performance of a lifetime, and here you are talking about gods and rubbish like that. Can't you be a bit positive, woman?'

Oh God. They were off again. Sure, Bridget thought Betty was an uptight snob, and Betty thought Bridget was an attention-seeking show-off, but it was the last thing I needed. Where was Niall when I needed him? I turned to look for him, and then he was beside me.

'Ladies, let's try to stay calm for Antonia's sake, shall we?' he said in a tone which brooked no objection.

'Of course,' Bridget was the first to say. 'I'm sorry, Antonia, we just both want the best for you. Don't we, Betty?' She stood, arms crossed, and shot Betty a glare.

'Of course we do, Bridget,' Betty shot back grimly, arms folded.

242

I had to fight the urge to laugh, in spite of my tears.

'And now, ladies, if you don't mind, I'd like to give my girlfriend a hug,' Niall said, pulling me towards him, enveloping me in his arms, and murmuring, 'Well done, you,' into my ear, over and over again. He felt warm and solid, and I held on to him tightly, willing him not to let me go.

'Aww, isn't that just lovely? Could do with a bear hug myself,' I could hear Bridget say in the background.

'Sure I'd give you one, Bridget, only I'd be scared you'd crush me to death,' Billy was joking.

'You should be so lucky,' Bridget retorted.

After a while, Niall held me at arm's length and smiled. 'You did it.'

I nodded. 'I did it.'

'What was it like?'

'I can't describe it. Oddly calm, I suppose,' I responded. Really, I had no idea what to say to him in response. I couldn't explain to him just what it had been like: the lights, the tension, the audience. Maybe later, but now I was still shell-shocked.

'There, there,' Sister Monica was beside me now, patting me on the back. 'You've done all you can now, love.'

'I know,' I said, accepting her proffered tissue and dabbing at my tears. 'It's just, it feels weird that it's finally all over, after all these weeks.'

'I know,' she said soothingly. 'And it'll take you a while to come back to earth, but you gave that performance everything, and you should be proud of yourself, no matter what happens. You know, I can't believe you've come so far. Think about it, Antonia. Just a few weeks ago, well . . .'

I nodded. 'I know. And Mum was up there, looking down on me, I know she was.'

She nodded, and then Niall pulled me towards him again. 'C'mon, let's get you something to drink.'

I allowed myself to be led to a sofa in the corner of the room, feeling suddenly shaky, flopping down on the cushions and leaning my head back for a few moments. 'I need to take these shoes off.' I laughed.

Colette came bustling towards me. 'Gently, please. No yanking them off your heel and then wondering why they don't fit you properly the next time.'

At her bossy tone, everyone burst out laughing, and the tension was suddenly lifted.

'What?' she said, looking cross.

I shook my head, doubled over with laughter. 'Nothing,' I said, bending over to take them off as gently as I could. 'Thank God,' I sighed, wiggling my toes. 'Apologies for my sweaty feet everyone, but they're killing me.'

Niall attempted to grab one of my feet. 'Are they sweaty? Hmm, let me have a sniff,' and then he pretended to gag.

I mock-punched him. 'Cheeky.' I leaned back on the sofa again, realizing that I wanted him to kiss me, but he could hardly do so with the entire population of Glenvara standing over us. It would have to wait until later.

I closed my eyes for a moment, feeling myself relax just a

fraction. I've no idea why, when the audience vote was still coming in, but after the performance, I felt spent. Maybe Monica was right. I'd given everything and I had nothing left. I allowed the others to fuss over me, Betty offering me tea from her ever-present flask. 'None of that bog water they call tea in this place,' and Niall gently rubbing my feet.

And then I blinked and Karen was standing over me, her earphones on her head. 'It's time, Toni,' she said kindly. I looked at Niall, not wanting to leave him, but he smiled at me reassuringly.

'Go on, we'll all be here when you get back, and we can celebrate your win then.'

'Don't say that,' I said shakily.

'But it's true,' he said, squeezing my hand. 'It's yours, Antonia, believe me.'

I said nothing, not wanting to argue, just letting Colette help me into my shoes again, before Karen led me back to make-up. 'We'll just get Valerie to have a look at you before you go back out on stage,' she said gently.

Valerie for once was silent, merely nodding and offering a brisk, 'Well done,' before applying fresh powder and a slick of gloss to set my lipstick, then teasing my hair back into shape.

'Thanks, Valerie,' Karen said, leading me back out and down the long corridor to the backstage area, where Damien and the boys from 4Guys had gathered. We all hugged and congratulated each other, and then Damien winked at me and gave me that cheeky grin. I blushed bright red. Oh, no, had he read the rumours about us?

But then he gave me a brotherly peck on the cheek. 'Toni, you were fantastic. May the best man win.'

'Thanks, Damien,' I said. 'Good luck.'

'OK, everyone,' Karen was saying. 'Aaron will open after the ads and announce that the lines are closed, and then he'll cue you all on to the stage. You know your spots, so you just stand there and don't move, please, because it really puts the number-one camera guy off.'

We nodded like naughty schoolchildren, and she continued. 'Aaron will ask a couple of questions. Nothing major: how nervous are you, what'll you do if you win, etcetera? And then he'll announce the third place. Whoever gets third accepts the applause, then comes off the stage *quickly* so we can prep for the final announcement. Now, you know that whoever wins will be going straight into their song, don't you?'

We nodded. It all sounded so businesslike, so clinical, when in just five minutes, one of us would be winning *That's Talent!* I tried to focus on my breathing, because any wobble in my voice would be heard when I came to sing. And then I chided myself. Why did I assume that it would be me singing? It could be Damien or 4Guys. Tomorrow I could be back in Glenvara parish choir singing 'Hail Holy Queen'. But the steady breathing helped me to stay calm, focused. We all held hands and waited, and then the ad break was over and Aaron was bouncing on stage again.

'Here goes,' Damien said, and on cue, we all walked out on stage, taking our places and accepting the deafening applause. All of a sudden I was stricken with shyness, and prayed that Aaron wouldn't ask me a question. I hated all of that – I just wanted to sing, when the nerves would fade away and I could really be myself.

He must have read my mind, because he zeroed in on me, microphone in hand. 'Now, Toni, you've been the subject of much of the media speculation this week. That's a lot of pressure, isn't it?'

I tried to smile brightly. 'Well, I try not to think about it too much, Aaron. I just focus on the performance. That's all I can do: sing the song and leave people to make up their own minds.'

There was a huge round of applause, whistles and shouts, and I thought, Thank God, I've given the right answer – it feels like a school test. Aaron moved on to 4Guys and Damien in turn, who both answered much the same, because it was true. The judges could say what they liked, but in the end, the public decided, and all we could do was leave it up to them.

I only half-listened to the rest of Aaron's chat, because my heart was thumping so wildly in my chest and there was a roaring in my ears even louder than the audience's screams. And then he was about to announce the third-place act, and by this stage, the audience was yelling so loudly I only half-heard . . . it was 4Guys. Oh, God, there was only Damien and me left. A silence descended over the stadium again, broken only by the flashing bulbs of cameras. Maurice and Mary came down to the stage, Maurice standing with

Damien, Mary with me, to give us moral support. I found myself thinking that I would really have liked Maurice in my corner. There was something . . . trustworthy about him, I thought. But I accepted Mary's outstretched hand as we both stood there on the stage. 'Fingers crossed, Toni,' she whispered into my ear. I smiled back, but said nothing in reply. I was just too nervous to talk.

And then Aaron began his intro. 'Ladies and gentlemen, it's been eight weeks of highs and lows, fabulous performances, tears and laughter, but it all comes down to this. This one moment,' he said. 'The votes are in and the lines are closed. And the winner of *That's Talent!* is . . .'

Of course, there was an endless silence that seemed to stretch into eternity. Mary squeezed my hand and whispered into my ear, 'Good luck, Toni.' I didn't even react. It was beyond luck now. I had no idea how to behave. Colette had made me practise in the mirror, pinning a look of surprise on my face, and then a smile of acceptance if I lost, but now . . . well, I hadn't a clue what to do.

And then Aaron said, 'Damien!' and the audience erupted. I stood there, a smile pinned on my face, for what seemed like the longest time.

Mary was yelling above the audience, 'So sorry, Toni, so sorry.' I kept on smiling, remembering to applaud Damien as he came towards me and enveloped me in a bear hug.

'Sorry, Toni, it should have been you . . . honest.' He had to shout into my ear above the screaming.

248

'For God's sake, don't be silly. You deserve it,' I said, smiling and hugging him back, and then Aaron was coming towards me, microphone in hand. My heart sank. I didn't want to talk right now.

'Toni, you have truly won the hearts of the nation with your singing every week. It's been consistently just brilliant. Tell me, how do you feel?'

How did I *feel*? I had no clue as I was completely numb. I hadn't expected to win it, but now that I hadn't . . . I opened my mouth like a goldfish, then closed it again, trying desperately to pull myself together. Eventually, I managed, 'Well, Damien's a worthy winner, Aaron, and I'm truly glad to have got this far.' And that much was true, I thought, as I allowed Mary to lead me off the stage, in a complete daze.

That was it, I thought, as she let go of my hand and wandered off with a production assistant, who was fussing over her microphone. It was over, I thought, as I stood in the wings, watching Damien strap his guitar on and prepare to launch into his song. It was over, and I'd be forgotten about the very next day. And I didn't mind, I told myself. It'd be nice to get back to Glenvara and a bit of anonymity for a bit. And to process everything that had happened in the past few weeks. And I could hold my head up high. I'd got to the finals and given the competition everything I possibly could.

I watched Damien sing his number, tears rolling down his cheeks, and I was glad for him. He was a great singer and had stage presence. He'd go far, I knew that.

And then I felt someone at my side. I looked up to see Maurice Prendergast standing beside me, in his silver-grey suit and black shirt, every inch the record company mogul. He looked more polished than usual. Karen must have got hold of him for the 'tidy-up' she'd been threatening to give him all season.

'The surprise winner.' He nodded at Damien.

'No, he deserved it.' I was adamant.

He snorted with laughter. 'Everyone knows it should have been you, Toni. But you're a good sport, I'll give you that.'

'What do you mean?' I looked at him sharply.

'Damien's talented, sure, but there isn't much of a market for pub-circuit singer-songwriters. Now *you*, on the other hand . . .'

I shook my head. 'But I didn't win . . .'

He looked at me and smiled, and I suddenly thought how much he reminded me of Dad. 'Oh yes, you did.' And he waved his hand around the set. 'This isn't the end, Toni, not by a long chalk. Ring me tomorrow, will you?' And he thrust a small white card into my hand. And then he was gone.

I was alone all of a sudden, standing in the wings in my fuchsia dress. There was no sign of Karen. She was probably busy with Damien. Well, at least I know where to go, I thought, as I walked down the narrow, dark corridor off the set for the last time. And all I could think was: Thank God it's over. Thank God I'll never have to do this again.

21

NIALL FOUND ME FIRST. HE'D WANDERED OFF FROM THE green room and sneaked towards the backstage area. 'I knew you'd need a hug,' he said as I walked towards him.

'I do,' I said softly, walking into his arms and letting him hold me.

He rubbed my back and whispered into my ear, 'You're the greatest, do you know that?' over and over again.

I nodded. 'Thanks. Thanks for everything.'

'It must be hard to stand out there and . . . well . . .' he began.

I interrupted him, pulling out of his arms. 'It's fine, really,' I said. 'It's just . . . it's been such a surreal few weeks. My feet haven't touched the ground and . . . well, I can't tell you how glad I am it's all over.'

He looked sceptical. 'Not too disappointed?'

I shook my head. 'No, really. I never expected any of this. It's been beyond my wildest dreams, and now I can't wait to get back to normality. I want us to do ordinary stuff like climb Powerscourt waterfall . . .'

'You've got to be kidding.' He laughed. 'It nearly killed you the last time.'

I found the energy to smile. 'Well, I'll have plenty of time to practise my mountain-climbing technique, won't I?'

'Maybe.' He kissed me on the nose. 'If this is what you really want. But I have a feeling you won't be getting much time for mountain climbing.'

'Well, we'll see,' I said. I didn't tell him about Maurice Prendergast. I just wanted to sit down and have a cup of tea and forget about it all. 'Could I ask you a favour?' I asked him.

'Sure, anything.' And he was so gentle, so caring, that I felt like crying.

'Could you go first into the green room? I mean, ahead of me?'

He pulled me towards him and hugged me again, so tightly I could feel his ribs through his shirt. 'You have absolutely nothing to be ashamed of, do you know that?' he said.

I nodded. 'I know.'

'C'mon, let's go,' he said, holding my hand and squeezing it tight.

It was truly the worst thing of all, going back into the green room and seeing the disappointment on everyone's faces. They gathered around me, patting me on the back and telling me that I'd tried my best and, sure, wasn't I brilliant anyway? But I could tell that they all felt deflated. They'd put so much into supporting me, week after week, and now here we were. Not winning, but not exactly losing, either. It was clear that nobody knew what to do.

In the end, Niall took charge, insisting that I needed some food and drink, and that he was going to drive me home, after which I'd drop into the big celebration planned in Glenvara.

'Are you sure you wouldn't prefer to have some quiet time?' Sister Monica looked at me searchingly.

That's exactly what I would have liked, but the very least they deserved was a bit of a party, after all they'd done for me. 'No, I'd really like to celebrate. I got to the finals after all!'

'That's the spirit,' Bridget whooped, so loudly and enthusiastically that we all laughed, and the mood was lifted for a bit.

'I need to change out of this and clean off some of this make-up first, so I'll meet you all outside, OK?' I said.

'But they'll all want to see you in your finery,' Bridget protested. 'They'll want you to do the song again and—'

'I think Antonia's already done enough, Bridget,' Sister Monica intervened, placing a hand gently on Bridget's arm. She was lovely, as ever, but the message was clear.

Bridget shrugged her shoulders and smiled. 'Of course, pet, what was I thinking?'

Poor Bridget. She'd been my number one fan. I couldn't bear to spoil it for her. 'Bridget, I'd like nothing better than to go to the party, and I promise I'll sing whatever song you like. I'll just freshen up a bit first, is that OK?'

She cheered up immediately. 'Bless you, pet. We'll be outside,' she trilled, and led the gang off to the car park, like the Pied Piper.

Alone again with Niall, I sighed and managed a watery smile.

'You don't have to go, you know.' He took my hand and squeezed it gently.

'No, I want to,' I said, more enthusiastically than I felt. 'But I need to take some of this stuff off, it's driving me crazy,' I indicated the thick layer of make-up, which felt like concrete on my face.

'Sure—' he began, when there was a shuffling at the door, and in strode Karen, her earphones around her neck, clipboard in hand, as usual.

'Where on earth did you get to?' She fixed me with a glare.

'Sorry, I thought . . .'

'What? That we'd have no further use for you now that you're runner-up. Are you kidding?' She looked at me. 'I've a list as long as my arm of stuff I need you to do, beginning with the wrap party. You'll need a change, I think, and we'll get Valerie to have another look.' She wrinkled her nose. 'Where's that bossy stylist of yours?'

'Ehm, I think she's gone home.'

'For God's sake, doesn't she have a clue?' Karen looked impatient, before shrugging her shoulders. 'Sorry. It's just we're really tight for time, and you need to be looking your best. Let's see what Niamh in costume can do with you. Will *you* be coming?'

This remark was directed at Niall, who looked at her, open-mouthed. 'Oh, I don't know, I—'

'Good, great, fab, well, I'll just take Toni off now to change, and we'll hand you over to Steven, one of the researchers. He'll keep an eye on you and take you to the venue, OK?'

'Karen, the gang in Glenvara have a party planned for me—' I began, but stopped when she looked at me as if I was deranged.

'Well, we do have family and friends at the wrap party, but obviously not coachloads. It's more of a networking thing, you know? Give you the chance to meet interesting people.' And then she tapped her earphones and yelled, 'What? No, I've found her. Yep, will get her sorted and bring her to the back door in thirty. C'mon.' She tugged me by the arm. And then she looked at Niall. 'Don't move. I'll send Steven along in five.'

I hesitated, thinking of Bridget, and how disappointed she'd be. I couldn't let her down, not after everything she'd done for me. I needed to be in Glenvara, with the people who really mattered to me, the people who'd supported me all along.

In the end, it was Niall who decided for me. 'Go. I'll talk to Bridget.'

'I can't, I—'

'Better get used to this.' He looked at me kindly. 'I've a feeling this is the way it's going to be from now on.'

'No way.' I was adamant. I thought: This is just a one-off,

because I'm the plucky runner-up. What was it Dad used to say? 'Today's news is tomorrow's chip-wrappings.' Well, that's what I'd be tomorrow: chip-wrappings, I thought, as I allowed Karen to lead me to the dressing room for another costume change. And I was actually pleased about it. I could go back to the life I'd had before, couldn't I? Escape from all the madness of the past eight weeks.

So, why did the thought scare me so much?

I hardly saw Niall for a few hours, as I was dragged from one 'interesting' person to another in the packed nightclub. I didn't know who anyone was, but they all seemed so friendly, considering that I hadn't actually won. They congratulated me on my performance and told me I'd have a great career, and one or two even offered to manage me. I wasn't sure how to react – should I talk to these people seriously, or wait to consult Karen? I was bewildered. If I got this much attention for losing, God knows what it would have been like if I'd actually won the thing. I desperately wanted Niall by my side, but he was nowhere to be seen.

Damien was holding court in a circle of record company executives, charming them with his humour. I had to admit, he was every inch the rock star, with his edgy look and dark flashing eyes. I went up to him to say 'congratulations' again, and found myself blinded by flashlights.

'The two of you together,' one photographer yelled, encouraging Damien to put his arm around me.

'Fabulous, just fabulous.' Damien even gave me a cheeky

kiss on the lips, which of course made me blush. 'We'd make a great couple,' he said.

I laughed, thinking that he was joking. 'We would, except that I'm already taken.'

Damien looked at me searchingly for a moment. 'That doctor guy? Does he know what he's letting himself in for?'

'I'm not *that* bad,' I said, not understanding what he meant for a moment.

'Not you, this.' He waved his arm at the crowds. 'It's madness, and this is only the beginning. Is he ready for not seeing you for weeks and months on end?'

'Hardly. After this dies down, I'll be back at home in Glenvara, and that'll be the end of it.'

'You have got to be kidding. I won the thing, sure, but we all know who the real winner is, don't we?'

I didn't know what to say for a second, and just blinked at him. 'I don't know what you mean.'

He shook his head and grinned. 'Toni, you're a one-off, do you know that? With your talent . . . well, all I can say is that he's a very lucky man, your doctor. If only the rumours about us were true . . .' He looked hopeful, and I punched him playfully on the arm.

'Chancer.'

'Well, a guy's gotta try.' He gave me that cheeky grin again, before growing serious. 'Take it easy, Toni, won't you?'

'Sure,' I said, and pulled away before he could say anything more. What on earth had all that been about? I needed

257

to speak to Niall. I made my way through the crowds, finding it hard to breathe with the sheer press of bodies. There was a commotion for a second and the sound of raised voices. Heads swivelled in the direction of the noise, and I had to peer over someone's head to see what was going on. Jonny, the youngest of 4Guys, seemed to be yelling, tears streaming down his face, as another of the boys whispered in his ear, trying to calm him down. I tried to push forward to go to them, but my way was blocked by a press of people.

'God, the state of him,' someone was saying.

'Hmm,' a woman agreed. 'Too much of the free bar. And he's underage, I'm sure of it.'

Poor Jonny. He'd be 'tabloid fodder' in the morning, as Karen put it. I'd barely started in this business, but already I knew that. I was fond of Jonny and all the boys – they'd become like baby brothers to me. I suddenly felt that I'd had enough, and knew that I needed to go home. But first, I had to find Niall.

I found him at the bar, ordering what looked like a lemonade, a young girl in skinny jeans and a low-necked top chatting animatedly to him. He looked polite, but strained, and I put my hand on his arm. 'OK?'

'Sure,' he said, rolling his eyes in the direction of the girl, who melted away on cue.

'Groupie?' I teased.

'And I'm not even the famous one,' he joked. 'Would you like some of the champagne flowing freely here, or something else?'

I nodded at his glass. 'Don't tell me: lemonade.'

'Well . . . you'll need a lift home later, won't you? And you won't be in any fit state to drive yourself.'

'I love you,' I said, and the words were out of my mouth before I had time to censor them. My mouth was still open, a round 'o' of surprise. I'd only meant to say, 'Thanks for being so thoughtful,' but instead I'd said . . . this. Words I'd never said to any man in my entire life.

I didn't dare look at him as he put down his glass and reached out to me, cupping my chin in his hand.

'Look at me, Toni.'

'Don't call me that. That's not who I am,' I replied indignantly.

'Sorry, it's just . . . look, I love you too.'

I looked at my glass for a few minutes, thinking about what we'd both just said. 'You do?' I squeaked.

'I do.' His voice was warm. 'I really do.'

I nodded, and then, as if overwhelmed by the moment, Niall changed the subject.

'They sure don't make doctor parties like this,' he said, looking around at the packed room.

'Oh, really?' I smiled, relieved at the change of tone. 'What do they make them like?'

'As much drink as we can possibly consume in one sitting, and a handful of crisps for soakage.'

I burst out laughing. 'Sounds good. You'll have to invite me to one, one of these days.'

'If you're lucky enough, I might just do that.' He grinned.

259

I sighed. 'You know what? I want to go home.'

'Me, too. Will we just slip away?'

I looked around for any sign of Karen, who'd been watching me like a hawk all night, steering me in the direction of 'interesting' people and making sure that I was photographed with anyone who was anyone. Could I escape without her noticing?

'Sure,' I said.

Somehow, we managed to sneak out the side door of the nightclub, and found ourselves standing in a deserted alleyway. It was bizarre, after all the excitement of the night, that it was completely silent, not a photographer in sight. I looked up beyond the rooftops and there was a sprinkling of stars dusted over the chimney tops. I suddenly felt cold – it was winter and I was standing outside in a strapless gold-sequinned minidress, after all. It had been Niamh at Celtic TV's choice of outfit. 'Sex on legs,' she'd said enthusiastically, urging me out of my fuchsia number and into the tiny strip of gold.

'I'm not sure—' I'd said.

But she'd interrupted, 'Maybe you might bag yourself a star tonight at the wrap party – that Damien's a cutie!'

I'd just nodded. Best not to say anything further.

'Here, you'll be needing this.' Niall placed his jacket over my shoulders.

'What about you?'

'Oh, I'll survive,' he said. 'My mountaineering genes.'

'Very funny. Why don't we go for a walk?' I suggested.

'Are you sure that's a good idea?' he said. 'You might be recognized.'

I laughed. 'So what if I am? What are you afraid of, that people might say, "Who's the girl with that handsome doctor-type?"'

He shrugged. 'Well, can I help it if they all want a piece of me?'

'C'mon, you eejit. Let's go down to the river.' And I tucked my arm into his, and we walked against the icy wind until we'd reached the Ha'penny Bridge, climbing the steps over the white-painted Victorian bridge.

'I used to walk across this every single day when I was a student,' Niall said, taking me by the hand and leading me to the middle point, where we looked down the river. In this light, Dublin twinkled and glittered. It looked almost romantic.

As if reading my mind, Niall said, 'It should be Paris, really, or Rome.'

'But it's not,' I responded. 'It's home. And you're here, and that's all that matters.'

He was silent for a long time, and then he said, 'Did you mean it, earlier?'

'Mean what?' I leaned against his shoulder and let him slip his arm around me.

He kissed the top of my head. 'When you said you loved me.'

I turned my head to look at him, and his expression was

261

earnest, concerned. 'Of course I did. I've never said that to anyone in my entire life.'

He grinned broadly. 'Well, I meant it, too. I love you, Antonia. I love everything about you, your hair, your eyes, your funny feet, your habit of dunking your digestives in your tea.'

I laughed. 'And I love your horrible smelly fleeces and your mucky walking boots and your silly jokes.'

We kissed tenderly, and when we broke apart, he spoke again. 'Do you remember our promise?'

'Of course. We only made it last week.' I tried to keep the tone light, but he turned to face me, putting both hands on my shoulders and looking at me so intently, I knew how serious he was.

'We promised that no matter what happens from now on, we won't change.'

'I *know*.' I sounded a bit impatient because I wanted him to understand that I knew what I'd said.

He tucked a strand of hair in behind my ear. 'It's just, I think you're going to have to get used to a lot of new things in your life. It'll be different, Antonia, really different.'

'Well, whatever happens, I won't change. I won't forget my promise,' I said to him, squeezing his hand.

'I know,' he said softly. 'But I'd understand if you did. It's inevitable.'

'No it's not,' I protested loudly. 'I promised, and I won't change. And besides, this is me, Antonia. Toni Trent is someone else.'

His smile was firmer this time. 'Good, I'm glad. Because now I can kiss you.' He smiled, pulling me towards him, and enveloping me in his warmth. All thoughts of the past weeks faded as I melted into his arms. Nothing mattered except the two of us and the promise we'd made to each other. That was what was really important: Niall and me.

Later, much later, I crept into bed, and lay there for a few moments, looking out at the night sky, and the stars against the chilly winter blue. I'm not the same, I thought. I've changed. It doesn't really matter that I didn't win *That's Talent!* I'm not disappointed, I know I'm not. Everyone spent the whole night asking me if I was, even when I got back to Glenvara and they were all waiting for me in the village hall. It was the question on everyone's lips, 'Not too disappointed?' accompanied by a look of sympathy.

But when I replied, 'No, honest,' it was true. Because I've learned so much from all of this, I thought as I lay there – I've grown so much in the last few weeks, I hardly recognize myself. Miss Mouse really has become Toni Trent. And, you know what? It's fun. Scary, but fun.

And of course, there's Niall. I've never felt like this before in my entire life. It's the strangest feeling, like I have butterflies in my stomach all the time. That the only person I really want to think about is him – the way his hair sticks up, the way his eyes crinkle when he smiles, a smile which transforms his face. I'm lucky, I thought. Truly lucky. I snuggled down under the duvet, feeling its warmth envelop me, truly relaxed for the first time in months. Within seconds, I was in a deep sleep – so deep I didn't even hear the bleep of my mobile phone on the bedside table beside me.

I only got the message the next morning, when I was scrolling through the hundreds of messages in my in-box, deciding who to text back to thank. It was hidden amongst the 'congratulations' and 'well done's, the 'we're proud of you's, so this time, I wasn't even prepared for it – I'd opened it without even thinking.

'WELL, BITCH, HOW DOES IT FEEL TO BE THE LOSER? KISS GOODBYE TO YOUR DREAMS . . .'

I looked at it for a long time, blinking back the tears. Who could hate me enough to send me a text like that?

22

Two weeks later

'CHAMPAGNE, TONI?' KAREN'S VOICE INTERRUPTED MY thoughts.

'No thanks, Karen. I never thought I'd say it.' I laughed. 'But you really can have too much champagne.' I settled back in my seat and closed my eyes for a moment. If this was flying, well, I could get used to it.

Karen had been astonished that I'd never been on a plane before. 'You are kidding me?' She'd looked at me, mouth open in surprise, as we'd waited in the queue for the airport security check two hours previously.

'No, honest,' I'd said. 'I had to get a passport for the first time, can you believe it?' I'd smiled as I'd opened the maroon-covered booklet and examined my passport photo. I'd had to go to the passport office and beg them to give me one, first unearthing my birth certificate in a box in the attic. When I'd taken it out of the Manila folder, I'd looked at it for a long time. There was my name, in the careful script of the registrar, with two names above it. 'David Trent: engineer',

'Anna Trent: housewife'. My mum and dad. There was no clue that I'd been adopted. What would they have thought of it all? I'd wondered, as we waited in line. Here I was, about to get on a plane to sing at Wembley, of all places.

'OK?' Karen's voice had been gentle, nudging me to move forward in the queue, past a sad-looking Christmas tree.

'Oh sure.' I'd nodded, trying to smile. 'I was just thinking how much my mum and dad would have loved all this, flying first class, going to London to sing in a big show. Mum would have been so excited.'

'I know,' Karen had said. 'I'm sure she would have been really proud.'

I'd nodded, trying to keep the tears at bay. 'Oh, God, I don't know what's come over me. One minute I think I'm OK, and the next I'm in floods of tears.'

'Well, it's early days, you know, Toni. You probably haven't had the time to think about it, with everything that's been going on.' Karen's voice had been soft. 'I know that when my dad died, I threw myself into work, hoping that I could forget, but really, I was just storing up trouble, and it came back to bite me in the end.'

'Oh, I'm sorry, Karen, I didn't know,' I'd said, realizing that for all the time I'd spent with Karen, I didn't actually know her that well. I knew about her little dog, Toto, her boyfriend, who loved hurling, and that her favourite programme was *Mad Men*, but I'd suddenly realized that this was only surface detail. I'd felt a start of guilt – after all, I'd spent more time with Karen than with anyone else over

266

the past few weeks, and yet I hadn't thought to ask her about her family – maybe I was just another of those self-centred, egotistical singers, I'd thought, who simply obsesses about themselves. I hadn't always been like that – I used to think only of others, Mum, Dad, everyone – maybe I'd changed more than I'd thought.

She'd shrugged and smiled, pushing a hand through her blonde curls. 'No, of course you didn't. But it's hard, isn't it?'

'It is,' I'd said cautiously. 'Someone once told me that you only know what it's really like to lose a parent when you actually have lost one,' I'd ventured. 'Nobody can imagine the way it feels.'

'You know, you're right.' She'd smiled as the queue moved forward at last, and I'd felt her gently squeeze my arm. 'So how have you survived since the show ended?' she'd said, changing the subject.

'Oh, God, I can't believe it. I thought everyone would forget about me, because I didn't win, but it hasn't worked out like that.' I laughed. It seemed that Niall had been right – I'd promised not to change, and I hadn't, but my life had, beyond all recognition. After the night of the finals my phone hadn't stopped ringing, from Karen wanting to scold me for running off, to the head of Celtic TV, and about twenty journalists, all wanting interviews. It was totally overwhelming, and in the next two weeks, the press attention had grown, as had that of the public, as the messages of goodwill flooded in. I'd found myself invited to every single talk show, press call and opening, as well as being inundated by requests to help charities and open supermarkets.

'You'd turn up at the opening of an envelope,' Colette had teased me.

'But I didn't even win,' I'd protest every now and then. 'It was Damien, not me.' Once, Betty had overheard me saying the same thing to a journalist, and when I'd put the phone down, she'd taken me to task.

'Listen, Damien won, and that's fair enough, but you are the story here, and if people are still interested, well, the least you can do is be polite and answer their questions.' And when I'd looked shocked, she'd said, 'It's an opportunity, love. Don't miss it.' She'd even made me ring Maurice Prendergast when she'd realized that I hadn't yet done so. 'Are you mad altogether? Get on that phone, young lady, and take your chance, do you hear me?'

Two days later, I'd met Maurice at a hotel in Dublin, my knees knocking, hands trembling with nerves. He couldn't have been nicer, which was disconcerting, considering how hard he'd been as a judge. I'd wanted Niall with me, but he was on shift, so I'd taken Colette in the end, and, of course, she'd plied him with the kind of questions I didn't dare ask. Not for the first time, I'd wished I could be more assertive, but somehow, I never wanted to rock the boat. I preferred to get on with singing and let others do the talking for me. Cowardly, I know, but unless I was singing, I felt more comfortable being in the background.

'Look,' he'd said. 'My advice to you would be to sign

nothing – no management, no record contracts, not until you've been to London and seen how you feel after that. There's no rush at all. Karen's great, so let her guide you, and then, when you get back, you can get in touch if you're still interested.'

'Interested in what?' Colette had been like a terrier, digging away, and Maurice had given me a look, as if to say, 'Who's your friend?' I'd blushed, and he'd smiled.

'Interested in working with me. But I'd like it to be on your terms, Toni, once you've seen all the options and talked to people. In the meantime, if you want me to check out any offers and give you my honest opinion, I'd be happy to do that. Alternatively, I know a few good lawyers who'd help you out.'

'You'd do that for me?' I'd squeaked. 'Thanks, Maurice—'

'What's in it for you?' Colette had interrupted, and he'd smiled again, darting her a look.

'The chance to work further with Toni. She's a huge talent, but I want her to think before she leaps into anything.'

I'd wondered why I was being talked about in the third person, but I was glad Colette was there and in my corner. And Maurice Prendergast was one of the biggest players in the business. Even *I* knew that. I'd been flattered.

'Should I go with him?' I'd asked Colette when we were on the way home to Glenvara.

'Take his advice, Antonia. Do nothing and wait. Then you can make a choice.'

'I didn't know it'd be like this,' I'd said shakily.

'Hang on tight,' Colette had joked. 'It's going to be a hell of a ride.'

It was the singing that saved me, I thought now, as I tried to doze off in my seat. It was the singing that kept me calm, that helped me to remain centred in the eye of the storm. I'd even managed to take Colette's advice and ignore the nasty texts which kept coming, pushing themselves in amongst all the positive messages, like weeds in a bed of lovely flowers. They'd been sporadic at first, but soon, I was getting one every single morning. They varied, but the subtext was always the same: that I was a bitch who didn't deserve her success, that whoever it was hoped my career stalled, and that I'd lose my voice permanently. I tried to put them out of my mind, but they were really getting to me. I didn't dare tell a soul about them, either, because I knew that anyone I told would only get excited, insisting I do something instead of just pressing 'delete' and trying as hard as I could to forget about them. I felt that that was the only real way I had of rising above them – just to put them out of my mind and concentrate on getting better and better as a singer.

I'd been mortified to receive a round of applause as I'd got on the plane. I'd waved a bit, like the Queen, before diving into my seat and plugging my iPhone in as soon as I could, lying back in the seat and closing my eyes, letting the music carry me away. I hummed along with it in my head, the way I always did, and felt my shoulders drop as

I gradually began to relax. I looked at Karen now, leafing through the celebrity pages of a newspaper, and thought that it really had helped that I'd kept the same people around me. Karen was a tiger with the press, and held them at bay, and Colette and Mary made me look and feel a million dollars. I wished they were on the plane with me now, but the TV company had been snooty about them coming along, and said it was too expensive when they had their own stylists on hand.

'Who wants to fly to London on St Stephen's Day, anyway?' Colette had insisted when I'd broken the news. 'It's a day for watching TV in your pyjamas and eating the leftover turkey.' But I knew she was trying to be brave – that she and Mary would have loved it all. I was just lucky, I guess, that I'd chosen good people like them to be around me, because I knew that my instincts weren't perfect, and that I sometimes trusted too easily. But with them that trust had been repaid. They were my family.

But it was hard on Niall, I was aware of that. It was hardly the right way to keep a relationship going, was it, by jetting off for ten days? And I'd barely seen him since the night of the finals. I desperately wanted to ask him where we stood, now that the show was over. Maybe the intensity would wane, now that all the excitement was past. Maybe he wouldn't have a reason to take care of me any more? But surely that night by the river hadn't been just a dream? It had really happened, and I tried to keep the memory close.

271

*

'So what's on the agenda in London?' I asked Karen.

'Well . . .' Karen began, rummaging in her outsize leather bag and pulling a thick folder out, on the front of which was taped a typewritten sheet, with a moment-by-moment breakdown of my trip. 'We'll need to go to the studio first for rehearsals, because the London edition of *That's Talent!* is really thoroughly rehearsed, I can tell you.' The London *That's Talent!* had invited me along with Damien to their semi-final special, even though I hadn't actually won the Irish competition, which everyone kept telling me was a huge honour. I wasn't sure how Damien would feel about it, but I could hardly say no, could I? But all the same, I couldn't help wondering if I was stealing his thunder. I'd tried to distract myself by practising for the show, with Eithne, a new arrangement of 'Bridge Over Troubled Water', which they thought would go down a storm with 'their demographic' as Karen put it.

I gulped as she continued. 'And then after that we have a meet and greet with selected members of the audience, and then a record company bash, and then there's a dinner with the Celtic TV executives . . .'

As she went on and on, I tuned out, telling myself it'd be better not to think about it too much. Just to let her take control. That was her job, after all. And it all sounded so daunting . . .

'Oh, crap.' My thoughts were interrupted by Karen's swearing as she sat bolt upright in her seat.

272

'What is it?' I asked. It wasn't like Karen to swear. She was normally completely unflappable.

'Nothing.' She shook her head and carefully folded the newspaper she'd been reading.

'Karen, what is it? Another story?' I'd grown used to them by this stage, and the press had combed through every inch of my past: from my 'tragic' early life in the orphanage to my school days, dredging up comments from 'friends' that I'd never heard of. 'Aren't we supposed to sue?' I'd asked Karen once, and she'd guffawed.

'God, if we were to sue every time we read a lie about a client, the lawyers' fees would bankrupt us. No,' she'd shaken her head. 'We just have to pick our battles, Toni, and ignore the rest, because it's all just rubbish, really.'

Now, though, she was shifting uneasily in her seat, looking cross. 'Karen, you'll have to show me sooner or later,' I said gently.

Wordlessly, she passed me the newspaper and I opened it. There was nothing much, the usual recession stories and celebrity gossip. 'It's on page four.'

'Right,' I flicked to that page and gasped. 'IS THIS THE NATION'S SWEETHEART'S NEW LOVE?' The headline was huge, accompanied by a photo of Niall in his scrubs, looking harassed. It looked odd, as if they'd caught him leaving the hospital after a shift. 'He'll be mortified,' I managed, scanning the paragraphs, my mouth opening in horror as I did so. It wasn't that the story was nasty, exactly, just full of insinuation. It described how 'the handsome doctor who's been Toni Trent's rock over the past few weeks has a bit of a past'. And helpfully supplied grainy photos of Niall as a child with people I didn't recognize. I'd seen photos of his parents and foster siblings, so I knew it wasn't them. It must be his first family. Poor Niall.

And there were quotes from a wizened-looking elderly woman who said she was his granny, about how wonderful his natural parents were, and how he'd been wrenched away from them. 'It nearly broke their hearts,' she moaned. I felt my pulse race. From what he'd told me, they had never tried to get in touch with him, or made any effort once he'd been placed in care, so I knew that this would hurt.

'Dave Byrne. That little shit,' Karen was saying, two spots of red on her cheeks. Then she managed to compose herself. 'It's all just rubbish, Toni.' I felt her hand on my arm, saw the look of concern in her face. 'You have to put it out of your mind.'

I looked at her sharply. 'That's fine, Karen, when it's about me. I don't care what they say then. But Niall's done nothing except be a friend and a support, and this is what he gets. I don't know how I'll explain it to him.'

'You don't have to, because he'll know it wasn't you. You didn't write this crap. Dave Byrne did, having wormed his way into your confidence. Wait till I get hold of him. It'll be the last story he covers, if I have my way.'

I thought of Dave Byrne, smiling at me in his leather jacket, and I felt the colour rush to my cheeks. Oh, God, what had I said to him? I didn't remember ever having mentioned

Niall, but I couldn't be sure. I racked my brains, trying to think what I'd said to him over the past few weeks. He'd taken to calling me every so often, for a 'friendly chat' or to check some detail, and it had all seemed fairly harmless. I was sure I hadn't told him anything really private.

'I gave him my number,' I blurted.

'Oh, Toni,' Karen said, looking at me reproachfully. 'Didn't I warn you to let me deal with the press? What on earth got into you?'

Tears sprang into my eyes. 'I thought it was all harmless. And he was so friendly.'

Karen's mouth was set in a grim line. 'That's the way these people work, Toni. They sneak into your life, pretending to be a mate, but really, they're just gathering information for their nasty little stories.' She ran a hand through her blonde curls, and then attempted a weak smile. 'Look, don't blame yourself. You were just naïve. I'm sorry you had to learn the hard way, that's all.' And she patted my hand.

I shook my head. 'I do blame myself, Karen. If Niall wasn't going out with me, none of this would have happened. I need to speak to him.' I need to ask him if he spoke to anyone, I thought, because I know I didn't say anything. I *know*. But then, Niall was the last person to talk to the media, I was certain.

'I'm sure you do,' Karen was firm. 'But you'll have to wait until we land at Heathrow, and until then you can do nothing, so just put it out of your mind and concentrate on our plans.'

275

She was being harsh, but she was right, I supposed. And then she added more gently, 'I'll get Colman to ring them and tell them no more exclusives if they continue to print this kind of crap. And then I'll break Dave Byrne's legs.' She smiled. Colman was Celtic's lawyer, a small man in an expensive suit who was as tough as old boots. He had successfully threatened to sue over two particularly nasty articles about my childhood, and the papers had backed off. I knew that I could rely on him.

I nodded mutely. 'I'm sure it wouldn't stop Dave Byrne, but thanks,' I said, wondering why just wanting to sing could lead to *this*. But how on earth had the paper got hold of the story?

And then suddenly the penny dropped. The texts, the story. It all came together. Why hadn't I thought of it sooner? It was so obvious. The look on her face that last time we'd met. Amanda.

'Oh, God,' I said out loud.

'What?'

'I think I know who's behind the story.'

She looked at me sharply. 'You do?'

I nodded. 'I think so—'

I was about to tell her when she interrupted me. 'The thing is, it's not important, Toni. Believe me, there will be tons of people out there who will want to get at you, because you're so talented and successful, and this is one of the ways they can do so, by selling some half-assed story about you to the tabloids. But you have to rise above it, really you do, and focus on what's important: the sing-ing.'

But what about Amanda? I thought. Shouldn't I confront her, say something to her? I couldn't say anything to Karen, of course, or she'd think I was completely paranoid, so instead I just swallowed and nodded. 'You're right. OK.' I tried to relax, but I kept fidgeting, waiting for the flight to be over so that I could call Niall. I just needed to talk to him, to check that he was OK. He was the only person I could tell about Amanda – the only one I could trust with the information.

As soon as we landed, I dialled his number, but his phone was switched to voicemail. I didn't want to, but I had to leave a message in the end. 'Niall . . . not sure if you've read the papers, but if you have, I'm sorry. It wasn't me who told them that, honestly. I need to talk to you, so, ehm, will you call me back?'

I pressed 'disconnect' and sighed, while Karen pretended not to listen, her back turned to me at the baggage carousel. Then she patted me on the back. 'C'mon, Wembley awaits.'

'Wembley Arena – you know, I can't believe I'll be sing-ing there,' I said.

'Wembley Stadium,' Karen corrected me, a smile twitch-ing at the corner of her lips.

I looked at her, my mouth open. 'I can't sing *there*. It's huge.'

'Yes it is, and yes you can. This is the biggest show in the country, and you are in it, by special request, so get used to it.' She smiled, softening her tone when she saw the look on my face. 'And of course, you'll be fabulous.'

'Oh. My. God,' I said out loud when I got to the rehearsal studio, a vast warehouse in west London.

'I know.' Karen nodded. 'It makes the Irish production look as if it's been done in a matchbox, doesn't it?'

'It sure does,' I breathed, taking in the orchestra, the swarms of technicians beavering around in the vast, open space.

'Hi, you must be Toni.' A friendly looking guy came towards us, a large pair of earphones around his neck. 'Mac, the floor manager,' he said, extending a hand.

'This place is huge,' I managed.

Mac took one look at my terrified expression and smiled reassuringly. 'It is, but remember, it's only a rehearsal, and you're among friends, so try to relax, OK?' He smiled. 'Now, you have a runner assigned to you. She'll show you to your dressing room, and you can leave your stuff there. She is at your disposal for the day, so ask her for anything you need, OK?'

I swallowed, thinking of the tiny, cramped dressing rooms in Dublin, stuffed with hordes of performers, make-up artists and hangers-on. This was in another league. I had my very own runner. 'Thanks,' I said nervously, allowing myself to be led away by a lovely young girl who introduced herself as Sharon. She was tall and willowy and looked more like a pop star than a runner.

'How was the flight?' she asked as we walked down another of those endless corridors.

'Great, short,' I said, thinking suddenly of the tabloid story and wondering when I could try Niall again. I began to panic at the thought of it, looking at my mobile as if it would answer me back. Maybe I should ring Amanda, confront her? But no, what if it wasn't her? I'd have lost a friend for ever, then, even if I hadn't spoken to her since that coffee after the semis. Surely she wouldn't do this to me? But then I thought of the expression on her face when we'd been doing the photocall in St Stephen's Green. How weary she'd sounded, how cynical. Maybe that's how you feel if you chase a dream for years and it never comes true. She'd wanted it so badly, I thought. More than I did, and yet I was the one singing at Wembley, not her.

My heart fluttered with anxiety as I worried about what to do. I had no idea what I'd say to Amanda. After all, how do you broach a subject like that? 'Have you been sending me nasty texts? Have you been selling my story to the tabloids?' It sounded so paranoid, I thought, when you put it that way. No, I'd wait, I decided, until after I'd spoken to Niall. He'd know what was best.

Sharon showed me to a huge dressing room with a TV and its own bathroom. There was also a tray with fruit, water, a flask of coffee and lots of little treats to eat. It felt more like a luxury hotel suite than a dressing room. I couldn't believe it.

'Right, I'll leave you for a few moments to get comfortable, and then I'll be back with Karen, if I can track her down.' Sharon smiled. Then the door closed behind her and I was alone.

I tried Niall again, but there was no signal, so I gave up and just sat there for a few moments, unable to believe I was going to be rehearsing for a show at Wembley Stadium, of all places. No matter how often I thought about it, it seemed like a dream.

Then there was a knock on the door and Damien burst into the room, full of energy and high spirits as usual. Honestly, he was like a puppy sometimes.

'Toni!' He ran over to me and pulled me into a bear hug. 'Can you bloody believe it? You and me. Here. About to do Wembley! How bloody fantastic is that?' And he started dancing me around the room, singing, 'We are famous, we are famous,' over and over again.

Laughing, I had to beg him to stop. 'Calm down or you'll burn out before tonight.'

But he shook his head. 'No way, baby. I am here as winner of *That's Talent!* Ireland, and boy, am I going to make the best of it. You don't know how long this'll last, Toni,' he said. 'This time next week, you could be back in the middle of nowhere, and I could be packing supermarket shelves again. So we owe it to ourselves to enjoy it.' And he looked at me with that cute grin of his, his head cocked to one side.

All of a sudden I felt better. Damien always cheered me up with his buoyancy, his zest for life. 'You're right,' I said, managing a smile. His good humour was infectious.

'Great, so you'll come with me to the after-party tonight? After all, we are a *couple* . . .' he said mischievously.

'You mean . . . a date?'

I opened my mouth to tell him that Niall was on his way, but he interrupted. 'I know you've got that doctor fellah in Dublin, so don't worry. We'll just have a bit of fun . . . and I'll be the perfect gentleman . . . promise.' That cheeky grin again.

I laughed and said, 'OK. If you promise to behave.'

'*Me?* When have I ever misbehaved?' He pretended to be offended. 'Now, c'mon, let's check this place out.'

'I have to practise—' I began.

'Sure, sure, I know.' He looked crestfallen, then his expression brightened. 'Tell you what, why don't we see if we can knock out a duet while we're waiting?'

'A duet?'

'Sure, both of us singing together, you know?'

'I know what a duet is, Damien.' I smiled.

'Well, great, let's give it a shot. I'll go get my guitar,' he said, and bounded off out the door. God, he'd tired me out already, I thought, as I watched his retreating back.

In the end, I was glad of the duet, because we whiled away a couple of hours picking out a melody while we waited for rehearsals to begin. It was fun, working with Damien. Our voices meshed well together, and I found that I could actually contribute something to the process of creating the tune and lyrics.

He was pleasantly surprised. 'And there was I, thinking

281

that you were just a great cover singer. You can make songs, too. I'm impressed.'

I blushed. 'Thanks, Damien. I'd actually like to write more of my own stuff and this . . . well, it was fun. Thanks.'

To my embarrassment, he leaned over and pecked me on the cheek. He smelled of peppermints and aftershave. 'It was fun, wasn't it? We're more alike than you think, Toni.'

I didn't know what to say, so I did my usual, staring at my knees and blushing, wishing that I had something to say, something exciting and witty. Thankfully, I was saved by Karen and Sharon, who both appeared at the same time.

'Wow, that was fantastic,' Karen said. 'I heard it from outside the room. Maybe we could get you on together.'

I wasn't sure if she was joking, but Damien, of course, was enthusiastic. 'Brilliant, Karen. It's not ready yet, but there's something there, definitely. Will keep you posted.' He grinned his boyish grin and I wondered why I didn't have that confidence, to tell Karen that I wasn't quite ready yet. Instead, I just jumped to attention, obedient girl that I was.

'Sorry about the delay, guys, the director wanted to try a few things. So we'll have Toni first and then we'll call you, Damien, OK?' Sharon said.

As I got up, Damien grabbed hold of my hand. 'Hey, re-member our date?'

I was flustered. 'Oh, sure . . . well, we'll see what happens after the gig.' Then I realized they were all smiling at me, and I blushed again.

Karen came to the rescue this time. 'C'mon, Toni, we'll make our escape from this charmer. You'd want to be careful of him, you know,' she joked.

'You're just jealous.' Damien grinned, and winked at us both. I was totally mortified. What on earth would Niall think of this if he ever got to hear of it?

'He really likes you.' Karen was smiling.

'I have a boyfriend,' I said, more sharply than I'd intended.

'Oh, of course. Sorry, Toni, I didn't mean to offend.'

I turned to her and put a hand on her arm. 'I know that, Karen, but it's just . . . all of this is completely overwhelming, not to mind Damien. I can't deal with it all,' I said. Really, I was thinking of Amanda and of Niall, and whether our relationship was ruined.

'You poor thing,' she soothed. 'Well, just ease yourself into the number and you'll be flying, OK?'

As usual, singing gave me the confidence I didn't have in real life. The rehearsals went well. They were even fun, as the exacting director, a woman called Melanie – with bright red hair pulled into a tight knot and severe, black-framed glasses – put me through my paces. Every time I thought I'd given my best, she asked me to sing again, until my throat felt hoarse. 'I need a bigger sound, Toni,' she kept saying. I knew what she was getting at. It would need to be pretty big for Wembley Stadium, and I nodded, forcing myself to relax, to really open my diaphragm and sing from the pit of my stomach, as Eithne had taught me to. Slowly, I improved. 'Good, good,' Melanie said, until she was finally satisfied with me.

'God, she was a bit of a dragon,' Karen said, as I was led back to my dressing room after the rehearsal.

I shook my head. 'Actually, I enjoyed it. I feel I'm really stretching myself here. It's a whole new standard for me, and it's brilliant.'

'Well, great,' Karen said warmly. 'Good for you for rising to the challenge. Roll on Wembley!'

In the end, Melanie put us through rehearsals for the entire week, before deeming us ready for the concert on the Saturday night, New Year's Eve. Sharon had even dragged her along to my dressing room to hear me and Damien sing together, and she agreed that we were 'cute'. 'You make a nice couple. We'll see if we can make room for you, but only if the song's really polished. Keep practising.' With a half-smile, she was gone.

Damien punched the air. 'Fan-bloody-tastic!' And then he grabbed me and swung me around the room. 'We are about to be very famous, Toni, with a song we wrote off our own bat. Aren't you even a bit pleased?' And he looked at me with those puppy-dog eyes.

'Of course I'm pleased,' I said, grinning from ear to ear. 'I'm ecstatic, in fact.' And I hugged him, inhaling that peppermint-aftershave smell. He wasn't like Niall, who was clean and freshly scrubbed, but never wore aftershave. I liked Niall better.

'And we'll be able to celebrate tomorrow night. Remember our date?'

'Sure,' I said. I'd been hoping that he'd forgotten, because I was going to ring Niall and ask if he could make the concert. I hadn't been able to reach him for three whole days in this place – his phone had always gone to voicemail when I'd tried it – and in the end I'd managed a hasty text in the cab on my way back to my hotel the previous night. 'Rehearsals really full on, but worthwhile. Hope work OK for you. Can you make it to the concert on Sat night? Would really love you to come. Toni xx.' It was only once I'd sent it that I realized: I'd signed myself Toni, but to Niall I was Antonia. I'd promised him I wouldn't change, not one bit. I bit my lip with anxiety.

On the Saturday morning, I got a one-line reply. 'I'll be on the 4 p.m. flight. Have hotel booked. Will call you when I get in.' And nothing else. No 'love'. He hadn't even signed it. My heart sank. He must have read the newspaper piece, then. But still, I reasoned, he was coming and that was the important thing. I'd have to tell Damien not to overdo it, or Niall would get the wrong message and I'd be in trouble again.

Even though the Saturday was manic, with a photocall for the Wembley gig, and a whole raft of press interviews, I was on edge, waiting to hear from Niall. All morning I kept looking at my mobile, until Karen said, 'It won't ring if you stare at it continually, you know.'

'I know.' I sighed. 'I'm waiting for a call, that's all.'

'The doctor?'

I nodded. 'I haven't spoken to him since the tabloid story. I've been trying to, but he never picks up. I'm really nervous, Karen.'

'He'll understand, Toni, honestly. He must know what this business is like, how ruthless it can be.'

I shook my head. 'He doesn't, Karen. He thinks it's all just nonsense, full of people with egos.' Or people who were so jealous, they wanted to destroy you, I thought.

'I doubt it, somehow, Toni. After all, he's going out with you, isn't he? And you're a performer. I'll bet he understands better than you think.'

I nodded. 'Maybe you're right. I suppose I'll find out later.'

'Look, I don't know him, but everything I've seen of him makes me think he's one of the good guys. So give him a chance, will you?' She looked at me kindly.

'Me, give *him* a chance?' I laughed. 'Don't you think it's the other way around?'

Karen smiled. 'I don't, actually. You're assuming you know what he thinks. And you don't. So I'm just suggesting that you let him tell you what he thinks, before jumping to conclusions.'

I swallowed hard. 'You're right. Thanks for the advice, Karen.'

'You're welcome. I charge a small fee,' she joked, and then she looked at me more seriously. 'And look out for that Damien, will you? He's a chancer.'

I blushed. 'I know, but he's only messing, and I've really enjoyed singing with him.'

'That's great. And your voices really work together, but he's a bit of a bad boy, so be careful, will you?'

'I'm perfectly capable of looking after myself,' I said, so huffily that Karen burst out laughing.

'Toni, you are a complete innocent, do you know that?'

'You know, you're not the first person to say so,' I said ruefully.

'I'm sorry,' she said.

'No, you're right, but I'm learning,' I said. And as I spoke the words, I realized that they were true. I was growing in confidence every day, in spite of everything. After all, Amanda's texts hadn't stopped me, had they? I felt strong now in a way I never had before. The competition had given me that. Who would have thought, just over three months ago, that I'd be getting ready to sing at Wembley Stadium? Sometimes, when I thought of the days and weeks after Mum died, I could hardly believe I was the same girl.

'What are you thinking?' Karen interrupted my thoughts.

'It's just, I feel so much more confident than I used to . . .' I began.

'You are,' Karen said. 'I can't believe you're the same shy girl who came to the auditions. But you aren't tough, Toni, and you need a really thick skin for this business, so you need to be careful, OK?' She patted my hand.

I nodded solemnly. 'I will be.'

'And stick with Niall. He's a good guy, and he'll keep you steady. Damien . . . well . . .'

'Karen, I'm not interested in Damien,' I moved to reassure her.

'But he's interested in *you*. And he'll wear you down with his persistence. And sometimes his motives . . . well, they leave something to be desired.' She looked at me darkly.

I was baffled. Karen was talking in riddles, but I was saved from asking anything when the taxi pulled up at the rehearsal space for the final run-through. She put her hand on my arm. 'Just watch out, Toni, won't you?'

23

IN THE END, IT WASN'T DAMIEN I HAD TO LOOK OUT FOR. HE was a chancer, Karen was right, but he wasn't a bad guy, I could see that. She thought he was trying to piggyback on my success, and maybe she was correct, but what was really so wrong about that? And we sounded good together: we clicked as singers. No, in the end, the threat didn't come from Damien, nor even Amanda, but from someone else, someone who made Damien look like the naughty schoolboy he was. But Karen was right in one sense, I wasn't as tough as I thought I was. I didn't have a thick skin for the dark side of this business, and I found out in the worst possible way.

All that afternoon, I was distracted, glancing constantly at my mobile, until Melanie had to take me to one side. 'Everything OK, Toni?'

I tried to look in control, calm. Melanie didn't like panickers. 'Oh yes, everything's just fine.'

She looked at me closely. 'Good, because I'm going to go with that duet between you and Damien, so I want to be sure that you think you can pull it off.'

I could hardly believe what she was saying. Not only was I doing a solo, but I was getting the chance to perform original material, which is what I'd always wanted to do. I could show the world that I was more than just a cover singer. I was so astonished that I couldn't think of anything to say for a moment, my mouth hanging open like a goldfish, until Melanie shot me a glare.

'You sure you'll be up to this?'

'Yes, yes, I mean, of course, Melanie. I won't let you down.'

She smiled at me thinly. 'Good. Find that Damien and start practising and I'll try you out again in an hour.' And with that, she was gone, leaving me gobsmacked.

'She likes you,' Karen joked.

'I'd hate to see her if she didn't.'

'Ha ha. Go and find Damien, quick.'

Damien was nearly hysterical with excitement when I told him, lifting me up and swinging me around the dressing room, before planting a smacking kiss on my lips. 'Fan-bloody-tastic!'

'It's the song that matters,' I said, when I'd got my breath back.

'Yeah, yeah, whatever.' He grinned, but then, catching my expression, he was serious for a moment. 'You're right. If the song was crap, we would not be singing it at Wembley Stadium, but we sing it well, you've got to give me that. This could be the start of something beautiful!' And he gave me that charming, mile-wide smile again.

He's flirting with me, I thought, and I burst out laughing. 'Maybe, Damien. Let's just concentrate on the song for the time being.' And I gave him a playful shove on the shoulder.

'You're right,' Damien nodded, suddenly all business. 'This is our big chance, Toni, and we're going to ace it.' I had to admit that Damien was professional when he needed to be, and I was glad to have a distraction to take my mind off things. I hadn't heard from Niall, in spite of the fact that I'd kept my phone practically two inches from my ear all day. Oh, God, I thought, why did I never seem to do the right thing as far as Niall was concerned?

We were harmonizing the second chorus when my mobile bleeped. I stopped dead in the middle of a note and lost my concentration. 'Sorry, Damien,' I said.

'You'd better get that,' Damien said, strumming away on his guitar. 'Then we'll pick up from the second line, OK?'

'Sure,' I agreed, reaching for my mobile, fingers trembling.

'How's life for the rich and famous? Have u forgotten us all here in Dublin? (joke). Catch up when you get back? Good luck tonite! Colette xx PS Karen tells me ur duetting with a tall dark stranger. LOL'

I blushed and swallowed, texting back a brief 'xx'. 'Right,' I said then, 'let's continue, shall we?'

'Not from the doctor, then?' Damien nodded at the phone.

'None of your business,' I said, so huffily he burst out laughing.

'OK, Mum.'

I shot him a glare, and we spent the rest of the practice session dutifully singing our parts, until we could feel them mesh together in the way we'd planned.

'Perfect,' Damien said, at the end of what seemed like our hundredth run-through from the top.

'Yes, yes it is.' I nodded.

Damien put his guitar down, leaning it against a chair in the corner, as if it was a fragile and tiny baby. 'It's been great working with you, Toni,' he said quietly.

'And I've loved working with you, Damien,' I said. 'We should try writing something else together.'

He nodded, but the cheeky grin was gone, replaced by a look I'd never seen before. 'I'd love that. And there's something else—' he began.

'Oh yeah,' I was only half-listening, distracted by the sound of laughter and music in the corridor outside.

'Yeah. I think we're great together.'

'I know,' I said. 'You just said that.'

'Yes, but what if we really were together?'

'What, you and me?'

He grinned. 'Well, would that be so bad?'

I thought of Niall, of how well we fitted together, of how relaxed he made me feel, how I loved the simplicity of life with him. But would we ever get a chance to be together, with my life the way it was? It seemed more and more of an impossibility with every passing day. Maybe Damien was right.

'You mean, go out together?'

He gave me an amused look. 'Well, look, the press loves us, and if they thought we were an item, would it really do us that much harm? And it's not like either of us has the time for a proper relationship, is it?'

And then the penny dropped. He wasn't serious, of course. God, Karen had been right. He *was* a chancer, albeit a charming one.

'Damien,' I said, 'I'm not going to go out with you for the sake of getting my name in the paper. Neither of us needs that.'

'No, we don't right now, but think of it, Toni, if we were together, we'd be on page one for weeks, not page two and then three, until finally we're doing panto in Brighton. We've got something special, the two of us, something that can take us so far separately, but together . . . we'd be like Ike and Tina Turner or Sonny and Cher, or . . .' he began.

I didn't know much about either, but I wasn't sure they were exactly terrific examples of togetherness. And then I looked at his face, at the expression of puppy-dog enthusiasm on it. Damien was older than me, and this was probably his last chance at fame. I supposed I could hardly blame him for trying his luck. And of course it wouldn't be 'bad'. He was fun, and talented, and had a great sense of humour. But he wasn't Niall.

I smiled and shook my head. 'Damien, I'm flattered by the offer, but I think you know what I'm going to say.'

'Well, if you change your mind, I'm here.' He stretched

out his arms and gave me that cheeky grin. 'Waiting to welcome you into my arms.'

'You are completely insufferable,' I said, and he burst out laughing.

'And you have the measure of me, Toni. You might look innocent, but I think you're actually a tough cookie, do you know that?'

'Not tough, Damien. Just sensible.' I tried to sound brave, sophisticated, but all the time I was wondering how on earth I'd got myself into this. Miss Mouse.

Karen had been right. It was a strange world, and I'd need all my wits and a thicker skin to survive it.

24

OF COURSE, WEMBLEY WAS OVERWHELMING, SCARY AND fabulous, all at once. I could hardly speak for nerves, and in spite of Melanie's drilling, kept having blank moments as I practised in my dressing room before the show. Oh, God, I thought, as the time for my performance drew near, I'm going to dry. It's every artist's worst nightmare and haunts them constantly, and if they say it doesn't, they're lying. I kept forgetting bits of the new song Damien and I had written, and having to hum it to myself, because the words just wouldn't come. Finally, in frustration, I yelled, 'For God's sake!' so loudly I frightened myself.

'Anything I can do?'

I turned at the sound of the voice and there he was, standing at the door. Niall. He was dressed casually in jeans and an open-necked shirt, his hair, a little longer than usual, brushing the collar of his shirt. It was sticking up on top, though, and made him look like a duck. My duck.

'Niall!' I shrieked. I ran into his arms and he enveloped me in a hug.

He whispered, 'I love you,' over and over again, and I whispered it back, meaning every word.

'I thought you weren't coming,' I muttered into his shirt, feeling the warmth of him against my cheek. I suddenly felt safe, as if nothing could go wrong, not now that he was here.

'I wanted it to be a surprise, but then Karen rang me about the piece, and I thought I'd better say something, in case you thought I had the hump.'

My heart plummeted. 'Oh. The piece. You saw it.'

He shook his head and gave a small smile, running his hand through his hair. 'I didn't, actually, because I was on shift, but one of the other doctors helpfully kept it for me to read when I came back on again on Monday.' He winced.

'Niall, I'm sorry, it wasn't me—' I began.

He interrupted, tucking a strand of hair behind my ear. 'I know, you silly girl. Why on earth would you do something like that?' And he kissed me gently on the nose.

'I wouldn't, of course, I w-wouldn't,' I stammered. 'I'd never do that . . . it must have been Amanda, she was really upset to be knocked out, and she knows a lot of people in the media—'

He shushed me, pulling me towards him and stroking my hair. 'Please, Antonia, forget it. I'm a big boy and I know how the world works, OK?'

'And I don't, not really,' I said, holding his hand in mine. 'She's been sending me nasty texts for weeks, and I never twigged that it was her. I trusted her, and now I feel like a child, as if I know nothing at all about anything.'

'But you're learning.' He smiled down at me. 'And what's really good is that Amanda hasn't shaken that faith you have in others. Your innocence, it's special, Antonia. You don't want to lose it, and it'd be easy in this industry. I don't give a rat's, quite frankly, about tabloid stories.'

I nodded. 'Thanks, that means everything to me.'

He grinned, kissing my forehead. 'But I do give a rat's about *you*, and you've got a performance to prepare for, so what's it to be: gargling with vinegar, stuffing rosemary branches up your nose to clear the airways?' he joked.

I mock-punched him. 'You are quite ridiculous, and I love you.'

'I love you, too. And now, I want you just to relax, and focus on the performance, OK?'

'It'll be easy, with you here,' I said.

'It's never easy, Antonia, but thanks. I wouldn't have missed it for the world.'

Niall being there kept me going in that last hour before I went on stage. Karen had blagged him a backstage pass, so he was able to stay by my side for almost the entire evening. 'I'll leave you alone in hair and make-up – anything else would be creepy,' he joked. 'I'm just going to put my feet up in your dressing room and eat all that free food you've been given, and drink the champagne and then have a snooze.' And he waved cheerfully as I was taken off to the make-up artist, a silent, sulky-looking girl, who said not one word as she worked her magic. Where were Valerie and Colette when I needed them?

The London production team were much more strict about choosing my outfit, and they'd assigned me a stylist, insisting on supervising my costume choices for the night: a long black jumpsuit with a diamanté belt and silver high-heeled sandals, and a low-cut zebra-print minidress which was too risqué for my taste.

When Niall saw it, he did a double take. 'Wow, that's really . . .'

'Revealing?' I blushed. 'I feel as if I'm half-naked in the thing.'

Niall looked bashful for a moment. 'You look stunning,' he said diplomatically. 'I might prefer something more modest, but it'll make an impact, that's for sure.'

And it did. When I walked on stage, the orchestra playing the opening bars of 'Bridge Over Troubled Water', I was almost glad I was wearing it. It felt like a costume made for a bolder, sexier girl, the girl I could pretend to be as I stood in front of thousands of people on the vast stage, with nothing to prop me up except a microphone. The applause had been polite when I was announced by the presenter – after all, nobody knew the runner-up of *That's Talent!* Ireland, did they? – and I could sense that the audience was waiting, just marking time before the bigger acts came on, but then I remembered about how it was my time to shine. I stepped up to the mike in the middle of the vast stage, and listened for my cue from the orchestra, opening my mouth and murmuring the opening lines, conscious of the fact that I had to control the sound, to let it build and build over the course of the song. There were a couple of impatient whistles from the audience, used to more uptempo numbers, so I had to hold my nerve, to focus on the song and on letting the notes come out of my mouth, the way I always did. By the time I hit the second verse, the orchestra swelling behind me, I knew the audience was on my side. I could feel them. It's funny, maybe all performers have this sixth sense, knowing intuitively how the audience is feeling. I suppose you have to have it.

As the song drew to a close, I tried to keep my focus, tried not to think about Niall and how much he loved it, how often he'd played the Elvis cover for me on YouTube, about how we'd both loved Elvis's passion, his showmanship, about Mum and how she was always with me when I sang, always, hovering around me, making me feel strong, confident. About how much she'd hate my sexy costume. She'd insist I wear a cardigan, I thought, trying not to giggle, to bring my mind back to the closing notes of the song.

And then it was over and the orchestra was swelling for the closing bars. And there was that split second of silence before the audience erupted, a roar which went around the stadium, accompanied by so many flashbulbs, I thought I'd be blinded. I stood there for a moment, unsure of myself, until the presenter, a lovely blonde young girl with a cheery smile, saved me, tucking my arm into hers and saying, 'Wow, that was amazing. What a talent, everyone!' And she pulled me gently offstage as the audience erupted again.

'Well done, Toni, that was wonderful,' she trilled, placing a kiss on my cheek as she led me into the wings, where Sharon was waiting.

'High five,' Sharon yelled, holding her hand up to mine. 'You blew them away out there. I've never heard anything like that applause. You go, girl!'

I was a bit embarrassed at her shrieking, and tried to keep my voice low. 'Thanks, Sharon. I'm gobsmacked, I really am.'

'Of course you are,' she soothed, her expression one of concern. 'I'd say that was nerve-racking.'

'My legs are like jelly,' I said, taking a sip of the water Sharon had handed me. I looked frantically around for Niall. I'd told him where to stand to get the best view, but there was no sign of him. 'Have you seen Niall?'

She looked at me blankly. 'Sorry?'

'My boyfriend. Tall guy, blond hair.'

'Oh, him. He's cute.' She grinned. 'But Melanie doesn't let anyone apart from crew backstage, so we had to move him, I'm afraid.'

'Move him?' It made him sound like a piece of furniture.

'Yep, he's in your dressing room.' She smiled at me. 'C'mon, let's go and have a rest before the next number.'

I followed her back to my dressing room, opening the door to find him sitting on the leather sofa, waiting. He held his arms open and I collapsed into them, so overcome with emotion that I started sobbing loudly. 'You did it,' he kept whispering into my hair. 'Shush, it's over. You did it.'

'Did you see it?' I asked anxiously.

'I was right there, in the wings, until Melanie spotted me and had me booted off.' He smiled. 'But I saw it all, and I was amazed, yet again, by just how you do it.'

I blushed and said nothing, allowing the sobs to subside, feeling more relaxed now that I'd let the tension of the last few hours out. 'Maybe I should cry after every performance – I feel better already.' I smiled.

'Well, that's an idea,' he said. 'You really rose to the occasion, do you know that?'

I nodded. 'Thanks, Niall, do you really think so?'

He looked at me quizzically. 'Of course I do, haven't I just told you?'

'It's just, you know, in this business, everyone tells you that you're amazing and wonderful, and sometimes it can be hard to tell if they're being sincere, but I know I can rely on you to tell me the truth.'

'I know. It's the doctor in me.' He grinned. Then he looked around the room. 'All of this is completely over-whelming, don't you think?' He gestured to the tasteful cream leather sofa, huge bowls filled with fruit and pastries, and flat-screen TV mounted on the wall, the show running on it in the background.

'It seems a long way from the church loft in Glenvara and a nice cup of tea after Mass, that's for sure. I miss everyone, Niall. Sometimes I think I'm on a treadmill, and I just want to go home. But then I remember how lucky I am. I didn't even win the competition, and yet here I am, at Wembley Stadium.'

Niall took my hand in his and turned it over, running his thumb along my lifeline. 'It's a life-changing thing, all of this, but you don't have to go along with absolutely everything, Antonia. You can still say no, if you're tired or stressed.'

I shook my head. 'I can't say no to this,' I exclaimed. 'It's taken such an effort to get here that I feel I have to make the most of it, for everyone at home and for Mum. She'd be so proud of me, I know.'

'She'd be proud of you if you were washing dishes in a greasy spoon,' Niall said. 'You need to do it for yourself, nobody else, OK?'

I nodded. 'OK.'

'And remember our promise?'

'That this won't change either of us?' I laughed.

'It won't. Not inside.' He paused. 'I'm telling you the truth, Antonia. I think you're amazing, so amazing that I'll even let you sing a duet with that plonker, Damien.'

I burst out laughing, wiping the tears from my face with the tissue he'd given me. 'You're too kind.'

25

DAMIEN WAS HOLDING COURT, HIGH ON HIS PERFORMANCE that night, as the sexy young Irishman with the guitar. Our duet had been a success, earning a rare smile from Melanie, but I knew that he was really happy to have done so well solo. And I was happy for him too. He was a hard worker and a really talented songwriter, who just happened to be enjoying his five minutes. And who could blame him?

The after-party was typical of these things: hot, sweaty and overcrowded, full of self-conscious stars and hangers-on. There were groups of people clustered around the really famous performers, fetching them whatever they needed, throwing filthy looks to keep the groupies at bay. I felt like a complete impostor as I stood in a corner, clutching my glass of champagne. Niall had gone to the bar, and as I looked over I could see him deep in conversation with Damien. My heart skipped a beat. Please God, let them get on, I said to myself.

Suddenly, there was a presence at my side and a large man loomed over me, dressed all in black, an earpiece in his left ear, a pair of shades on his face, even in the nightclub, which was pitch dark.

'Miss Mayhew would like you to come over and say hello,' he murmured.

'*Alicia* Mayhew?' I squeaked, at which he glared at me and nodded imperceptibly. Obediently, I followed him over to a dimly lit corner, in which were huddled the usual crowd, Alicia Mayhew looking tiny in the middle of them.

When she saw me, she stood up. 'Toni!' She grinned, and extended her arms to me.

I realized that we were expected to embrace, and air-kissed her awkwardly. Her hair felt soft and clean and her face was just lovely, so pretty. And yet she looked so frail. She mustn't eat at all, I thought, wondering when someone would tell me it was time to lose a few pounds. I wasn't big, by any means, but in this business, normal just didn't cut it.

'Sit. Let's have some more champagne,' she suggested, moving over on the velvet banquette to make room for me. Magically, two glasses of champagne appeared on the table in front of us. 'I loved your cover. Elvis himself would have been proud.' She smiled.

'Thanks,' I said, wondering why I felt so tongue-tied. 'I love your songs,' I managed, thinking that it just sounded so lame. 'They're really so sophisticated, and yet uplifting at the same time.' Oh, God, it was getting worse.

She smiled again. 'Thanks, Toni. Maybe we should try working together some time. I'll get my people to talk to your people.'

I nodded dumbly. Who were my people? But then she shifted slightly in her seat and I realized that the conversation was over. Was I expected to get up and leave now? I supposed I was. 'Well, it was great meeting you, Alicia,' I said shyly, extending my hand this time. I could feel the tiny bones in her hand as she returned my handshake, and then I was making my way back across the room, looking frantically for Niall.

Eventually, I caught sight of him. He was sitting at a table, underneath a glittering disco ball, Damien beside him, and I didn't like the expression on his face. Oh, no. What had Damien said? He was capable of saying anything just to rile Niall. I'd better sort this out, I said to myself as I walked over to the table, pinning a bright smile on my face. 'Hi, guys, you'll never guess who I just met—'

'Hi, Toni!' Damien looked as if he was up to no good, and my stomach started fluttering. 'I was just filling Niall in on our little arrangement.' His voice was slurred, and I realized that he'd been drinking, or worse.

I tried to stay calm. 'Oh, really? And what's that?' I shot a glance at Niall, but he wouldn't catch my eye. My heart sank.

'Just, you know, that we're an item, so to speak.'

I shook my head and pretended not to understand.

'I mean, it's purely for the media, of course. A few shots of us kissing, leaving some nightclub or other. A bit of hand–holding, or maybe something more.' He winked lasciviously. And then he leaned towards Niall, wobbling slightly as he did so. 'But it's OK, you can have her the rest of the time . . .'

I was about to reply, to tell Damien to get lost, to reassure Niall that he was just winding him up, but I didn't get the chance. The next thing I knew, Niall's fist was connecting with Damien's chin and everything seemed to be in slow motion. There was a look of terror mixed with surprise on Damien's face as his head flipped back and he hit it against a stone pillar. It made a huge crack and I gasped in fright. 'Niall, you'll kill him.'

'That's the idea,' Niall said, clutching his fist, which he'd obviously hurt, as Damien leaned forward on the table, groaning loudly. And then two huge security guards were hauling Niall out of the club, with me following behind, tears streaming down my face. 'Niall, for goodness' sake, it's not true. You know what he's like . . .'

But I didn't have time to say anything further, because the two men bundled Niall out the door and on to the pavement, and then stood in front of the door, blocking my way. 'Best leave it, madam,' one of them said to me.

'But I have to see him,' I shrieked, feeling the panic rising in my chest.

There was a hand on my shoulder and I tried to shake it off, but the person was insistent. 'Toni, c'mon, let's go and sit down and calm down for a few minutes.' I turned around to see Karen.

'Oh, Karen, Niall hit Damien, and he's been thrown out and—'

'I know, I know,' she said soothingly, leading me away from the crowds and down the corridor, to a door marked 'Staff Only'.

'In here.' She ushered me into a tiny room about the size of a broom cupboard, and made me sit down on a hard plastic chair, while she busied herself making me a cup of tea. She said nothing at all until she'd handed me the steaming mug, along with a tissue. 'Your mascara.' She made a gesture towards her eyes.

I nodded and dabbed at my cheeks, before wailing, 'Karen, what am I going to do?'

She knelt down in front of me. 'Look at me, Toni. You are going to forget this happened. Damien is a plonker, a chancer who can't believe his luck that after years on the pub circuit, he's finally made it into the inner circle. And the pub circuit is exactly what he'll be doing a year from now. He knows it, and we know it. But until he does, he's going to act the eejit and try to milk every situation for maximum publicity. You've just got caught up in that.'

'But Niall—' I began.

She shot me an impatient look. 'Niall's a nice guy, Toni, but you don't need hassle right now. What you have to realize is that you are the one with the talent, and you can either waste it, throwing it away on Damien and your boyfriend who can't hold his temper, or you can become a real professional, who behaves impeccably at all times and who never invites even a moment's controversy. This . . .' She waved her hand at the door and the scene

307

outside. 'Is a one-off. We won't be seeing it again.'

I nodded silently. I knew she was right. If I was to stand any chance at all of lasting in this business, I couldn't be involved in nightclub fracas. As it was, it'd be all over the papers tomorrow morning.

As if reading my mind, Karen said, 'Now, I have Rebecca at Celtic working full-time to keep this out of the tabloids. It won't be page one, but all the showbiz pages will carry it, and it won't exactly get your career off to a flying start. We'll have to see what we can do, but in the meantime, I'll get Sharon to take you back to your hotel, via the back entrance, and we'll talk again in the morning. OK?'

I nodded once more, feeling like a naughty schoolgirl. There was silence again, before Karen spoke, and this time her voice was softer. 'Toni, it's not your fault. You're a lovely girl, but you're an innocent, who has a lot to learn about this business. Just stay out of trouble for a bit and let me take care of things, will you?'

You mean take care of my mess, I thought, as I allowed myself to be hustled from the office and out the back door of the club, where a limousine was waiting for me. Sharon shoved me in and slammed the door behind us, barking, 'Knightsbridge,' to the driver, who nodded and drove off.

'Thank God, no press,' she muttered as we pulled out of the lane behind the club and into the busy London traffic. I looked out the window at the lights of the Savoy Hotel, at the people thronging the pavements, at the gloomy outline of Green Park behind the ornate wrought-iron gates, and

I wondered how a performance at Wembley, the highlight of my professional life, could have ended in such a mess. Perhaps Karen was right. It was simpler to cut Niall out of my life if this was the way things were going to go. But it was so unfair, I thought. It wasn't Niall's fault, it was Damien's. He'd wound Niall up.

And then in my mind's eye I saw Damien's chin snap back as Niall's fist connected with it, and I knew. He could be moody, Niall, as I was well aware, but I'd never seen a look like that on his face before.

'How's Damien?' I ventured.

'Oh, he'll live . . . unfortunately.' Sharon grinned. 'He's such a little oik, even if he is cute.' She looked at me sympathetically. 'Look, I know he wound your boyfriend up—'

I interrupted her. 'Sharon, I don't mean to be rude, but Karen's already explained it to me. And she's right. It's not even the publicity, it's just that I can't concentrate on singing with all this . . . stuff going on.' As the words came out of my mouth, I realized that they were true. The only thing that really mattered to me was singing. Without it, well . . . it was singing that had got me through the last few months since Mum's death, it had saved me, had revealed to me things I didn't know about myself. But did I really have to sacrifice Niall into the bargain? The thought scared me more than I thought possible.

Sharon wisely said nothing, just patted my hand and looked out the window. The next twenty minutes were spent with her pointing out the sights to me, from Kensington

Palace to Sloane Street. 'The things you can buy here are just amazing,' she breathed, pointing out row after row of designer shops. 'Maybe we could cheer ourselves up with a little shopping at the end of the trip. There's space in the schedule, I think, after the meeting with Marc Davidson.'

I was only half-listening, but at the sound of that name, I turned my head. 'Isn't he a record-company executive? I think Karen mentioned him.'

'Yep, he's one of the best. A real sharp cookie with a great sense of the market. And he wants to see you. And Damien, for some unknown reason,' she muttered. 'But we'll stagger the meetings, Toni. Don't worry, you won't be running into Damien again.'

'It's not Damien I'm worried about,' I said, thinking suddenly of Maurice Prendergast. What would he have to say about Marc Davidson? I tried to remember Maurice's advice about not agreeing to anything until I'd consulted him first. But surely it wouldn't do any harm just to meet Marc Davidson? I didn't have to sign a contract.

I hardly opened my mouth for the rest of the journey, just managing to mutter goodbye and thanks to Sharon. I'm sure she thought I was rude, but I felt so upset because of what had happened after the show. All I wanted was to hide. I stumbled into the lift and out again, fumbling for my hotel swipe card as I did so. Once in my room, I leaned against the door, sliding to the floor, where I sat for a while, feeling the silence envelop me. After that evening, it was a balm to my soul.

And then my phone bleeped and my heart started racing. I debated for a while whether to open the message, knowing who it was from. Eventually, I rummaged in my tiny bag, pulling out the handset, the centre button flashing. In the dark, I fumbled around for the 'read' button.

'I'm sorry. I love you. Niall xx.'

I leaned my head back against the door and cried my heart out.

26

I DIDN'T SLEEP MUCH THAT NIGHT, TOSSING AND TURNING, my mind spinning, reliving every moment of the previous evening, until it was all a huge jumble in my head: Niall, Mum, Amanda, the show, everything. Eventually, I gave up on sleep and got up to look out my hotel window. The hotel was on a quiet Knightsbridge Street, all tall white buildings and swanky cars – London really was amazing – but all I could think was that I was going backwards somehow. Sure, I was growing stronger, and more confident as a person, but what good was that when I couldn't understand the world around me? How on earth had I not seen the real Amanda? And not noticed how jealous she was of me? I'd thought she was a great friend, and all the time she was sitting at home, composing nasty text messages. And then Niall – how had I never noticed his temper? He'd always seemed so . . . controlled. Maybe that was the problem. He was too controlled.

I sighed. It was as if I'd been living in a convent all of these years, even after I'd left the orphanage. It would have been easy to blame Mum and Dad, to say that they'd sheltered me too much, but in fact, I knew that I was partly to blame. I'd hidden away in Glenvara, happy to be in the background, to look after Mum and to let life pass me by.

But now it was different. I'd been given a chance in a life-time. I owed it to Mum to make the best of it, no matter how hard it was. I owed it to myself. And so, as I stood, looking at the dawn break over London, I resolved that from now on, the singing would be the star, and that I'd focus all my energies on making the most of this opportunity. That was what I really wanted, and nothing came without a sacrifice, did it?

It was funny – my decision not to text Niall back, to try to move on, made me stronger. With every day that passed on the London trip, I missed him more than I thought possible, but I also found that I was capable of more than I'd imagined, fielding all the press conferences and photocalls that came with the British show with as much aplomb as I could muster. And if I felt lonelier than I'd ever been in my life, longing for home and my friends around me, I didn't let on.

Karen approved. 'You've grown up,' she said to me after one tough encounter with a journalist.

He'd asked me about the nightclub, of course, but I'd pulled myself together and smiled at him. 'That's all in the past. I'm focusing on my music now, and on making the most of this great opportunity I've been given.' I'd cringed as I'd said the words, but he'd seemed to be convinced, nodding and jotting them down on a pad.

He'd even smiled at me. 'Good luck.'

'God, you charmed him.' Karen was pleased, I could tell.

'Thanks, Karen. I'm trying,' I said to her. Even though my heart feels as if it's been broken into a million pieces.

My meeting with Marc Davidson was scheduled for the last full day of my London trip. Karen was jubilant at having got 'anywhere near' him. 'You've no idea, Toni, how big this guy is. He can make your career.' She insisted on taking me to one of the best hair salons in London for a new cut. 'Something sexy and sophisticated. Less country girl,' she explained to the hairdresser, an intimidatingly trendy young girl with fabulous blonde hair, called Wendi.

Wendi looked at me dubiously, running a comb through my hair, which had grown long and curly again. 'Hmm – it's beautiful. But it's very . . . thick.' She announced diplomatically.

I nodded. My hair was my pride and joy, and I prayed that she wouldn't want to give me anything too radical.

'How about a crop?' She looked at me. 'They're all the rage at the moment, and it'd really work with that lovely little face of yours.'

Oh, God. I wouldn't have a hair left on my head, I thought, fingering my thick curls.

'I was thinking of a few layers.' I laughed.

She looked at me again. 'Are you a singer?'

'Yes, I am.'

'Well, it depends on what your market is, but don't you want to look a little less . . . middle-aged?'

'Middle-aged?' I squeaked. I looked at myself in the mirror. Did I look middle-aged? Well, I supposed it was a little conservative, having waves of golden brown to my waist. Maybe I could try something new. And before I could think twice about it, I heard myself say, 'Go ahead.'

She looked at me and her jaw dropped. 'Are you serious?'

'Take it all off,' I insisted. 'I need a complete change of look.' As I said the words, I knew that I was right. I needed a whole new me to match my new direction in life. I needed to shed the old Antonia and be Toni.

Karen had popped out for coffee, and when she came back, clutching two cardboard cups of cappuccino, she screamed so loudly the entire salon turned in our direction. 'What the hell are you doing?'

'Me?' I said, unable to turn my head in her direction, because Wendi was in mid-snip. 'I'm having a haircut.'

'I can see that. I meant a trim, a bit of shape, not a Buddhist-monk job. Toni, for goodness' sake! The photo work we've done will be useless now.'

'Well, they can do new ones.' I stuck my chin out, determined. 'It'll give them all the more reason to take my photo now, won't it?'

'You really have changed,' Karen said, giving me a faint smile and handing me my coffee.

I didn't answer. I had changed, she was right. I looked at myself in the mirror, my golden-brown hair a close crop

315

around my head, making my eyes look huge, and I didn't even recognize myself. A new look for a new life, Toni, I told myself, unable to understand why I suddenly felt so sad.

My new haircut demanded a whole new wardrobe, of course. 'Less pageant queen, and more foxy chick,' as Karen said grimly, dragging me along to the boutiques on Sloane Street. 'What Simon at Celtic will say to this, I don't know,' she muttered.

'He'll be thrilled at the fresh publicity,' I said. 'And I'm paying for these myself, Karen.' I shot her a warning look as she rummaged in her handbag. 'I can afford it, and I want to buy them.' I hadn't made any money from the show yet, in spite of all the predictions, which was understandable considering all the money Celtic was spending on me, but my inheritance meant that I didn't really have to struggle. I was lucky, I knew.

My tone brooked no objection, and so she just sighed dramatically and said, 'Oh, well, I suppose I'd better get into the vibe here,' and started pulling at the rails.

Two hours and much laughter later, I had a look to match my cut, much younger and funkier. 'My God,' I said, gazing at myself in the mirror. 'I look about nineteen.'

'That's what I'm afraid of, Toni. It's not the nation's sweetheart look that won you all those votes. Take it easy, will you?'

I suddenly felt sorry for putting her through this. She'd done nothing but support me and here I was, giving her a hard time.

'Look, I promise I'll grow it out, Karen. It's just for this meeting with Marc Davidson. I don't want to resemble a middle-aged beauty queen. I can't think that he'd want to take me on looking like that.'

She nodded. 'You have a point, I suppose. But for God's sake, when you get back home to Dublin, tone it down a bit, will you? You won't have a fan left.'

'I will, Karen. I promise.'

27

THE FUNNY THING WAS, AFTER ALL THE FUSS, I TOOK ONE
GLANCE at Marc Davidson and knew that I didn't like him.
He looked good, sure, like a lot of people in this business,
who had the money to dress well and have an expensive haircut: in his case a messy half-Mohawk that was too young for
him. He had an all-over tan, and when he smiled his teeth
were blindingly white.

'Toni, I've been dying to meet you,' he gushed, standing
up as I entered his office, on the twenty-second floor of the
Samroy Record Company building in the City. The views
were astonishing: of St Paul's Cathedral and the brown swirl
of the Thames, all the way down to Tower Bridge. It was
breathtaking.

'You are just exquisite,' he said as he came around his
huge black desk and leaned in for a kiss, placing a hand in
the small of my back. I resisted the urge to wriggle from his
grasp, turning my head so the kiss landed on my jaw. He
stood back then, and gave me a penetrating look, as if he
could see into my soul. 'Utterly exquisite,' he repeated, in a
way which made me cringe inside.

He didn't greet Sharon at all, merely throwing her a look. I wanted to introduce her, but didn't have the nerve. Not for the first time, I wished Karen was there, but she'd been taken ill that morning. 'It's all the stress,' she'd managed to joke down the phone to me, her voice muffled with the symptoms of a cold. 'Now, don't sign anything,' she'd warned me. 'Just go and see what he has to offer and we'll discuss it, OK? And be careful, will you? He has a bit of a reputation.' Looking at him now, I could see why.

'Sit,' he gestured, going around his desk and sitting in his outsize chair again. I pulled out one of the chairs, a heavy straight-backed one covered in cream damask, which made a loud scraping sound along the floor. Mortified, I perched on the edge of it.

'You seem nervous.' He smiled.

'I am a bit,' I admitted. 'I've never met a record-company executive before.' Oh, God, I sounded so naïve.

'Well, relax, Toni. You're among friends.' And he smiled, a smile which didn't reach his eyes. The 'friends' he was talking about were a beautiful thin Chinese woman in skinny jeans and a white fringed T-shirt, who was tapping at a mobile phone, and who hadn't looked up since we'd come into the room, and another man, who, although he was sitting beside Marc, made no move to introduce himself. If I was among friends, it sure didn't feel like it, I thought. But maybe that was just after the week I'd had; I was too paranoid. This could be an opportunity, Toni, don't muck it up, I thought.

'Well, we've seen the tapes from the Irish talent show.' He smiled patronizingly, as if it was a local agricultural show he was talking about. 'And I can see you've got talent, but the material . . . well, it's only right for the grannies, to be honest. It might work where you come from.' He grinned. 'But for this market, we need something funkier. I like your cut, by the way.' He nodded at my crop and I blushed. 'I mean, you *look* right, but the songs . . . well, you need something, that's for sure. What do you think, Nick?' He turned to the silent man beside him, who nodded, but said nothing. Maybe he couldn't speak, I thought, fighting the urge to giggle. I could feel the hysteria mounting, and prayed that I wouldn't burst out laughing from sheer nerves.

'What kind of songs did you have in mind?' I ventured.

He gave me the kind of smile which told me that I wasn't supposed to have spoken, but his reply was polite enough. 'I'm thinking less Leona Lewis and more . . . Alicia Mayhew.'

'I love her!' I exclaimed.

'Well, great.' He laughed. 'Tell you what, I'll have a little think about material in that area.'

'Great . . .' I began.

'And I'll be in touch, OK?'

'OK . . .' I said doubtfully, wondering if this was it. There was a rustle around me as everyone got to their feet, and I had to conclude that it was.

'Thanks for stopping by, Toni.' Marc didn't kiss me this time, thank God, just extended a hand. It felt moist to the touch, and my stomach turned.

'Sure.' I gulped. 'Thanks for seeing me.'

'Pleasure. Mai, will you show the girls out?' The thin girl moved for the first time, still not looking up from her phone, and opened the door, which she then closed behind us without another word.

Sharon and I travelled down in the lift in complete silence. We didn't speak until we had walked through the vast marble foyer and out of the revolving doors.

'What the hell was that all about?' I said once we were safely outside in the street.

'I think he likes you.' Sharon grinned.

'That's him "liking me"?' I said.

'You betcha. He's a real cold fish, Marc Davidson, but he knows his stuff. Just wait and see. Now, I really fancy a fry-up, after all this rabbit food I've been eating. How about you?'

'You're on!' After my meeting with Marc, I couldn't think of anything nicer than to tuck into bacon, egg and sausage. I remembered Betty's legendary Sunday morning fry-ups after Mass. Every once in a while, she'd invite the choir over for a huge feast of unhealthy food, washed down with lashings of hot tea.

I stood there for a moment on the pavement in London, longing for home and for a bit of chat and a laugh with the gang from the choir. I wondered how Sister Monica was. She wasn't a texter, and I hadn't heard from her since the final – Mum would kill me, I thought, if she knew that. After everything Sister Monica had done. I'd ring her as soon as I got home, I told myself. Home, where I suddenly wanted to be more than anywhere else in the world.

I only saw the card when I got back to the hotel that afternoon. I wondered how I hadn't noticed it before. It was plain white, expensive, with 'Marc Davidson', written in neat black ink in the middle, and an address in Kensington. He'd scribbled a note on the back: 'A party at mine tonight. You might meet some interesting people. Marc xx.'

I sat down on the bed and stared at the card. He must have slipped it into my bag, I thought, when we were saying goodbye at the office. And yet, he hardly knew me, so why the invitation? I was in a quandary. If I went, I'd be alone: Karen was sick with a cold, and I didn't dare ask Sharon because she was having her first night off in months with her boyfriend. Well, I'd promised myself I'd seize every opportunity, I reasoned, and there were bound to be all kinds of interesting people there. If I was serious about having a singing career, I couldn't hide any more. Right, I decided, getting up from my bed and sorting through the outfits I'd bought on Sloane Street, I *was* going. And I was going to knock him dead.

Eventually, I decided on a black tuxedo jacket with a sharp, knee-length pencil skirt. It looked modest and businesslike, yet trendy at the same time. I applied just a few touches of make-up – mascara and some lipgloss – and then stared at myself in the mirror. With my sleek new haircut, I hardly recognized myself. 'Who are you?' I said out loud in the gloom.

It took me a while to find Marc Davidson's house. Even the taxi driver struggled to locate the tiny back street in Kensington, taking several wrong turns before finding it. 'Need to do my knowledge all over again, love,' he joked. Once he'd heard my accent, he'd kept me entertained with a stream of Irish jokes, and I'd found myself relaxing, so by the time he let me off on a dark corner, I felt almost carefree. I tottered unsteadily in my high heels down a lane which had no streetlights, thinking that there couldn't possibly be anyone living in it. It felt spooky, deserted. Maybe the card had been a hoax. For a second, I felt like turning back, but I forced myself to go on, until I spotted the outline of a building a little further on. A solid block of shiny grey concrete with tiny windows slashed in the side, it looked like a bunker. Just right for Marc Davidson. I spent another few minutes trying to locate the bell, rummaging around in my handbag for my mobile phone and cursing myself for my stupidity, until eventually the door just clicked open. Startled, I stood there for a minute, until a voice said, out of the darkness, 'CCTV.'

I jumped and let out a little scream. There was a small laugh and Marc Davidson appeared out of the gloom. 'I'm sorry to have startled you, Toni. I thought I'd better come down to you. It's very hard to get in here.'

He seemed warmer than he had that morning, and I allowed myself to relax and return his kiss in greeting.

'Great that you could come. You alone?'

I nodded, wishing that I wasn't, that I'd brought some-body with me, anybody. I could feel the colour rising to my cheeks as I followed him up a narrow set of stairs, in the shiniest marble, and in through a black hall door into the whitest, most modern home I'd ever seen. Every surface seemed to gleam under the bright lights in a way which made my eyes hurt. He led me into a vast open space, furnished in white, grey and cream, at the end of which crackled a fire in an open grate. There was nothing on display on the walls except one large and expensive-looking modern painting. The room was gorgeous, but it didn't feel as if anyone lived there. It was more like a corporate headquarters than a home, I thought.

'Wow, this is amazing,' I managed, craning my neck for any sign of the other partygoers. 'Where is everyone?'

'Oh, they'll be along soon. There's a party on in town for Alicia. I thought we could have a chat first.'

'Oh. OK,' I said, wondering if I could make an excuse and leave. I didn't like this one little bit.

'Champagne?' he offered.

Did anyone drink tea in this business? I wondered. 'Water would be just great, thanks.'

He laughed, flashing those teeth. 'You can't come to a party and drink *water*.'

'Oh, right, then. Well, just a little drop of champagne, thanks.'

He smiled and I expected him to go into the kitchen and

fetch a couple of glasses, but instead he sat down on the grey suede sofa and stretched an arm along it, until it was just inches away from my shoulder. Instinctively, I moved, and he gave me a sly smile. 'No need to be nervous.'

'I'm not,' I said, with more bravado than I felt. We waited for a few moments in silence, and I was wondering what on earth to say, when the door opened and a man, dressed in a white jacket and black trousers, entered with a drinks trolley. He was a uniformed servant – I'd thought no one had them any more.

'Thanks, Sven.' Marc accepted the two glasses of chilled champagne, handing one of them to me. 'I'll give you a call when we need anything further.'

The man nodded silently and disappeared.

I clutched my glass of champagne and took a sip. The bubbles popped and pinged on my tongue. Champagne was great, I thought. I could get used to it. 'It's lovely,' I managed.

'Good.' Marc put his glass down on the plate–glass coffee table. I noticed he hadn't taken a sip.

'So, Marc, thanks for inviting me,' I began, trying to sound businesslike. 'I really appreciate the opportunity . . .'

To my astonishment, he just laughed. 'Slow down, Irish girl. We can get to the business bit later. Just relax. Enjoy your champagne.'

I took another sip, more of a gulp, and felt it settle in my stomach. I really needed to get out of here. 'Marc, this is lovely, but I have to be somewhere.'

'Oh? What could possibly be more fascinating than being here?' He grinned at me in a way which made me feel uneasy. Seeing my expression, he said, 'Just joking. I really did ask you here to discuss your career. So tell me about it.' He looked at me expectantly, as if I was the most interesting person in the world.

Here goes, I thought. 'Well, I'm an amateur, really. I've no formal training or anything, apart from the church choir at home. Eithne's taught me everything: how to interpret the songs, which ones suit my voice, that kind of thing.'

He nodded, but I could tell he wasn't really listening. 'This . . . Eithne.' The way he said it made it sound like 'Etnee', and I fought the desire to laugh, in spite of the situation. 'Who is she?'

'The choir leader.'

'Ah,' he said, and I could see he was stifling a smile. 'So, the only training you've had is from the local choir mistress.'

'Well, yes,' I answered, thinking that it sounded so dumb the way he put it.

He leaned back on the grey sofa and stretched his arm along the back, until it was uncomfortably close to my shoulder. 'It's a really quaint story, Toni, country girl who makes the big time. I understand that you're quite the star in Ireland.'

'Well, I suppose so,' I said, thinking of all the fans who lined up outside the stadium in Dublin to say hello and get an autograph, of how hard they cheered as I made my way into the rehearsal room, of just how warm and kind people

326

were, always wishing me the best. I suddenly felt lonelier than I'd ever been before. I want to go home, I thought. I took another sip of champagne and realized that my glass was almost empty. I hadn't eaten since the fry that morning, and with my empty stomach I began to feel a little bit woozy. I opened my mouth to say something, but no words came out.

'I'm just wondering how hungry you are for success. I mean, you seem a nice girl and everything, but I'm not sensing a burning ambition.'

'Oh, I am ambitious,' I said, more loudly than I'd intended. 'There's nothing I want more than to record and do concerts and sing. It's the only thing that I really, truly enjoy.'

Marc smiled that wolfish smile again. 'Easy, tiger,' he joked. 'Seriously, it's great that you have ambition, because that's really what counts in this business. Talented singers are ten a penny, but drive . . . that's what separates the men from the boys . . . or the women from the girls,' he said. 'Now you . . . I think you need some original songwriting and a fresher image. That middle-aged market is saturated now . . .' He leaned forward in his seat, and before I could do anything he reached out and touched my hair, just above my ear. 'You have a bit sticking out . . . there, that's better.'

Instinctively, I edged away, and he said softly, 'There's nothing to be afraid of, you know. We're just chatting.' And he leaned back in his seat, for all the world as if that's what we really were doing.

I swallowed nervously and put my glass down on the

table. When I stood up, my legs felt wobbly, my head swimming. 'Thanks for the champagne, Marc. It was great. But Karen's meeting me for a drink later, so I'll have to go. Maybe we can chat another time?' I tried to keep my tone steady.

'How about now?' he said, reaching up and grabbing my hand. 'Karen won't mind. She knows how important your career is.' And he pulled me gently back down on to the sofa.

I tried to pull my hand away, but his was clamped over mine. I began to panic. 'Marc, you're hurting my hand.'

'I thought you'd like a little pain.' He smiled thinly, leaning towards me and grabbing my chin in his free hand, squeezing it tightly. 'Isn't that what you all like, a little pain?'

'Ow, you're hurting me,' I said, but he wouldn't stop, and then he was pushing my head back on to the sofa, and then he was on top of me, pressing me down into the expensive suede fabric. I tried to scream, but his hand was clamped over my mouth.

'C'mon, Toni, why are you here, really? It's not for a record chat, that's for sure.' He was looming over me now, my chin still in his vice-like grip, his breath hot on my cheek. And then he was trying to kiss me, his lips burning into mine as I tried to turn my head away. I struggled to break free, but he was too heavy, too strong. Oh, God, I thought, I'm going to have to lie here, to give into him. But then he was struggling with my clothes, trying to pull my top down with one hand while he stuck the other up under

328

the hem of my skirt, making hideous snorting noises, like a pig, in my ear, and I don't know where I got the strength from, but I thought: No! And I lifted my knee up as hard as I could, pushing it into his groin with as much force as I could muster.

He let out a roar. 'Jesus fucking Christ!' and made to grab me again, but I'd managed to push him aside by kicking my heel repeatedly against his shin. 'You bitch,' he said, making to grab my hair, but I had the momentum now, and managed to push myself off the sofa and on to the floor, scrabbling furiously to push myself to a standing position. He lunged forward again, but I swung out with my fist and my ring caught his eye. 'Oww, oww, Jesus, wait till I get you!' he roared.

But I was too quick for him, running to the door and fumbling with it. I cursed the modern door with its hidden catch, pressing and pushing until at last it opened. Why hasn't he caught me? I wondered, unable to stop myself glancing back as I closed the living-room door behind me. But he was just lying on the sofa, clothes dishevelled, a hand over his eye, muttering 'Jesus Christ' over and over again. Maybe I've really hurt him, I thought, as I let the door swing behind me with a bang and ran as fast as I could.

I ran so fast down the cobbled lane that one of my heels snapped, and I had to take the shoe off, breaking into a half-run, half-trot as I did so. Eventually, I gave up and threw both shoes behind me, running in my bare feet around the corner and into the busy street. I stood at the corner, gasping and sobbing, clutching the edge of the wall, feeling my stomach heave. It's OK, it's OK, I kept saying to myself. He won't come after you here. Not on a busy street.

People were passing me by, staring at me, before walking on. God, nobody cares, I thought. I could be half-dead and no one would even ask if I was OK. I decided to ring Karen. I needed to talk to someone. But then I realized, to my horror, that I'd left my handbag back . . . there, in that place. I burst into tears, sobs racking my body. I had to wipe my nose with my hands because I had no tissue. I looked around for any familiar landmark, and then I remembered that I was in London, for God's sake. I had no clue where I was.

I started walking, the pavement damp and cold under my feet, tears streaming down my cheeks. I just want to go home, I just want to go home, I kept repeating to myself. I scanned the faces of the other people thronging the pavement, hoping desperately that someone would come to my aid, but I didn't dare ask for help. Eventually, I saw a pleasant-looking middle-aged woman coming towards me. 'Excuse me,' I said. 'I need to find my way back to the Knightsbridge Hotel.'

She looked at me doubtfully, obviously weighing up whether to talk to me, before saying politely, 'Well, it's quite a walk . . .'

'That's OK,' I managed. 'I feel like walking.' And I attempted a smile, which must have appeared crazed to her. I was sure I looked a complete mess.

'Right, well, if you follow this road for the next mile or so, you'll come to Brompton Road, and then you'll need to take a left . . .' the woman went on giving me instructions, for all the world as if I was a lost tourist, and I smiled, nodding and thanking her for her time.

I walked and walked, in a complete daze, through the streets of London, past shops and taxis and Tube stations, until at last, I spotted a familiar landmark – a row of shops that I knew were near to my hotel. I walked on, my feet sore and bruised, my tongue dry, my chin sore from where it had been grabbed – I tried not to think of Marc looming over me, pushing me down, using his strength to defeat me. I was free, I thought. I'd escaped.

I walked through the hotel doors and across the lobby, feeling suddenly wobbly, as if I might faint. Out of the corner of my eye, I could see the receptionist look up from her desk and gasp. 'Miss Trent, are you OK?'

I nodded, feeling too traumatized to respond, until I realized that I'd need my room key. I went over to the desk and swayed there, unsteadily, until the receptionist, who had the name 'Samira' written on her uniform, came around the desk and took hold of me. 'Here, take it easy, just lean on me.'

I didn't even manage to say thanks, just rested against her. Eventually, I said, 'I need a drink of water.'

'Of course, of course,' she said. 'Let's go and sit down over here, shall we?'

She was leading me to one of the comfy sofas in the lobby, but I shouted, 'No! I want to go to my room. Please.'

'OK,' she said soothingly, sensing my distress. 'Just let me get someone to cover for me. John,' she yelled across the lobby.

A tall man emerged from the office behind reception, darted me a look, and decided not to ask the question which was obviously on his lips.

'Can you take over for a sec?' Samira said to him. 'I just need to see Miss Trent up to her room.'

At this, he gave me a knowing look. Bet he thinks I've just had a few too many, I thought. If only he knew. 'I'm sorry, I just can't bear to sit in public like this—' I tried to explain.

Samira interrupted me, patting me on the arm and shushing me gently. 'Take it easy. It's fine. Let's just go upstairs, shall we?' she said soothingly, leading me towards the lift. When we were both inside, I caught a glimpse of myself in the mirrored wall and nearly screamed in fright. My mascara had run down my face in deep, black rivers, my lipstick was smeared around my mouth and my top had a large rip at the neck. I looked down at my feet, which were black with dirt and covered in scratches. I glanced at Samira and saw that she was trying to hide her alarm. At that moment, she felt like my only friend.

The bell pinged for my floor and I jumped. 'It's OK,' Samira soothed. 'Let's go to your room and we'll have a nice cup of tea.'

A cup of tea, the solution to all ills. I allowed myself to

be led to my room, Samira slotting my card into the door handle and standing to one side to let me pass.

'Would you like me to come in?' she asked.

I nodded silently, and she followed me into the room, drawing the curtains and switching on the low bedside light, before guiding me on to the bed. She then filled the kettle, flicking on the switch, before sitting gingerly beside me. I was grateful that she never once asked me how I'd ended up in such a state.

She took a deep breath. 'Miss Trent. I don't mean to pry, but should I call the police?'

I sat bolt upright on the bed. 'No, please, no. Don't call them, don't.' Panicking, I looked around for the telephone. 'I need to ring Karen, she'll know what to do.'

Samira shifted uneasily on the bed, then got up and came over to me, placing an arm around my shoulders. 'Whatever's happened, Miss Trent, I can help you. You won't be alone.'

At that, I cried, great big sobs, and tears poured down my cheeks. 'There, there,' Samira soothed.

'But I am alone,' I wailed. 'This is why this happened to me, because I'm alone and I've no one, and everyone else is at home in Glenvara, and I just want to go back there now . . .' I rambled.

I could see Samira didn't understand what I meant, but wisely she just nodded her head. 'Can I phone this . . . Karen for you?'

I looked up and managed a half-smile. 'That'd be great.'

But then I remembered that her number was programmed into my mobile, which I'd left . . . in that place. 'Oh no, I've lost it,' I said, my hands covering my face.

'Not to worry,' Samira said calmly. 'If you've rung her from your room, we'll have a record of the number on our computer. Let me just ring down and get it for you.'

Thank God for Samira. My hand was shaking as I punched in Karen's number. 'Please pick up. Please,' I muttered, but it went straight to voicemail. Only when I got her cheery message did I put my head in my hands and sob my heart out. I cried so long and so hard I thought I'd burst.

'Oh, dear,' I could hear Samira's voice in the background. 'Are you sure I can't call the police? You seem so distressed, Miss Trent.'

'No, no!' I screamed so loudly that she jumped back on the bed and put her hands up, as if in defence. 'OK. OK. But please let me get you some help, you look really unwell.'

I shook my head, adamant. 'No, I just want to have a bath and sleep.'

She looked at me for a long time. 'Are you sure?'

'Yes,' I said, hugging myself because I suddenly felt cold. 'Yes, I am. Thanks, Samira. Thanks for everything.'

She hesitated for a moment. 'Well . . . I don't want to leave you alone . . .'

I tried a smile, to reassure her that I was just fine. 'Thanks, Samira, what I really need now is a long soak.'

'Well, if you need anything, just call. I'll be on all night.'

'Thanks, Samira, I really can't thank you enough.' I

practically pushed her out the door, promising to call down if I needed her. I almost felt bad shoving her like that, after everything she'd done, but I needed to be by myself. And then I sprinted into the bathroom and ran the hot tap until the room filled with steam, pulling my tuxedo jacket off so hard that two of the buttons flew off, and hurling it into a corner along with my skirt, top and underwear. And then I jumped into the water, almost screaming at the heat. It was a scalding, pure heat that made me forget everything for a moment as I sank down into it, holding my nose to submerge, until at last I felt safe. I held my breath for as long as I could and then came up, gulping for air. I felt strong enough then to reach for the soap and begin to scrub and scrub, washing away all traces of that man, until I could scrub no more. I pulled the plug and crawled out of the bath, my limbs suddenly like lead, my head feeling as if it was too heavy for my shoulders. I barely pulled on a bathrobe before collapsing on the bed, my mind suddenly, blissfully blank.

28

I BLINKED IN THE HARSH SUNLIGHT, PULLING MYSELF UP ON my elbows. I turned to check my bedside clock for the time and then screamed. There was someone sitting on the bed.

'Oh, God, Karen, it's you! How on earth did you get in? What time is it?'

'The receptionist rang me first thing this morning, before her shift ended, and it's half past nine.' Karen's voice sounded muffled because of her cold.

'Oh, no, no, no.' I lay back down on the pillows, the memory of the previous night hitting me like a tidal wave. I felt the suede of the sofa against my cheek, Marc's hand on my neck, my jaw, the other one scrabbling around at the bottom of my skirt . . .

I must have looked terrified, because Karen leaned towards me and said, 'Toni, what's wrong? The receptionist said you turned up last night in a very bad state and she practically had to carry you up the stairs.' I could tell that she was irritated, thought I'd been out on the razz. 'When she told me that, I called your mobile, and it rang and rang. Where the hell were you?'

At her tone, the tears came again, streaming down my face. I couldn't do anything except just cry. 'Oh, pet, what's the matter? You're just stressed, that's all . . .' Karen's tone was kinder now, but I shook my head and gulped, huge sobs racking my body. I couldn't speak, couldn't open my mouth to tell her, because I felt so stupid. I knew she'd think I was even more of a fool, a liability.

'C'mon, Toni, tell me,' Karen pressed. 'You're scaring me now.'

I took a deep breath and blurted it all out, closing my eyes when memories of the night before became too strong. As I spoke, it was as if I was reliving everything, frame by frame. Tears poured down my face and I found myself clutching my robe tighter around my neck.

Karen listened in silence, her mouth hanging open, until I got to the bit where I tried to escape.

'How did you get away from him?' she asked.

'Well, I kicked him in the . . . you know, privates, and I bashed his eye, I think, and then he let go and I managed to make a run for it.'

At this, she gave a thin smile. 'You should press charges, Toni. You have to. Bastards like that need to be stopped.'

I shook my head. 'I just want to go back to Glenvara, Karen, that's all . . .'

'You can't let people like him win, Toni. Think of all the other girls in your position. I'm sure he's done it to them, and he'll do it again.'

'And I stand absolutely no chance of working in this

industry again if I say anything . . .' I snapped back at her. 'Please, Karen, will you just leave it?' At that moment, I just didn't have the strength. The very thought of taking any kind of action made me feel panicky, my stomach churning. I clutched a hand to my throat, which felt constricted and tight.

Karen looked at me and her features softened. 'I'm sorry, Toni, I'm pushing you. Look, take your time, and if you want to do anything . . . well, I'll support you a hundred per cent.'

I shook my head. 'Karen, there were no witnesses, there's nothing I can do.'

'Oh, I don't know, it's a small industry. Word gets out about these things. But keeping silent . . . well, it just allows people like Marc Davidson to continue to get away with it.'

I knew that she was right, that I had to be strong and stand up to him, if not for my sake, for other girls who might fall into the same trap. Just not now, I told myself. Now, I wasn't strong enough.

'At least you have the consolation that you injured the little shit. Hope he never walks again,' she muttered.

I managed a watery smile.

'So, what do you want to do now?' she asked.

I knew that she'd judge me, but I took a deep breath and said, 'I want to go home. Now. This morning.'

She looked at me and smiled, taking my hand in hers and squeezing it tight. 'OK, then, we'll do that.' And she pulled out her iPhone and began tapping the screen. 'I'll put a stop on that magazine photoshoot, it's not essential, and I'll rebook our flights . . .' she muttered to herself as she got to work.

I let her do her job and lay back on the pillow, closing my eyes, feeling myself relax. And then I was back in that room, feeling his weight pressing me down. I sat bolt upright in the bed, my forehead clammy.

'OK?' Karen said.

'OK,' I answered. Only, of course I wasn't. I wondered how the last few weeks had come to this. How the euphoria of singing to all those people had been replaced by feelings of depression and terror. I wondered how on earth I'd ended up in a place where people could come across me in a complete state on the street and not ask me a single question – like how I was? Or what had happened? In Glenvara, the entire village would have come to my rescue, and the gardaí would have been called, and I'd have been taken into someone's home for a nice cup of tea. I needed to get out of this place, I thought, as soon as I possibly could. I needed to get home to Sister Monica and Betty and Bridget and all my friends in Glenvara, and never come back.

'Right, that's done. We'll leave at midday.'

I nodded. 'Thanks, Karen. Thanks for everything.'

'You're welcome. I'm sorry this happened to you, Toni. Really sorry. But don't let it defeat you. You'll come back stronger, I promise.'

'I know,' I said. 'But now, the only thing I can think about is going back to Ireland.'

29

AS SOON AS I ARRIVED IN GLENVARA, I KNEW I'D DONE THE right thing. As the taxi rolled down the main street, past the post office and the church and the primary school where I'd spent five happy years, I felt my heart lift for the first time in weeks. I was safe at last. The nightmare of the last few days didn't seem as vivid here. I got out of the taxi, drinking in the soft evening air, and looked around me, at the familiar street with its sweet little houses. My front garden looked surprisingly neat, and I realized that Betty must have been working hard to keep it tidy while I was away. I felt a surge of love and sheer relief. I was home.

The first person I rang when I got in the door was Sister Monica. I just wanted to hear her comforting voice. She'd been like a mother to me all those years ago, and I suppose I needed her again, now that Mum was no longer here. If the last few weeks had proved anything to me, it was that I couldn't manage alone. I'd thought I could, that I was a big girl, as Mum used to say, but I wasn't. I was still Miss Mouse, and I'd learned that in the most painful way.

'Hello?' As soon as I heard her voice, I felt a jolt. Because

I realized I really wanted to speak to Mum. To tell her what had happened to me in London, and to have her give me a hug and tell me it'd all be all right and that we'd tackle it together. I've let you down, Mum, I thought. And I couldn't possibly tell Sister Monica what had really happened, no matter how close we were. I just knew she wouldn't understand. She was a *nun*, for goodness' sake.

'Antonia,' Sister Monica exclaimed. 'I thought you were too famous altogether to be ringing me.'

I managed a laugh. 'I'm sorry, Sister. It's just been so crazy for the past few weeks. I've hardly had a moment—'

'Ah, sure, will you stop?' she interrupted me. 'I'm only teasing you. How's life in the fast lane? Tell me everything. I'm starved of any excitement in this place.' I felt like laughing. Sister Monica was always complaining about the convent – how boring and crotchety all the other nuns were: 'Old bags, like myself,' she'd joke – but I knew she loved it, that she was truly happy there with all the 'girls' around her.

I managed to make it all sound just as she'd expect. Glamorous, fun. I told her about the Stadium and how it felt singing in front of thousands of people, and about the after-show party. 'Alicia Mayhew came up and congratulated me. Can you imagine? *Me?* And she said she wanted us to work together.' I laughed.

'Don't knock yourself, pet. With your talent, people will be queueing up to collaborate with you, or whatever it is they call it,' she said.

'Thanks, Sister,' I said. In truth, until that moment, I'd

forgotten all about Alicia's offer. I suppose I should have done something about it, but I had no idea how to do so, and doubted she'd be asking me again any time soon. And even the thought of going back to see her made me feel physically sick.

'You sound a bit . . . low-key, Antonia . . .' Sister Monica's tone was gently enquiring, the way it always was when she was trying to draw me out.

'It's nothing, Sister, it's just been a really hectic few weeks.'

There was a long pause. 'Is there anything else?'

'No, why?'

'Antonia, I understand that it's a tough world, the one you've chosen,' she said. 'It can take its toll. Don't be afraid to ask for help and support if you need it.'

Sometimes it felt as if I'd done nothing but ask for help and support, I thought. And the one time I hadn't, look what had happened. 'Thanks, Sister, if I need help, you'll be the first I'll ask. I promise.'

'Good. I hope so, pet. You can always talk to me, you know that.'

I thanked her and put down the phone and wondered, not for the first time, if she was psychic. If she had an instinct for knowing when I was upset or down. But then, I supposed, after Mum, she knew me better than anyone.

I was ashamed of it, after everything everyone had done for me, but for the next week, I hid away in my house. I don't think anyone even suspected I was there, because I was careful not to venture outside, waiting until it was dark and then driving to Arklow for milk and groceries, even though it was half an hour away. It was somewhere no one would know me, and that was what mattered. It was daft, I knew, but I just couldn't face my friends, not yet. I was still getting texts from everyone, asking me how I was, and how life was in the big smoke. If only they knew, I thought. That I'm not in the big smoke at all. I'm here, at home, hiding from them.

And I was hiding from someone else, too. I hadn't called Niall since that night in London. And he hadn't called me. I'd told myself that it was better that way, and that I had to take Karen's advice about not letting anything get in the way of my singing. What a joke that seemed now! And yet, I couldn't call him. I had no idea what I'd say. How I'd tell him about Marc Davidson and what he'd done to me.

In the end, it was something Mum used to say that changed things for me. I was passing the time at home tidying up her bureau, which I hadn't had the time to do since she'd died. I was filing all the letters and cards she'd received into a box folder, when I came across a photo of her and me. It must have been not long after I was adopted, because I looked about seven. We were on a visit to the zoo and we were standing side by side, huge ice-cream cones in our hands. I remembered that I'd been terrified of the elephants that day, and she'd tickled me under the chin and asked, 'Are you a man or a mouse, Antonia?'

I remembered that I'd thought it was the funniest thing: 'I'm not a *man*, Mum,' I'd said, and she'd given me a huge bear hug because it was the first time I'd called her 'Mum'.

And I had to ask myself that now, kneeling down on the living-room floor, a pile of cards in my hand. 'Are you a man or a mouse, Antonia?' I said it out loud, feeling the sound of the words on my lips. And I found myself giggling, just like I had with Mum all those years ago. And I knew that I didn't want to be a mouse. Not any more.

So I picked up the phone to Maurice Prendergast. When I punched in his mobile number, I kept asking myself what on earth I was doing. I mean, why *him*, why another music-industry professional? You'd think I'd have had enough of them. But there was something about Maurice, he was solid, like Dad. And anyway, it was too late. Before I could disconnect, he'd answered.

'Toni! Good to hear from you.' He was brisk, crisp, businesslike, and immediately I relaxed, because I knew I'd done the right thing. I'd trusted my instincts and had been proved right. He was tough, but he was a pro. 'How was London?' he asked.

'Well, that's just what I wanted to talk to you about,' I began. Careful, Antonia, no blubbing over him, I thought. 'I'd love to meet up with you, if I could. I'd really welcome your advice about a few things.' I was careful not to go into detail on the phone. I needed to see him face to face.

There wasn't a moment's hesitation in response, just, 'Sure, let me check my diary.' Followed by, 'Saturday is the only day I can do . . . breakfast, say seven thirty?' And he mentioned a little café in the city centre, which did a roaring trade in fried breakfasts. Who would have thought that Maurice Prendergast would have meetings there?

I didn't dare joke about him not having a lie-in on Saturday morning, just responded in an equally businesslike manner. 'Perfect, and thanks, Mr Prendergast.'

When he responded, he sounded amused. 'Call me Maurice.'

'Right. Maurice. See you then.'

I drove up to Dublin early that Saturday morning, when the mist was still swirling around the Sugar Loaf Mountain, the fields a deep shade of winter grey and brown. And I realized how much I loved the countryside here, the beautiful hills and woods, the sea, everything. I felt at peace here. I didn't fit in in London – and not just because of that . . . man. I just felt like a fish out of water. And even though singing made me feel happy, truly happy, I wasn't sure I could live that life. That was why I needed to see Maurice Prendergast, to see if there was another way of doing things. Something that would let me do what I loved, but not end up a burnt-out wreck in the process.

For the first time in weeks, as I passed through the thick wooded hills of the Glen of the Downs, I was exactly where I wanted to be. There was only one thing missing, but I couldn't do anything about that. Not yet anyway.

*

'It's my local.' Maurice Prendergast smiled as he stood up to greet me. He was sitting at a corner table, his mobile and a scattered bundle of paper spread out before him. He looked older than on stage, his sandy hair sprinkled with grey, his dark-purple shirt wrinkled.

'I like the food here, and they leave me alone. Isn't that right, Anto?' He smiled at the young man behind the counter, who was frying eggs and sausages.

'That's right, Mr Maurice.' Anto smiled back. 'Anything for you.'

'Do they know who you are?' I asked.

He shrugged. 'Doesn't matter. Who cares who I am? I only manage singers. It's no big deal.'

'Some of the biggest singers in the business,' I ventured.

'True, but I like them to have the limelight. Not me. I'm more comfortable here, with my rashers and sausages.' He smiled again. 'Like the "do".' He nodded at my hair.

'Thanks. I'm trying out a new look.'

'Well, it works.' He nodded approvingly. 'Anyway, I'm glad you came to see me. I thought you'd got carried away by all the offers in London.'

I froze. I opened my mouth to say something about how fantastic it had all been, but nothing came out. And then suddenly I felt the tears spring to my eyes. Don't cry, Toni, for God's sake. Don't cry.

Maurice had the grace not to press me further, pretending to examine his menu for a few minutes. 'I'm going to have the works,' he announced. 'Sausage, bacon, egg, mushrooms, and fried bread, because it's Saturday and I deserve it.' He grinned. 'Now, what about you, Toni? You look undernourished, wan.' He eyed me sharply.

I took this as a signal that I was supposed to order the works too, even though I wasn't sure I could stomach them. 'Ehm, maybe some poached egg?'

'You know, girls often make the mistake of starving themselves in this business, thinking that they have to look slim and perfect, but they need stamina.' He was waving his fork now, and I realized that he was really quite eccentric. I was warming to him more and more.

'I know. I'm not on a diet. It's just the stress of the last few weeks. I normally have a great appetite.'

'Good. Keep it that way,' he said, leaning back in his seat as a huge plate of fried food was placed before him. He speared a portion of sausage on his fork. There were a few moments of silence while he chewed, and I sipped my tea – which had been offered to me by the kind young man behind the counter without me even having to ask.

'So, what happened in London?'

I looked up at him sharply. 'What do you mean?'

'I mean, something clearly went wrong there.' He looked at me kindly over the top of his glasses. 'Tell Uncle Maurice.'

I looked down at my breakfast and suddenly lost my appetite. I didn't know where to start.

'You know, it's a small business, Toni. I hear all kinds of things. So why don't you tell me, and we'll see if we can sort it out, eh?'

I swallowed. Surely he didn't know about Marc David-son? I looked at him for any sign that he did, but he just gazed back at me steadily.

'Karen rang me,' he said finally. 'She didn't go into detail, but she told me there were a couple of . . . incidents.'

I nodded silently.

'You look scared.' He was studying my face.

I nodded again, and the next thing I knew, I was telling him about Niall and Damien in the nightclub. 'I couldn't believe it, how Niall just . . . lost it,' I finished.

He rolled his eyes to heaven. 'That Damien is a little scut. He's always looking for trouble. That's why I don't manage him. He's far too much hassle.' He smiled. 'Now you, on the other hand . . . but I don't think you're this down because your boyfriend socked that eejit in a nightclub, are you?'

I shook my head. 'No.'

'So?' His tone was gently enquiring, and after a moment's hesitation, I took a deep breath.

'Do you know Marc Davidson?'

He leaned back in his seat and put his knife and fork down on his plate. 'Ah.'

'He invited me to his flat for a party and . . .' I began.

Maurice raised his fork in warning. 'And I know exactly what happened next.'

'You do?' I said. Maybe Karen had told him, I thought, wishing that she hadn't, and that she'd kept her promise not to tell another soul.

'I do. Because he's done it to every single girl starting out in the industry. I'm sorry, Toni. If I'd known, there's no way I'd have let you go anywhere near that little shit.'

'Oh.' I felt better and a fool at the same time. 'I had no idea.'

'Of course you didn't. And I can tell you, I'll be having a word with whoever arranged the meeting. They should know better at this stage.'

I winced, and he continued. 'You blame yourself.'

'Yes,' I managed. 'If I hadn't been so naïve . . .'

'Don't, Toni.' His voice was softer now, and he patted my hand. I wasn't sure how to react until he said, 'It's OK. I'm married. Six kids, would you believe it? And I'm fifty-nine in February.'

I breathed a sigh of relief. 'You hardly look a day over forty,' I joked.

'Cheeky girl.' He smiled.

'Thanks for not telling me to put it all behind me,' I said. 'And for listening. I feel a little better, believe it or not.'

'Good, I'm glad to hear it. I've daughters of your age, Toni, and if Davidson tried it on with any of them, I'd chop his nuts off!' He mimed a karate chop, and I felt like laughing out loud for the first time in three weeks.

'Well, ehm, I sort of did that myself,' I said, not looking Maurice in the eye.

'You didn't!' He snorted with laughter. 'Toni, you surprise me more every time we meet.'

I looked up from my plate, and the look in his eyes was warm. 'Thanks, Maurice. Must have been my survival instinct.' And then I took a deep breath. 'But I feel so guilty—'

'Don't. People like Marc Davidson give the industry a bad name. They need to be stopped. But there are ways of doing this which don't involve you sacrificing your career.' He grinned at me. 'Now, you let me take care of that. I'll put a call in to a few gossip columns in London and see where we go . . .' He gave a mischievous smile. 'And now . . . let's talk about you.'

'Haven't we been talking about me?' I said, feeling suddenly hungry. I tucked into my poached egg with more appetite than I'd felt in weeks.

'Not about your talent or where you want to take it. So, tell me, I'm all ears.'

'Oh, God. Well . . . to be honest, I hated London. I felt that I was getting chewed up and spat out again.'

He nodded. 'But you made a good impact at Wembley, so all wasn't lost. A few people noticed you, like Alicia Mayhew. She'd be good to work with.'

'Hmm . . .'

'You sound doubtful.'

'No, it's just, well, she asked me, actually, but I thought she was only being nice.'

He shook his head. 'No. You know, people like that rarely make offers out of the goodness of their hearts. It's in their interests to work with talented young people. It makes them look good, and the results can be interesting, so we can pursue that . . .' He made a note on a bright-pink pad with flowers on it, which had been hiding under his newspaper. 'Mary-Ellen, my youngest, gave this to me. Said I wouldn't lose it on account of it being floral.'

I was beginning to like Maurice more and more, and I decided to bite the bullet. 'Maurice, I love the singing, really love it, but the whole merry-go-round with *That's Talent!*, well, it was just exhausting. I'm not sure I can keep that up.'

He looked up from his floral notepad, a surprised look on his face. 'Nobody's asking you to. Everyone knows those shows are complete car crashes. No sane human would have anything to do with them. But I suppose we're not sane humans, are we? We want people to notice us and see that we've got talent. And it worked for you, Toni. You got people to recognize your talent, so we can build on that now. Do you know what I'd suggest?'

'I'm dying for you to suggest something.' I smiled.

'Well, that you get off the merry-go-round for a while, fade away for a bit, because otherwise, you'll use up your fifteen minutes of fame, and soon no one will be able to stand the mention of your name. You'll end up doing pet-food commercials.' He gave a sly grin, a reference to Damien, whose gravelly voice graced Pet Surprise dog food ads on the television.

'Actually, Damien and I did a duet at Wembley.'

'I know. I saw it. It was quite good. I was surprised that the little git had some talent.'

I giggled. 'Will I get in touch with him?' I remembered Karen's words, that he was a snake. But he wasn't really.

He was just a silly boy who'd had too much to drink. Marc Davidson had made me realize what a snake really was.

'I'll get in touch with him, otherwise he'll start to pester you again. Much though I hate to encourage him, I think you two might just have something. And I'll put together a list of other songwriters that we could work with. You can't build a career with covers of "Bridge Over Troubled Water", you know, although you did it nicely.'

I wasn't sure if this was a compliment or not, so I said nothing.

'That was a compliment,' Maurice added with a smile.

'Oh,' I blushed. 'Thanks.'

'Look, the plan is, I think, just to stay away from the limelight and focus on singing and recording for the next few months. Only go out into the market when you're ready, and when you have something strong to sell. It's got to be right. You only get one chance in this business.'

'Thanks, Maurice. I don't know what to say—' I began.

'You can thank me by letting me be your manager,' he said.

'What?' I jumped up out of my seat. 'You want to manage me?'

'Yes, believe it or not. You may be accident-prone, but you have real talent, Toni. Take it nice and slow, and you'll be fine.'

I threw my arms around him and gave him a huge bear hug. 'Thanks, Mr Prendergast . . . I mean, Maurice. I won't let you down.'

'Easy, you'll give an oul' fellah a heart attack,' he said, into my hair.

'Sorry,' I sat back down.

'Good, well, that's a few things sorted, then,' he said. 'I'll get Sophie in the office to draw something up. I do have an office, you know. I don't always work out of a greasy spoon. Only when I want to schmooze people.' And he winked. 'Now go home to that boyfriend of yours, and forget about all of this crap for a while, will you?'

At the mention of Niall, I looked down into my half-eaten food again. 'Ah,' I could hear him say. 'What is it about you young women? My girls are the same. Meet a nice guy who'd move the sun and the moon for them, and what do they do? Make a mess of it all.' He was filling his cup with thick black tea. 'Want some advice?'

I shook my head.

'OK, no advice then. Just that you're stronger than you think you are.' He smiled and patted me on the hand again. 'Now, off you go and we'll talk during the week.'

I stood up. 'Maurice, I just want to say—'

He raised a hand. 'No pathetic gratitude, please. Save it for the Grammys.'

I grinned and walked out the door, feeling as if I was walking on air.

'Toni?' he called me, just as I was about to step out on to the street.

I turned and he smiled and said, 'When things are right, you know they are.'

Maurice was right, of course. Maybe I was stronger than I'd thought. I could give myself some credit for having survived the last few weeks, at least. I'd tried my best, and I'd made the most of the opportunities I'd been given, and if things had gone a bit haywire . . . well, I'd try not to blame myself. I also tried not to think about Marc Davidson, and when I did, I felt a sense of shame that I hadn't done anything more about him. That the same thing might happen to another girl. But I just didn't have the strength to deal with him right now. For the time being, I'd have to leave it to Maurice.

Maurice was right in another way: if something is right, you know that it is. Only, of course, I didn't realize it at the time. I was so confused about everything that had happened in London. I needed the dust to settle for a while, to focus on not doing much, apart from tidying Mum's affairs and fixing all the little jobs around the house that I hadn't had time for. Missing Niall had become a dull ache now, and I'd have to put up with it. In the meantime, I needed to make it up to all the people who'd given me so much support in the competition, to show them how much they meant to me.

I took it easy at first, just inviting Betty over for tea, because I knew that she wouldn't be over the top, like Bridget. She'd be happy to talk about the garden and the seasons and all the gossip in Glenvara. Betty was her usual tactful self, not asking too many questions, just complimenting me on my hair – and the scones I'd baked for the occasion.

'Your mammy would be proud,' she said, biting into one. 'They're delicious.'

'Thanks, Betty. I'm enjoying being domesticated for a bit. Getting the chance to relax after everything . . . you know.'

Betty nodded. 'I know. You must be worn out, pet. Was it worth it, do you think?'

I looked at her, startled, for a while, before responding. 'Gosh, well . . . I don't know, to be honest. I mean, I've proved to myself that I can sing, and I've surprised myself by being more capable than I'd thought . . .'

Betty nodded. 'Oh, you have, pet. You've surprised everyone in Glenvara, too. You know, you were always such a good girl, Antonia, so pleasant and kind, and the way you looked after your mum . . . well . . .' She looked teary for a moment. 'Suffice it to say that we were all glad that you had your moment in the sun.'

I laughed. 'I did, Betty. And yes, it was worth it.'

'Good, well, that's good, pet. Now, will you be gracing us at choir this Sunday?'

'Aha, I knew there was an ulterior motive for the visit,' I joked.

Betty grinned. 'Well . . . we were just wondering. That awful Fidelma Ferguson has the ears burnt off us with her tuneless warbling. I can't stand it.' She held her hands up to her ears and chuckled.

'Will you tell the others I'm just wrecked?' I said. 'I'll come back soon, though, promise.' I didn't want to admit to Betty that I was too shy to face them all, that I felt I'd let them down in some way.

'Of course I will, pet. And go easy on yourself, will you? You've given it your all over the last few weeks and you deserve a break for a bit. Promise?'

'I promise, Betty.' I smiled.

Next on my list were Colette and Mary. I arranged to meet them for sushi in Dublin the following Saturday. 'My treat,' I'd insisted. 'It's to say thanks to you both for all the help.' It was a real girls' night out, in a busy sushi bar in the city centre. They both screamed when they saw my hair, and after they'd calmed down a bit, and decided it was a success, we sat on high stools and ordered off the conveyor belt. Mary had never eaten sushi – 'Dave's idea of dining out is McDonald's,' she joked – and she oohed and aahed like a child over the sashimi and nori rolls.

'I got a taste for it in London,' I said, marvelling as I said it that I was able actually to mention the name now without feeling short of breath, as if it was all a distant memory. 'We went to this amazing sushi place one night with the TV crew from the London show. The chefs prepared the most elaborate sushi in front of you – I ate all kinds of things I'd never touched in my life before, like sea urchin. Mum would have been proud of me, that's for sure.' I laughed.

'She would, Antonia, considering you were the child who'd eat nothing,' Mary said, slurping her miso soup. 'I remember you wouldn't eat chicken at one stage, so she started to tell you it was poultry instead.'

'God, was I that bad?' I said.

'You were a little angel, all soft curls and big eyes. And you were so sweet, Antonia – who would have thought you'd change so much?' Mary giggled, as I mock-punched her on the arm. 'Seriously, though, if your mum could see you eating sushi . . .'

'I know, she'd be proud of me.'

'She'd be proud of a lot of things, if she could see you now,' Mary said.

I blushed and examined my plate.

'Bet none of those celebs actually ate the food, of course,' Colette said, tucking into her fifth California roll.

'Not like you, Colette,' Mary joked.

'Well, there's nothing wrong with a healthy appetite, is there?' Colette said, unapologetically. 'Besides, no man likes a skinny ass, do they?' We nodded in agreement.

'Speaking of which, how's Niall, Antonia?' Colette said, and both she and Mary guffawed, and I was pleased that they were laughing so much that they didn't notice that I hadn't replied. I tried to think of something – to say he was busy at work, or my schedule had been too hectic, but instead I just sat there, chopsticks in hand, feeling that I missed Niall more than anything in the world. It was so sudden, this feeling, that it took my breath away.

Mary was the first to notice. 'Sorry, Antonia, we weren't making fun of him, honest.'

I shook my head. 'It's not that, it's just that . . . well, I haven't seen him in a while.'

'You *haven't?*' Colette squeaked. 'But you two were perfect together. What happened? Does he wear women's underwear, or what?'

I had to smile. 'No, it's just, well, there was an incident in London.'

'An incident?' Colette lifted an eyebrow.

'Yes . . . we were in a nightclub after the Wembley gig, and Damien—'

'Ooh, I fancy him,' Colette interrupted.

'He's an eejit,' I shot back.

'Oh, now you've ruined my illusions about him. I thought he was kinda sexy.'

I rolled my eyes to heaven. 'If only you knew—'

'So, what happened?' Mary interrupted impatiently.

'Well, Damien saw a story about us going out together in one of the tabloids . . . it was all just a joke, really, and he was messing and said something to Niall about it . . . just nonsense, but Niall . . . well, he decked him.'

'Nice Niall, the ER doctor and all-around saint, punched someone?' Colette's jaw hung open.

Even Mary, who was more tactful, gasped.

I nodded silently.

There was a moment's pause and Colette said, 'Bloody fantastic!' and Mary burst out laughing.

'I didn't think he had it in him. Good old Niall, showing some backbone.'

'It's not funny, girls,' I said indignantly.

'Well, it is, kinda.' Colette grinned. 'Mind you, a bit of an overreaction, don't you think?'

I tried to explain it to them, the overheated atmosphere at the gig, not being able to get in touch with him all day, him being ushered back to the dressing room. 'He was just stressed by it all, I think, and, well, Damien was the final straw.'

'But why never see him again? Isn't that a bit harsh?' Mary said gently. Good old Mary, she was always so tactful. Once again, I thanked God that we'd become friends again.

'Oh, God, it was Karen, really. Said I shouldn't, that I had to become a 'real professional', whatever that is, and, well, I went along with it and . . .' I was about to talk about Marc, but stopped. I didn't want to tell them, because I knew they'd be so sympathetic, so caring. And I couldn't bear it.

'Jeez, it sure is a strange business,' Colette said. 'Do you miss him?'

I nodded. 'Yes. I do. I kept telling myself that I'll forget him, but I can't really. Life just isn't the same without him.' And with that, my eyes filled with tears. 'I really like him, girls,' I said, reaching for my handbag and rummaging around for a tissue to stem the tears.

Colette shot Mary a look. 'So, ring him up. Ask him out. Do something,' Colette said impatiently. 'Antonia, he's a catch, for goodness' sake, a handsome, caring doctor with all his own teeth. Some girls would just kill for that.'

'I know,' I snuffled. 'It's just, I'm afraid that he won't want to see me any more. Not when I dumped him like that, after everything he'd done for me.'

'He'll understand, I know he will.' Mary wrapped an arm around my shoulders.

'Hmm,' I said, 'knowing Niall, I'm not so sure.'

'What do you mean?'

'Look, things haven't always been easy for Niall, in spite of appearances. He takes things to heart, and I'm not sure he'll forgive me that easily.'

'Forgive you?' Colette raised an eyebrow. 'How about you forgiving him for making an eejit of himself and you in public? Sounds to me like he has to accept some of the blame.'

I raised my hands. 'I know, I know, but girls, I just want to forget about all that . . . stuff, please. Just for one night.'

'Of course, of course, Antonia, I'm sorry,' Colette was immediately apologetic. 'Tell you what, let's order some more of this sake and get smashed, shall we?'

'You know, Colette, for once I'm with you,' Mary agreed. 'Let's drink to the next stage in Antonia's career.'

'Hear, hear!' Colette raised her cup of sake and clinked it against mine and Mary's. 'Here's to singing, and men and life.'

'I'll drink to that,' Mary said. 'Cheers.'

After Colette and Mary, I knew that there was something else I still had to do. Well, there were a lot of things, but this one I knew I had to put firmly behind me. I thought about it for a while first, deciding what I would say, and how I would say it. Would I be angry? Indignant, self-righteous? But I didn't feel angry, not any more. I just wanted to get it over with.

My hand shook as I dialled the number, and when the voice said, 'Hello?' I debated whether to hang up.

Instead, I took a deep breath. 'Amanda?'

'Yes?' her voice was cautious.

'It's Antonia.'

There was a long pause at the other end of the line, before she said, 'Antonia, it's so good to hear from you!' Her tone was one of false cheer, and I felt my teeth grit. 'I've been meaning to ring you for ages to see if we could meet up, but it's just been busy, busy, you know?'

'I know,' I replied, as warmly as I could manage. 'Why don't we have another coffee somewhere in town? It'd be great to catch up.' And then I can meet you face to face, I thought, and ask you why you sent those nasty texts. Why you wanted to undermine me so badly, when I thought we were friends.

There was another long silence, before she responded. 'Look, ehm, I'm kind of busy right now—'

I took a deep breath. Clearly, I wasn't going to get the chance to confront her, so I'd need to say what I had to right now. 'I know about the texts, Amanda,' I blurted.

'You . . . what? What texts?'

'Amanda, I know you sent them, and I can't pretend to

361

understand why you'd want to do that to a friend, but, well, I just wanted you to know that it's fine.'

'What, that you forgive me?' Her voice was suddenly harsh on the other end of the line.

'No,' I said, more firmly than I felt. 'I don't actually. I thought what you did was just nasty, but I wanted to let you know that you don't need to do it. You have lots of talent . . .'

'And you think I should be grateful that you've thrown me a bone. *Please*.' Her voice dripped sarcasm. 'I don't need your forgiveness.'

I took a deep breath. 'Look, I'm sorry we can't be friends, but I wish you all the luck in the world, I really do. And, well, I just called to say that you didn't win, Amanda. You tried, but you didn't succeed. And that's what really matters. Goodbye, Amanda.' And, before she could reply, I pressed 'disconnect'.

I had to sit down for a few minutes, to catch my breath. Never in my entire life had I confronted anyone, not like that. I'd never needed to. My hands were shaking, and my entire body trembled with fright. But I'd done it, I thought. I'd stood up to her. I wasn't Miss Mouse any more.

30

THE FOLLOWING FRIDAY, I MADE MY WAY IN THROUGH THE church doors and slowly up the steep steps to the choir again. I'd forgotten how high up it was, and by the time I reached the top step, I was out of breath.

'You need to get more exercise.' The voice behind me was warm, amused.

'Billy!' I turned around and gave him a bear hug. 'Boy, am I glad to see you.'

'Easy, girl! I'll fall down the stairs,' he joked. 'And is it good to see you? That Mrs Ferguson, she has the ears—'

'Burnt off you, I know. Betty told me.' I smiled. 'Thought you could do with a bit of help.'

'Lord, we could. I prayed to the Blessed Virgin Mary, and she's answered our prayers.' He smiled. 'C'mon, every-one else will be thrilled to see you,' he said, bounding ahead of me through the door. 'Everyone, look who's here.' He yelled so loudly my ears were ringing.

I was nervous at first, taking a deep breath before I walked through the door. I needn't have worried. There was a round of applause and I felt the colour rise to my cheeks. Billy gave a piercing whistle and everyone burst out laughing, and exclaimed at my new look. Then Eithne came forward and took my hands in hers. 'Antonia, you did us proud, and we're thrilled that you're back, aren't we, everyone?' There was another round of applause, and loud whooping and cheering, all with the exception of Mrs Ferguson, who was sulking quietly in the corner. Poor woman, she loved doing the solos and I was just spoiling it for her, I knew.

Eithne looked at her, then winked at me and mouthed, 'Thank God you're back.'

I grinned. 'It's good to be back, Eithne. I thought you wouldn't want me any more.'

'Don't be silly,' Eithne said, ushering me to my place as if I'd been there only last Friday, and not ages ago.

Only Bridget was frosty. 'We thought you wouldn't want to sing in our little choir any more, that you were too famous for us here in Glenvara altogether.' She sounded upset, and I supposed I could hardly blame her. The choir was Bridget's life, after all.

'Bridget . . .' Eithne shot her a warning look.

'It's OK, Eithne. Bridget, I'm sorry I wasn't around for the last few weeks. It all got a bit crazy for a while, but if you'll have me back, I'll be here every Friday and Sunday from now on. Promise.'

She gave me a stern look. 'Well, I suppose—'

Billy interrupted. 'Oh, for God's sake, Bridget, get off your high horse. We should be glad Antonia's back, not giving the girl a hard time. I'm not sure what sin you think she's committed, but I can tell you, she's done wonders for this place. She's really put Glenvara on the map, and we should be thanking her.'

I felt like hugging Billy all over again.

Bridget looked a bit emotional for a few moments, as if she was wrestling with her conscience. Then she came over to me and patted me on the arm. 'Antonia, you're welcome back.'

I knew she wouldn't say anything more, so I just smiled and said, 'Thanks, Bridget. I appreciate that.'

'Well, if the shoot-out at the OK Corral is over, perhaps we can do some singing,' Eithne said dryly.

'Hear, hear,' Billy said, and as the choir shuffled into position, whispered to me, 'That old bat, honest to goodness . . .'

'She means well, Billy,' I whispered back. And she did. I knew she'd given me all the support in the world, and I was grateful to her for it. And then I caught the expression on his face, one which didn't match his disdainful comment. He *likes* her, I thought. Oh my God! I tried not to giggle.

'Right, everyone, "Hail Holy Queen",' Eithne said crisply, and the practice began.

I managed to keep my promise to Bridget. The following Sunday, there I was at Mass, and Father O'Hanlon got so excited, he made everyone give me a standing ovation. I was mortified, of course. He insisted I sing 'Bridge Over Troubled Water'. 'As a special treat for us all. I'm sure God is looking down on you now and smiling upon this daughter of Glenvara, for did he not say, "a man's gift will make a way for him"? Well, Antonia's gift has made a great and distinctive way for her, and of this we are truly proud.'

Everyone burst into applause, and I was so embarrassed – it was worse than any talent show, I realized, standing up to sing in front of all my friends. I made sure that my performance equalled that of *That's Talent!*, the choir swelling behind me, even managing to drown out Mrs Ferguson, and when I'd finished, there was another round of applause, whooping and cheering. Please God, make it end, I thought to myself, delighted and mortified at the same time. After everything that had happened over the last few weeks, I was home at last. Really and truly.

Of course I just couldn't forget about Niall. With every day that passed, I thought about him more. About how he made me laugh, about the tuft of hair that stood up on top of his head when he hadn't had a haircut, about how he loved soccer and hated rugby, about how chicken korma was his favourite Indian dish. I wondered what he was doing and how busy he was at work. Several times I found my hand reaching for my mobile, but at the last minute, I'd always decide that no, he wouldn't want to talk to me. And so the weeks passed and I didn't ring, and I kept telling myself that, sure, neither had he, so what did that tell me? I'd just have to try harder to forget him. It'd be better that way.

One thing that *was* working was my singing. True to his word, Maurice set up a couple of meetings for me with songwriters he liked, and I began to work with them and, for the first time, to really enjoy the business. It felt liberating, as if, at long last, I was truly myself as a singer. I'd enjoyed working with Eithne and rearranging classics to suit my voice, but working on original material, I knew I'd finally come home.

One of the first people Maurice arranged a meeting with was Damien. I hadn't given him much thought since London, but there he was, in Maurice's café, as cheerful and bouncy as ever, like the puppy he was. He stood up as I came towards him, throwing his arms around me and giving me a bear hug. 'Hiya, kiddo,' he said cheerily, for all the world as if we were the best of friends.

'Hi, Damien,' I said cautiously, trying to extract myself from his embrace.

He let me go, grinning. 'It's OK, I'm not going to try to steal you from your boyfriend again. Maurice warned me,' he said.

'Too late,' I said dryly.

'You mean there's still a chance for you and me?' he said cheekily, sitting back down and stirring his cappuccino.

'Shut up and don't push your luck,' I replied tartly, pulling out a seat for myself and smiling at the owner, Anto. I didn't talk to anyone else in this way, but there was something of the annoying little brother about Damien. It made me want to smack him and hug him at the same time. If only Niall knew, I thought, that he had absolutely nothing to worry about on that score.

He had the grace to laugh. 'Look, Maurice suggested we meet up, see if there's still some of that "chemistry" there. We might even do something together . . . you know, make sweet music?' And he winked.

'For God's sake, Damien, if you keep this up, I won't talk to you ever again,' I said, exasperated.

I made to get up out of my seat and walk out the door, and he burst out laughing, holding his hands up in a gesture of surrender. 'OK, OK, I promise. Seriously, Toni, I think we'd make a good team. That duet we did, well, it was pretty good, and I think we can do better. Let's give it a shot. It can't do any harm.'

'Less of the puppy-dog eyes,' I said sharply.

'Aww . . . *please*.' He looked at me mournfully.

'You are a complete chancer,' I said, managing a smile.

'I know.' He grinned cheekily.

'I'm willing to give the partnership thing a go, and that's it,' I said crisply. 'So no messing, OK?'

'You love me really.' He grinned.

I rolled my eyes to heaven.

But we did make a good team. Even though I wanted to kill him, we clicked creatively, Damien and I, and true to his promise, he didn't say another word about 'us'. We just spent the next few weeks at a little recording studio on the quays in Dublin, working on our songwriting. It was funny: even though Damien was officially the most irritating person in the world, I found myself really opening up as a singer with him, trying out things I'd never thought I would, stretching my voice and taking a few risks. After a few weeks, I found myself almost becoming fond of him. He was really quite nice, once he stopped all the messing.

'Do you know, I'm grateful to you, Damo,' I said one night. It was late and everyone in the studio had gone home, except Dave, the sound engineer, who'd wandered off to make coffee.

He put a hand to his heart. 'See? I knew you'd thank me one of these days.'

'I mean it. Without you, I wouldn't have tried half the things I've tried recently. You've given me a new lease of life.' I smiled. And it was true. After Marc Davidson, I didn't think I'd be able to open my mouth and sing a single note, and now, here I was, writing my own material, albeit with help.

He looked at me for a long time. 'Thanks, kiddo. You know, I should be thanking you, too.'

'Oh, really? Why?'

'Look, we both know that you should have won *That's Talent!* I'm just a club singer. I know that. But you, on the other hand . . .'

I shook my head. 'No, that's not true, Damo. You won

fair and square. You've a great voice and lots of . . . stage presence—' I began.

He burst out laughing. 'Thanks, love, but I know what I am. And I don't mind, honest. But working with you, well, it's shown me that I can do something else really well. Write songs. Thanks to you, I have a whole new career.'

'Oh. Well, you're welcome, I suppose.'

There was a long silence then, as we both sat side by side on the sofa. The room was quiet, and all I could hear was the tick, tick of the clock on the studio wall. Neither of us moved for what seemed like the longest time, and then Damien leaned towards me, cradling my head in his hand, and kissed me. And I kissed him back. It was nice, nicer than I'd thought it would be. His lips were warm, and his breath smelled of peppermints. But all I could think was that he wasn't Niall. It just wasn't the same.

I pulled away. 'Damien, I—'

'Don't say it.' He smiled, pulling his guitar on to his knee and strumming. 'It's that other guy, isn't it? That uptight doctor with the killer punch.'

I nodded. 'Yes. Sorry.'

For a moment, I thought I saw a flicker of real pain cross his face, but then the boyish grin was back. 'Oh, well. A man can dream . . .' he said, and then he broke into song. 'Oh, Toni, baby, you broke my heart, right from the start,' he sang, in a falsetto warble.

'You are a complete pain, do you know that?' I laughed. And we were back on steady ground again. I was more relieved than I'd thought possible. Because Damien was actually a nice guy, and it would have been perfect really, to fall for him, but I just didn't feel that way about him. What his kiss had made me realize was that I missed Niall more than ever. Now I had actually to do something about it.

31

I REMEMBER I USED TO LAUGH AT MUM, SITTING IN HER comfy chair, watching *When Harry Met Sally*, or *Maid in Manhattan*, and sniffling into her hankie at the mushy bits. She was a great believer in romance, Mum. It was the only thing we ever argued about. I'd say, 'It's just nonsense, Mum. Things like that don't happen in real life.' Of course, there was no way I could possibly know, but perhaps that was why I was so adamant, because I'd never experienced it.

Mum would be quite sharp with me. 'You know, they do, Antonia, and if you dismiss it all as nonsense, you'll never get the chance to experience real love. It can pass you by if you're just too cynical to be open to it.' Mum was usually so gentle that it always came as a shock to me that she would get so agitated about romance. Of course, I knew how much she'd been in love with Dad, because she'd often told me stories about how they'd met, and the sweet things he'd done for her, but crying over movie stars struck me as ridiculous.

'Just you wait,' she'd say smartly, pulling her cardigan around her shoulders.

And she was right, of course. That night with Niall after the finals was the most magical of my life. And of course, I'd made a mess of it. I'd let other things get in the way, things that I realized now just weren't important. Because, when it came down to it, love was all that really mattered. I could see that now. But I had no idea how I was going to sort it all out.

And then, as in all the best romantic movies, fate intervened, in the last week of January. Mum would have been delighted, but I couldn't help wondering afterwards if she'd had a hand in the whole thing. It sounds silly, and I don't believe in ghosts, but there was something so . . . unexpected about it that there had to be some kind of magic at work.

I was leaving the newsagents' after Mass, and the sun was low in the sky, blinding me for a second as I stepped on to the pavement. And then I bumped into Niall. Literally, slap, bang, so hard that I fell backwards on the pavement. I lay there for a few moments, until I found him leaning over me. 'Are you going to stay there, or can I help you up?'

I'd actually prefer to lie here until you're gone, I thought to myself, looking up at him. He was dressed in a suit, which I'd never seen him in, a smart blue charcoal with a bright-blue shirt which brought out the colour of his eyes. My stomach flipped, and I felt myself begin to shake with nerves.

Silently, I extended a hand and allowed him to pull me up, brushing the dust and dirt off my clothes. I thanked

God and Mum that I looked all right anyway, having just been to Mass. I was wearing a new winter coat, a smart black one that Karen had helped me to buy in London, and my severe pixie crop had grown out a bit, so it looked softer now.

'I hardly recognized you,' Niall began. 'You look . . . different.'

'I might say the same about you.' I nodded at his suit.

'Yes . . . well, it's Gerry and Sally's wedding anniversary, and we're going to lunch in Wicklow. Ten years.'

'Wow, ten years.' I couldn't imagine what that would feel like. Niall and I had lasted just over two months, and it had ended badly. 'Well, please tell them I said congratulations.'

'Sure,' he ran a hand through his hair in that way he loved, and I suddenly felt that I wanted to reach out and kiss him. 'Listen,' he said. 'Why don't you come up to the house with me and say hello? I'm going now – I just came down to get the paper.'

'Oh no, no, I don't want to intrude. But thanks for the offer . . .' There was a long, awkward pause while both of us wondered what to say. Eventually, we both spoke at the same time.

'Well, it was good seeing you . . .'

'Yes, you too . . .'

I wanted to say, 'This is silly, Niall. Can't we talk?' but the words just wouldn't come out of my mouth and so I didn't.

Like a fool, I let him say, 'Well, goodbye, then,' and walk

off up the main street towards Gerry and Sally's. As I looked at his retreating back, I thought my heart would break.

I spent the rest of the afternoon feeling sorry for myself, watching an old movie on television, curled up on the sofa in my pyjamas. It was called *The Philadelphia Story*, and was about a woman whose ex-husband comes back to woo her. Mum loved Cary Grant, which is really why I started watching it, and it was so funny and smart. And yet for some reason, I found myself weeping as Cary Grant and Katharine Hepburn exchanged wisecracks. I've missed my chance, I kept telling myself. And I won't get a better one. And then at the end of the film, the two warring partners got together, and I cried even more.

I didn't hear the knocking at the door at first, until it was quite loud. Must be Betty, I thought, shuffling into the hall, not even bothering to check myself in the mirror. Betty wouldn't mind, I told myself. She was used to seeing me like this.

I opened the door, 'Betty—' I began. Then, 'Oh.' Because it wasn't Betty.

'I'm sorry, I didn't realize you were . . . resting,' Niall said politely. He scratched his head and shuffled from foot to foot. I noticed that he'd changed out of the suit and was wearing his old hiking boots, jeans, and a thick fleece which had seen better days.

At the word 'resting', I found the giggles bubbling up inside me, until they came out in a burst of laughter. 'Thank you for being so polite,' I managed. 'I look a total disaster.' I looked down at my pyjamas and blushed to the roots of my hair.

'No you don't. You look perfect, as usual.'

'Thanks,' I looked up at him and he was smiling at me, that smile that I couldn't resist. And I thought of all the smart things that I could say in reply, just like Katharine Hepburn in the movie, but instead I just said, 'I really missed you.'

'Oh, I missed you too.' And then he was over the threshold and pulling me towards him, nuzzling my hair and kissing the top of my head. 'You're smelly, but I love you.'

'I love you too,' I found myself replying. 'And I'm sorry that I'm smelly.'

He laughed and took my hands in his. 'Look, before we go any further, I want to apologize to you, Antonia. I've spent the last few months thinking of every single way I could say sorry and none of them seemed to be good enough. I've never hit anyone before in my entire life, and to embarrass you in public like that . . . well.' He put his hands in his pockets. 'I'm truly sorry, and it'll never happen again, I promise.'

I shook my head. 'I know. I can't say you didn't frighten me, Niall, but instead of talking to you about it, I just bolted. Karen said . . . well, that I should just focus on my singing, and it seemed easier that way. At least I kept telling myself it was.'

He nodded. 'I know. Karen was probably right. What I did was unforgivable, and I wouldn't have blamed you if you'd never spoken to me again.'

I looked up at him, at the fine lines around his deep-blue eyes and knew. 'I spent the last three months trying to pluck up the courage to ring you, but I thought you wouldn't take my call.'

He squeezed me tight again. 'Never. I just wanted to give you some space, and I needed to think about what I'd done. Because it truly will never happen again.'

'I know,' I said.

'Look, can I come inside?'

I nodded. 'I thought you'd never ask.'

Later that day, we were both standing on top of Powerscourt waterfall again, me huffing and puffing and Niall hardly having drawn breath. We'd brought Gerry's large lab, Lola, with us, and she had helpfully pulled me up the last bit.

'I am really out of shape,' I laughed, patting the dog's head. She whined gently and licked my hand.

'Well, we'll soon sort that out,' Niall said. 'A few Saturday-morning hikes up here, and you'll be right as rain.'

I groaned. 'There is absolutely no way you are dragging me back up this mountain, do you hear me?'

'Ah, go on, you know you love it, really,' he teased me. 'Bet you missed it over the last few months.'

I shook my head. 'Not one little bit.' But the mention of the past few months made us grow silent for a while. Eventually, Niall broke the silence. 'Did you ever think we'd be doing this again?'

'No.' I shook my head.

'I thought I'd lost you after London. And it was all my own fault.' He stood behind me and put his hands on my shoulders, bending his head to give me a kiss.

'I was too caught up in it all,' I blurted.

I expected him to react badly, but instead he just smiled and shook his head. 'I'm not surprised. It's hardly what you need if you're the nation's sweetheart, is it? A marauding boyfriend?'

'You weren't marauding . . .' I began. 'Niall, there was nothing going on with Damien. He's a complete twit—'

But he interrupted. 'Antonia, I know that. It's not you, it's me. I have a temper, and I have to work really hard to control it. It used to get me into trouble as a teenager, but Mum and Dad put a lot of effort into helping me overcome it. And I did. I focused all that anger into doing positive things, like this—' He indicated the mountains around us. 'And my studies. But that night in London, I thought I'd gone right back to the guy I used to be. I felt that I'd lost everything. You – and that I couldn't trust myself around the patients any more. It was scary, and I needed time to work it out. To make sure it wouldn't happen again.'

I didn't say anything this time, just nodded, and he put an arm around my shoulders and pulled me towards him. 'Antonia, do you think you could ever make room for me in your life again?'

I swung around to face him. 'Of course I could,' I said indignantly. 'It's my fault, too, Niall. I was so obsessed with the show and the merry-go-round of it all that I just never

378

stopped to think. I thought that being successful meant losing you, and now I see that it doesn't. I'm in a great place, now, Niall. I'm working with really good people' – I decided not to mention Damien just yet – 'and my singing is really coming along. I feel as if I've been given a new lease of life. London wasn't for me, Niall, I can see that now. I want to be here . . . with you.'

He nodded. 'In that case, there's only one thing to do.' And, taking my hand, he went down on one knee, wincing as he hit a stone in the soggy ground. 'Antonia, you're the love of my life. Will you marry me?'

I was silent for a minute, in absolute shock. 'Niall, I—' My hands flew up to my mouth.

'You don't have to say yes, just say you'll think about it.'

'Oh, you eejit, the answer's yes, of course.'

'Oh, great, my knee's killing me,' he joked, pulling himself back up and wrapping his arms around me.

'On one condition,' I said, looking into his blue eyes.

'Anything.'

'That we don't do it just yet. We've been through a lot and . . . well, I'm not ready. I know I'm not. I want to marry you, I promise . . . but when the time's right. When we've got to know each other properly. Maybe you won't want to wait, but . . .'

'I'll wait, Antonia. If I know you'll marry me eventually, I'll wait a hundred years.' And then he pulled me to him again, and kissed me deeply, and I wondered how on earth I'd ever kissed Damien. It just hadn't been the same. The kiss went on for a long time, until the dog, clearly distracted by a rabbit, bolted off down the mountain.

'Oh, no, if we lose her, Gerry'll kill me,' Niall said, breaking into a run. 'Lola, Lola, wait!' He whistled and called as he ran, with me staggering along behind him, out of puff after a hundred yards.

'I am never doing this again, do you hear?' I yelled after him.

'You love it really,' he threw over his shoulder, and I stood there and laughed until my stomach hurt.

32

One year later

'BRIDGET, WILL YOU EVER HURRY UP WITH THAT BUNCH OF irises?' Betty was yelling as she made her way gingerly along the track towards the waterfall. She was dressed head to toe in pale lilac, a purple fascinator at a jaunty angle on her head, which was a mass of tightly permed grey. 'Just like that Kate Middleton,' she'd said, when I'd complimented her on it. 'They were all the rage at the royal wedding.'

'You look wonderful, Betty,' I said now, trying to distract her from her anxiety about Bridget, who'd promised to bring the bridesmaids' bouquets up with her. 'Any man's fancy, as Mum used to say.'

Betty looked chuffed and embarrassed at the same time. 'Well . . . you told me to mix the practical with the glamorous, because of the location, and I've tried my best.' She looked ruefully down at her sensible walking shoes. She shuffled along beside me, huffing and puffing, and I could see that she was trying not to complain, to ask why we'd decided to have our wedding at the top of a waterfall, of all places.

381

Bridget hadn't been as reticent, of course. 'You just have to be different, don't you?' she'd said. 'All that singing has turned you into some kind of New Age hippy. What Father O'Hanlon will say, God only knows.' She'd only been slightly mollified when I'd told her that Father O'Hanlon would be doing the ceremony and had been delighted to be asked.

'I know you have, and thanks,' I said to Betty now, smiling at her, taking her hand, and squeezing it tight. 'Look at what I've got on underneath my dress.' I laughed, lifting the hem of my cream silk number to reveal a pair of hiking boots. 'Niall will be pleased, anyway.'

'Sure, Niall would be pleased if you turned up wearing a plastic bag,' Betty said warmly. 'He's such a lovely man. I can't believe it took you this long to marry him.' There was a note of reproach in her voice, and I had to stifle a laugh.

'Well . . . we could have got married sooner, I suppose,' I agreed, 'but it's been such a mad year, with the album and everything. I really wanted to wait for things to calm down so that we could do it properly.'

'You're right, pet. Sure, you both have the rest of your lives to be married. If you can't live a little first . . . well, you might get the seven-year itch later, or something,' Betty said resolutely, before adding, 'not that I'm an expert, of course, not having gone down that road myself.'

'Do you regret it?' I asked her.

She shook her head so that the little flower on top of her fascinator wobbled. 'No. I did for a bit, when I was younger, but now I realize it wasn't for me. That I have other things

382

to do in life, do you know what I mean? And I'm happy with my gardening and the choir and helping out around the place.'

I nodded, pretending that I understood, even though I couldn't imagine how anyone would want to get through life without love and the support of someone beside them. Although I had to admit that I'd felt the same as Betty, just twenty months ago. If someone had told me then that, within the space of a year, I'd have fallen helplessly in love – as well as released a number-one album and toured the country – I'd have told them they were completely mad, so who was I to talk? And now here I was, making the climb up to the top of the waterfall, just as I had every free Sunday I could manage for the previous year. Except that this time, when I walked down again, I'd be married.

I'd kept my promise to Niall, that when the time was right we'd do it, we'd tie the knot. And even though the tour was in full swing, I'd known that it had to be now. What was it Maurice had said, that when things are right, you know it? Well, that happened between a gig in Galway and Waterford, as it turned out. It didn't matter that Niall spent every spare moment in my house anyway; I wanted to spend my entire life with him.

Niall had been surprised at first, when I'd called him after the Galway concert, a wobble of emotion in my voice. 'Let's do it,' I'd said to him. 'Let's get married.'

'Why now? I mean, I'd marry you tomorrow, but don't you want to wait until the tour's out of the way?' He'd been amused, I could tell, at my impulsiveness, but he was getting used to me now. I was still quiet – I hadn't changed *that* much – but I was beginning to discover things about myself and who I was that I reckon I must have kept hidden for all those years, trying to be the kind of daughter that any mother would want. It was strange, but since Mum had died, I'd come out of my shell. Sometimes I felt guilty about it, but mostly I tried to see it as a gift she'd given to me, the ability to live my own life, to make mistakes and learn from them. I discovered that I was decisive and stubborn, and that once I got an idea into my head . . . well . . . I was like a dog with a bone, as Bridget would say.

'You've decided, haven't you?' Niall had said, a tremor of laughter in his voice.

'Yep,' I agreed.

'Do I have any choice in the matter?'

'Not if you want to become Mr Toni Trent, you don't,' I'd teased him. The press were always going on about the doctor who'd captured the heart of Ireland's singing sensation, how steady he was, always by my side. 'Mr Toni Trent,' they'd labelled him. To his credit, he hadn't really minded.

'Well, then. Let's do it.' He'd laughed down the phone.

The choice of venue was equally easy. 'It has to be the waterfall,' he'd said, on one of the rare days we both had off, a week after I'd popped the question. We'd curled up in front of the fire with the papers, steaming mugs of tea and some of Betty's fruitcake, to while away an afternoon.

'It means such a lot to us that I couldn't think of having it anywhere else.'

When I'd looked startled he'd added hastily, 'And the ceremony will be the same, I promise.' Niall wasn't religious in any way, and although I loved the parish choir, I wasn't, either, though I had dreamed of a church wedding. But I did know how important it was to meet him halfway. After all, that's what marriage is about, isn't it? Compromise.

'You are quite mad,' I'd said to him, resting my head on his shoulder. 'How are we going to drag Betty and Billy and Bridget up there, for God's sake?'

'We'll take the easy route to the top, the one that loops around the back of the waterfall. It's a much more straight-forward climb,' he'd said. Then he'd added, 'What?', as I'd sat bolt upright beside him on the sofa.

'You mean there's an easy route to the top of that blessed mountain, and you never told me about it?' I'd picked up my copy of the paper and proceeded to whack him play-fully over the head with it.

'I thought you could do with the exercise,' he'd said. 'Ouch! You're hurting me.'

'Serves you right,' I'd said, pretending to be angry, pull-ing hard on the newspaper as he'd tried to grab it out of my hand. 'Give it back. It's mine.'

'How badly do you want the sports section?' he'd joked, making a lunge for me and starting to tickle me as hard as he could.

I'd collapsed in giggles. 'All right, all right, I give up,' I'd protested. 'You know I hate tickles.'

'All the more reason,' he'd said, and persisted, until I was weak with laughter. Only then had he pulled me towards him and wrapped his long arms around me, pressing his nose to mine and looking at me with those deep-blue eyes. 'Do you know how happy you make me?'

'I can't move my head.'

'Well, do you?'

'No, I mean yes. As happy as you make me.' I'd grinned, and tried to kiss him.

His expression had grown serious. 'It's been a hell of a year, hasn't it?'

'It sure has,' I'd agreed. 'Let's make it a wedding to remember, shall we?'

'You betcha.'

'Oh, for God's sake, woman, I'm coming.' Bridget scuttled up behind us in her heavy tweed coat with a fox-fur stole wrapped around her neck. The stole was obviously ancient, as the fur was matted and in some places had completely worn away, the fox's eyes a glassy brown.

'What's *that*?' Betty looked at it askance. 'And where on earth are the flowers?'

'It's a stole, Betty,' Bridget snapped. 'Ever seen one before? And Colette and Mary insisted on taking the irises themselves. Said they couldn't let an old woman climb a bloody mountain with a huge bunch of flowers under each arm, unlike some people.' Her face was bright red now, and I thought for a moment that she might have a heart attack.

'Bridget, I——' I began.

'Oh, will you whisht, woman, and stop complaining? The exercise will do you good. Might knock off a few pounds,' Betty interrupted, glaring at Bridget. I looked at Betty askance. I'd never heard her talk to anyone in this way, but then, Bridget always did get on her nerves.

'Speak for yourself,' Bridget responded. 'At *least* I have a man in my life.'

'OK, ladies, I think that's enough,' I intervened, wondering if Billy would really like to admit that he was 'doing a line', as he put it, with Bridget.

'She railroaded me into it,' he'd said ruefully, the one time I'd asked him about it, but I think he was secretly quite chuffed, though he hadn't quite wanted to share it with the world just yet. And who could blame him? Bridget was scary at the best of times.

'Sorry, Antonia,' Betty murmured. 'It's your special day. I didn't mean to spoil it.'

'Yes, sorry,' Bridget agreed, looking slightly crestfallen.

'It's OK.' I laughed, pulling them both towards me. 'I couldn't have made it through the last two years without you both, do you know that? You've both been absolute rocks, and I can't thank you both enough,' I said, hoping that my words would smooth their ruffled feathers a bit.

'Yes, well . . .' Betty looked mollified, her fascinator bobbing up and down on her head again as she nodded.

'Oh, for God's sake, Betty, can't you take a compliment?' Bridget began, before I interrupted.

'Oh, look, here we are!'

Distracted, they both followed me to where the path evened out at the top of the mountain, and I gasped. 'Wow, the view!' All around us, the mountains were that rich, purple-green of spring, clumps of trees wearing bright green leaves, the waterfall from that angle just a flash of silver in the rocks. It was beautiful, and I had to stand for a few moments to drink it all in. And I knew then that we'd chosen the right place. And that Mum didn't mind that it wasn't in Glenvara Church. I could tell.

The group waiting for us at the end of the path was a small one, just our families and closest friends. Well, really, Niall's family, because, as I realized with the same jolt I always felt, I didn't have one, at least not in that sense. What would Mum have made of this? I wondered, although of course, I knew. She would have loved every minute of it.

All of Niall's brothers and sisters were there, all six of them, three stunning women, Elizabeth, Susan and Mary, with their gaggle of children, and his three brothers, Gerry, of course, and Sally, Mike, and Niall's 'blood' brother, Matt. Matt was just as I'd thought he'd be: a mischievous joker with a twinkle in his eye.

'So you're marrying Niall, eh?' he'd joked when we'd first met, when Niall had brought me home to meet his family for Sunday lunch. 'Has he told you his deep dark secret?'

I'd looked at Niall askance. 'What secret? I didn't know

you had any secrets . . .' I'd begun, my heart sinking. Oh, no, I'd thought, not *another* secret. What on earth could it be this time?

But Matt's lips had twitched. 'He likes musicals,' he'd said, and snorted with laughter as his brother mock-punched him on the shoulder. 'You wouldn't know it, would you? He seems quite masculine, really, but scratch the surface and he knows all the words to *South Pacific*.' And he'd guffawed as Niall just rolled his eyes to heaven.

'My brother,' Niall had said, shaking his head. 'The guy with the back so hairy no girl will even look at him,' ducking as Matt returned with a punch of his own. They were like two little boys, mock-wrestling on the sofa.

'Honestly, you two,' Niall's mother, Eileen, had said, coming into the living room, smoothing her hands on her apron and announcing that lunch was served. But it was clear how much Niall and Matt loved each other. Looking at them together, I'd wondered if the fact that they were actual brothers gave them a special bond. I think it probably did, maybe because of what they'd gone through together. But then Niall was close to Gerry, and when I'd met the rest of the family I'd realized that they were all the same: all confident, joking, fun. Eileen and Jim had obviously done a brilliant job with them, because it was clear that they shared a love that was rock solid.

Sitting down with them to a huge lunch of roast lamb with all the trimmings, I'd felt a momentary pang. How I would have loved a big family like this, all gathered around

389

the table! I'd watched them all, laughing and joking and teasing each other, passing the potatoes and vegetables, and it had been hard not to feel like an outsider. That was, until Niall's mother had squeezed my arm. 'Welcome to your new family, Antonia.' And she'd smiled at me as if I was the most special person in the world. I was truly lucky to have her as a mother-in-law, I knew.

She was smiling at me now as I walked towards them all, pulling my warm cream stole around my shoulders. Colette had helped me to buy it, ensuring that it matched my dress. 'And feathers are very directional,' she'd joked. I was glad I had it now, because even though it was spring, there was still a chill in the air. Colette was the first to break away from the crowd, grinning at me and holding a sports bag aloft in her hand. I nodded, and pretending to ignore everyone for a moment, darted towards a clearing in the woods.

'You look as if you're taking a loo break,' she joked, as she ducked between two huge horse chestnuts, their leaves almost fully out. 'Right, got the cream Jimmy Choos, but only on loan, so for God's sake don't get grass stains on them,' she said as she helped me to unlace my boots and slip my feet into the gorgeous silk shoes.

I gasped. 'They're fabulous, Colette!'

She grinned up at me as she tied the strap around my ankle. 'That's what six hundred euro will get you, pet.' And then she looked at my leg. 'Crap, you've got a sock mark on your ankle,' she chided me. 'Honestly, did you have to wear woolly hiking socks on your wedding day?'

She rubbed my ankle frantically, trying to remove the red elastic mark around it, until I stopped her. 'Colette, I had to wear my boots to get up here, and anyway, no one's going to be looking at my ankles.'

'*I'll* know, though, won't I? And I won't be able to concentrate on the ceremony, thinking that you have two big red marks around your legs which make you look like a football player. I won't even be able to concentrate on that brother of Niall's. He's a bit of all right, isn't he?'

'Colette . . .'

She looked at me and gave that cheeky grin beneath her pixie haircut, her dark eyes dancing. She was so pretty, Colette, so fun and lively. She'd actually make a good match for Matt, I thought.

'So what? He looks kinda dangerous, don't you think? I like that in a man.' She giggled.

'Oh, for God's sake.' I rolled my eyes to heaven. 'Don't make a show of me, please?'

'Would I? On your wedding day?' She looked innocent for a moment, as she pulled herself upright, until she was standing in front of me, in her deep-blue dress, the colour of irises. And then she was serious for a moment, taking my hands in hers. 'Antonia, you look beautiful, radiant. Niall is a very lucky man, elastic marks or not.'

'Thanks, Colette,' I said, accepting her outstretched hands. 'It means a lot to me, coming from you. Thanks for everything. I owe you such a lot—'

She waved her hand and I could see there were tears in

her eyes. 'Don't start, will you? Weddings make me weepy.'

And then Mary was beside me, golden and beautiful in her bridesmaid's dress, my bouquet in her hand. 'All set?'

I nodded, and made my way towards the huddle of people gathered at the top of the mountain, towards my family. Sister Monica was there, having been escorted by Niall's father, who was as keen a mountaineer as Niall, and Billy and Eithne and Betty and Bridget, who'd put their differences aside for a moment just to smile at me. I'd even invited Damien, with Niall's blessing. They hadn't really spoken since the nightclub incident, but it was more out of embarrassment than anything. Niall couldn't get over the loss of control, and Damien was mortified that he'd been a drunken eejit. But Damien and I had really gelled as a songwriting partnership, and as I'd got to know him I'd realized that underneath all that silly stuff was a really nice guy, and a talented one too. We'd become friends, proper ones, and I was delighted that Damien had invited his girlfriend Maureen. She was a beautiful blonde dancer he'd met at Wembley, to whom he'd given his number – of course – except that, unlike all the other girls he'd given it to, she'd had the nerve to ring him a month later and ask him out. And the rest was history.

'I'm off the market.' He'd grinned at me when, at the end of one of our recording sessions, he'd told me that they'd started seeing each other. 'Are you devastated?'

'My life will never be the same again,' I'd said, putting my hand on my heart, and we'd both exploded with laughter.

But I was pleased for Damien, as pleased as I'd be for any little brother.

Only Karen wasn't there. Our friendship, such as it was, had cooled since I'd come back from London. Just because we had spent so much time together hadn't meant we were friends, I suppose, but it was more than that. I think she was disappointed in me, somehow, felt that I hadn't got what it took to last in the business. Maybe she was right, but I knew that I had to succeed on *my* terms.

Maurice was waiting for me, to escort me to the altar, wearing a grey suit which looked too small for him, and which he'd probably borrowed, being too cheap to actually buy one. Maurice, I'd learned, was very careful with his money, which I suppose wasn't a bad trait in a manager. He'd been chuffed to be asked. 'Sure, none of my daughters will get married, they're all happy to live in sin, God help them. So it'd be an honour,' he'd said. Maurice had become a friend over the past year, a friend and a father figure, and I knew I could trust him. I was getting better at that, knowing who to trust, I thought, as Maurice tucked his arm into mine and winked, turning so that we both faced forward.

And then we walked to where Niall was waiting for me, at the makeshift altar – a clearing of stone at the top of the waterfall – Colette and Mary, my bridesmaids, behind me. Niall was standing with Matt, Father O'Hanlon in front of them. Matt was grinning, of course, but Niall had an anxious look on his face and was hopping from foot to foot, but he looked so handsome in an open-necked shirt and smart black trousers. No ties, we'd both agreed. It wasn't that kind of wedding.

'It's OK,' I mouthed as I reached him, and he managed a nervous smile.

Maurice melted away into the background, and Niall reached out and took my hand, squeezing it briefly and tightly in his. 'You look beautiful. Stunning,' he whispered.

All of a sudden, I couldn't answer. There was a lump in my throat, and I felt the tears spring to my eyes. After everything that had happened in the last year and a bit, here I was. It was another one of those moments, a moment that would change my life for ever and for the better, I knew that. I felt that I was the luckiest woman in the whole world.

'Ready?' Niall said, scanning my face for any trace of second thoughts.

I smiled at him, to reassure him, and I could see the corners of his eyes crinkle in that way I loved as he relaxed. 'I'm ready.'

Acknowledgements

Sadly, Anita became ill shortly after completing this novel.
Her husband, Gerry, has written the following
tribute and acknowledgements.

Anita always felt that to complete a book and have it published was not just down to professional assistance but also to the advice of friends and loved ones who played such an important part in her life, so, naturally, she would want to thank them all. Now that she is ill I am attempting to do this on her behalf.

To begin with Anita would want to say that she would not have written a single word were it not for Patricia Scanlan who initially spurred her on to risk everything, to follow her dream, and who has been a friend ever since.

She would hate it if I forgot to mention the team at Transworld for all their support. In 2002, editor Francesca Liversidge left a phone message to enquire about more chapters of *Back After The Break*, and that happy partnership was responsible for her first four books. She saw Anita's potential as a writer and Anita treasured her. Linda Evans took over as editor in 2009 and has been hugely supportive. Thanks, too, to Larry Finlay, who has given Anita great support over the years, and to Eoin McHugh at Transworld Ireland. It's been a rollercoaster of a decade.

Marianne Gunn O'Connor agreed to represent her and right up to this moment continues in the role of both agent and friend. The close bond between them proves that you can combine business and friendship. Thanks to Vicki Satlow and Pat Lynch in Marianne's office who have always been a huge support.

Anita was never shy of doing publicity and Declan Heeney and Helen Gleed O'Connor at Gill Hess Ltd took full advantage and made sure she was on the promotional trail as each publication date approached. Thanks also to Simon and Gill Hess for all their hard work on her behalf.

RTÉ meant so much to her for nearly twenty years and she continues to be supported by ex-colleagues, Claudia Carroll in particular.

As a couple we've been very lucky that we both came to the relationship with great friends whom we now both share. Everyone has supported Anita throughout her literary career but in particular this book benefited from the warm and caring relationships she has with all the Brittas Bay wives. Her next book would have been about them all and would have been her best ever. However, particular hugs have to go to Judy, Mary, Karen and my sister-in-law Claire who helped us carry on when things started to get complicated.

Anita's dad, Mark, died shortly after she turned twenty

and her mum, Teresa, died six weeks after we were married. They were such a good influence on Anita and she prayed for them both every night. Teresa also brought up three other girls, Madeline, Lorraine and Jean, who have all been amazing through good times and now through bad. Three special sisters that Anita loves wholeheartedly.

My dad, Arthur, never failed to turn up with a bouquet of flowers for Anita to celebrate all the good times in her life. He is immensely proud of her success and bought many copies of each book so that Anita could sign them for his friends. She loved cooking for him, she loved hearing his stories about the cinema business and mostly she loved the fact that he was always there for her.

As our situation has changed we now rely on the kindness of other people, and Edel, Berni and Sally bring care, comfort and relaxation to our daily lives. Myself and Anita simply could not keep going without them.

Throughout life we all have intense relationships that come and go and if we are lucky we have some that never go away. Anita is blessed with the friendships of people who have always relied on her support and who have given theirs freely over many years. Anita always enjoyed that Ursula, Dave, Caroline, Niamh and Dee remained an important part of her life but Derv is the one, the BF, that she could never be away from for too long. They shared so many things over the years. Derv is everywhere in our house. They continue to have an amazing connection.

The good thing about writing these acknowledgements

is that I can thank Anita herself. She has brought joy to everyone she has met and has given of her time selflessly. She has always had such an interest in everything that was important, and the clarity of thought not to be concerned about things that didn't matter. I thank her from the bottom of my broken heart for her love, her trust, her company, her laughter and the experiences we've had together.

Anita has always loved writing. She was always thrilled that people wanted to read her words. She always felt privileged to be able to get lost in her stories and was delighted when readers got in touch to tell her what they thought. She knew that her readers were the most important people when she set out to write each book. On her behalf I thank you all for being a part of this journey. It would be her sincere wish that you enjoy this final book.

NO ORDINARY LOVE
Anita Notaro

When Lulu wakes up one morning and realises that she's in crisis, she knows she must rethink her life completely. She just needs more time – time to relax, time to have fun with her friends and, most importantly, time to find the perfect man who's eluded her for far too long. So she packs in her job as a therapist, ditches the swanky apartment, waves goodbye to her soft-top car and embraces a simpler life.

But then a terrible tragedy strikes and Lulu realizes that it isn't that easy to escape the past after all. Can she deal with her unfinished business and make the perfect life she longs for?

Out now in hardback and paperback